It was dead calm until...

Aaron kissed me, one brief kiss and another, and then another, longer this time. He was right, I was the Wicked Witch: melting, *melting*.... Then several things happened at once, none of them pleasant. A scream. A splash. A shout of alarm.

Below our railing, in the green-black water of the harbor, we saw a wavering luminous shape trailing strands of fair hair, and edges of pallid cloth that rippled just below the surface, slowly sinking and rising. Two ghostly arms spread wide, the pale fingers parted as if to conjure something from the depths. A cacophony of shocked, excited voices filled the night.

I stepped back from the melee and called 911.

Lavish praise for Veiled Threats.

"Always a bridal consultant, but seemingly doomed to
never be a bride, Carnegie Kincaid is the kind of woman
anyone would want for a best friend."—April Henry

"Reminiscent of Donna Andrews's *Murder, with
Peacocks,* this zany mystery is a bubbly blend of farcical
humor, romance, and intrigue. First-time author
Donnelly will beguile readers with her keen wit and
mint descriptions, but it is her characters that make
this a stellar debut."—*Publishers Weekly*

"Donnelly's fast-moving story and likable sleuth
will please readers."—*Booklist*

"*Veiled Threats* is a solid start for what could be
an entertaining edition to the cozy ranks. With her
charm, intuition and the unpredictability of weddings,
Carnegie could find herself a very busy sleuth."
—*The Mystery Reader*

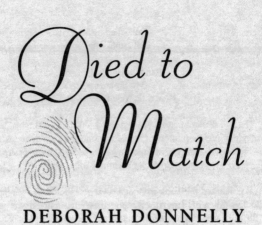

Died to Match

DEBORAH DONNELLY

A   DELL   BOOK

Also by Deborah Donnelly

Veiled Threats

Published by
Dell Publishing
a division of
Random House, Inc.
1540 Broadway
New York, New York 10036

This is a work of fiction. Names, characters, places, and incidents
either are the product of the author's imagination or are used
fictitiously. Any resemblance to actual persons, living or dead,
events, or locales is entirely coincidental.

If you purchased this book without a cover you should be aware that this
book is stolen property. It was reported as "unsold and destroyed" to
the publisher and neither the author nor the publisher has received
any payment for this "stripped book."

Copyright © 2002 by Deborah Wessell
Cover art copyright © 2002 by Deborah Campbell

All rights reserved. No part of this book may be reproduced or
transmitted in any form or by any means, electronic or mechanical, including
photocopying, recording, or by any information storage and retrieval system,
without the written permission of the Publisher, except where permitted
by law. For information address: Dell Publishing, New York, N.Y.

Dell® is a registered trademark of Random House, Inc., and the colophon
is a trademark of Random House, Inc.

ISBN: 0-440-23704-1

Manufactured in the United States of America

Published simultaneously in Canada
October 2002
10 9 8 7 6 5 4 3 2 1
OPM

For my parents,
Ginny and Fred

Acknowledgments

My thanks to the usual suspects, and also to some new ones: to Liz for wizardry, to Joanne for writerly camaraderie, and to Julie for her lively support. Thanks to Annie, who bakes a mean cake. Most of all, and always, my love and gratitude to Steve.

Died to Match

Chapter One

MASKS ARE DANGEROUS. THE MEREST SCRAP OF SILK OR SLIP of cardboard can eclipse one's civilized identity and set loose the dark side of the soul.

Trust me. You take a pair of perfectly well-behaved newspaper reporters, or software engineers or whatever, dress them up as Spider-Man and a naughty French maid and *whammo*! It's a whole new ball game.

Which is why this party was getting out of hand. Free drinks can make people crazy, but free costumes make them wild. Two hundred big black envelopes had gone out to Paul and Elizabeth's friends and colleagues, inviting them to a Halloween engagement party in the Seattle Aquarium, down at Pier 59 on Elliott Bay. And tucked inside the envelope was a very special party favor: a coupon for the persona of one's choice at Characters, Inc., a theater-quality costume shop.

So tonight, more than a hundred and fifty reasonably civilized people were living out their fantasies among the fishes. And the fantasies were getting rowdy. It all started innocently enough: Madonna flirting with Mozart, Death with his scythe trading stock tips with Nero and his violin, Albert Einstein dirty dancing with Monica Lewinsky. And everyone toasting the engaged couple with affection and good cheer.

Paul Wheeler, the groom-to-be, was news editor at the

Seattle Sentinel; he made a skinny, smiley swashbuckler—
sort of Indiana Jones Lite. His fiancée, Elizabeth (*"not* Liz")
Lamott, was a tough-minded Microsoft millionaire who had
retired at twenty-nine. Dressed as Xena the Warrior Princess,
Elizabeth looked drop-dead sexy, and more than capable of
beheading barbarian warlords. The Wheeler and Lamott fam-
ilies would all be at the wedding in two weeks—an extravaganza at the Experience Music Project—but tonight's bash
was more of a coed bachelor party.

And like so many bachelor parties, headed straight to hell.
Luke Skywalker was juggling martini glasses, quite unsuc-
cessfully, near *Principles of Ocean Survival.* A well-tailored
Count Dracula had knocked over the sushi trays at *Local
Invertebrates.* Various members of the Spice Girls and Sgt.
Pepper's Lonely Hearts Club Band were disappearing into
the darkened grotto of *Pacific Coral Reef* and returning with
their costumes askew. And at all the liquor stations, masked
revelers had begun pushing past the bartenders to pour their
own drinks—a danger sign even when the crowd is in
civvies.

I wasn't wearing a mask, and I certainly wasn't fantasizing, except about keeping my professional cool and getting
our damage deposit back from the Aquarium. It was my
hands the party was getting out of: "Made in Heaven
Wedding Design, Carnegie Kincaid, Proprietor." I usually
stick to weddings, too, but business had been iffy ever since
I'd been a suspect in the abduction of one of my brides.
Everybody reads the headlines, nobody reads the follow-up,
and now my name, besides being weird in the first place, had
a little shadow across it in the minds of some potential
clients.

So an extra event with an extra commission had been

hard to turn down. And the formidable Ms. Lamott had been impossible to turn down. When Elizabeth wanted something, she got it, whether she was launching products for Bill Gates or, more recently, harvesting charity donations from Seattle's crop of wealthy thirtysomethings. Elizabeth asked me to manage her engagement party in person, I explained that I really don't do costumes, and suddenly, somehow, there I was in a long jaggedy-hemmed black gown and a crooked-peaked witch's hat, stationed by the champagne at *Salmon & People*, and reminding my waiters that cleaning broken glass off the floor comes first, no matter how many guests are demanding more booze.

"Carnegie!"

"What?" I snapped. "Oh, sorry, Lily. I'm losing my mind here."

Lily James, my date for the party, was a statuesque black-skinned Cleopatra, rubber snake and all, with her wide eyes and arching brows elaborately painted into an Egyptian mask of gold and indigo. By day, Lily staffed the reference desk at Seattle Public, but tonight she was every inch the voluptuous and commanding Queen of the Nile. Of course, Lily could be voluptuous and commanding in sweatpants—I'd seen her do it any number of times.

Why was my best friend also my date? Because I'd had a spat with Aaron Gold, my who-knows-what. The spat was about Aaron's smoking, which I found deplorable and he found to be none of my business. But it went deeper than that. We were teetering on the brink of being lovers, and life on the brink was uncomfortable. At least it was for me; I kept hesitating and analyzing and wondering if we were right for each other. Aaron's view was that we could analyze just as easily lying down.

Aaron was at the party, of course. All of the *Sentinel*'s reporters were there, gleefully adding to the pandemonium. I could see a laughing, breathless bunch of them now, escorting Paul and Elizabeth up the tunnel from the Underwater Dome room, where the dancing was. As they headed for the martini bar, Aaron put his arm around Corinne Campbell, the paper's society writer. A handsome couple: he was quite dashing in a Zorro mask and cape, and she made a blonde, bosomy Venus in a filmy white gown crisscrossed with silver cords.

I knew Corinne professionally—she often wrote about my brides—and I'd been seeing more of her now that she was one of Elizabeth's bridesmaids. She wasn't the sharpest knife in the drawer, but she could be pleasant enough, in an overeager kind of way. Especially to men. I bet *she* found the scent of cigarettes manly and exciting.

"I said, I'm having a fine time." Lily's voice broke through this sour speculation. "You're not listening, are you? You're mooning after Aaron."

"I am not! I'm keeping an eye on all the guests. He just happens to be one of them."

"Whatever you say." Her glittery makeup caught the light as she gazed around and let loose the deep, provocative laugh that often startled the library's patrons. "This is a fabulous place for a party!"

"You bet your asp it is," I said, scanning the crowd over her shoulder. "But it's tough to supervise, with all these corridors and cul-de-sacs. I've got a couple of off-duty cops here as security and I haven't talked to either one in hours except on the two-way radio. Makes me nervous."

I was especially nervous about *Northwest Shores*, a narrow grotto behind the martini bar. I'd already had to shoo some

Visigoths off the handrail of the shorebird exhibit down at the end. The water in the little beach scene was only a foot deep, but if anybody tumbled over backwards it would terrify the long-billed curlews and they'd never let me rent this place again. The management, I mean, not the curlews.

"Well, everyone but you is having a blast," said Lily. "Even Roger Talbot, in a quiet sort of way. I'm surprised he came."

Talbot, publisher of the *Sentinel* and a prominent Seattle Democrat, was making a brief appearance to toast the happy pair. It was generous of him; he'd recently lost his wife to cancer, and could hardly be in a party mood. We watched him join the little crowd of newspaper people, shaking hands with Zorro, giving Venus a quick hug, raising his glass to lead a toast to Xena and Indy. In his black tuxedo and carrying a black topcoat, Talbot looked grave and distinguished among all the gaudy costumes.

"He's really fond of Paul," I told Lily. "And he's on his way home from a medical fund-raiser. I guess if you're going to have a public career, you've got to put your private life aside."

Not long before his wife's death, Talbot had announced his candidacy for mayor of Seattle. He had a fighting chance, too, despite the incumbent's popularity. He looked like a statesman, for starters, with the height and grace of a former college basketball star. More than that, he had a scholar's grasp of detail and a reporter's knack for crystallizing ideas. The word around town was that if Talbot did make it to the mayor's office, he'd soon be packing a suitcase for the other Washington, the one back East.

"Carnegie, there you are!" Talbot raised a hand to me above the crowd and came over. Even with his air of strain and fatigue he was a handsome man, with a bold Roman nose and dark eyes and brows below thick, prematurely silver hair. "I understand you created this wonderful event. You do good work."

"Thank you, Roger. Thanks very much." I'm leery of politicians, as a rule, but still I found myself glowing at the praise. There was something about Roger Talbot's gaze that made you feel special, singled out. I introduced him to Lily, and watched the magic take effect on her. That kind of charm must be money in the bank to an ambitious man. Talbot listened intently to Lily's comments on the controversial design of the new downtown library, added a few well-informed remarks of his own, and then moved on.

"Well, he could eat crackers in *my* bed," pronounced Lily as we watched him walk away.

I was about to agree, when we heard an angry shout from the martini bar. A knot of people tightened suddenly, their backs to us, intent on a scene we couldn't see.

Over their heads, arcing high in the air, rose the scythe of Death.

Chapter Two

I SHOVED MY WAY THROUGH THE CROWD. I'M ALMOST SIX feet tall, so I can shove with the best. Lunging like a fencer, I parried the scythe with my broomstick just in time to save Zorro from having his hair parted right through his hat.

"What on earth is going on here? Syd? Aaron?"

Death's hood had fallen back, revealing the fat and furious face of Sydney Soper, a big-shot local contractor and personal friend of the bride-to-be. That explained what was going on. Aaron had done an article, the first in a series, questioning Soper's methods of winning state highway contracts. With Seattle and Bellevue booming, and traffic approaching Los Angeles levels, those contracts ran into the millions. According to Aaron, a lot of millions were being misspent, if not actually swindled.

So now Death was pissed off at Zorro, and Zorro was standing his ground and grinning, a lock of raven-black hair flopping down beneath his black gaucho hat. I knew from personal experience how infuriating that grin could be, and I felt for Soper. Especially since, unlike me, Soper probably didn't appreciate the sexy brown eyes above the grin. His own eyes, hard and pale as pebbles, were bulging with anger. God knows what Aaron had said to provoke the Grim Reaper, but he was lucky the scythe was plastic.

As I hesitated, wondering how to cast a soothing spell, the scene was stolen from me by a gypsy queen. Mercedes Montoya, another of Elizabeth's bridesmaids, stepped up in a swirl of bright skirts and a chiming of bracelets. She was a classic Castilian beauty, via Mexico City, with a mane of midnight curls framing cheekbones so sharp you could cut yourself. And a mind to match. Mercedes had recently decamped from the *Sentinel* for the headier world of TV news, and she was already making a name for herself. The camera, as they say, loved her.

"Mister Soper," she murmured, with the faintest hint of an accent in her caressing, dark-chocolate voice. "This is a party. Come dance with me."

She held out a slim brown hand, sparkling with costume jewelry. Soper glared at her, breathing hard, but Mercedes' hand never wavered and the smile never left her narrow, aristocratic lips. I marveled at her self-assurance, even as I waited for the burly contractor to snarl her off. We all waited, Zorro and Cleopatra and the rest of us, through a long, uncomfortable moment. And then damned if Soper didn't take her hand and walk away, with a flush rising up the back of his thick neck. Taming the fury of Death, now that's what I call magic.

The knot of guests unraveled, many of them following Mercedes and Soper to the dance floor. I saw Mister Rogers hand in hand with Lady Macbeth, and Dracula bowing gallantly to a hippie chick in love beads and granny glasses. As he swept her down the tunnel with his black cape fluttering around her tie-dyed shoulders, Lily went off to boogie with the Visigoths, and I was left with Aaron Gold. Behind the Zorro mask, his eyes were cold and angry. But not at me. Our latest argument was the farthest thing from his mind, at least for now.

"That *bitch*," he said.

"Aaron! She was just smoothing things over."

"No, she was just worming her way into Soper's confidence." His usually flippant East Coast voice was harsh and flat. "Montoya's working up her own exposé on construction fraud. In a couple of weeks, Soper's going to turn on the TV and wish he'd used that sickle thing on her."

"Well, you're trying to expose the fraud yourself. So what if it gets TV coverage, too?"

He sighed. "In the long run, it's better for John Q. Taxpayer if this all comes out as publicly as possible. But I've been dogging that story for months. Our favorite fortune teller there waltzed off to KPSL with all my research in her pretty little pocket."

"What do you mean?" I asked.

"I mean, she stole my notes right off my hard drive!"

"Couldn't she be fired for that? For unethical behavior?"

"Well, I can't actually prove it. But I got a very confidential lead about Soper bribing someone at the DOT, and now Montoya has lined up an interview with that same someone. And she was at my desk one night before she quit, fooling with my computer. Said she was interested in one of my programs, but that's bullshit. She hates computers. I'd bet money she read those notes."

"You're beautiful when you're angry." I couldn't resist; he needled me often enough.

"Very funny. She better not tip her hand to Soper, though, or he'll really freak. He thinks he's untouchable, but this bribery deal could bring him down for good."

"Mercedes seems so talented," I continued innocently. What a relief to be back on teasing terms after the chilly anger that had sent us to this party separately instead of together. "I saw her interview Roger Talbot on that afternoon show the other day and she was brilliant."

"Brilliant?" he yelped. "How brilliant do you have to be to bat your eyelashes? 'The people of Seattle are so grieved for you, Roger.' 'Roger, how will you pursue public office without Mrs. Talbot at your side?' What a phony."

I giggled at his rendition of Mercedes' soulful on-camera manner, and he narrowed his eyes.

"Wait a minute, you never fall for that kind of crap. You're just giving me a bad time, aren't you? Wicked witch."

Down below, the DJ cued up "Respect"—Otis, not Aretha. Time for a peace offering. "Look, Aaron, the Dome room's next on my rounds, and I'm due for a break anyway. Come dance with me?"

He looked away uncomfortably, straightening his shiny black cape. "I promised Corinne, when she gets back from the rest room. If she ever gets back. She's spending half the party in there."

"Oh. Well, don't let me keep you." Corinne, with her golden curls and her syrupy Southern drawl and her ice-cream-scoop cleavage. I have long red hair, which I'm regrettably vain about, but I'm also skinny as a broomstick, and in my witch's hat I towered over Aaron's middling height. The difference in our statures bothered me, and amused him. He just called me silly nicknames and insisted that he didn't have to be bigger than me, only smarter and more charming.

"Corinne's kind of my date tonight, Stretch," he was saying. "I'm trying to keep an eye on her. She's been really down since she broke up with that Russian guy."

"She's been looking kind of rocky," I agreed. "But I think it was Boris who broke up with her."

Actually, I knew it was. Boris Nevsky—Lily called him Boris the Mad Russian Florist—had given me the gory details as we planned Paul and Elizabeth's wedding flowers. "She vanted to get *merried!*" he'd announced, mournful and astonished, shaking his shaggy Slavic head over the parrot tulips and the hellebores. Having dated Boris a couple of times myself, I was astonished too, but there's no accounting for taste.

"I wondered about that," said Aaron. "Corinne claims *she* dumped *him,* but she's awfully depressed about it. And I think this wedding stuff is making her feel extra-single. Funny how weddings do that to women. Us bachelor groomsmen feel just fine."

"I bet you do."

He chuckled. "Hey, I meant to ask you, aren't the bridesmaids supposed to be close friends of the bride? I didn't know Corinne and Elizabeth were such buddies."

"Sorority sisters at the UW, along with Mercedes," I said. "Though frankly, I think Elizabeth's main criterion was looks. She'd already picked out these slinky bridesmaids' dresses, she just needed bodies to fill them. Says she doesn't have time for girlfriends."

"Too busy cashing out stock options at the top of the market. So it's Mercedes the bitch and Corinne the goddess, and who else?" He glanced around as he spoke, keeping watch for Corinne. "I know you told me the lineup, but I keep forgetting."

"Funny how you remember batting averages but not bridesmaids' names."

"Matter of priority, Slim. Help me out here, in case I miss the rehearsal. I go in by myself, and then out with a bridesmaid, but which one? Tell me it's not Mercedes."

"No, it's not, but why should you miss the rehearsal? This is important, Aaron."

"I know, I know. But I might have to go back East on short notice. So who's my partner?"

"Well, we're matching you by height, so you go with Corinne, and Paul's brother Scott gets Mercedes."

There's often a glow of romance around the paired-up bridesmaids and groomsmen. Aaron and Corinne would be walking arm in arm, dressed to kill, up the aisle through the beaming crowd. I wasn't crazy about it.

"Great," he said. "And who's the lucky girl who gets young Zack?"

"Angela Sims," I told him. "She was Elizabeth's assistant at Microsoft. Angela's the pregnant nun tonight, you can't miss her. She looks like Princess Di and talks like a trucker. She was the life of the bridesmaids' luncheon."

There was still no sign of Corinne, so we drifted back to the champagne bar. I figured I could take my break there and check the Dome room later. The harried barman set a bottle in front of us and returned to his customers. It's nice sometimes, being the boss at a party. Aaron poured for us both, touched his glass to mine, and took a sip, gazing at me over the rim of the glass. He really could be charming, when he tried. And he could look sexy without even trying. So why did I get cold feet every time he got hot hands?

"You were at the bridesmaids' luncheon?" he prompted.

"Oh, I was there all right. It was supposed to be a working lunch, to talk about dresses and hairstyles and manicures. But instead, we ate fajitas and drank tequila shooters for about three hours. Even Patty got happy." Patty Lamott, Elizabeth's older sister and maid of honor, had missed tonight's party, claiming a schedule conflict, and Elizabeth had shrugged off her absence. No love lost on either side, apparently.

"Wait, wait, I heard about this," Aaron was saying. "The

famous purse-snatching incident at La Corona? The newsroom was still talking about it when I got back from my last trip to Boston."

"That was it." I shivered a little and sipped some bubbly. "This creepy-looking guy grabbed Elizabeth's bag. It had the wedding rings in it, she'd just picked them up at the jewelers. We all froze except Angela, who went sprinting after him like a racehorse. He sprained his ankle tripping over a trash can, and we all stood around guarding him and talking hemlines till the police came."

Aaron laughed. "What a story!"

"Well, it seemed funny at the time, after all that tequila, but really, what if he'd pulled a knife or a gun or something? You should have heard the disgusting things he said, sitting there on the curb. And now we'll have to testify at his trial. He had tattoos on his *skull*, for God's sake."

"Take it easy, Slim. Lots of people have tattoos. *I've* got a tattoo."

"You? Where?"

"If you were more cooperative, you'd know that by now." He grinned wickedly and reached out to take my hand. "I could arrange a viewing tonight...."

"Gosh, look at the time," I retorted, but I didn't take my hand away. "I've got to go supervise. If I see Corinne I'll tell her you're waiting for her."

"Thanks, Wedding Lady," said Aaron. He ran his fingers in little circles across the inside of my wrist. I could feel my blood shifting. "Save a dance for me, OK?"

"I'll save two."

What's wrong with this picture? I asked myself as I pushed open the ladies' room door a short while later. *I'm at a party, Aaron's at the same party, and what am I doing? I'm keeping an eye out for his date. What a world.* Still, I felt for Corinne. Weddings are hard when you're brokenhearted, and I'm a sucker for broken hearts. That's why I started Made in Heaven, I suppose. What better business for a hopeless romantic who likes to throw parties?

Inside the rest room, preening in solitary glory, was Mercedes Montoya. I wondered if Syd Soper was outside somewhere, resting his scythe and hoping for another dance. If so, he was a patient man; a fortune in designer cosmetics lay spilled across the counter, and Mercedes was employing all of it. No wonder the camera loved her. She obviously loved herself.

"The wedding planner!" she announced gaily, shaking back her midnight hair. Her eyes, meeting mine in the mirror, were suspiciously shiny and hugely dilated. Was it only alcohol flying her kite, or a little something extra? I really didn't want to know. "I was just thinking about you! About hiring you."

"Really? I didn't know you were getting married. Who's the lucky man?"

Mercedes clapped a hand to her lips. With the other hand she clutched my arm, tight enough to hurt. "No! It's a secret! You can't tell a soul. Not a single *Sentinel* soul!"

She gave a long peal of melodious laughter, then blinked vacantly and seemed to forget why she was laughing. Definitely something extra. I retrieved my arm. "I won't breathe a word."

"Good," she murmured. "Good. Roger would be furious."

"Roger?"

She gasped again. "How did you know? You have to keep it secret!"

"Keep what secret, Mercedes?"

She leaned close, her ropes of beads clicking and swaying. *"I'm going to marry the mayor!"*

I thought I'd heard her wrong. "Mayor Wyble's already married."

"Not *him*. Roger Talbot! Roger's going to be mayor next year, after I help him beat Wyble." Mercedes was suddenly cold and shrewd. She was cycling through moods like a kaleidoscope. "We'll have the wedding right before the primaries. The grieving widower finds happiness. People will eat it up."

Apparently the widower wasn't all that grieved, not that it was any of my business. Brides were my business, but I wasn't sure I wanted this volatile prima donna as a client.

And yet, I thought, while Mercedes went back to fluffing her hair and humming a Motown tune. Landing another big-budget, high-profile wedding could put Made in Heaven in the news, maybe even in the trade magazines, and definitely in the black. I was still several thousand dollars in debt from starting up my business, and the dock fees on my rented houseboat were killing me. Well, time for those calculations later. I couldn't very well hold her to a decision made under the influence.

"Congratulations," I said, wondering if she'd apply my comment to the engagement or the election. Probably both. "But there's plenty of time to plan. You don't want to choose a bridal consultant on a whim. Think it over."

"You don't believe me," she pouted. Mercedes had a superb pout. She slid a hand down her ragtag gypsy bodice and drew out a long gold chain with twisted herringbone links. Suspended from it, swinging inches from my astonished eyes, was a monster diamond on an ornate platinum band. "You'll believe a girl's best friend, won't you?"

"Mercedes, that's stunning!" I wanted to get away from her and her secrets, but for a moment I was mesmerized. The diamond swung back and forth, like a hypnotist's watch. "It must be nearly three carats! Is it antique?"

"Family heirloom," she said complacently, and lowered the treasure back into its cozy hiding place. X marks the spot. "It was his grandmother's engagement ring, and now it's mine. I told Roger, I'll keep our secret, but I have to have something to put under my pillow, don't I?"

"It's a wonder you can sleep."

She laughed. "I sleep very well. Roger makes sure of that."

I wasn't going anywhere near that one. "Well, like I said, think it over—"

"I don't have to, I want *you*." The kaleidoscope was turning faster; now she was sulky and stubborn. She rummaged in her patchwork shoulder bag and pulled out a wad of bills. "Here, take this. For a deposit."

"Mercedes, you don't have to—"

"Take it!" she said shrilly.

"OK, OK." Anything to calm her down. I took the money; there were twenties, and at least one fifty. "Let's count it and I'll write you a receipt."

"No, no, I trust you. Oh, Carnegie, isn't it exciting? I'm getting married!" Looking suddenly girlish, Mercedes gave me an impulsive hug, laying her head against my shoulder. Her hair was perfumed, sweet and musky. Then she wrenched herself away.

"Just remember, wedding planner . . ." She fixed me with a dark, straight stare—a tiger's stare. "You keep your mouth shut."

Chapter Three

MERCEDES SWEPT UP HER PAINTS AND SWEPT OUT OF THE room. A black-and-gold powder compact lay overlooked under the balled-up paper towels. I picked it up but didn't go after her. I'd had enough schizophrenic gypsy glamour for the moment. Instead, I stood pondering this unexpected glimpse into Roger Talbot's private life. His wife had only been dead a month or so. If Mercedes and Talbot had a whirlwind courtship, it must have blown at gale force, unless they'd gotten involved while Helen Talbot was still alive. A nasty thought. Aaron had mentioned once that Mercedes was constantly in the publisher's office. Maybe she'd been negotiating more than her salary. Maybe her move to television was really part of Talbot's campaign. I hated to be that cynical, but—

A sudden sound, at once revolting and unmistakable. The room had appeared empty, but someone was in the farthest stall being spectacularly sick. I heard ragged breathing, then a moan.

"Hello?" I called, sliding the cash and the compact into the ample pocket of my witch's gown. "Can I help?"

The stall door swung wide to reveal one very unkempt and unsteady Greek goddess. In wordless sympathy, I ran a paper towel under the faucet and handed it to Aaron's long-lost date. Corinne dragged it across her mouth, her long fake fingernails a startling crimson against her pale, trembling lips. How much champagne did it take to drown the memory of Boris Nevsky? A double latte had done the trick for me, but then, I never wanted to marry the man.

"I'm going to die," said Corinne. She looked at herself bleakly in the mirror—hairdo in ruins, satiny toga crumpled and soiled—and took a long, sobbing breath. "I want to die."

"You'll get over him," I offered. "You'll feel better, really you will."

She glared at me. Her eyes were a weak, watery blue, almost aquamarine, and the look in them was somehow scarier than Mercedes'. "What do you know about it? How do you know how I feel?"

"Corinne, I just meant that you'll find somebody else—"

Her eyes went wide and rolling, like a panicky horse about to bolt. "I'll never find anyone like him. *Never!*"

Then she pushed past me and was gone. *Aaron,* I thought, *Aaron, she is all yours.* While I waited for the gypsy queen and the drama queen to get a good head start, I belatedly remembered *Northwest Shores*. I radioed Marvin, one of my security guards, and asked him to close it off. Then I left the ladies' room and went back to my rounds, checking on each of the bars and food stations. The Halloween menu I'd designed with Joe Solveto, my favorite caterer, was definitely a hit, especially the all-chocolate dessert bar. Good thing we had generous reserves; running out of food is an event planner's highest crime.

As I worked my way through the party, I could see that Lily was right: people were having a blast. Down in the eerie green gloom of the Underwater Dome room, the dance floor was overflowing. Ropes of thick green weed wavered like

ghosts behind the curved glass walls, and sharks floated omi-
nously over the heads of the gyrating dancers. Perfect for
Halloween. I stood for a while admiring the DJ in action.
Rick the Rocket was a chubby fellow whose bald pate rose
from his ring of untidy blond hair like a big pink egg in a nest
of straw. His costume matched his hairline: he was dressed
as a tonsured medieval monk, with a rough-spun black cloak
and a rope belt around his ample middle.

Rick Royko was new in town, but he was doing a first-rate
job for me tonight, gauging the mood of the crowd with skill
and accepting requests with a friendly smile. A music-snob
DJ can really kill a party, but this guy was good. *I know how to
pick 'em, if I do say so myself.* I watched happily as the dancers
outdid themselves to Gladys Knight's "Grapevine." What
were a few smashed glasses, after all? If we could just get to
midnight without a serious mishap, I'd call the whole party a
smashing success.

Before I could pat myself on the back any harder, I was ac-
costed by a large leprechaun.

"Carnegie, you look glorious! Who are you supposed to
be, exactly?"

Tommy Barry, the *Sentinel*'s legendary sportswriter, was
sixty-five or so, and a legendary drinker of Guinness. The
costume was appropriate, because when Tommy drank he
got very Irish. A shamrock-bedecked hat sat askew on his
bush of grizzled hair, and one of his curly-toed leprechaun
slippers was missing. I had gently suggested a more reliable
best man—and Elizabeth had demanded a more photogenic
one—but Paul was adamant. Tommy was his mentor and his
pal, so Tommy it would be.

"I'm supposed to be a witch," I told him, "and you were
supposed to be here at eight. We had to do the toasts

without you. The maid of honor is working tonight, so I was depending on you. You will be on time for the wedding, won't you, Tommy?"

"Of course, of course. Tonight I gave Zack here a ride," he said proudly, as if this were quite a feat. In his current inebriated condition, maybe it was.

Zack Hartmann, the young Internet whiz working on the *Sentinel* web site, was Paul's third groomsman. He was sometimes shy and slouching, but not tonight. Tonight Zack was the Prince of Thieves, with a quiver of arrows over his green-cloaked shoulder and a couple of martinis under his belt. Tall and rangy, with crisp fair hair and long-lashed cobalt-blue eyes, he stood next to the sportswriter/leprechaun with his shoulders back and his head high. Maid Marian would have been thrilled to bits.

"We were a tad late, perhaps," Tommy was saying, "but now we're raising the roof and showing the girls a good time, aren't we, Zack? You go dance with Carnegie, and I'll just stop by the bar."

"I'm really awfully busy," I began.

"Nonsense!" he rasped. Tommy had a voice that could strip paint. "Too busy to dance with Robin Hood? Off you go, both of you."

I liked Zack, and I didn't want to hurt his feelings. "Sure. Just one dance."

As I followed him out onto the dance floor, Rick ended the Motown set and changed musical gears with the Righteous Brothers, "Soul and Inspiration." I hadn't bargained on a slow dance, but it had been a long night, and if I couldn't have Zorro's arms around me, Robin's looked like a decent substitute. For a few minutes I even relaxed and enjoyed myself. But once the song ended I'd have to go check with Donald, the other security guard, up on the observation deck, to make sure no one had gone skinny-dipping with the seals or was feeding pâté to the puffins or some damn thing. Not that my presence would prevent them, but—

"Is something wrong?" Zack blurted. I realized he was trembling a bit, and there were spots of hectic color on his cheekbones. What I'd taken for head-high confidence was just a rigid façade. Whether it was the drinks or the awkward social situation, Robin Hood was strung up as tight as piano wire.

"Nothing's wrong. I was just wondering how the rest of the party is going."

"Well, if you're too busy to dance with me, I totally understand." He sounded miffed, and very young.

"Not at all. You dance very well."

Actually, he just danced very tall. Try as I might, slow dancing with a shorter man always made me self-conscious. Aaron had wanted us to go as Rocky and Bullwinkle tonight, for crying out loud. What was he thinking? We were clearly incompatible. Oil and water. Chalk and cheese. High fashion and low comedy. Comedy was the operative word, though. Aaron could always make me laugh. I liked that.

"Tommy was right," said Zack, bringing me back to the moment. "You really do look beautiful tonight."

Right words, wrong guy. Still, nice words.

"Thanks, Zack. You're pretty gorgeous yourself."

In the shifting underwater light, I couldn't quite see him blushing, but I could feel it. He began to reply, then settled for holding me a little tighter, with one large strong hand spread across the small of my back. It felt good, and when I subtly tried to put a bit of space between us, I wasn't all that sorry when the press of bodies kept us close. I gave up, and peeked over Zack's shoulder to check the crowd. No sign of Aaron and Corinne, but Paul and Elizabeth were there, clinging as close as they could given the bride's bronze-and-leather breastplates. Paul's thin, good-humored face was lit up with laughter, and Elizabeth, with his Indy fedora perched on her long black Xena wig, was smiling dreamily.

Happy clients, that was the ticket. Happy clients who would recommend me to their happy, wealthy friends. My silent partner, Eddie Breen—never silent for long—was always pushing me to advertise more, while I favored word-of-mouth among brides and their mothers.

One thought sparked another. "Zack, are you full-time with the *Sentinel* now or do you freelance elsewhere? My partner's been pestering me about jazzing up our web site."

It was like flipping a high-voltage switch.

"Sure!" Zack's face lit up, and he seemed to forget all about my charms for the moment. "I'd do it for cheap, too. I need more stuff in my portfolio. We could start right away."

"Whoa! Eddie and I need to brainstorm a bit first. Right now the site is just a scan of our print pamphlet—"

"Brochureware!" he groaned. "That is so lame."

"Well, excuse me!"

"I'm sorry, I didn't mean . . . that's what everybody starts with, really. But you can do, like, tons more than that. I'll help you brainstorm. I'll come tomorrow afternoon, OK?"

"Well, OK. Eddie's not usually there on Sundays, but he's wrestling with some new software, so he said he'd be in."

"Oh. Will you be there, too?"

"Yes, as a matter of fact. So tell me, what could we do that wouldn't be lame?"

The Aquarium's rental rules called for low-volume music

in the Dome room, which made dance floor conversation possible, and Zack took full advantage of the fact. He regaled me feverishly with the on-line wonders he could perform for Made in Heaven, becoming almost agitated as he raved about JPEG files and animated GIFs and why frames, like, totally suck. Amused, I made fascinated and admiring noises.

"You're really interested in this stuff, aren't you?" he asked at one point.

"Sure," I lied. "Why wouldn't I be?"

"Well, some people think it's boring. Or, like, nerdy or something."

"Who thinks that?"

But the song ended and he fell abruptly silent, unsure of his next move in this adult ritual. I could almost read his mind: *Do we just go on dancing, or am I supposed to ask her, or what?* Or maybe Zack had forgotten he was dancing at all, lost in cyberspace.

I took the lead. "That was nice. Now I'd better get back to work."

"I'll come with you," he said. "Maybe I can, you know, help you and stuff."

"There's really nothing for you to do, but thanks." He tagged along anyway, and as we took the stairs to the pier level, I privately admired his well-filled doublet and hose. *Hmm. Must lift weights.*

"What made you choose Robin Hood, Zack?"

"Oh, stories, I guess. When I was a kid, we had this book of stories. When I got to that shop and saw the costume, I remembered. Robin Hood was always riding to the rescue and everything. How come you're a witch? I mean, *dressed* as a witch."

I laughed. "I've been feeling a little witchy tonight! But no reason, really. By the time I got around to picking, the glamorous stuff was all taken."

He stopped abruptly at a landing and gazed into my eyes, too close for comfort. "I think you're always glamorous."

It was an absurd situation, made more so by the fact that I was suddenly and warmly aware of Zack's body, and my own. If he'd had a little finesse, I might have forgotten the gap in our ages, at least for the moment. Instead he lurched forward and kissed me, clumsily but with great gusto. It was like being leapt upon by a huge, overfriendly young Labrador retriever. One who tasted like gin.

"Zack, cut it out!" I pulled away and my witch's hat rolled to the floor. When I stooped for it I bumped heads with someone in black: Aaron, coming right behind us. As Zack muttered an apology and continued on upstairs—*good, let him go cool off*—Aaron returned the hat with a flourish and a laugh.

"Cradle-robbing, Mrs. Robinson?"

"Oh, shut up. He's just a kid."

"Some kid." Aaron fell into step beside me. Despite the laugh, he looked annoyed. "Young Zack spends more time coming on to women than he does working."

"Well, nobody's working tonight but me. Did Corinne find you?"

"No. You saw her?"

"In the ladies' room. Aaron, I think she's drinking too much."

"That's funny. I've been fetching her Perrier all night."

"Well, it wasn't Perrier she was chucking up. Do you want to go look for her?"

"No," he said, as we came out onto the pier. He stopped

and faced me, and the party guests milling around us seemed to disappear. "No, I want to stay right here and gaze at the city lights and say romantic things to you. For instance, I've noticed that you walk in beauty like the night of cloudless climes and starry skies. Plus, as a bonus, all that's best of dark and bright meet in your aspect and your eyes. I admit you're not quite as dark as Lord Byron's girlfriend must have been, but you know what I mean."

I sagged against the wooden railing and took a deep breath of the damp night air. Elizabeth had insisted that the rain would hold off tonight, and she was right. Maybe she cut a deal with Mother Nature. Far out on Elliott Bay, a ferry was lit up like a birthday cake against the black mirror of the water. Aaron and I had begun our current spat on a ferry ride, and continued it back at my houseboat a few days later, with encores on the telephone after that. But I never fought with the men I dated, never. What was going on?

"Aaron, I'm working tonight. And besides . . ."

"Besides what?"

"I'm just not sure. About the romantic part." I noticed I was kneading the brim of the witch's hat in my hands, round and round, and made myself stop. "Aaron, I like you a lot. I care about you, but we keep arguing."

"Then let's not, Stretch. Let's do this instead."

He'd been moving closer as he spoke and now he kissed me, one brief kiss and another, and then another, longer this time. He didn't touch me at all except with his lips, warm on mine. He was right, I was the Wicked Witch: melting, *melting* . . .

Then several things happened at once, none of them pleasant. A scream. A splash. A shout of alarm. "Somebody's in the water!"

People surged toward the railing, roughly jostling me and Aaron as we peered downwards. The green-black water of the harbor was dappled with light and dotted with debris: cigarette butts, a paper coffee cup, chunks of sodden driftwood. And one wavering luminous shape, trailing strands of fair hair, and edges of pallid cloth that rippled just below the surface, slowly sinking and rising. Two ghostly arms spread wide, the pale fingers parted as if to conjure something up from the depths.

Then the man who made the splash diving in—it was Donald, the security guard, I recognized his crew cut—reached the body, hooked an elbow neatly under the chin, and towed it to a wooden ladder that rose up along a piling. A cacophony of shocked, excited voices filled the night, and people fell over one another in their haste to help him hoist his dripping burden to the pier.

I stepped back from the melee and called 911.

Chapter Four

THE MEDIC ONE GUYS SAVED CORINNE CAMPBELL, BUT IT was touch and go. They say King County is the best place in the world to have a heart attack, and it's an auspicious spot for a near-drowning, too. We had a fire truck on the scene in minutes, and the paramedics shortly after. Aaron and I stood rooted, our hands knotted in each other's, while they resuscitated Corinne and swathed her in blankets.

When they went for a stretcher, we crouched beside her on the deck. Rivulets of water snaked from Corinne's hair and costume, making a puddle that soaked through the thin skirt of my gown. I was distantly aware of Marvin, my other guard, directing the crowd back out of the way, and of Lily, ever practical, borrowing a blanket for the soaked and shuddering Donald. Elliott Bay is deep, and deadly cold.

Through all this I chafed at one of Corinne's hands, trying to will some life into her. Her hand was icy, the nails bitten to the quick, and her face was a blue-white mask, violated by grotesque smears of mascara and lipstick, and traces of blood from a deep abrasion on one cheek. She was silent at first, then began an agonized muttering.

"How *could* he!?" Her head swung rapidly from side to side, as if she were being slapped. "How could he, how could he..."

"Corinne!" said Aaron, his features contorted with distress. He cupped her face gently in his hands. "Shhh. Don't think about Boris. Everything will be all right."

I felt a pinprick of jealousy, and guiltily suppressed it. They were coworkers, of course he cared about her. As a friend. The paramedics reappeared and shunted us briskly out of the way. Elizabeth, stiff with shock but self-possessed, climbed into the ambulance with Corinne, her broadsword and leather kilt bizarre among the high-tech medical gear. Paul, hovering nearby, moved forward as if to follow but she waved him away, in command as usual.

"Follow us in the car," she told him as the doors swung shut. "Carnegie, handle everything!"

Paul turned to me with a dazed air. "What about the party?"

"Party's over," I told him. "Marvin and I will clear the building. You just take care of Corinne."

The ambulance rolled away at the stroke of midnight, so we were actually on schedule, though we ran a bit behind because of the explanations. Everything's fine, Marvin and I repeated endlessly. Yes, someone fell from the pier but she's now getting help, and please, the party's over, drive safely, thank you for coming, yes, everything's fine, she's getting help, good night. Some of the revelers, especially the *Sentinel* crowd and the people who'd seen Corinne in the water, went away with shocked expressions and hushed voices.

Other guests had left before it happened: I didn't see Syd Soper, with or without Mercedes, or Roger Talbot either. I did talk to the Visigoths, but not Dracula, and I wondered idly if he had scored with the hippie chick. Zack, apparently, had taken himself and his romantic impulses out of the way, which suited me fine. The rest of the guests now departed calmly enough, strolling out into the night, trailing their costumes and props, and calling boisterously to each other as they headed for their cars. I saw Angela, the third bridesmaid, departing with Barney the Dinosaur. She had her pregnancy-pillow under her arm and her nun's habit in black billows around her, and she was laughing. A good time was had by almost all.

Corinne got help, but it was almost too late, I kept thinking. If only I'd helped earlier. Whether she was drunk and lost her balance or was distraught enough to jump, as her words suggested, surely I could have hung on to her in the ladies' room for a heart-to-heart talk. I said as much to Aaron as he accompanied me on my final walk-through of the Aquarium. The grottos were empty, the corridors dim, and our footsteps echoed on the decking.

"She was taking this breakup much too seriously," I said as we passed the marine mammal tanks. The wavering upward light sent little rings of brightness and shadow chasing across our faces. "There are lots of men who'd be interested in Corinne. I should have warned her about Boris in the first place. He's strictly good times and no strings. I should have—"

"Carnegie, you can't take charge of this, too," Aaron exclaimed.

"What do you mean, too?"

"I mean you're always stepping in, taking charge, knowing best. You can't manage everybody's life for them."

"I don't manage people's lives! Just their weddings. If I happen to have an opinion—"

He snorted. "You *always* have an opinion."

"Aaron, is this about Corinne or about us? It's not my opinion that smoking can kill you. It's a fact. But you won't even try to quit—"

"Why the hell should I?" He reached reflexively for a cigarette, remembered the no-smoking rule, and smacked the railing instead. His mouth was tight with anger. "You keep me at arm's length, and then you want to dictate my behavior. We might as well be married!"

"*What?!* Is that your idea of marriage?"

"I didn't say that."

"Well, what are you saying? If I sleep with you, then you'll stop smoking? Is that the price tag on the deal?"

"There's no deal, Stretch." He sighed and stared down into the tank, tired and discouraged. His dashing black costume was damp and smudged and his hat, along with mine, lay forgotten somewhere back on the pier. A harbor seal, huge and sleek, cut a sudden arc on the illuminated surface just below us, but Aaron didn't seem to notice.

"I'm sorry," he said at last. "The truth is I'm mad at myself, not you. Corinne was my date, I knew she was depressed, I should have stayed with her instead of wandering off with you. Christ, if she'd killed herself—"

"Well, she didn't," I said, pushing away the image of her pale, pale face. "We don't even know if she meant to. She could have just fallen. Either way, blaming yourself won't do anyone any good. Look, why don't you go on home? I'll be here for another hour at least; I've got a cleaning crew coming."

"You don't need a ride?"

"Nope. Lily took Donald home in a cab, so I've still got Vanna White." That was my aging but faithful white van.

"All right, Stretch. I'll call you." No good-night kiss, not tonight.

The moment Aaron left, I wished he had offered to stay. I was tired and discouraged myself, and we'd left so much unsaid. Well, I'd be home in bed soon enough. I went through the exhibits on automatic pilot, making mental notes for the cleaners. The Aquarium contract requires only that the floors be vacuumed, but I like to leave my venues spotless—you never know when you'll need a last-minute reservation somewhere, or just a good word on the grapevine. And after a fiasco like Corinne's fall, the word would not be good, for the Aquarium or for me.

I was determined to call it a fall.

Busily fretting for my reputation and checking for damage, I inspected the length of *A Watershed Journey,* starting with the artificial marsh, whose hollow plastic log had earlier sheltered Florence Nightingale, giggling madly, and a remarkably vocal mime. It was empty now, I was happy to see, with no bits of nursing apparel left behind. Along the artificial stream, wire mesh had prevented a blob of carpaccio and a couple of caviar blini from joining the ecosystem. So far so good.

I checked the river otters' playground near the artificial waterfall, then stood by the cascading water, staring into its endless foaming descent, while my troubled mind went blank and still. I even closed my eyes for a moment, pleasantly deafened by the roar, nearly asleep on my feet. Then I started awake when someone laid a hand on my arm.

It was Marvin, a look of concern on his comfortable, old-shoe face. "Everything all right?"

"Fine!" We could hardly hear each other over the roaring water, so we stepped outside. "Did you check the shorebird area for trash when you closed it off?"

"Not really, just looked around that nobody was in there. I was kinda busy—"

"No problem. Let the cleaners in when they get here, OK?"

"Will do." He went back inside. I made my way down the corridor, through another entrance, and past the post-and-rope barrier he had erected across the *Northwest Shores* grotto. Not much litter on the floor here, that was good, but I wanted to be sure no one had flung anything into the tide pool or onto the little beach. You can't have the marbled god-wit eating caramel brie for breakfast.

The tide pool was unsullied, but when I rounded a broad concrete pillar to check the beach, I stumbled over something that shifted, soft and heavy, under my feet. Kneeling down, my eyes adjusting to the dimness after the brighter light outside, I made out grizzled hair and a Kelly-green jacket very much the worse for wear. A mushroom cloud of Guinness fumes clinched the ID.

"Tommy? Hey, Tommy, wake up!"

His head lolled silently, and for a moment I thought we were due for another ambulance. Then the bleary Irish eyes flickered open and a palsied hand lifted high.

"Stop it!" said Tommy hoarsely. "Stop it, you're killing her!"

"Stop what? What are you talking about?"

But the hand dropped down, the eyes rolled up, and Tommy was no longer with us. I laid him gently back against the pillar and straightened up to use my radio.

"Marvin, we have a stowaway. There's a gentleman passed out near the door to . . . to . . ."

"Carnegie? Hello? I'm losing you. Should I come over there?"

"Yes," I whispered, staring down into the shorebird ex-hibit, and going slowly cold all over. The radio slid from my hand and I spoke into the air. "Yes, come."

A garish heap of patchwork and ruffles lay on the little

beach exhibit, half in and half out of the water. Slim brown legs extended from it among the coarse tufts of salt grass, and one slender outflung arm, still adorned with showy bracelets, stirred gently in the shallows. Long hair, midnight-black, curled and twisted like weeds beneath the surface, obscuring the downturned face of Mercedes Montoya.

I vaulted the handrail and hit the sand with a jolt that clapped my teeth together. As I hauled at Mercedes' shoulders to roll her clear of the water, elusive scraps of CPR training scattered from my mind like minnows from a shark. *There was an ABC, wasn't there? A, what was A? Airway! Tilt the head back to open the airway. Then B, check for breathing, or is B for bleeding? Oh, please, what do I do?*

Mercedes wasn't breathing, so I crouched low and pressed my mouth to hers, forcing air into her, again and again. No response. When I sat back, dizzy with the effort, her head fell lifelessly to one side. Sand had crusted in the scrapes and scratches on her cheeks. I positioned my hands on her chest to begin pumping, then stared at my fingers in disbelief. They were blotched with dark smears that spread over my hands and up my wrists. Dark, sticky red smears . . .

Then I saw the blood on the sand and the stones, and the way the perfumed mane of Mercedes' hair was matted against the nape of her neck. I lifted the curls aside tenderly, like a lover, afraid and yet certain of what I would see. And there it was. Behind her left ear was a ragged concave wound the size of my fist, dark with blood but showing pale glints of bone. Mercedes hadn't drowned in those few inches of water. Someone had bashed in her skull.

Chapter Five

THROWING UP AT A MURDER SCENE IS APPARENTLY NOT UNCOMmon, though the police, when Marvin called them, made it clear that they wished I hadn't. Things were enough of a mess, what with my footprints all over the sand and my inconsiderate handling of the corpse.

Being SPD himself, Marvin had done all the right things, and done them fast. He made sure I was unhurt, secured the body and the exits, and checked warily around for the presence of the murderer.

"Long gone," he assured me, wrapping his windbreaker around my shoulders. Marvin looks like your favorite uncle, portly and graying. I was grateful for his presence as the other officers arrived and went about their grisly business. Their voices seemed loud and callous, and when a Polaroid flash went off, I nearly jumped out of my skin. They had a video camera, too, but I kept my back resolutely turned on the scene they were recording.

Marvin brought over Lieutenant Michael Graham, a weedy, dark-haired fellow in parka and sneakers. He wore a look of intense disappointment, which I later learned was a permanent feature, not a reaction to queasy witnesses.

"Ms. Kincaid, I'll need a brief statement now, then a more detailed account tomorrow morning. OK?"

"Whatever," I said numbly. "Is Tommy all right?"

"Who?"

"Tommy Barry, he's over by the pillar. He's drunk. He said 'You're killing her,' and then he passed out."

But Tommy, it seemed, was also long gone. He must have slipped out the exit to the dock, and gone around to the street on the outside walkway. I was asked urgently for his description, which I provided, and for a description of his car, which I'd never seen. Some officers left in a hurry, and only then did Lieutenant Graham ask me about finding Mercedes. I made a calm, step-by-step statement, and when it was done I erupted into sobs.

Graham watched me mournfully for a minute, then dispatched Marvin to take me home. I made a stop at the ladies' room to scrub off the blood. Marvin came in with me, and a good thing. As the pink-tinged water spiraled slowly down the drain, I nearly fainted clean away.

"Carnegie, you all right?"

"Sure. Fine. No problem." I clutched the counter, gulping air. Mercedes had stood here, only hours before, vain and scheming and alive. My newest almost-client. *She would have made a glorious bride. We could have woven flowers into her hair.* "I just want to get out of here."

But first we had a gauntlet to run: a little crowd of reporters at the building entrance, barking at us like dogs. How had they found out so quickly? There were more camera flashes, blinding in the darkness, and a dozen shouted questions.

"Who got killed?"

"Officer, can you tell us what happened?"

"Miss, did you see anything? Miss, what's your name? Hey, Miss!"

"Hey, Stretch!"

One of the baying newshounds had a familiar face. Aaron. He reached out to me, but there was a pencil in his hand and a question on his lips. *Not you, too.* I turned away, disgusted. He'd always be a reporter first, and a friend—or a lover?—second. If I needed some direction about our relationship, I'd just gotten it. Marvin hustled me into Vanna and drove me home.

Home is a houseboat on Lake Union, with Made in Heaven's two-room office on the upper floor. The houseboat itself has seen better days, but my slip is priceless: right at the end of the dock with a view of downtown Seattle to the south and Gas Works Park to the north, and a constant parade of watercraft and waterfowl in between. Renting home and office in one waterborne package had been just barely affordable when I started Made in Heaven, and now with the dock fees escalating and Vanna in need of round-the-clock nursing, I was perpetually broke. But I loved my shabby little place, and I'd never been so glad to see it as tonight.

Marvin walked me to my door, along the worn wooden planks of the dock. I assured him one last time that I didn't need a friend to come stay with me, so he called in to the station for a pickup and went out to the parking lot to wait. Numb with exhaustion and shock, I stepped out of my gory witch's gown and left it on the bathroom floor. With my last bit of energy, I called up to the office and left a message for Eddie to hear in the morning. Then I crawled under the covers and fell fathoms deep into dreamless sleep.

The next morning it was raining, a dense mournful rain that drummed on the wooden stairway as I trudged up to the office, and sheeted down the picture windows of Made in Heaven's reception area. The "good room," with its fresh paint and wicker love seats, was where I met with clients to talk cakes and bouquets. To help them daydream. The work-room, through a connecting door, was all secondhand desks and file cabinets, but boasted the same stellar view of the lake. Eddie rarely met with the clients—he objected to marriage, and therefore to weddings, or so he claimed—but this morn-ing he stood in the good room pouring coffee for Lieutenant Graham and a dimpled young Asian-American woman in po-lice uniform, who sat stiffly with a notebook on her lap.

Eddie Breen and my father had been inseparable, back in their hell-raising merchant marine days. He's little and leath-ery, with fine white hair, a limited but immaculate wardrobe, and a tetchy disposition. Eddie keeps my books and negoti-ates my vendor contracts and bosses me around, and I let him, I guess, because Dad's no longer alive to do it. He looked me over as I came in, his steel-gray eyes on high beam.

"Carnegie! Sit down before you fall down. Have some cof-fee. You look like ten miles of bad road."

Coming from Eddie, this was a wealth of tender solici-tude. I accepted a cup and sat across from Graham, who wore a jacket and tie, with wingtips nicely polished and crinkly brown hair neatly combed. He looked like a well-groomed, disappointed man who'd been up all night. After introducing Officer Lee, he turned to Eddie.

"Thank you, Mr. Breen," he said, in polite but positive dismissal. "You've been very helpful."

Eddie rose. "I'll get back to answering the phone, then. Carnegie, I've been saying 'No comment' to everybody. That OK?"

"Perfect. If you need to, just put it on the answering ma-chine and let it ring."

He nodded and turned back to Graham. "Don't go getting her all upset. She's got work to do."

Officer Lee smiled to herself, but Graham just nodded solemnly as my fire-breathing champion left us. I barely waited for the workroom door to close before I demanded, "Lieutenant, have you talked to Tommy? Did he recognize the murderer? Who was it?"

"Let's start at the beginning," said Graham, as if I hadn't spoken. "What time did you arrive at the Aquarium last night?"

"What does it matter what time I arrived! What did Tommy say?"

"Ms. Kincaid," he said quietly. "This is not a conversation. It's a witness interview in a homicide investigation. Please cooperate."

So I did. Graham asked me about my relationship with Mercedes, and if I knew of anyone who might have wanted to harm her. Then he had me reconstruct the events of the party, hour by hour. He unfolded a visitor's map of the Aquarium on the glass-topped table that usually holds bridal magazines and photographers' portfolios, and I traced my movements on it, with approximate times. Marvin reported closing off the shorebird corridor at about eleven P.M., which jibed with my recollection of when I'd radioed my request to him.

"So Mercedes must have been killed after eleven?" I speculated. But I got no response from Graham. "The corridor would have been too public before then. Either she crossed the rope barrier with someone else, or she went alone and the murderer followed her. Don't you think?"

Still no response, except for more of his steady, methodical questions. "You say that Ms. Montoya invited Sydney Soper to dance with her. Did she remain with him for the rest of the evening?"

"I have no idea, Lieutenant. I spoke with her briefly just

before I radioed Marvin to close off *Northwest Shores*, and I don't think I saw her at all after that. Or him either. But that doesn't mean they were together."

"What exactly did you do between eleven o'clock and the time you discovered the body?"

I described my circuit through the party, my dance with Zack, the people I recalled seeing on the dance floor, and then meeting Aaron on the stairs and going out on the pier with him. All the while, Officer Lee scribbled away. Graham seemed unsurprised by Corinne's fall into the harbor; maybe it happened all the time at waterfront parties. I continued on, explaining about my final walk-through routine, and mentioning Aaron's departure. This time I managed to describe the corpse without tears.

I thought we were finally finished, but instead, the detective began to skip around in the chronology of the party, repeating questions he'd already asked, probing at my memory like a man with a poker stirring at a fire. It's surprising what you can remember if someone asks the right way. Graham coaxed out details I hadn't even registered at the time, like the triangular gap in the rocks near Mercedes' shoulder—the source of the murder weapon, I surmised, though he wouldn't say—and the damp patch of drool on Tommy's leprechaun jacket.

"Would you assume that Mr. Barry had been lying by the pillar for some time?"

"Well, long enough to sit down and then pass out, but it might not have taken long. I expect he was pretty well plowed when he first arrived. Marvin was at the front entrance, he could tell you."

"He already has. I'm double-checking. Mr. Breen gave us the guest list, and we'll be interviewing everyone on it, as well as the staff from Solveto's and the cleaning firm and so forth." The lieutenant smiled sorrowfully. "Too bad it wasn't a smaller party. Let's go back to your encounter with Ms. Montoya in the rest room. Was she taking drugs?"

"What?!"

"It's a simple question." Graham sat remarkably still and composed, as if he could do this all day. I suppose he often did. Outside, the rain went on raining, a muffled drumroll against the windows.

"I . . . didn't see her doing anything like that." Of course, I suspected that Mercedes blabbed about Talbot only because she was high. But suspicions aren't facts. "Why do you ask? Were there drugs in her system?"

As before, he ignored me. "You said the two of you talked a bit. What about, exactly?"

I was dreading this question. I'd deliberately glossed over the conversation in my step-by-step account. Mercedes had confided in me—I thought of her now as one of my brides—and it seemed cruel to expose her private life. But facts *are* facts. And murder is murder.

"She told me she was engaged to be married. To Roger Talbot."

Graham was startled, though he hid it well, merely elevating one eyebrow a millimeter or two. His voice stayed level. "That's . . . quite a piece of news."

"She said it was a secret, no one knew about it yet."

"Did you believe her?"

"Well, I didn't think she bought that ring herself."

"Which ring? She was wearing several."

"That was all costume jewelry. She had a diamond ring on a long chain around her neck. She waved it at me and then hid it down her blouse. . . ."

Lightning struck both of us at once. Graham leaned forward. *"There was no diamond ring on the corpse."*

"Oh, my God." I pictured again the bloody rent in Mercedes' skull, the vulnerable nape of her neck. "No. No, it was gone. I should have realized that last night—"

"Never mind. Can you describe it?"

I closed my eyes and took a breath to steady myself. "A marquise diamond, between two and three-quarter and three carats. Six-prong setting. Pear-cut side stones. Platinum band engraved with leaves. I'm not sure of the size on the side stones, maybe half a carat apiece."

"Ginny, call that in. And find out if Talbot's in his office today." She went to the window and spoke quietly into her cell phone. Graham was looking at me curiously. "She *waved* it at you and you saw all that?"

I shrugged. "It's my business."

"Really. And you didn't see any sign of it when you found her? No ring, no gold chain?"

"No. But maybe if you search the exhibit—"

"Ms. Kincaid, we are sifting the goddamn *sand,* grain by grain. Excuse my French." He sighed heavily. "So she asked you to plan her wedding. Was she happy about this secret engagement? Any anger at Talbot for keeping it secret?"

"She seemed fine with it, as far as I could tell. She was kind of . . . excitable."

"Excitable. What was she excited about?" Graham's tired brown eyes were expressionless, but I could sense the active intelligence behind them as he weighed my words.

"Well, about Talbot's running for mayor, and about their wedding. She was very insistent that I agree to work for her. She even gave me some cash as a deposit."

This brought both eyebrows up. "Cash? How much cash?"

"I don't really know. I didn't want to take it out and count it during the party, and then after I found her I forgot all about it. It's still in the pocket of my costume."

Another sigh. First the ring, now this. I was definitely flunking Witness 101. "Ms. Kincaid, we'll need to take the money in as evidence. You'll be given a receipt. All right?"

"Of course." *But still, she meant to hire me. She meant to be my bride.*

"Let's go back to Mr. Barry. Tell me again what he said."

I shifted in my chair. Wicker's not that comfortable. "Tommy said 'Stop it.' I think he said that twice. And then he said 'You're killing her!' "

"So he believed that you had killed Ms. Montoya?"

"Is that what he told you? Lieutenant, Tommy couldn't even focus his eyes at that point, he was dead drunk! I think he must have been repeating something he'd said earlier, during the murder."

"And yet if he had spoken out earlier, the killer would hardly have left him alive as a witness."

"Well maybe he didn't say it out loud, except later, to me, only he didn't know it was me, he was just raving! Look, I know you're supposed to be cagey about testimony, but *please* tell me, who did Tommy see? Did he recognize the murderer?"

Graham stood up. "We'd very much like to know that ourselves. Unfortunately, after leaving the crime scene, Mr. Barry drove his car into a concrete abutment under the Alaskan Way Viaduct. He's currently in intensive care at Harborview. In a coma."

Chapter Six

MY MOUTH AND THE OFFICE DOOR SWUNG OPEN SIMULTANE-ously. Nothing emerged from me—I was too stunned—but what emerged through the door was a large rosy-cheeked man, his medium-sized rosy-cheeked daughter, and his diminutive but equally rosy-cheeked wife. You could have fit one inside the other inside the other, like those painted Russian dolls. All three were dressed in jeans, cowboy boots, and "I Love Seattle" sweatshirts, and laden with damp Nordstrom's bags, Starbucks cups, bridal magazines, and paper cartons of what smelled like rain-soaked kung-pao chicken.

"Carnegie!" hollered the man. He managed to laugh and holler simultaneously. "I know we don't have an appointment, but we brought you lunch to make up for it! You need to eat more, girl, you're thin as a fence rail, isn't she, Mother?"

He rotated like a benevolent lighthouse to beam at my other visitors, shedding parcels on the table as he seized Graham's hand with both oversized paws and pumped it fervently.

"Bruce Buckmeister! Call me Buck! My wife Betty, my daughter Bonnie! Hey, congratulations! Is this your blushing bride?" He leered roguishly at Officer Lee, who stood frozen at the window trying to keep a straight face. "The bride wore a nightstick, how 'bout that! Better not leave her at the altar or she'll bust you!"

"Buck, please, can you come back later? Or wait in your car?" I hardly knew what I was saying; all I could think of was Tommy. "I have to talk with Lieutenant Graham—"

"We're done," said Graham, nodding at Officer Lee, who gathered up their jackets and went to the door. "If we could just pick up that one item?"

"Sure. Um, folks, I'll be right back. You go ahead with your lunch."

Lee hurried down to my front door, but I halted Graham on the covered landing at the head of the stairs. The rain formed a hissing silver curtain around us.

"Tommy *drove* away from the Aquarium?" I demanded. "In his condition?"

"Apparently," said Graham. "He only got a few blocks. Fortunately, no other vehicles were involved."

"Will he be all right? Is he going to live?"

"Unknown." The detective was watching me closely, and his expression softened. "You're a friend of his?"

I recalled the old sportswriter beaming at Zack by the dance floor, and kissing my hand in the *Sentinel* newsroom back when Aaron first introduced us, and his pleased and proud surprise when Paul asked him to be best man. A charming, exasperating fellow, Tommy Barry.

"Yes, we're friends."

"I'm sorry to bring you the bad news, then. Look, Ms. Kincaid, a murder scene can be pretty traumatic. We have a Victim Assistance section; they can help you with counseling and so forth. Let me have someone call you—"

"No, thank you, I'll be OK. My best therapy will be getting back to work."

"All right, then. Let's get that money."

Graham and Lee waited in the kitchen while I retrieved

the little bundle of bills from my witch's gown, which was still on the bathroom floor. As he counted out the money on the kitchen table, and Officer Lee prepared a receipt, I began to get goose bumps. There were tens and twenties, all right, but several fifties, not just one, and the inside of the roll was all hundred-dollar bills.

"Two thousand, nine hundred and fifty dollars," said Graham. "Not exactly pocket change, is it?"

"That's bizarre! Why was she carrying so much cash at a party?"

Graham was really very good at not answering questions. He signed the receipt and handed it to me along with his card. "Call me if you change your mind about Victim Assistance. Meanwhile, we'll get a statement typed up for you to sign. And Ms. Kincaid, it's important that you don't discuss the details of the case with anyone."

"What do you mean, details?"

"Cause of death, condition of the body, Mr. Barry's presence at the scene, and so forth. That won't be released to the press just yet. For now, a party guest was found dead, that's all."

"Of course. Whatever you say."

After they left, I went back to hang up the gown, just until I could get it to a dry cleaners. As I lifted the crumpled black folds, I heard a faint clatter against the tiles of the bathroom floor, and remembered: Mercedes' powder compact. I pulled out the little square of black enamel and gold trim, and felt tears welling up. Just a bit of female frippery. Souvenir of a dead woman. I took a shaky breath, set the compact gently on a shelf, and returned upstairs to discuss details of a very different sort with Buck, Betty, and Bonnie.

The Buckmeisters were a living, laughing, hollering argument for charging an hourly rate instead of a commission. I figured that by the time Bonnie said "I do," Buck and Betty would have paid me about fourteen cents an hour for my services. They popped in to see me almost daily, had me pursue every new fad and feature that showed up in the magazines or on-line, and changed their minds as often as Buck changed the bandannas that he invariably wore, pirate-fashion, wrapped around his broad red forehead and knotted in back above his scraggly gray ponytail. Today's bandanna was blue with yellow polka dots. Buck was from El Paso, where he'd made a fortune in hot tubs, and moving to Seattle hadn't changed him one little bit, no siree.

Daughter Bonnie was to be a Christmas bride, and we'd already worked through four or five entire scenarios for the wedding, from food to flowers to music, each of them increasingly Yule-ish. The only constants were the church and country club sites, the ornate wedding gown, and the invisible groom. Invisible to me, that is, because he'd been out of the country for the entire planning process, setting up a computer center for his company in Milan. I hoped he wouldn't throw me any curves at the last moment. It was remarkable enough for a father of the bride to be as immersed in wedding minutiae as Buck was; grooms and dads usually just showed up and said "Yes, dear."

"Yes, dear," Buck was saying now. "I did too bring the chicken, it's in this bag, no it isn't, wait a darn minute, here it is! Carnegie, we brought you your favorite!"

"You eat up, dear, and we'll tell you this wonderful idea we've had about the bridesmaids," said his wife. Betty's hair was dyed black as patent leather, and permed into curlicues that framed her round, kindly face just like a painted doll's. "Instead of bouquets they could carry little silk purses, dyed to match their shoes, with flowers peeking out the top. Wouldn't that just be sweet?"

I sank into a wicker chair, wondering how Boris would respond to yet another change in plan. "Very sweet. I bet you have a picture to show me."

"As a matter of fact, we do!" Bonnie was the round, curly image of her mother, amplified with some of her father's height and heft. "We found this at the library. Look!"

She opened a glossy volume authored by the sort of florist-to-the-stars that Boris claimed to disdain and, I suspected, secretly envied. The thought of Boris brought Corinne's face, deathly pale, floating before my eyes. Should someone tell Boris about her fall, or would she be embarrassed if he knew? *Damn her anyway for being so melodramatic.*

"See?" said Bonnie. "It's a bride's purse in the picture, but all the girls could carry them, and we'd have Christmas flowers instead of these tiny little pansies or whatever they are."

"Primroses!" Buck boomed. "Caption says they're primroses and forget-me-nots. Hmph. I'd like to see anybody forget my little Bonnie. Anyhow, we'd want holly and mistletoe, wouldn't we, to keep it Christmassy, or maybe poinsettias?"

Betty squealed at her husband in affectionate glee. "Why, Father, you know how big a purse you'd need for a poinsettia? We'd have bridesmaids with tote bags!"

"Well, little poinsettias then. Carnegie, can't your Russian fella come up with some kinda mini-poinsettias?"

"Amaryllis," I said faintly. My head was swimming. Conversing with the Buckmeisters was odd at any time, but utterly surrealistic today. "We had planned on ruby-red amaryllis blossoms, with cedar fronds and red hypericum berries. If you don't want them we really need to let Boris know."

"Oh, that's right," sighed Bonnie. "I do like those amaryllises. Well, we'll decide later. Oh! And I saw this article about tiaras. They say a tiara can be a bride's crowning glory. Carnegie, I could wear a tiara!"

"Well, yes, you could. Although we have already ordered your headpiece and veil." *Twice, in fact. We've ordered everything for this bloody wedding at least twice.*

Bonnie knit her brows. "Maybe a tiara on top of the veil?"

I smiled inwardly at the notion of all that sparkle and drama perched above Bonnie's rosy, sweet-natured face. A tiara calls for a woman with a certain confident carriage, a certain aristocratic air . . . a woman like Mercedes Montoya. Suddenly Bonnie's voice faded to a distant murmur, as the events of last night crowded around me, and I knew if I sat still much longer I was going to lose it.

"Folks, could you excuse me for just another minute?"

I went into the workroom and closed the connecting door behind me. "Eddie, if you love me, go out and talk to the Buckmeisters."

"Oh, no," he said, his feet planted on his desk and an unlit cigar clamped in his teeth. No smoking in the workroom, by order of the proprietor. "Ohhh, no, not the Killer B's. If you're too shook up to work, then get rid of 'em and take the day off."

"I'm not shaken up; I'm going to Harborview."

"What the hell for?"

"Tommy Barry's had a drunk-driving accident, I want to try and see him. Please, Eddie, just take some notes and don't promise them anything for sure until I check it out."

He grumbled, but he did it, and within minutes I was fleeing through the downpour to climb into Vanna. As I drove, Tommy's voice sounded in my head: "You're killing her!" But who? Who had he seen with Mercedes, and did that person know they'd been seen? Was there someone out there hoping that Tommy never woke up? Or planning to make sure that he didn't? The police should be guarding him. The morning news had only hinted at foul play and said nothing of witnesses, but if the killer knew about Tommy, he could easily track him down.

I maneuvered into a tight spot behind a pillar in the hospital's underground garage, and fumbled in my purse to be sure I had Graham's card handy. I could call him from the lobby after I'd seen Tommy. A grandmotherly volunteer told me what floor Mr. Barry was on, then began to say something about restricted visiting. I didn't stay to listen.

Hospitals try so hard to be efficient and cheery, like office buildings crossed with day-care centers. Soothing watercolors, potted plants, even espresso carts, for revving up the staff and calming down the visitors. But every time I enter one of those double-wide, slow-moving elevators with their indefinable hospital smell, I can taste Styrofoam and the thin, bitter vending-machine coffee that Mom and I drank by the quart at St. Luke's, in Boise, as my father failed to recover from his third heart surgery.

Dad gave me my red hair and also my name. He had educated himself in the public libraries endowed by Andrew Carnegie, and conveniently overlooked the fact that old Andy was a robber baron. But Dad gave me so much more, and I still missed him. Mom and I practically lived at the hospital, that last time. She knew all the nurses' names, and I knew every waiting-room watercolor by heart. Dad was buried in the veterans' cemetery there in Boise. Mom went to see him every Sunday.

The elevator began to fill, and I squeezed back in the corner and tried hard to think of something else. You couldn't get more "else" than the Buckmeisters, so I thought about them, and the Great Christmas Cake Conundrum. The dinner menu was shaping up fine; Joe Solveto was planning on roasted halibut with a macadamia crust and mango chutney, and he was fine-tuning a vegetarian entrée as well. But the Killer B's wanted the cake to be a special event in itself, some kind of colossal Christmas concoction that they couldn't quite describe, but they'd know it when they saw it.

Buck, Betty, and Bonnie had done tasting after tasting—these folks just loved to eat cake—but none of my usual bakeries had really wowed them. So far, they'd rejected a traditional tiered cake with holly trim, a forty-pound brandied fruitcake, and a fantasy forest of fir-tree-shaped *croques en bouche* in a blizzard of spun sugar. Time was getting short. I had one more baker, deep in my Rolodex, who might just do the trick. . . .

The doors swooshed open on the intensive care unit. Surprise, surprise: the police knew their job better than I did. At the end of the corridor I could see a brawny officer planted on a folding chair beside a door. Tommy's room. I made a beeline for it, past a waiting area full of family members with strained expressions, despondently doing jigsaw puzzles or rereading magazines. I tried not to see them, not to imagine who or what they were waiting for. A tiny, sharp-nosed black supervisor with bloodshot eyes intercepted me, demanding my full name and relationship to the patient.

"You're not Mr. Barry's daughter, then," she said. It sounded like an accusation. "Immediate family only at this time."

"Tommy has a daughter? Can I get her phone number? I'd like to help."

"We can't release that information."

"Can you at least tell me how he's doing? Or could I talk to his doctor?"

"The doctor would tell you that Mr. Barry's condition is critical," she said, glaring up at me, "and there are no visitors allowed except immediate family."

In another minute she'd call the cop over to evict me; he was already watching us suspiciously. Well, at least I knew Tommy was safe. I stopped in the hospital gift shop on my way out and tried to order a bouquet for his room, but they told me flowers weren't allowed in the ICU. As I bypassed the elevator and clattered down the fire stairs to the van, I vowed to myself that I'd bring an armful of blossoms when Tommy woke up. Surely he'd wake up soon. At the moment, I didn't even care if he could identify the murderer. I just wanted Tommy Barry back in the land of the living.

Preoccupied as I was, I must have pulled out of my parking space too fast. A bang like a gunshot coincided with a shock that flung me forward against my shoulder belt. I sat still for a moment, unsure at first of what had happened. Then I realized and groaned aloud, not in pain but in sorrow. *If my insurance goes up I'm screwed.* I scrambled out. My fender was a mess, but the occupants of the other car, a Catholic priest and a drab young woman, seemed to be intact.

"I'm so sorry," I babbled as they climbed out of the shiny blue sedan. The priest, a burly man in his sixties, had been driving. "Honest, I thought I looked, but the pillar was blocking me. I'll pay for any—Corinne?"

Drab and washed-out, matted hair pulled back with a rubber band, lush figure bundled in an oversized parka, the passenger was indeed Corinne Campbell. I'd never seen her without her face painted and her hair styled, but those round, slightly bulging aquamarine eyes were unmistakable. *Of course, the ambulance must have brought her here, and then they kept her overnight.* She stood hugging herself as if she were cold, looking dazed and miserable, staring at nothing.

"Do you know each other?" the priest asked, in the rich, confident voice of a born public speaker. He held out his hand. "What a very small world. I'm Father Richard Barnstable. And you're—?"

"Carnegie Kincaid." We shook hands and I nodded at Vanna's copper-colored Made in Heaven logo. Wedding professionals often do pink, so I try to stand out. "I'm an event planner. I was at the party last night where Corinne . . . that is, the party at the Aquarium. One of the guests had a car accident."

Corinne snapped to attention. "Who?"

"It was Tommy Barry. He's in critical condition, I couldn't get in to see him. Listen, Corinne, how are you? I mean, are you OK now, and are you all right from last night?"

And did you jump or fall? That's what I really wanted to ask, though I'd feel guilty about it either way. Either I failed her as a friend or I failed to spot a safety hazard at the party venue. Maybe I should call myself a disaster planner.

"I'm fine," she said absently, gnawing at a thumbnail. "Father Richard is taking me home. Father, you're not hurt, are you?"

"Not at all, not at all. And the car seems to be undamaged, though Ms. Kincaid's van looks the worse for the encounter."

"It's just a little body work," I said, bending down to inspect the fender. It wasn't quite scraping against the wheel, but it looked awful, with bare metal showing through the white paint. Poor old Vanna. Nothing like a dilapidated vehicle to make a really classy impression. "It's drivable."

Corinne wasn't interested in the state of my van. "What happened to Tommy?"

"He was drunk and he tried to drive himself home. He's still unconscious. Corinne, has anyone told you about Mercedes?"

She stared at me. Corinne never seemed to blink. "It was on the news this morning. What happened? They didn't really say."

I'm used to counseling hysterical brides and soothing their irate mothers, but explaining this kind of news to this kind of person was above and beyond. To complicate matters, a behemoth SUV full of teenagers came down the ramp and honked at us; the priest's car was blocking the aisle. He hastened to move it, and Corinne stepped aside with me.

"I can't say much either," I told her, remembering Graham's admonition. "She died some time during the party, or right after. I found her. The police are questioning everyone, so you'll probably get a phone call. They, um, know about your fall."

A hand shot out from the baggy sleeve of her parka and gripped my arm. "Carnegie, I didn't fall."

"Oh, Corinne, I'm so sorry. I knew you were upset about Boris, I should have come and found you so we could talk. Aaron feels really bad about it, too. Is Father Richard going to stay with you this afternoon? You can always call me, you know."

"What are you talkin' about?" Her Southern accent had grown stronger.

"Well, I don't want to butt in, but if you're still feeling like you might harm yourself, you shouldn't be alone."

"Y'all think I jumped?" She shook my arm impatiently and her eyes got even rounder. "Carnegie, *somebody tried to drown me.*"

Chapter Seven

IT WAS MY TURN TO STARE, INTO THE AQUAMARINE SHALLOWS of Corinne's wide, wild eyes. The SUV lumbered off, and we were left in echoing silence.

"Are you sure? Maybe it was a joke. People were drinking a lot—"

"I don't know who did it, but it wasn't a joke. I was sitting on the edge of the pier, over where the guests weren't supposed to be, you know? I went around the barricade. I just wanted to be alone. Somebody in a black cape, or a cloak or something, came up behind me. He bunched it over my face and we wrestled around and then I hit my head. Next thing I knew, that guard was hauling me out of the water. I didn't jump, honestly. You believe me, don't you?"

Father Richard joined us at this point, and Corinne's demeanor changed abruptly. Her expression went blank, and she turned quickly away from us to get into his sedan and slam the door.

"I'll take her home," the priest told me, as I gazed after her in consternation. "We'll just forget the fender bender, shall we?"

"Father, has Corinne told the police she was attacked?"

He moved closer, his back to Corinne, and spoke softly.

"She plans to," he said. "Unfortunately."

"What do you mean?"

"You have to understand," he said, "she's told stories like this before. I've known Corinne since she came here to the university, and she's always had, well, call it a vivid imagination. She gets a bit dramatic when things aren't going well. There was a young man once, she was angry at him, and she made an accusation that wasn't quite true."

"An accusation? . . ." I couldn't quite say "rape" to a priest.

He nodded significantly. "We settled it quietly enough, but the police are unlikely to take her seriously a second time. Nor should they, I'm afraid. I think Corinne just needs a different way to explain what happened last night. Self-destruction is a sin against God's love, you know, and she's a very devout girl."

"I understand," I said, though I wasn't sure I did. "Well, here's my card, in case there's a problem about your car. Thanks for being so reasonable about it."

"You're welcome. God bless you."

They left, and I drove away with my thoughts spinning like a whirlpool. It was certainly possible that one woman tried to kill herself on the same night that another woman was murdered. Corinne might well have repented her suicide attempt, then gotten the idea for her "story" from the report of Mercedes' death on the news. She'd been all alone out there in the dark, beyond the barricade, with no witnesses. Simple enough, last night, to slip into the water in drunken despair. Simple enough, this morning, to pretend there was a killer stalking the party, and play the victim instead of the fool. Or the sinner.

But wasn't the boy who cried wolf devoured by one? Was Corinne's wolf in a black cloak imaginary, or all too real?

I needed time to think, and I wanted to give the Buckmeisters time to vacate the office, so I swung out of my way to do a drive-by of the Experience Music Project. Even if Paul and Elizabeth decided to postpone, I'd have to check off this chore eventually. For each of my weddings, I drive to the site pretending I'm a guest with no special knowledge of one-way streets or parking-lot entrances. It gives me a better sense of where to put signs or set up valet parking, and serves as a double check if we've put a map in with the invitation.

Eddie harrumphs that people should fend for themselves, but I believe that your experience as a wedding guest begins when you walk out your front door. Inconvenient dates, un-reasonable distances, or incomprehensible driving directions are just as bad as wilted flowers or a lackluster cake. So I drove through the thinning drizzle, and parked Vanna just as the faint, moist sunshine began to gleam on the vast curves of the Experience Music Project, where it reared up from the Seattle Center grounds.

I had mixed feelings about the EMP, at least the outside of it. Inside, the rock-and-roll museum was fabulous: 140,000 square feet of interactive exhibits, memorabilia from doo-wop to Hendrix to riot grrrls, and various innovative per-formance spaces. And, of course, it made a hip venue for a wedding.

But the outrageous Frank Gehry design for the building it-self gave new meaning to the phrase "You either hate it or you love it." Inspired by the shapes and colors of electric gui-tars, it's a multi-colored metal-skinned train wreck of dark gold, red, and silver sections, with rippling blue and green bands and iridescent pink bulges in between. I was leaning toward loving it, but mostly I found myself wondering how it was going to look covered with frosting.

Because, unlike the Buckmeisters, Elizabeth knew exactly

what she wanted for her wedding cake: an architecturally perfect model of the EMP. The cake itself would be bitter chocolate, laced with raspberry liqueur and filled with mocha mousse and French buttercream. Rolled fondant, carefully dyed to match the EMP's in-your-face colors, would form the shell of the building. And a tiny marzipan monorail would wend through it, heading for a chocolate-and-gum paste Space Needle. The price tag was exorbitant, but people would talk about it for weeks.

Before they could eat cake, though, they'd have to navigate their way to the wedding site.

I pulled out again and made three passes, coming at the EMP across town from the freeway, then south from Queen Anne hill, and finally north from downtown on Alaskan Way.

Then I pulled over on Fifth Avenue to record my findings in the spiral notebook that's always in my tote bag. Eddie keeps suggesting some kind of digital gizmo, but paper works fine for me. And concentrating on practical matters helped me to keep from worrying about Corinne and Tommy.

"Hello there!"

The voice, and the simultaneous tapping on my window, made me jump. My favorite pen leapt from my fingers and hid itself down near the pastry crumbs at the base of the gear shift. Swearing silently, I rolled down the window, and a matronly woman with a pleasant smile handed me a parking ticket.

"I wasn't parking!" I protested. "I was just sitting here thinking for a minute."

"Well," she chirped, "you should have thought about putting money in the meter. Have a nice day!"

A parking fine and body work both, on top of the overdue overhaul on the engine. Wonderful. If only my mechanic would plan *his* wedding, so I could trade for his services.

At least the Killer B's had left. They drove a purple Cadillac with, heaven help us, a pair of steer horns mounted on the grille, so you always knew if they were around. I went wearily upstairs to check in with Eddie. I owed him big time for taking them off my hands. I considered telling him what Corinne had said, but Eddie has this funny notion that I read too much into things, and see mysteries where there aren't any. Like the time I thought a guy courting Lily was married because he wouldn't show her his house, and it turned out he just never vacuumed the place. Eddie would tell me to mind my own business.

"Carnegie!" he bellowed from the workroom as soon as I cracked the door. "This boy's a genius! He's got this planning software working like a charm!" There were printout pages heaped around the room like snowdrifts: checklists, budget graphs, pie charts labeled "Bride's Expenses" and "RSVPs to Date."

Eddie was at his computer, with my erstwhile Robin Hood standing behind him, puffed up with the praise. He *was* awfully good-looking. Maybe I should have kissed him back. At least he didn't smoke.

"Zack!" I said. "I forgot you were coming, after what happened last night."

"You mean that thing with Corinne? Bummer. She OK?"

"I haven't told him," Eddie said quietly, his hands still on the keyboard. "I didn't know if I should."

I moved a sheaf of pages and dropped into my desk chair. "Zack, you haven't seen the news today, have you? Or talked to anyone at the *Sentinel*?"

"Nah. My TV's dead anyway. I slept in and, like, dinked around until now. What's going on?"

"It's Mercedes Montoya." *How do I say this?* "I was walking through the exhibits last night, after everyone left, and . . . Zack, she's dead. I don't know if you knew her very well— Zack? Eddie, catch him!"

Zack had gone white to the lips, as if every last ounce of his blood had been drained away, and then he began to tremble and sway. Eddie leapt from his chair and guided Zack into it, then pushed his head down between his knees.

"Slow breaths," he said gruffly. Eddie has different degrees of gruff, though, and it stuck out a mile that he liked this youngster. "Carnegie, for God's sake, get a glass of water."

Zack had to sip at it for a minute before he could speak. "What happened? Did she drown?"

"I'm not supposed to talk about it until the police say I can. Sorry." He nodded vaguely. "Listen, maybe you should go home. Eddie can show me what you've been working on, and we'll get back to it later. Did you drive over?"

"I took the bus," he said hollowly. "Yeah, I think I'll go home. Sorry."

"Don't worry about it," Eddie told him. He walked Zack to the door, then came back to his desk and began to gather the printouts into stacks.

"I wondered if he had worked with the Montoya girl," he said. All females under fifty were girls to Eddie. "Must have liked her a lot. They're all in an uproar over at the *Sentinel*, according to your boyfriend."

"Eddie, I asked you before. Please don't call Aaron my boyfriend."

"Well, then, your 'acquaintance' called, to tell you the Campbell girl is all right. He tried to see her at Harborview but she'd already gone home." He sat at his desk and laid the paperwork aside. "How's the best man? Sobered up?"

"He's in a coma, Eddie!" My partner had never met the *Sentinel*'s sportswriter, so I couldn't expect any serious sympathy, but still I bridled. "They don't even know if he's going to live."

He winced. "Sorry. Well, there goes the wedding. Shall we divvy up the cancellation calls?"

"Not yet, not till I talk to Elizabeth and Paul. I told you about Paul's great-aunt, didn't I? She's ninety-eight, and apparently she's been hanging on just to see him get married. I don't know what they'll want to do. We have a meeting scheduled for tomorrow, so I assume we'll decide then."

"Good enough." He glanced at his watch, a racy silver affair below his crisply turned-back cuff. Eddie wore a white shirt every day, starched rigid, and you could slice bread with the creases in his khakis. "Well, get going. You've still got time to change before dinner. Did you ever eat lunch?"

"I wasn't hungry. Why should I change for the movies?" Every few weeks Eddie and I went to a big-budget flick and ate junk food. I was looking forward to it tonight, though I planned to insist on a comedy, or even a cartoon—anything without blood.

"Rain check," said Eddie. "Aaron's coming for you in half an hour. I told him you needed cheering up."

"Eddie, who asked you to set up my social life?"

"You're welcome," he said. "Now scoot. Put on something pretty."

"I will not! He just wants an interview."

"He told me he wouldn't pester you with any questions."

I snorted. "Fat chance."

"Now, don't get on your high horse. Aaron just didn't think you should be alone tonight."

"I wasn't going to be alone, I was going to be with you!"

"Scoot."

Boy, do I hate a matchmaker, I thought as I descended the stairs. If Eddie nudged me any harder, I'd fall overboard myself. I wasn't even sure if he liked Aaron, or if he just wanted me settled with a man, any man.

No, that wasn't fair. Eddie had made his distaste for Boris Nevsky quite plain right from the first date. And before that there was Wayne, the hot-looking videographer. Eddie had him pegged for the self-centered type within ten minutes. It took me two weeks.

Holt Walker had been another matter. Smitten, I'd kept Holt to myself, away from Eddie and his opinions. And then my handsome and successful suitor had turned out to be a particularly unsavory sort of criminal. *I sure can pick 'em.*

I was still getting over Holt, in more ways than one. Maybe that was the real reason I was hanging back with Aaron. That and the fact that all he really wanted now was some juicy quotes about a murdered corpse. I dumped my jacket on a chair and did what I always do when I'm tangled up inside my own brain: I poured a glass of cheap white wine and, ignoring the message light on my phone, I called Lily.

"Hey, you caught me just coming in," she said. "I took the boys to their friend Dylan's for a campout."

"A campout? Lily, it's raining again, or hadn't you noticed?"

"Calm down, Honorary Aunt. They're in Dylan's basement. Kids have no nerve endings, they can sleep on concrete and love it. Now, what on earth happened to that

Montoya person last night? She's the TV star, right, the gypsy?"

"She was." I gulped some wine and gave her my tired little routine about not discussing the details.

"I get it," she said. "But you must be in shock. You want some company?"

"No, that's all right. . . . Actually, yes, I would like company. If you don't mind having dinner with Aaron Gold?"

"Aha, the cute reporter. Cute guys always welcome. Don't you want him all to yourself?"

"No," I said. "No, tonight I definitely do not want Aaron all to myself."

Chapter Eight

DINNER STARTED OUT AWKWARD AS HELL. STANDING IN MY living room, faced with a trio instead of a duet, Aaron masked his surprise with a bland and off-putting courtesy that was worthy of Zorro, and Lily responded in kind. The two of them had heard plenty about each other from me, so I knew there was some sizing up going on as they shook hands and commented on the weather.

Lily looked smashing, in a royal-purple sweater and skirt that set off her statuesque figure and coffee-colored skin. Aaron was less rumpled than usual in yellow dress shirt and spiffy black leather jacket. I wore jade silk and an uncomfortable smile. Despite my second—and third and fifth—thoughts about Aaron, I really wanted these people to like each other.

My two companions did have one thing in common: both of them assumed I was upset by what I'd witnessed and persisted in treating me with kid-glove kindness. If Aaron was going to tackle me for an interview, it wouldn't be tonight.

"I made reservations at Toscana," he said as we walked out to the parking lot. The rain was thinning again, to the sloping mist so typical of Seattle. "I hope that suits you, Lily?"

"Sounds wonderful, Aaron," she replied graciously, but then frowned at the sight of his vintage Volkswagen Bug, recently acquired third-hand from someone at the *Sentinel*. It was banana-yellow, with appropriate brown spots of rust. "Umm, how about if I drive?"

I was just as glad—at least Lily's Volvo had some legroom—but that left the brave caballero scrunched in the backseat with her sons' toys and soccer gear. Hardly the way to start a romantic evening. *Serves you right for conspiring with Eddie,* I thought, but without much spirit. Then, as we drove to the University District making the smallest of small talk, I stopped thinking about Aaron and thought about whether I was truly as upset as he and Lily believed me to be.

Certainly I felt sad for Mercedes, and revolted by the horrible way that I'd found her. But as more time passed, there was also plain old vulgar curiosity. Who, of all the masked revelers at the Aquarium last night, had gone home with blood on his hands? And did those same hands try to drown Corinne, or was she fantasizing? Was the killer's motive as deep and murky as Elliott Bay, or as simple and sharp as the glint off a diamond ring?

The Italian bistro Aaron had chosen was dim and intimate, perfect for lovers but a bit much for new acquaintances. We had our choice of tables on a Sunday evening, so we settled ourselves into a corner booth flanked by shelves of wine bottles and hanging plants. The waiter lit our candle, poured our Chianti, and left us. We reviewed the menu, then fell into an uneasy silence.

"So, Lily," said Aaron after a moment. We both turned to him brightly, a couple of nice girls waiting for the boy to start the conversation. "Carnegie tells me that you're African-American."

Lily gaped, stared, and let out a whoop of laughter. Aaron stayed deadpan, but his eyes were sparkling.

"Yes," she replied, once she got her breath back. "Yes, I've been Black for quite some time now. And how about yourself? One of the Chosen People, are you?"

Aaron grinned. "As Chosen as they come. Pass the wine."

An hour later we were all full of penne puttanesca and the two of them were arguing about jazz.

"Chuck Mangione?" Aaron protested, flourishing his fork. He'd shed his jacket and rolled back his cuffs. I vaguely recalled the musician's name, but mostly I was busy admiring Zorro's sword arm, which was very brown and strong-looking. "Mangione is a sure cure for insomnia! You can't listen to his stuff and operate heavy machinery."

"It is beautifully hypnotic," Lily insisted. "I used to fall asleep listening to him."

"You weren't falling asleep, you were falling into a stupor. Mangione isn't fit to tie Coltrane's shoes."

"Oh, not another 'Trane snob!"

"Bite your tongue," Aaron shot back. "Next thing you'll be telling me you listen to Yanni and Kenny G!"

Lily bridled. "And what's wrong with Kenny G?"

"A lot of brides want Kenny G played at their weddings," I chimed in. "But only *after* the ceremony."

They looked at me, puzzled. I think they'd forgotten I was there.

"Why after?" asked Lily.

"They don't believe in sax before marriage."

They both chortled, and Lily threw her napkin at me, saying, "Bad jokes from the woman who hates jazz."

Aaron looked at me in horror. "You hate *jazz*? Say it ain't so, Slim. Say it's only Sominex jazz like Mangione's."

"It's true," Lily insisted. "Carnegie loathes everything except Dixieland. She's hopeless."

I tried to take a dignified sip of wine, but my glass seemed to be empty again, so I put it down. "Just because I don't like irritating music with *no* melody and *no* rhythm—"

"Philistine!" said Aaron. "She's beautiful, but she's a philistine. What am I going to do with her?"

Lily snorted. "I bet you could think of something, a Chosen guy like you."

"I bet I could," he said, doing Groucho Marx with his eyebrows.

"OK, time out," I said. "No more of this."

"Well, then," said Aaron, "let's talk about murder."

I could swear the candle flickered when he said the evil word, but maybe it was just the shadow that descended on our spirits. Then the flame rose again, and I got mad.

"Dammit, Aaron, I should have known—"

"Hey, it's no crime to be curious. Besides, I'm just wondering how you're doing, after what you've been through."

A likely story. "Aaron, this evening is off the record."

"Of course it is."

"I'm serious," I told him. "If I see one word in the *Sentinel*—"

"Look, if you think I'm so unscrupulous, how come—"

" 'Scuse me!" Lily, her diplomacy radar on full alert, made off for the ladies' room and left us to argue in private.

Aaron sat back, breathing hard, and folded his arms. "Stretch, when I say something is off the record, it's off. You can bring along a chaperone if you want, but don't question my integrity, all right?"

"It's just that after seeing you there last night, it's hard to separate the person from the reporter."

"Well, I've done the separating for you. I took myself off the story, as soon as I realized you were involved."

"Really?" I said, abashed.

"Really. Paul assigned it to someone else. We hashed it all out in the newsroom this morning."

"Oh." I thought about Zack's reaction to the news. "How's everyone at the *Sentinel* feeling about Mercedes?"

"They're shocked, of course. But they're news junkies, they're fascinated. And, of course, some of them weren't crazy about Mercedes in the first place, including me. But nobody wanted her dead."

"Well, somebody did." It occurred to me, for the first time, to wonder if Mercedes' secret fiancé was as blissful about their engagement as she was. Suspicion is a poisonous thing. "How did Roger Talbot react?"

"He wasn't there, just left a message asking everyone to cooperate with the police, and tapping Paul to do the obituary. To tell you the truth, I think everybody's mostly concerned about Tommy. More wine?"

"I'd better not."

We ordered cappuccino for three, and when the waiter was out of earshot I asked, "So, who do you think killed Mercedes?"

"Soper," said Aaron promptly. "Gotta be. Look how he came at me with that sickle thing."

"But he wasn't trying to *kill* you."

"Of course not, but it shows how short his fuse is. I think Mercedes let on that she knew about the bribery, and he went ballistic. I think Death killed her."

Lily overheard him as she slid back into the booth. "That's what kills everybody. But you're talking about that guy with the scythe, aren't you? Why would he kill Mercedes Montoya?"

"She was working on an exposé about his company," Aaron said quickly, with a significant look at me. I got the message: the bribery story was still under wraps. "So it's a scythe? I thought it was a sickle."

"A sickle's got a small handle," Lily told him. "Death carries a scythe."

"You librarians, you just know everything, don't you?"

"Never mind that," I said impatiently. I probably shouldn't be doing this, but I just had to talk about Corinne, and these were two of the smartest people I knew. "Why would Syd Soper have attacked Corinne?"

They stared at me and spoke at once.

"Corinne was *attacked*?"

"That woman who almost drowned?"

I held up a hand. "Wait, I'm coming at this backward. I went to see Tommy Barry this afternoon—"

"Who's Tommy Barry?" Lily set her elbows on the table and her chin in her hands. "If you're going to tell me about this, tell it from the beginning."

So I did. I began with Mercedes' startling announcement about marrying Roger Talbot, and the equally startling amount of cash she was carrying. The former seemed to overshadow the latter, at least for Aaron.

"Engaged?" he said. "With the guy's wife barely cold in her grave? Or maybe even before then. Man, Talbot can forget the mayor's office if people find out he was cheating on a dying wife."

"I assume that's why the engagement was secret. And it's got to stay secret, OK? I'm only telling you two because I'm trying to figure out what was going on at the party."

"Sure, we won't go spreading rumors," said Lily. "But

what about all that money? Maybe someone killed her for that."

"Maybe," I said, "or maybe for something else."

I described the disappearing diamond, Tommy's disappearing act from the murder scene, and Corinne's little bombshell about being attacked. And, of course, Father Richard's skepticism about Corinne. The only thing I left out was exactly how Mercedes was killed; I meant to keep to the letter of my deal with Lieutenant Graham, even if I was violating the spirit. After all, what harm could it do to puzzle it over a little with Lily and Aaron? So we drank cappuccino and ate tiramisu, and contemplated the trustworthiness of Corinne Campbell.

"Because what it boils down to," I said, "is that either Corinne's lying, and somebody killed Mercedes specifically, or else she's telling the truth, and somebody was sneaking around the party in a black cloak trying to murder people in general."

"A serial killer dressed in black?" said Lily. "That's pretty far-fetched."

"And what do Corinne and Mercedes have in common," Aaron chimed in, "that would make them targets of the same murderer?"

I shrugged.

"Listen," he continued, "I know Corinne. She's a professional victim. Everything's a crisis, and nothing's ever her fault. She craves attention in a major way. I felt sorry for her after she got dumped this time, because she seemed so happy for a while and then she crashed and burned. But that doesn't mean I'd take her word for anything. You know, when I was first hired at the paper, I heard that she accused some poor SOB of rape, and then went back on it."

"I heard that, too," I admitted. "Apparently her name is mud with the police. But even if you believe that she'd tell such a serious lie, do you really believe she'd try to kill herself over Boris Nevsky?"

Lily frowned into her coffee cup. "I'm no fan of the Mad Russian, but it's not his character we're looking at, it's hers. This woman sounds kind of unstable. And people do crazy things for love. Carnegie, you went out with Boris. Would he be really nasty about breaking up with her? He is *such* a megalomaniac. Maybe that's what pushed her over the edge. Sorry, bad pun."

"Whoa!" said Aaron, setting down his cup with a clatter. "You dated the guy that Corinne's been moping around about? The flower seller?"

"Briefly! Very briefly, quite a while ago. And Boris is a floral designer, a very good one."

"My, my," said Aaron. I could see him trying to cover his first reaction with flippancy. "I must meet him one day."

"You will, smart-ass," I said. "Elizabeth invited all the principal vendors. I think she wants to be able to yell at them in person if anything goes wrong. Meanwhile, I'm going to talk with Boris about Corinne."

"Why?"

"Well, to see if he thinks she's lying."

"No, I mean why are you getting involved?" Aaron looked over at Lily. "Back me up here, Ms. Know-It-All Librarian. The three of us speculating is one thing, but with a murderer running around, shouldn't Carnegie mind her own business?"

"Of course she should!" said Lily. "Doesn't mean she will."

We were quiet on the drive back to the houseboat, lost in

our own thoughts. Mine were still focused on Corinne, and the fear in her eyes there at the parking garage. Aaron knew her better than I did, and his argument made sense, but surely this was a woman in serious trouble.

Lily dropped us both near the head of my dock and drove off.

"Thanks for the company," I said. "Sorry about the chaperone."

Aaron smiled, his teeth gleaming white in the half-light of the parking lot. "Lily's great. In fact, she's brilliant, because she agrees with me. Mercedes is not your problem."

"But she was almost my bride. And if Corinne's telling the truth, there was someone stalking people at my party! I can't just forget about it."

"Sure you can, Stretch. You just need something to take your mind off things."

"Like your tattoo, I suppose?"

"Well, now that you mention it—"

Aaron slid his hands around me, under my coat, and pulled me to him. I went willingly, and for a few moments the parking lot disappeared from my consciousness along with the rest of planet Earth. Then a pager sounded, the beeping muffled somewhere between us. It wasn't mine.

"Damn." Aaron disentangled himself and glared at the unit's tiny display screen. "Hell and damn. Stretch, I've got to make a call."

"No problem. Come on inside and have a drink."

"No, I mean I have to go home and call. I'm sorry. It's, well, it's complicated."

"Don't worry about it." I rearranged my coat and forced a smile. "Good night, then."

But he was already heading back to his car, pulling out the ever-present pack of cigarettes as he went. I walked resolutely down the dock, hearing his door slam and the VW go putt-putting out of the lot and away in the night. I was at my door, fumbling in my purse for my house key, when Roger Talbot stepped out of the shadows.

Chapter Nine

I'VE TAKEN THOSE SELF-DEFENSE CLASSES FOR WOMEN, SO I can state with authority that I should have a floodlight installed over my door, and that when surprised by a man on my doorstep in the dark, I did exactly the wrong thing: I dropped my keys. Luckily, Roger Talbot didn't follow the script either. He scooped them up and offered them to me, with an apology.

"I'm sorry. I should have waited till tomorrow, I know, but I've been calling from my car, and then I thought perhaps you'd left your machine on and gone to bed. I didn't want to be seen, but I just had to speak with you."

I opened the door and gestured him into the kitchen. "What about?"

"About *her*." His voice was anguished, and his unshaven face, under the fluorescent light, had aged a decade since we spoke at the party. Under the dark, commanding brows, his eyes were red and swollen. He smelled of whiskey. "I heard about it on the news this morning. They had film of you leaving the Aquarium. Did you . . . find her?"

"Roger, I'm sorry, I'm not supposed to talk about it."

"Tell me!" He grabbed my upper arms and shook me, just a little, but I could tell how strong he was, and how frantic. But was he desperate to know if the secret was out and his career ruined? Or to find out if I'd seen the murderer? A black cloak, Corinne had said. Could it have been a black topcoat?

"Roger!" I rapped out in my best ordering-people-around voice. "Let me go this second or I'll scream the place down."

He obeyed, turning away from me, and leaning his hands on the kitchen counter. His head hung low, defeated, and his clothes were dripping with rain.

"Listen," I said gently. "I really can't talk about the details."

He whirled around. There were tears in his eyes.

"Dear God, I don't want to hear the details! Just tell me, please, *did she suffer*?"

I blinked back my own tears. He really had loved her, then. "No. No, I don't think she did."

"But you're not sure?"

"Actually, I am sure, Roger. It was very sudden. She wouldn't even have known."

All the strength seemed to go out of him with a long, shuddering sigh. "The police wouldn't tell me, the bastards, they just confirmed it was murder. I knew that anyway, the minute I saw Graham. I know he's Homicide. He said they'd keep our 'connection' confidential if they could, but he wouldn't tell me what actually happened to her. I've been imagining the most hideous things."

"Roger, come sit down." I led him to the couch facing the glass doors that open to the lake. Night made a mirror of them, reflecting the living room and my tormented visitor, so I pulled the drapes. "Can I get you something to drink?"

"No. Well, yes, thanks. Scotch rocks?"

I smiled in apology. "I've only got girl drinks: white wine, light beer, and V-8."

"Of course, sorry. And I've come barging in on you." He ran a hand through his thick silver hair, and seemed to notice for the first time that he was wet and chilly. "If I could have some coffee?"

"Coming up."

I made two big mugs and we sat over them, leaning into the fragrant steam. Roger began to talk about Mercedes, at first like a man talking to himself. But I think he needed me there. Who else could he tell? He'd regret this in the morning, but right now the words poured out, unstoppable.

"Her father was a policeman in Mexico City," he said. "Corrupt, like most of them, taking bribes and stealing confiscated goods. They lived well. Then, when she was fourteen, another officer shot him down. She never knew why, but he had made enemies, and within months the family was out on the street. Can you imagine what that was like for a sensitive girl like Mercedes?"

"Sensitive" wasn't a word I associated with her, but I shook my head in silent sympathy.

"She was determined to get out. She worked hard in school, polished her English. I met her when I was covering an economic conference down there; she had a job as a tour guide out at the Aztec pyramids. She was eighteen, and so beautiful. More than that. Exquisite."

Was your wife beautiful? I felt like asking. But it's hard to condemn someone who's already in hell.

"We were together for a week," he continued. "It was a fling, that was all. I'd think about seeing her again, sometimes, but it would have been impossible. I was married, with children, I was building my career. Then one day I received a phone call. She was in Los Angeles, she had a job at a Spanish-language magazine. My wife was away, so I flew down. I told her it was just for the weekend, but after that I couldn't stay away from her. Mercedes made other women seem so ordinary, so tedious with their petty little games. I pulled a few strings and got her a fellowship up here at the university. Then I hired her for the *Sentinel*."

"But she went on to television."

"Yes." He smiled fondly, lost in the happy past. "I helped her write her pieces for the paper, but she was impatient with writing. For her, it was all personal. She loved attention, she loved connecting with people with her eyes, her voice. Mercedes Montoya could get an interview out of anyone. She would have gone national, I know it."

"She told me you planned to marry," I said carefully, and watched his face melt in misery.

"Yes," he whispered. "She was so thrilled when I gave her the ring."

He looked at me sharply, coming back to the present. "Graham was asking about the ring. He said it wasn't on the . . . he said she didn't have it. She was supposed to keep the ring hidden, until we waited a reasonable time, but if he knew about it, someone must have seen it. That was you?"

I nodded. "Mercedes showed it to me in the ladies' room. She asked me to plan her wedding."

That snapped the last cord of his self-control. He dropped his face into his hands and sobbed. I found myself stroking his shoulder, making soothing noises.

"I'm sorry. I'm so sorry."

Then suddenly, shockingly, I was back in my own past, comforting Holt Walker about his wife's death. Playing the role he set up for me, playing the fool for him. Now here was another wealthy, successful, handsome man, and here I was acting as the sympathetic audience for his little drama. Helen Talbot had been dead just a few short weeks, and the fine romance Roger was recounting had gone on while she was alive, and then while she was dying.

"The ring was a family heirloom, Mercedes said. Did your wife ever wear it?"

He glared at me with those bloodshot eyes. "Don't bring Helen into this!"

"Seems to me she was already in it."

"You're just like everyone else," he said in disgust, rising from the couch and pacing the room with a long, athlete's stride. "Everyone thinks they can judge; they think they know what goes on in private—"

"You've just told me what went on in private! You had an affair—"

"I had several affairs, and so did Helen, and it's none of your goddamn business! Mercedes was different."

I stood up myself, unsteady from fatigue, the coffee curling painfully in my stomach. I couldn't quite believe I was debating ethics in the middle of the night with a dead woman's lover. I was in shock. Delayed reaction to a traumatic experience. Lieutenant Graham's Victim Assistance people would have come in handy just about now.

"Roger, I want you to leave my house. I'm sorry about Mercedes, I really am. But—"

"Please," he said. He was in shock, too, of course, and tomorrow he had to put on his public face and show only moderate grief, appropriate for a colleague. I didn't envy him. "Please, I want you to understand."

"Understand what?"

He sat down again, and spoke quietly. "Carnegie, you may

not believe me, but Helen and I loved each other once, when we were young, and we always respected each other, right to the end. First with the newspaper, then with politics, she was beside me all the way. She was a better strategist than I was."

"Then how could you—?"

"Do you have any idea what it's like to care for someone who's dying?" he demanded. "To be there every day, every hour, doing things for them that you'd do for a child? It's agonizing, but it's also exhausting, and it makes you impatient because you have your own life to deal with, and guilty for being impatient, and angry because you can't save her life, no matter how well you care for her."

I stayed standing, ready to show him out, but of course I was thinking about my father. What my mother went through was far more of an ordeal than anything I had suffered. I always thought of Dad as my hero, but it was Mom who was heroic in the end.

"It must have been terribly hard. But you did it."

"I couldn't have done it without Mercedes!" he said, and somehow I believed him. "She kept me sane, she encouraged me and cried with me and listened to me rave against the doctors, and against the unfairness of it all. She didn't want Helen to die."

That was harder to believe. Roger Talbot was Mercedes' ticket to success, to wealth and prominence and even political influence, in Seattle and maybe beyond. And maybe she had even loved him the way he obviously loved her. No, Mercedes would have been glad to see the last of Helen Talbot. I was still sorry about her death, but now I was sorry I knew so much about her life. And about his grief.

"Well, she was very happy about your engagement, I can tell you that. She cherished the ring you gave her."

"But where is it now?" He looked up at me piteously. "Did they kill her to steal it? I want it back, I want it as a memento of her."

The phone rang and I picked it up automatically. Roger rose and stepped into the kitchen, reflexively courteous even at a moment like this. He'd do well in politics, all right.

"Hey, Stretch, how you doing?"

"Aaron. Um, I'm doing fine."

"Oh, shit, I woke you, didn't I? I'm sorry. I just wanted to apologize for taking off like that. I suppose it's too late for that drink?"

I sighed. "Actually, Aaron, I'm just going to bed. Maybe I'll see you tomorrow. I've got a meeting at ten with Paul and Elizabeth at the *Sentinel*."

"I'll be prowling the halls sighing your name. Sleep well."

"You, too."

As I hung up, Roger reentered the room with a stiff, embarrassed air.

"Thank you for listening to all this. I shouldn't have . . . well, it doesn't matter."

"Don't worry about it," I told him. "Get some rest. Try not to think about it."

He smiled grimly, a death's-head smile, and went out into the night.

Chapter Ten

ENTERING THE *SENTINEL*'S NEWSROOM, I FELT LIKE BLACK Bart coming through the swing doors at the Red Dog Saloon. As I threaded the labyrinth of cubicles, gazes followed me and conversations stopped, only to resume behind me in hushed murmurs. I could practically hear my spurs jangling. *Why's everyone staring?* Then I heard a whispered phrase— "the one who found her"—and understood why. I had walked in the shadow of violent death, and I brought a little of that darkness with me.

At last I saw Aaron at the end of an aisle. He was tipped back in his swivel chair, eyes shut, lost in whatever was piping through the oversized headphones he wore. With his forefingers as drumsticks, he beat out a quick, intricate rhythm on the front edge of his desk, bobbing his head slightly with the beat, blissing out.

"Coltrane?" I asked.

Aaron swiveled toward me and smiled, eagerly pulling off the headphones and leaving a cowlick of crow-black hair angled out above one ear. I resisted the impulse to smooth it back—and the urge to ask him about the phone call that had interrupted our embrace last night. Not that we would have had much of an evening anyway, with Roger Talbot hanging around, but still...

"Nice try," he said loftily, and I was so lost in thought that I wondered what he meant. Then he continued, "It could have been Coltrane, but I'm surprised a woman of your caliber doesn't recognize the drum solo from that all-time surf guitar classic, 'Wipe Out.' It's the number one choice of finger drummers across the nation. Have a seat."

He nodded at the easy chair dominating his cubicle. It was upholstered in something that had once been plaid, and gave off a delicate bouquet of tortilla chips and long-dead coffee. The cube's fabric walls were covered with Red Sox posters, clipped headlines, and typed quotations. Most of the quotes were about writing and journalism, but one by Benjamin Disraeli caught my eye: "Every woman should marry—and no man."

I sat. "I've only got a minute, till Elizabeth gets here and Paul's off the phone. Um, nice cube you've got here."

"Not exactly *The New York Times*, is it? But it'll do till I get on with *The Seattle Times* or *The Oregonian*. Listen, you want coffee or something? Tea? Me?" He lowered his voice. "Seriously, Stretch, are you OK about last night? You sounded kind of odd on the phone."

"I'm fine. Did you say *The Oregonian*? You're thinking of moving to Portland?" The idea was oddly distressing.

"It depends," he said casually. "Meanwhile, are you going to be a good girl and let the police do the murder-solving around here?"

My casual and untruthful reply was interrupted by the bride-to-be. Elizabeth came striding through the newsroom like a warrior princess in Spandex, a bicycle helmet dangling from one hand and a cell phone in the other, her cropped chestnut hair slick with sweat. She nodded to a few people as she passed, and gave Aaron a friendly but peremptory smile.

"Hey, Carnegie. Paul's still tied up. Come talk to me."

But for once I was determined not to let Elizabeth rush me with her multi-tasking, time-is-money, what-have-you-done-for-me-lately manner.

"Say, Aaron, are you free for dinner Thursday?"

"That depends, too. No chaperones?"

"No chaperones. No pagers?"

"Promise."

"Great. I'll call you tonight. So, Elizabeth, where shall we talk?"

She frowned impatiently. "I'll show you."

She led me out through the lobby and into a rest room near the reception desk. It opened onto a locker room; apparently the *Sentinel* had a lot of joggers and bicycle commuters. Elizabeth dropped her gear on a bench and began to strip for a shower.

"I could wait outside—" I began. I was used to the locker room at the Y, but standing there fully clothed while she undressed felt funny.

"Why?" She peeled off her thermal vest and jersey, then her sports bra, and for just a moment I was back in high school, flat-chested and envious, complaining to my mother. *Don't let it bother you, Carrie. You have nice red hair and a pleasant personality.*

"I wanted to ask you something in private," Elizabeth went on, bending down to untie her flat-soled riding shoes. I don't know what I expected—a morbid question about Mercedes' corpse, maybe, or a discussion of Corinne's state of mind. Instead she said, "Does that wedding insurance you got us cover this kind of thing?"

"You mean, 'this kind of thing' as in murder?"

She straightened and faced me. "Carnegie, Mercedes' death was horrible and shocking. We all feel that. But you know damn well that she and I weren't close friends, and I won't be a hypocrite about this. I've got four hundred people and almost a hundred grand tied up in this wedding. Now, can I postpone or not?"

"Sure you can. But you'll lose your deposits and plane tickets, and probably your first-choice photographer and band. These folks are booked up pretty far ahead. The special-event policy covers things like vendors failing to deliver, or your reception being cancelled because of bad weather. It doesn't cover postponing out of respect for someone's death."

"That's what I figured." She nodded thoughtfully and stepped out of her bicycle shorts. *I have really got to hit the gym more often,* I thought. *Like, twice a day.*

"Does Paul want to postpone?"

"Yes and no," said Elizabeth. "He thinks it's kind of cold-blooded to keep going, though of course he's clueless about the cost of rescheduling. The main thing is, he doesn't want to disappoint Enid."

"That's the great-aunt?"

"Yeah. Nasty old bitch."

I must have looked startled, because she added, "Just because someone's nearly a hundred doesn't mean they're doddering and sweet. Enid's sharp as a tack and she hates me! But Paul's lined up a nurse to drive her down from Vancouver and stay with her through the whole wedding, and apparently that's all she's talked about for months— how she's going to live to see her darling boy on his wedding day. Hand me a towel?"

I complied, and she dug out some travel-size soap and shampoo from her knapsack.

"Well, that's it, then. I can't get my money back, so Auntie

Enid gets her heart's desire. I'll be ready in a minute if you want to wait in Paul's office."

After the newsroom and the locker room, Paul's office was refreshingly ordinary, with piles of file folders on the desk and credenza and a rain-streaked window looking out at the mushrooming condos of Belltown. He was still on the phone, but he waved me to a chair at the little conference table wedged in the corner. As I laid out the wedding paperwork, I took a long discreet look at him. What did hard-charging Elizabeth see in soft-spoken, sweet-tempered Paul? Good looks, certainly, and a keen mind, and a shared enthusiasm for long-distance bicycle races. But as time went by, would he chafe against her bossy ways, or would she find a safe harbor in his easygoing calm? Weddings are wonderful, but marriages are utterly mysterious.

Elizabeth joined us just as Paul hung up the phone, flushed and fresh from her shower. They kissed in the easy, happily-sated manner of two people who are getting absolutely all the sex they want, and we got down to business. I asked them how they wanted to proceed, Paul talked about his great-aunt, and Elizabeth made a gracious show of pressing on for Enid's sake without mentioning her nonrefundable deposits.

So we went ahead and reviewed the buffet menu, the flower arrangements, and the band's playlist, almost as if nothing had happened. Almost.

"I talked to Corinne again," said Elizabeth. "She says she's feeling OK and she'll be at the dress fitting. Good thing, too. She's put on weight lately."

"Did she tell you what happened on the pier?" I asked.

"You mean that somebody pushed her in? Yeah, she's telling everybody."

"But you don't believe her."

"I don't know what to believe. People were drinking, but they weren't drunk, except maybe Corinne herself. So who would do that?" Elizabeth raked her hands through her hair, helping it dry. "I'm thinking maybe she stumbled and fell in, and then when she heard about Mercedes she got carried away with the thrill of being at a crime scene. She used to pull this kind of shit back in college."

"Take it easy on Corinne," said Paul, ever the kind heart. "She's still upset about that guy Boris. That's probably why she's eating so much."

His beloved, ever the cynic, shrugged. "Whatever. Angela is convinced that she's lying, but Patty is really rattled. She thinks there's a stalker around. Either way, Corinne's getting on my nerves. I made her sign a nondisclosure about the wedding, but she keeps asking if she can't write just one little article."

"Paul," I said, to change the subject, "I don't want to be pessimistic, but have you thought about who you're going to want as best man if Tommy's still in the hospital?"

"I'm sure your brother would step in," Elizabeth offered. Paul's brother Scott was a city planner in Baltimore.

But Paul shook his head. "I'd rather not. Scotty understood why I chose Tommy instead of him in the first place, but I don't want to rub it in by substituting him at the last minute."

"But anybody you ask is going to be a last-minute sub," protested Elizabeth. "You can't stand up there by yourself."

"Well, you could," I said, just thinking out loud. "Judge Overesch could mention Tommy in his remarks. You know, our good wishes are with him today. Or would that be too much of a downer?"

"No," said the bridegroom.

"Yes," said the bride.

I riffled diplomatically through my paperwork while they had a telepathic conversation. She frowned, he smiled ruefully, she sighed fondly, and the thing was done.

"No," Paul repeated. "It wouldn't be a downer, it would be exactly how I'm going to feel if Tommy's not up and around by then. We better cancel the bachelor party, though, that is, if Tommy actually planned one."

"He picked a date and drew up a guest list," I told him, "but that was all. I'll make the cancellation calls."

"Thanks. Of course, when Tommy *is* up and around, I'm going to knock him flat for driving drunk. Did you see him leave the party, Carnegie?"

"No," I said. Misleading, but accurate. The police were keeping mum about Tommy's role as a murder witness, and so would I. "No, I didn't see him leave."

"I'm just sorry you had to see Mercedes," he said. "It must have been awful. I don't suppose you can give me a short statement—"

"No!" I said, more vehemently than I intended. I stood up and began to gather my checklists to cover the awkwardness. "I'm sorry, the police asked me not to discuss it, especially with the press, and that means you, doesn't it? I'll let you get back to work. Elizabeth, I'll see you at the dress fitting—"

"Hang on, Carnegie," she cut in. "Aren't you forgetting something?"

My mind went blank. We had all the contracts, the valet parking, the final head count . . . "What?"

"I need another bridesmaid."

"Of course. I don't know what I was thinking. Do you have someone in mind?"

"Yes," she said decisively. "You."

Chapter Eleven

MY FIRST THOUGHT SHOULD HAVE BEEN ETIQUETTE. INSTEAD it was breasts.

Sure, the etiquette was tricky. Would it really be proper for a professional wedding consultant to fill in as bridesmaid, a role traditionally taken by the bride's sisters and girlfriends? Would it compromise my work as wedding-day coordinator if I were also a member of the wedding party?

But those thoughts came second. What came first was an image of myself in the bridesmaid's gown, which was pink, plunging, and painted-on snug. The daring décolletage would have displayed Mercedes' ample charms quite nicely, and Corinne and Angela were going to look like scrumptious confections. I, on the other hand, would look like a celery stalk draped in bias-cut rose-petal satin. When it comes to cleavage, I have very little to cleave.

"Well?" demanded Elizabeth.

"The thing is," I stalled, hugging my notebook to the bosom in question. "The thing is, I'm going to be so *busy* that day. And besides, we don't really know each other, not as friends. Are you going to want me in your wedding photos for years to come?"

"What I *want* is a third bridesmaid." She stood as well, and picked up her knapsack and helmet. "Having a gap is going to remind everybody of what happened at the Aquarium. Come on, you're going to be there anyway, and you won't be all that busy during the ceremony itself. It's the obvious solution."

"But I'm sure you have friends who—"

"Let's face it, Carnegie. Anybody else I ask is going to be freaked out by the idea of wearing a dead woman's dress."

"And you think I'm not?"

"It can't be any worse than finding her body!"

Paul, who'd begun to look concussed, was saved by the bell: his phone rang. He snatched it up eagerly and turned away from us with an eloquent show of body language: *I'm busy working, see? Leave me out of this female stuff.* My bride and I obliged him, heading out to the lobby and into an elevator. It was empty, though I'm not sure the presence of strangers would have deterred Elizabeth. Bulldogs could have taken tenacity lessons from Elizabeth.

"Will you do it?"

"I'm sorry, I don't think it's a good idea."

"Bottom line," she said. "How much?"

"You want to *hire* me as your bridesmaid?"

"Call it a bonus. I can cut you a check today. How does two grand sound?"

"Honestly, I'm just not comfortable—"

"Three, then."

The elevator set us down at street level, offering escape.

"Elizabeth, I'll think about it, really I will. Right now, I've got an appointment with your florist. Are you sure you don't want to be there?"

"Too busy," she said. "You know the look I'm after. But don't think too long. The bridesmaids' fitting is tomorrow."

"I know that. I'll see you there." *And I'll put on that pink dress when hell freezes over.*

Rather than walk in the strengthening rain, I battled the traffic down to Pioneer Square in Vanna. A brand-new engine noise, a sort of muffled clank, reminded me once again to call my mechanic. Or maybe I should call a faith healer. The metered spaces were all full, so I used an exorbitant parking lot on Occidental and walked along a block of restaurants, blues bars, and touristy shops, most of them closed on a Monday, to reach Nevsky Brothers Flowers, which was open seven days a week.

Boris Nevsky's floral business was unusual—just like everything else about Boris Nevsky. For starters, he didn't have a brother in the flower business; he just thought the name sounded good. A small army of young men, most of them named Sergei and all of them darkly handsome, joked and squabbled in Russian as they hauled in wholesale flowers, assembled them under the master's savagely perfectionist eye, and trucked away the finished creations. If someone inquired about the Nevsky siblings, Boris just collared the nearest Sergei and introduced him ardently as "my only family here in your country." It worked like a charm.

Boris also didn't have a typical retail showroom, with display coolers of the standard flower arrangements and racks of hard goods—vases, mugs, picture frames—or impulse buys like greeting cards and scented soaps. Instead, he ran a tiny bucket shop out front, tended by a tiny Russian crone named Irina who sold blooms by the stem, bought wholesale for the purpose or left over from his design work.

I greeted Irina, shook the rain off my jacket, and braced myself for the patented Boris bear hug.

"Kharrnegie!" Sure enough, when Boris emerged from the workroom, he clamped me to his broad, sweater-clad chest and expelled all my oxygen. Then he held me at arm's length—quite a length, too, given the simian stretch of his arms—and beamed at me with blue-flame eyes that gleamed beneath his thatch of wiry hair like lanterns in a cottage window. "You luke rravished!"

I ducked the big wet kiss that often followed the hug. "I think the word you want is ravishing. Nice to see you, too, Boris. How are things?"

He frowned. "My things are well, but not your things, I think. A corpse at your party, that is very bad for you."

"Pretty bad for her, too."

He shrugged. Strangers were nothing to Boris, friends were everything.

"Come inside and have tea."

The Mad Russian Florist was an oversized man, and his workroom was built to scale. There were long sturdy design tables and vast humming storage coolers, with skylights high overhead and exposed brick walls bearing shelves of supplies and photographs of various floral triumphs. The fanciest restaurants in Seattle relied on Boris, and savvy wedding planners booked him a year ahead.

Boris' private office, as far as anyone could tell, was in his car, and his employee break room was a samovar in the corner and an alley behind the building, perpetually blue with the smoke of Russian cigarettes. The workroom itself smelled like springtime, like roses and freesias and lilies of the valley all at once, which was why I loved to visit. And today, of course, I had an ulterior motive.

"I must work while we talk," he said, nodding at a half-completed biedermeier on one table.

Biedermeiers are formal bouquets made in concentric circles, each tightly-packed ring composed of a different flower. This one had a center of creamy white tulips surrounded by pink lisianthus, then a ring of deeper pink sweetheart roses. A pile of hydrangea blossoms, white and palest blue, lay ready to form the lacy outer border. At the far end of the room the Sergeis came and went, but this bouquet was getting the Boris touch. He never staffed out the bride's flowers.

I perched on a stool to watch. "That's charming. Who's it for?"

"Bah, a silly liddle girl who will not appreciate. I should give her kharnations and cabbage leaves. Bring us tea."

The deep-seated belief that women were born to serve had been a sticking point when I dated Boris, but now that he was just one of my top vendors, I had no problem with drawing him a steaming glass from the samovar.

"None for you?"

"Not just now." I knew from sad experience what the smoky devil's brew would do to my stomach lining. We talked briefly about Mercedes, and I explained that the wedding was proceeding despite her death. "So what's the plan for the EMP flowers?"

"The sketches are over there. Bring them."

Some florists just list the plant variety and number of stems for each vase or bouquet, but Boris made these wonderful colored-chalk sketches. I fetched the folder marked "Lamott" and spread them out on the worktable.

"Wow! Double wow."

"EMP is big and loud, it needs big loud flowers."

These were loud, all right. Elizabeth's gown was sizzling orange chiffon, strapless, with a shoulder wrap of cherry pink gauze. Sort of Academy Awards meets the Tequila Sunrise. The bouquet Boris had envisioned was a thick pillar of frilly red-orange gloriosa lilies, rising like a snow cone from an electric green cloud of lady's mantle. Strange, but perfect for the dress. The bridesmaids, in their glamour-girl gowns, would each carry a dozen coral calla lilies clasped around a hot magenta heart of parrot tulips. The centerpieces for the buffet were equally audacious, mixing peonies, poppies, ranunculus, and amaryllis in a splendid clash of pink, crimson, orange, and scarlet.

"Very nice, Boris. Very cutting edge. And the boutonnieres?"

"Tiny calla lilies, with a *puff* of lady's mantle." He gave a puff of air as he said it, just to make me laugh. "You can approve this for Lamott?"

"Yep. Where do I sign?"

"Only to initial the sketches, please. Next week I have sketches for you for the Christmas wedding, the Buckmeister." He looked up from the snowdrift of petals on the table, his blunt brown fingers deft and gentle among the pale blossoms as he nestled each one in place. "She trusts you, Lamott. Everyone trusts you."

"Even you, Boris?"

He grinned wolfishly. "I trust no one but Boris and Irina. But you, a little, yes. I have a question for you. Private question."

"Shoot." I was impatient to work the conversation around to Corinne. I didn't have long to wait.

"Someone from Solveto's tells me," he said, "that Corinne Campbell is almost drowning. She fell from pier at your party?"

"Almost drowned," I corrected automatically. Boris liked

help with his English. "Well, she ended up in the water, yes. I'm not sure how."

"She is all right now?"

"Yes, she's all right. She was in the hospital overnight—"

"This I know! I hear of it in the morning and I think, I should go to her bedside! She needs me! But I don't go."

"Why not? You two were pretty close for a while."

He gave a rumbling growl. "Not close enough, for Corinne."

"Yes, you mentioned that she wanted to get married. That's not so unreasonable, is it?"

"Unreasonable all of a sudden!" he protested. "We are having fun, we are making frequent love, then like *that*"—he snapped his fingers—"she is different voman. Tears, sighing, no making love, merry me, merry me."

"And why didn't you want to marry her?"

He shrugged. "If I wanted or not wanted, no difference. I am married already."

"*Boris!*" I exclaimed, forgetting Corinne momentarily. "You and I . . . we . . . you're *married*?! Why didn't you tell me?"

He waved his arms and the biedermeier nearly went flying. "Do not shout at me, Kharnegie! Did you vant to merry me? Did you?"

"That's not the point."

"No, you did not vant. So what does it matter to you if I have wife in St. Petersburg? Besides, I have asked her for divorce."

"Did you tell Corinne that?"

"Of course not! Would only encourage her."

I gave up. "OK, just tell me this. Do you think Corinne was so upset about breaking up with you that she would try to commit suicide?"

"She fell on purpose?"

"I really don't know. I'd like to help her out, if I can."

Boris pursed his lips, giving the question judicious thought. "Why drown? Why not shoot?"

"You mean shoot herself? For starters, she'd need a gun—"

"She *has* gun."

"She does?"

He nodded. "For protection, for woman living alone. Liddle gun, but she had lessons for it. Bring more tea."

When I returned with his glass, he was frowning intently as he tucked florets of hydrangea in a final lacy ring around the sweetheart roses. "Of course, Corinne is upset when we break up. I am magnificent lover, she said so. Why did you not ever say how magnificent I am, Kharnegie?"

"It must have slipped my mind. Seriously, Boris, would Corinne drown herself over losing you?"

The blue-flame eyes narrowed. "Seriously . . . no. To drown for love, you must have a big soul, a Russian soul. Corinne, she is perfect for fun, but her soul is small. It must be that she fell. You are sure she is not harmed? You are the one who I can ask."

"I promise, I saw her with my own eyes. Her priest was taking her home. Maybe you should call her?" If someone really tried to kill Corinne, she could use some big, strong company. And who knows, maybe there were divorce papers on the way from St. Petersburg. "I'm sure she'd like to see you."

"No, no, no. I wish her to be well, I do not wish her to be with me. Not now." He lifted the biedermeier and twirled it in one hand, an exquisite little carousel. Then he strode across the room to a rack of ribbon spools and pulled off two lengths, one of narrow pink brocade and the other of white velvet cord. He twisted the two loosely together and tied them in an intricate bow around the stems, leaving four long fluttering strands. Then he presented the finished bouquet to me.

"As I said, it's charming."

"It is yours."

"Mine? Boris, that's for a bride!"

"I make her another." He pressed it into my hands. "This one is yours."

I lifted the flowers to my face, pink and cream and misty blue with a heavenly scent. "But why?"

He reached over and touched my cheek. "Because Kharnegie, your soul is not so small. You are in love these days?"

"No! Well, maybe. Maybe I am."

"I thought so. Be happy, Kharnegie."

Irina's twinkling eyes followed me as I left with the bouquet, and I caught some admiring glances on my way back to the van. I set the flowers carefully on the seat beside me, and was so entranced with them as I pulled out of the lot that at first I thought the hideous clanking noise was coming from somewhere else. But no, it was Vanna White, issuing a violent racket that didn't stop even when I hit the brakes and pulled to the curb. The clamor was unbearable, which I found out later is not unusual when an engine throws a piston rod that impales the oil pan like an arrow through an apple.

People up and down the block stopped to stare as Vanna gave a final *bang*! and expired in agony. A gray-haired woman rushed out of a T-shirt shop, her eyes huge with alarm.

"What was that noise? Was it a gunshot?"

"No, ma'am," I said sadly. "That was the sound of hell freezing over."

Chapter Twelve

"WHAT DOES THAT MEAN, YOU THREW A ROD?"

"It probably means a couple thousand dollars."

"Good heavens, Carrie! Do you have enough money?"

I do now. "Don't worry, Mom. I've got it covered."

It was Tuesday, the day after my visit to Nevsky Brothers, and Mom had called to chat. Having just gotten off the phone with Pete, my mechanic, I unwisely mentioned to her that Vanna was due for major surgery. As I sat in my living room, admiring the biedermeier bouquet, I hastened to find a less alarming topic.

"Listen, Mom, you'll like this. I'm going to be a bridesmaid for one of my clients."

"Oh, fun!" My mother had a somewhat oversimplified view of what I did for a living, so she saw no problem in my pulling double-duty for Elizabeth. She also believed that I had a lovely figure. "Is it the Christmas wedding?"

"No, the November one, at the Experience Music Project."

"Well, how nice. You'll send me one of the wedding photographs?"

"Absolutely."

"What's your gown like?"

"It's...pink. Very pink. In fact, I have to go get fitted

right this minute. Lily's working a late shift today, so she's going to drive me there. I haven't gotten a rental car yet. I'll call you later, OK?"

In the Volvo on the way up to the Capitol Hill neighborhood, I filled Lily in on my conversation with Boris, and she played devil's advocate. It's good to have a friend who's willing to challenge you, but Lily was more than willing.

"So," she summed up, "this Corinne person claims she was pushed in the harbor to drown. Most people, including her priest and the Seattle Police Department, think she's just covering up the fact that she got drunk and tried to kill herself. But *you* believe that whoever killed Mercedes Montoya also tried to kill Corinne."

"Yes."

"And what makes you a better judge of the situation than the cops and the church?"

I thought that over while she found parking around the corner from Stephanie's Styles, a stately little 1920s home tucked into a long block of brick-front businesses on Olive Way. It had finally quit raining, but the sky was still low and leaden.

"Lily, I keep thinking about the look in Corinne's eyes when she told me about it. She didn't seem self-pitying or deceitful. She was terrified." I reached into the backseat for my tote bag, which today contained a selection of lingerie and a pair of low-heeled, not-yet-dyed silk pumps. "Actually, you'll meet her in a minute, so you can form your own impression."

"You sure the bride doesn't mind my being here for this?"

"She's just relieved that I agreed to do it at all. Wait till you see these dresses."

Stephanie Stevens was quaint as a cameo, small and pink,

just the person you'd want to order your wedding gown from. She bustled cheerily around her lavender-scented, flowered-chintz shop with a tape measure dangling from her neck and a wristband pincushion at the ready, and she liked nothing better than to serve up tea and currant scones on her favorite Limoges china. The fact that her split-level on Vashon Island boasted a giant satellite-TV dish so that Stephanie could catch every basketball game ever broadcast on Earth, was a fact that rarely came up over tea. She also raised Rottweilers. Go figure.

"Carnegie! How nice to see you, as always. And this time you're going to wear one of the dresses that you ordered! The other girls are already here."

Stephanie had kept the original living room of the house as a reception area, adding only a long wall mirror and a small platform for the customers to stand on while she adjusted their hems. The dining room beyond was filled with racks of dresses and beautifully gowned mannequins, and a study to one side served as a changing room. We could hear Elizabeth's voice and Angela's laughter through the paneled oak door. I was introducing Lily to Stephanie when the "other girls" filed out, falling self-consciously silent when they saw they had an audience.

Elizabeth came out first, followed by her sister and maid of honor, Patty Lamott. At close range and without accessories, the bride looked rather garish in her movie-star satin gown the color of orange sherbet, and her cherry-popsicle chiffon stole. But after all the fittings I'd seen, I could easily imagine Elizabeth in full makeup, bearing her avant-garde bouquet. Not every bride could carry off this kind of look, but she was going to be dynamite.

Her sister was more of a fizzling fuse. Patty was a single

nurse who worked at the VA hospital, and she looked like the first draft for Elizabeth. You could tell they were siblings, but Patty's features were coarser, her long unkempt hair a dull brown to Elizabeth's cropped and glossy chestnut, her figure stocky rather than strong.

I suspected that Patty wasn't thrilled about her kid sister's successes, financial or romantic. And she certainly wasn't thrilled about her own rose-colored gown and stole, which did nothing for her skin tone and less than nothing for her figure. She nodded sullenly to me and frowned a little at Lily, who had relaxed into a wing chair to enjoy the show.

"Come on through, girls," Stephanie burbled. "Let's line you all up."

Corinne came next. Elizabeth was right, she had put on a few pounds. Instead of draping fluidly, the satin pulled in taut creases across her stomach and hips. But you hardly noticed, because the rosy shade was so exactly right for Corinne's porcelain skin. The pink set off her golden hair and pale blue eyes to fairy-princess perfection, while the plunging neckline would command the attention of every prince in the neighborhood.

Corinne knew it, too. The disheveled waif I'd run into at the hospital was gone, replaced by this confident Southern belle. She gave me a complacent little wave, and struck a pose that would have gone over big at the entrance to the Academy Awards.

Last in line was Angela Sims, tall and fair. She paced into the room with her long boyish stride, her stole hung round her neck like a huge, gauzy pink muffler. Angela moved like a jock, but she looked almost as good as Corinne.

"Well?" she asked with a good-natured grin. "What's the verdict?"

"Wonderful!" If I was going to be a bridesmaid for hire, I might as well be a good one, and concentrate on their feelings instead of my own. This was still a joyous occasion. "Elizabeth, I've signed off on your bouquet. It's spectacular. All the flowers are, and all of you look wonderful. Let me get into my dress and then we'll talk about shoes and hair."

Stephanie produced a long garment bag—Mercedes' gown, though all of us were determined not to think about that—and made as if to follow me down the hallway.

"Um, Corinne, could you give me a hand getting dressed?" I asked.

Stephanie looked puzzled, but stepped aside to let Corinne through. A positive mention in Corinne's newspaper column would do wonders for dress sales. I closed the changing-room door behind Corinne and hung my gown on a stand. Our eyes met in the three-way mirror.

"How are you doing?"

"Fine," she said absently, peering over her shoulder to get a rear view of herself. "Do I really look all right? I think they sent a size too small."

This took me aback. "I mean, how are you after what happened at the Aquarium? Good lord, if someone tried to kill you—"

Corinne dropped into a love seat piled with clothing, and covered her eyes with one hand. Ever the drama queen, even when the drama was deadly.

"Of course I'm worried!" she moaned. "I'm just trying not to think about it. I talked to the police, but I could tell they didn't believe me. Elizabeth doesn't either."

I sat beside her. "Well, I believe you. And we're going to figure out who attacked you, and then the police will listen."

She sighed heavily, then groped for my hand and squeezed

it. Her false fingernails, rose-pink to match her dress, stabbed into my palm. The trivial section of my brain wondered if Elizabeth would expect pink nails on me, too. *Of course she will. Get over it.*

"Thank you, Carnegie!" Corinne whispered. The waif was still in there, hiding behind the glamour-girl façade.

"I haven't done anything yet."

"No, I mean for believing me. I know people think I'm just an airhead, or that I make things up, but it was so horrible!" She lifted moist, childlike blue eyes, and I gave her a hug. *Poor kid.*

"I'm sure it was. And I'm sure it's hard to talk about, but can you remember anything specific about him? His size or age, the smell of his aftershave, anything at all? For that matter, are you sure it was a man?"

"Pretty sure." She shook her head, her blonde curls dancing. "It happened so fast. He dropped some black cloth around my face, and I tried to fight back but he was too strong. That's all I could tell. He was really strong."

"How about the black cloth, then, was it smooth or rough? Did it have seams and pockets, do you think, like a coat?"

"N-no," she said. "No, it wasn't a coat. It was all one piece, like a cape."

How many black capes were at that party? I wondered to myself. Syd Soper wore one as Death, but who else? Aaron as Zorro, but that was absurd—

"Are you two ever coming out?" It was Elizabeth, with an eye on the clock as always.

"In a minute!" I called. "Corinne, we'll figure this out, I promise. Meanwhile, get my gown out of the bag, would you?"

I shucked my jeans and sweater and slithered into the
pink satin, averting my eyes from the mirror and concentrating on the dress itself. The fabric was delicious on my skin,
lush and smooth, and the cut and construction were the
high quality to be expected from this particular designer. I
hitched up the spaghetti straps, stepped into my silk pumps,
and checked the skirt length. The bottom of the dress was
unfinished, ready to be hemmed up to suit Mercedes' height,
which meant that it hung barely to my ankles. Good enough,
if Stephanie gave it the narrowest possible hem. She could
also take in the bodice, which had enough room for two of
me. Or rather, one of me and four of my breasts.

"Your bra shows in back," said Corinne. "You need a
strapless bra or a bustier."

She gave the word the proper French pronunciation, but I
didn't. "No, I need to be a whole lot busty-er."

We giggled, and I patted her shoulder. "That's the spirit,
Corinne. Listen, I'm sure that whoever it was in the black
cape, he didn't choose you personally to attack. But you
should probably be extra-careful for a while, OK?"

"Don't worry," she said solemnly. "I'm not going anywhere alone, especially at night. Neither's Patty or Elizabeth.
I don't think Angela believes me."

I had a brief vision of Roger Talbot—or someone else—
stepping out of the shadows by my front door. *Time to put up
that floodlight.*

"I think that's wise. Come on, let's join the rest of the
babes."

When we came out, Lily and Stephanie were tucking pins
into Patty's hair, wrapping it up and to one side in a sophisticated French twist. Suddenly Patty's features were not
coarse, but strong and interesting. When she caught sight of

her reflection, she actually smiled and stood up straight, and that, too, worked a minor miracle. Pink was still not her color, but she looked quite nice.

Pink was apparently not my color either. Stephanie gave me a frozen smile that spoke volumes, and Lily actually snickered.

"It needs a little work—" I began, and Lily laughed out loud.

"A *little*?"

"It's fine," declared Elizabeth. "Stephanie, can't you do something with her neckline?"

"Of course," said Stephanie, coming at me with her pincushion. She shored up the bodice reasonably well, and then marched me back into the changing room to fit me out with an "invisible" padded bra that was not only strapless but backless, with tape at the sides to anchor it to my rib cage.

"Stephanie, this is ridiculous! I didn't know they made such contraptions. Are the others wearing this?"

"They don't need it." She silenced my protest by sliding the gown back over my head, then stepped back to let me view the result.

"Hey, that looks pretty good." I peered over my shoulder, just as Corinne had done. "That looks *very* good."

Stephanie dropped into a naughty whisper. "Carnegie, it looks sexy as sin."

I had to admit, she was right. The bodice of the gown dipped alluringly over my newly created cleavage, and the low, open back showed off my shoulders. When I walked, the bias-cut satin slid and swirled around my legs in a definitely femme fatale kind of way. This bridesmaid deal wasn't so bad after all.

Back in the living room, the other women were fluttering

around comparing lipstick colors and putting on identical pink pearl earrings and pendants, their gifts from the bride. Even Elizabeth got into the spirit of it all, and helped Patty do her eyeliner with a sisterly camaraderie I hadn't seen in her before. In the end, we lined up in processional order before the long wall mirror, and Lily pronounced us fit to be seen in public.

As we trooped back to change into our street clothes, I put on my wedding planner hat. "So, we're settled on lipstick and nail polish. I'll get my shoes dyed, Patty will schedule with a hairdresser for a French twist, and I'll see you all at the rehearsal dinner Friday."

"But the rehearsal isn't this Friday, is it?" said Corinne, flipping through her little pocket diary.

"No, just the dinner," I reassured her. "We changed the date because Paul's parents are coming through on their way to Hawaii. The rehearsal itself is still a week from Friday. I'll e-mail everyone with the updated schedule."

My head was still full of times and dates as Lily and I stepped outside Stephanie's shop and walked back to her car. But then, suddenly, I couldn't think at all. Just down the street, leaning on a phone pole and dragging on a cigarette, was the purse-snatcher with the tattooed skull.

Chapter Thirteen

LILY CHATTED TO ME THE WHOLE WAY BACK TO HER CAR, and I didn't hear a word. I was busy trying not to stare at the purse-snatcher. His tattoos, murky blue-black against the coarse, pallid skin, flowed down from his shaven head, disappeared into his torn and filthy sweatshirt, and emerged again on both forearms. I glimpsed snakes, spiders, and homely little sayings like "Only Death Is Real." On one side of his head, above the ear, a bat spread blue-black wings over a giant eyeball. I was transfixed by the bat when the man turned his head to stare at me, with malicious little eyes that were clenched in a face as bony and muscled as a fist. I knew that face, and I was dead certain that he knew mine. By the time we got to the Volvo I was cold all over.

"—never saw so much pink in my life!" Lily concluded, buckling her seat belt. "Hey, did you catch the tattoos on that guy back there?"

"Lily, that was him!"

"Him who?"

"The guy who tried to steal Elizabeth's purse after the bridesmaids' luncheon, the one I told you about!"

"Oh, my God, he looked absolutely *poisonous*." She pulled away from the curb. "Why isn't he in jail?"

"He's out on bail until the trial. Lily, I think he's following us."

She checked the rearview mirror. "I don't see him."

"No, I mean following Elizabeth and her attendants. Everyone who was at La Corona that day, and saw him get arrested, was at Stephanie's this morning. Elizabeth and Patty, me, Corinne and Angela. Everyone except... Mercedes."

Lily's eyes were wide. "You don't think—"

"I don't know, but I'm calling Lieutenant Graham. Circle the block, would you?"

I rooted around in my bag for the detective's card and punched the number into my cell phone. He picked up on the first ring.

"Homicide, Graham."

I identified myself and began to babble about the man I now thought of as Skull. Graham knew about the purse-snatching attempt—he knew a lot about Mercedes by now—but he was strangely calm.

"He didn't speak to you, or threaten you in any way?"

"No."

"And what is he doing now?"

Lily cruised slowly by Stephanie's, where the other women were piling gaily into Elizabeth's SUV. "Well, it looks like he's gone. But Lieutenant, I have to talk with you. You're in your office?"

"On my way out. I've got to grab some lunch before a briefing at the Federal Building. I'll call you later this afternoon."

"No, wait! We're on our way to First Avenue now. I have a meeting down there myself. Where are you eating?"

His voice was amused. "Sounds like you're going to tell me."

"By Bread Alone, the bakery on Seneca. They have great sandwiches, you'll love it. Fifteen minutes?"

"Fifteen minutes."

I ended the call and remembered my manners. "Lily, thanks for the lift. You were a big help at the fitting, too. You can just drop me on First—"

"Are you kidding?" she countered. "You're not leaving me in suspense. I want to hear the rest of the story. And besides, I'm hungry."

By Bread Alone was an organic, communal, whole-grain, save-the-whales bakery that had begun life in an obscure building in the south end. The business was already rising like yeast when their *pain au levain* was written up by a gourmet magazine, just at the magic moment when the foodies of Seattle discovered artisan breads. Now BBA, as the regulars called it, had a bustling bakery operation downtown, with a cheery little six-table café up front.

Lieutenant Graham, traveling on foot, was already seated by the time we stashed Lily's car. He stood up when we joined him, shook Lily's hand, and even took our coats over to the rack in the corner. Chivalry was alive at the SPD. Graham wore a two-button Ralph Lauren faille suit in dark olive, and an intriguing tie. Must be a high-level briefing. He looked better rested than he had on Sunday, though he still carried that perpetual air of disappointment. *Nice shoulders*, I thought absently, and plunged into my brand-new, made-up-on-the-spot theory about Skull.

"What if *that's* the connection between Corinne and Mercedes?" I said. "Some kind of weird vendetta that started the day we got him arrested? He had plenty of time to get to know our faces, sitting there on the curb waiting for the police. Elizabeth's wedding plans have been in the papers, along with her picture, so he'd know about the engagement party. He could have sneaked into the Aquarium carrying some kind of black cloth, killed Mercedes, and then tried to kill Corinne. And now he's stalking the rest of us!"

The waitress arrived and we ordered. A smile tugged at Graham's lips as he asked for the Wholey Grail Whole Grain special, but he turned serious again as he began to tick off points on his fingers.

"That's an interesting hypothesis, but it's got a few problems. First of all, why would Lester Foy—that's his name, by the way, though I like Skull better—why would he plot this drastic revenge just because you saw him commit a robbery for which he's already been arrested and booked? Serial murder is a very big-time enterprise to take on, and Foy is very small-time. In fact purse-snatching in daylight is not just small-time, it's stupid."

"But—"

"Second," he went on, "how could someone as stupid *and* bizarre-looking as Skull—I mean, Foy—sneak into a party with security guards at the door? And third—"

"Now, you can't say he's not stalking us!"

He took a bite of his sandwich and wiped his mouth carefully with a napkin. He had a narrow mouth and a nice square-cut jaw. "Sure I can."

I was indignant. "You think it was just a coincidence that he was standing right outside the dress shop this morning?"

"Well, it could have been. Coincidences do happen. But as a matter of fact, Lester Foy lives about two blocks from the address you gave me. I looked it up. It's no crime to hang out in your own neighborhood." As I sat back, deflated, the detective ticked off his final point. "Fourth, I'm not convinced that anyone at all assaulted Ms. Campbell on Saturday night. She and I had a brief conversation about it, and she declined to file a complaint."

"That's because she's upset—" I began, but Lily cut me off.

"Lieutenant Graham, listen to me," she said, with that imperious Cleopatra look she can summon at will. "Someone stupid and desperate enough for a daylight robbery could easily be stupid and desperate enough for murder. And even if he does live on Capitol Hill, it's still quite a coincidence that Skull was watching the dress shop like that. And besides—"

"Besides," I jumped in, "the boy who cried wolf was devoured by one. What if Corinne is telling the truth, Lieutenant? She may be a flake, but how are you going to feel if she's murdered, too?"

"Ms. Kincaid," he said, "things happen every day in this city that I feel just terrible about."

Suddenly I understood Graham's air of disappointment. It came from constantly being appalled at the sins of mankind, and constantly watching them committed all over again.

"So you won't pursue this."

"I didn't say that." He stood up, wrapped the rest of his sandwich in a napkin, and dropped a bill on the table. "I'll see if I can find out what your friend Skull was up to on Saturday night, and I'll talk to Ms. Campbell again. And then if you don't mind, I'll continue to do my job and investigate why one of your party guests killed Mercedes Montoya. Now, I'm late for my briefing. Thanks for your input. Nice meeting you, Lily."

We finished our lunch in discouraged silence, and then Lily had to go to work.

"Thanks again for carting me around today."

"No problem." She chuckled. "It was worth it to see you all dolled up like that."

"And thanks for sticking up for me with Graham. You made my case better than I did, even if it is a pretty feeble case. I'll take care of the check."

She left, and I sat folding sugar packets into origami and thinking about Corinne. I *knew* she wasn't just telling a theatrical fib, I could feel it. Professional victims, to use Aaron's phrase, feed on the attention and concern that they create with their histrionics. They revel in victimhood. Corinne was trying to go on with her day-to-day life, doing her interviews and writing up her columns, but she was hardly reveling. She was badly shaken, I could see it in her eyes.

The question was, now that I'd alerted the police, what else could I do? Elizabeth and her attendants were already on the alert; no point spooking them further by telling them my theory, which was probably wrong anyway. These were sensible women, after all. They weren't about to go strolling down dark alleys with a guy who looked like Skull.

"Hey, Kincaid. My shift is over. What's up?"

Standing before me was a spherical young woman wearing tiny cat's-eye glasses with huge rhinestone frames. Her hair was dyed chartreuse and shaved into a checkerboard pattern like clear cuts in a national forest, and when she spoke, you could see the steel stud through the end of her tongue.

"Hey, yourself," I said. "How'd you like to bake a wedding cake for me?"

Chapter Fourteen

JUICE NUGENT WAS EVEN MORE INTERESTING THAN SHE looked—and considering her outfit today, that was saying something. I was only five or six years her senior, but my linen trousers and tweed jacket came from a different planet than her ebony leather bustier and heavy denim jacket, and the startling stretch of plump, milk-white leg between the raveled edges of her very short shorts and the scalloped tops of her purple snakeskin boots. The jacket's shoulder seams were stitched with dozens of earrings, fishing lures and other trinkets that quivered and jangled at her slightest move, and a button on the lapel read "Queer and Proud. Any Questions?"

"You bet your ass I want to bake a wedding cake for you!" she said. Juice had a raspy voice with a lot of mileage on it. "I've only been telling you so for months. Wait, I'll get us some coffee."

As a teenage runaway, Juice had lived on the streets of Seattle for almost a year before hooking up with FareStart, a program that trains homeless people for food service jobs. They discovered her genius for baking, and she discovered self-respect. Now Juice was the diva of Danish and the goddess of galettes, and more than that, flat-out obsessed with becoming a sought-after wedding-cake designer. Her bosses at BBA, a middle-aged lesbian couple, loaned Juice cooler and oven space for freelance cake projects. She made a mocha mousse filling to die for, and did remarkably elegant work with tricky material like poured fondant.

The trouble was, Juice scared the clients. Green hair and blue language worked fine at a counterculture place like BBA, but not with your typical mother of the bride.

"So who's the lucky girl?" she demanded, returning with a refill for me and a cup for herself.

"Her name's Bonnie Buckmeister, and it's a very Christmassy wedding. She and her folks have looked at several designs, but so far nothing seems quite right."

She snickered. "So it's last-resort time, huh?"

"Juice, I've told you before, your cakes are fabulous, but cakes aren't everything. People need to be comfortable with you."

"And I've told *you*, Kincaid, people are gonna get comfortable with me once my reputation takes off. I just need to prove myself."

"Well, here's a chance to start. Do you want to take a crack at it?"

"Hell, yeah!" The jacket jingled as she leaned forward, her arrogant expression suddenly earnest. "You're not going to regret this, you'll see. I'm gonna be famous. I am going to be the freakin' Dale Chihuly of cake."

"I'm sure you will, Juice, but meanwhile could you do me a favor?"

"What?"

"When I bring the Buckmeisters in for a tasting, lose the tongue stud?"

She agreed, reluctantly, and I gave her the rundown on

the Buckmeister/Frost nuptials: number of guests, buffet menu, reception decor, and what I was able to surmise of the Buckmeister aesthetic approach. We made a date for the tasting, and then as we were leaving the table a thought struck me.

"Juice, you live on Capitol Hill, don't you? Have you ever seen a guy near Olive and Broadway, with tattoos all over his head?"

"On his face, you mean?"

"No, his skull is shaved and tattooed. There's a big one above his left ear, a bat hovering over an eyeball."

"Cool! I woulda noticed that if I'd ever seen him. I love tattoos."

"But you don't have any yourself."

She shrugged. "My girlfriend Rita likes my skin the way it is. How come you're looking for this guy?"

"Oh...I just wanted to talk to him about, um, a band he's in. For a client party. It's no big deal, forget it."

Which was what I needed to do myself. Lieutenant Graham was going to check out Skull's alibi, and I was going to forget about him and get back to work. But first I bussed up to Westlake and rented a car. My current finances restricted me to a charming little vehicle, lovingly crafted in Eastern Europe, that combined the roomy elegance of a soup can with the horsepower of a sewing machine. *Vanna,* I vowed, *I'll never complain about you again. All is forgiven, come home soon.*

As I stitched my way back to the houseboat, I reflected on the classic entrepreneur's dilemma facing Made in Heaven: when you've got business in hand, you're too busy to drum up new clients. But when the feast is over, the famine is there waiting. Eddie and I had to do our very best for Elizabeth and Bonnie, but we also had to line up some brides after

them. It was enough to make me nostalgic for a paycheck.
Sometimes.

Up in the office, Eddie was covered in smiles and my desk
was covered with paper.

"What's all this?"

"Our new software!" he crowed. "Now that Zack got it to
work, we're going to save all kinds of time and trouble. Look
at this. It's a graph of revenues versus expenses for the last
six months."

I took the sheet he handed me and sat down. "We lost
that much in just six months?"

He wasn't listening. "And this one charts the RSVPs for
Lamott/Wheeler, with columns for gifts received, thank-you
notes sent, the whole shebang. You check off which columns
you want visible on the screen."

"Hmm. His relatives back East still haven't answered. I
need to give Joe a final head count soon."

"...and *this* one is a pie chart of expenses allocated for
Buckmeister/Frost. You can edit the captions for each wedge,
see?"

"Are the flowers really running that high? Those amaryllis
must be made of platinum."

"*Carnegie!*" Eddie glowered at me and chomped his cigar
so hard it nearly imploded.

"What?"

"Are you interested in this software or not? I've been bust-
ing my butt at the computer all morning while you went
around trying on clothes, and now all you can do is pick nits!"

"Of course I'm interested!" The only treatment for this
kind of computer fever was to feign enthusiasm and pray for
a quick recovery. "This is just what we need to get a handle
on the business. Why don't you e-mail me some of these, so

I can see them on-screen? Save a little paper, anyway. . . . Hey, did Zack call?"

"Yeah, he's coming by tomorrow afternoon. He apologized all up and down about how he acted the other day, but I told him it was only natural seeing how a friend of his just got killed. He's a nice kid. Smart."

"According to Paul, he's a genius with web-site design. I can't wait to see what he comes up with for Made in Heaven. Anything else going on?"

"Joe Solveto wants to talk to you, so I told him to come on over. And that Talbot fellow called, but he wouldn't say why. Too bad about his wife. I remember reading about it."

"Yes. Yes, that really was too bad. I'd better make some calls before Joe gets here."

I started with Roger Talbot.

"Carnegie, about this rehearsal dinner on Friday," he said. His voice sounded ghastly.

"Roger, if you'd rather not be there—"

"I promised Paul I'd meet his parents. And I don't want people to think"—Mercedes' name hung in the silence between us—". . . to think anything. But I just can't do it. I'm not sleeping, I can't seem to pull my thoughts together."

"Don't worry about it, really," I said, privately grateful that he wouldn't be at the Salish. He was hardly the ideal dinner guest at this point. "You can spend some time with Chloe and Howard at the reception."

"I knew you'd understand. You're the only one who knows what I'm going through. Thank you, Carnegie."

First an unwilling confidante to Mercedes, and now a reluctant co-conspirator with Roger. This wasn't the role I signed up for. Mindful of Eddie's presence—he claimed he didn't eavesdrop but I knew he did, and he knew I knew—I made a brisk and businesslike farewell, and reached for my next phone message slip, from Pete the mechanic. But Eddie couldn't resist a comment.

"Talbot bailed out, huh?" Before I could come up with an explanation, he provided his own. "Delayed reaction to his wife dying. It happens. Your mother went along fine for a couple of months, keeping up a good front, and then she kinda folded up for a while. Probably the same for Talbot."

"I'm sure you're right, Eddie. Excuse me." I punched in Pete's number. The news was not good.

"We're looking at twenty-five, twenty-seven hundred here, Carnegie!" Pete had to shout over the din of engines, tools, and the Christian radio channel that blared eternally in his tiny office next to the garage. "Then there's that rear right fender. You want that in the estimate, too?"

"How did I know this would be three thousand?" I mused aloud. I might as well just sign over Elizabeth's check.

"Can't hear you!" he said.

"Never mind. Estimate the whole thing, including the fender, and fax it over, OK?"

"Okeydoke!"

Then I got on e-mail and reviewed Eddie's new hobby of chart creation for fun and profit. He was right, the new software would save us some time, and provide a nice professional format for keeping our clients updated on budgets, vendors, and guests. In my previous life—doing public relations work for a bank—I'd been project manager for some fairly major publications and events, but none of them held a candle to the logistical complexities of a large formal wedding like Bonnie's or Elizabeth's. For instance, very few executives throw hissy fits about who they're seated next to at the annual stockholders meeting.

A jaunty rap on the outer office door announced Joe Solveto. He let himself in, along with a gust of saltwater air and the cries of gulls.

"Victory is mine, boys and girls! I hold in my hand the final menu for Lamott/Wheeler, and it is a triumph of the culinary arts."

"If you do say so yourself?" I smiled. "Good to see you, Joe."

Joe was always good to see. For one thing, he was a beautiful man, from his cunningly mussed sandy hair, down past his diligently sculpted dancer's physique, to his impeccably polished, hand-crafted Italian shoes. Joe and his partner, Alan, made a lovely couple. They also made a lot of money. Alan was a media buyer for the biggest ad agency in town, and Joe had built up Seattle's premiere catering firm. I loved it when my clients could afford Solveto's; he was a prince to work with, and they always adored his food. I accepted the menu he offered with my mouth already watering.

"Let's see . . . spinach salad with feta and golden raisins, the haricots verts you told me about, Penn Cove mussels . . . ooh, crab cakes with dried cherries and cilantro, topped with chile aioli? That sounds scrumptious."

"It *is* scrumptious." He folded himself elegantly into a visitor chair. "As is the peppercorned New York strip on foccacia with arugula and Parmesan. Oh, and I've had an epiphany for the Buckmeister/Frost entrée, the vegetarian one."

"Tell, tell."

"Two epiphanies, actually. Number one is a torta di verdura, and—"

"What the hell is that?" Eddie wasn't quite as fond of Joe as I was. Back in his day, on the high seas, men didn't admit to homosexuality unless they were very good swimmers. But

Joe answered him with perfect courtesy. He had told me once in private that he found Eddie's attempt to embrace diversity quite touching.

"Torta di verdura is a 'cake of greens,' in this case brioche stuffed with spinach and citrus-scented ricotta."

"Oh," said Eddie, embracing away. "Well, that sounds pretty good. What's number two?"

"Baby arugula salad with figs. And polenta rosemary breadsticks to go with. The torta has dairy, the salad's completely vegan."

Eddie nodded grudging approval and went back to his reports.

"Joe, you've done it again," I told him. "I wish you were doing the rehearsal dinner, too."

"Oh, the Salish will do you proud," he said. "Even if the food was bad, the location is divine. And actually, the food is quite good."

The Salish Lodge overlooked Snoqualmie Falls, a Northwest beauty spot that's higher than Niagara, though not as broad. I'd reserved a private room for the dinner, with a fireplace and terrace, and French doors we could open to join the after-dinner dancing in the foyer.

"That's high praise, coming from you," I said. "I'll be sure to bring my appetite."

Joe cocked his head. "You're attending?"

"I'm an attendant." I told him about the bridesmaid bribe.

"Goodness! For that kind of money I'd put on a pink dress myself." That was aimed at Eddie, who snorted faintly. "Well, be sure and order the duck breast salad with blood orange vinaigrette. Their venison is excellent, too."

As I made a note about that, Joe pulled his chair closer to my desk. "Carnegie, I heard that you found Mercedes."

"You know her? I mean, knew her?"

He shook his head. "Not really. But her kid brother Esteban works for me. She moved him and her mother up here from Mexico a while ago. Bought them a nice house in Renton, and helped them both get citizenship."

"Oh, God. They must be devastated."

"Yes, indeed. Stebbie's English isn't that good, so he asked me to ask you something—"

"She didn't suffer," I said, for the second time. "It must have been over very quickly."

"Thanks. I'll tell him. It'll mean a lot to his mother. How are you holding up after an experience like that?"

"I'm fine. Well, not fine, but OK."

"You take care of yourself, Carnegie." His slender fingers tapped on the menu—which he could easily have faxed to me instead of coming by in person. Joe was a good guy. "I'll send you this with a cost breakdown. By the way, have you found a cake yet for the Killer B's?"

"Buckmeisters," I said automatically, though it was a losing battle. "Yes, I think so. Juice Nugent."

His high-boned, theatrical face twisted in dismay. "That bizarre child at BBA? Oh, please."

"Have you seen her cakes? She's quite talented."

"She's quite Martian, if you ask me. She keeps calling me for referrals, and I tell her to put on a wig and a dress and I'll think about it."

"You're a snob, Joe."

"And a good one." He stood up. "I'll be in touch. Strange as it may seem, I'm convinced that Lamott/Wheeler is going to be a huge success."

"I hope so. It certainly can't get any stranger than it has already."

Chapter Fifteen

WEDNESDAY PASSED UNEVENTFULLY, EXCEPT FOR THE BAD news that Vanna would be dry-docked at Pete's for at least a week. At least I didn't have dresses or cakes to transport this week, as I sometimes did. And I'd always meant to take a yoga class someday; folding myself into the soup can rental car was a good warm-up.

Thursday the Buckmeisters descended upon us again like a plague of cheerful, indecisive locusts. This time I was in better shape to handle them, so I let Eddie escape to lunch. Buck, Betty, and Bonnie had yet another wonderful new idea for the reception: Christmas carol karaoke.

I kept a straight face and lobbied for chorals rather than solos, and they agreed that Aunt Min doing all twelve days of Christmas by herself might be a bit much. That was a relief. I'd met Min, and based on her speaking voice, I figured the lords a-leaping would leap right out a window if they had to sit through the swans and the golden rings. Then I solved a little etiquette problem for Betty. Bless her heart, she had a tender regard for the feelings of every single guest.

"It's the table numbers," she explained. "Everyone expects the head table to be One, of course, and then the family sits at Two and Three, but then the people who get put at Nine and such might feel like they came lower down in our hearts, do you see what I mean? And they're *all* our friends."

" 'Cept for my business buddies," Buck rumbled. Today's bandanna was an unbusinesslike international orange, with pink paisley swirls. "They're not exactly friends, but I still want to treat 'em right. What about it, Carnegie? What's the official way to do it?"

It's funny how many people believe in the existence of some almighty etiquette bible, handed down on engraved deckle-edged vellum instead of stone tablets, and specifying everything from how to fold the napkins to how much to tip the kid in the parking lot. I kept introducing the principle of Good Sense Plus Thoughtfulness, and clients kept asking for the official rules.

"Tell you what," I said, flinging myself into the holiday spirit. "Let's do away with the numbers altogether. We'll call the head table Santa Claus, and name the rest of them after the reindeer. Once you get past Dancer and Prancer, no one's going to remember whether Cupid or Comet comes first."

"Well, *we* would," Bonnie the bride pointed out, gnawing a rosebud lip. Then her face regained its usual sunny expression. "But that's just because we love Christmas so much. We're sort of Christmas experts."

"I noticed that. But the rest of your guests will just enjoy seeing the holiday names there on the place card table. If we have more tables than reindeer we'll use, I don't know, Snowflake and Icicle?"

"Perfect!" said Betty. "Carnegie, you're just wonderful."

If only all mothers of the bride were so appreciative. I continued being wonderful for another half hour, and then when Eddie came back with Zack in tow, I ushered the Killer B's gently out the door.

Zack, I was surprised to see, didn't look any better than he had on Sunday. Worse, if anything. His usual shy smile had vanished, replaced by a heavy, stolid silence. His website demo was pretty stolid, too: our logo on a home page, our brochure copy rearranged a bit, and a request form where potential clients could ask for more information. No animation, no razzle-dazzle, no nothing. As Zack himself would say, it was, like, so lame.

"Well," said Eddie. "Well. It's certainly a start. Isn't it, Carnegie?"

"Yes, a good start. Zack, if you're really busy at the *Sentinel* these days, we could postpone—"

"That's OK," he said dully. "I pretty much quit this morning."

Eddie and I exchanged glances.

"Was there a problem, Zack?"

He shrugged, looking sullen, and younger than ever. "Um, Carnegie, could we, like, take a walk or something? I kind of want to talk to you."

"I could leave you two alone—" Eddie began, but I rolled my eyes at him and he got the message. "Except that I'm awfully busy right now. And anyway, Carnegie's got a dinner date. With her *boyfriend*."

This time the word was fine with me. The last thing I wanted was to be left alone with Robin Hood. He obviously needed comforting after losing his coworker, but I wasn't the one to provide it.

"I sure do," I said brightly, "and I'd better go change. Zack, you and Eddie do a little brainstorming, why don't you, and see what else you can come up with. I remember you had all those great ideas at the Aquarium." *Including the bright idea about kissing me.* "I'll see you Friday night, OK?"

Zack's face was stony, and he didn't reply. Downstairs in the kitchen, with more time than I needed to get ready, I poured myself some Pinot Grigio and sat looking out at the lake. It was gray and wintry, the color of November, with brushstrokes of whitecaps out in the middle. A few die-hard sailboats went swooping across my field of vision, but I hardly noticed them. I was gearing myself up for an uncomfortable conversation.

I'd come to a decision, or rather a nondecision, and tonight I meant to tell Aaron about it. Much as I hated to rank myself among the walking wounded—along with the recently divorced, the perpetually lonely, and the otherwise emotionally traumatized—I had come to realize that I just wasn't ready for a new lover, after that dreadful tangle with Holt Walker earlier in the year. A silly flirtation with a younger man, sure. But a serious love affair that might turn out to be permanent? Not yet. I had to ask Aaron to give me some time. And I was dreading his answer. What if he wasn't willing to hang around and wait?

I refilled my glass and called Lily. The wonderful thing about our friendship was the way we could slide from the big picture to the tiny details of life and back again, like a movie camera smoothly shifting from the far horizon to a single raindrop quivering on a leaf. Lily and I could analyze mortality, mutual funds, and mascara without missing a beat.

Still, as I heard her phone ringing, I decided not to talk about my nondecision, not till I knew the outcome. So I stayed on safer ground.

"Guess what, Lily? I'm now officially an older woman." I told her about Zack. "He's looking sad and soulful, but I'm relying on Eddie to snap him out of it."

"Well, don't go messing with minors, or I'll report you to my detective."

"Your what?"

"Lieutenant Graham called me yesterday," said Lily, "and then came by the library on my lunch hour today. He wanted to know all about you: how long I'd known you, how we met, all kinds of things."

I pondered this uneasily. "You think he's trying to figure out if I'm trustworthy?"

"I guess. You're asking him to believe Corinne Campbell, after all, and she is not his favorite citizen. Did you know that detective lieutenants aren't usually out in the field like this? He was downtown when the call came in about Mercedes Montoya, and then he stayed with the case."

"That's very interesting, but what about Skull and his alibi? That's who Graham should be checking on, not me!"

"I asked him, but he was pretty vague. He has this trick of not hearing questions he doesn't want to answer."

"I know that trick," I said. "Well, I'm seeing Aaron tonight, and he's got sources in the SPD. Maybe he knows something."

"You don't want me along this time, I take it?"

"No offense, Lily, but I think I better handle this one myself."

"None taken. Have fun."

But fun was not in the forecast. Aaron picked me up in his banana-mobile, commented appreciatively on my winter-white wool outfit, and then proceeded to scoff at my theory about Skull all the way downtown. I found myself defending the idea, even though I'd almost given up on it anyway.

"I don't *care* if you think it's far-fetched," I grumbled.

"Honestly, if looks could kill, I'd be lying dead on the sidewalk in front of Stephanie's Styles."

"Well, it must have been humiliating, a tough character like him getting busted by a bunch of bridesmaids. He runs into you on the street, remembers where he saw you last, and glares at you. Big deal. Where should I park?"

"Right here on Fifth. We're taking the monorail." I'd billed tonight's dinner as a mystery destination, my treat. We continued to argue for the short journey to the Seattle Center, then, as we emerged into the open air, I tried to shift gears. I wanted a calm, friendly atmosphere for the conversation I was planning.

"We're dining in the clouds tonight!" I pointed overhead at the Space Needle, with its glass elevators rising 500 feet up the tapering shaft to the circular observation deck and the SkyCity restaurant, lit up like a flying saucer against the overcast sky.

But Aaron didn't follow my script. Frowning, he shoved his hands in the pockets of his black leather jacket and said, "Up there? I heard it's overpriced, strictly for tourists. You don't want to go there."

"Yes I do, as a matter-of-fact. They revamped the restaurant quite a while ago, and I've been meaning to check it out. My clients keep asking about it. Besides, I've got a dinner-for-two gift certificate my mom sent me for my birthday."

"Look, if you're short of cash, I'll pick up the tab tonight," he said stubbornly. "Let's go to that café at the EMP."

This was bordering on rudeness, and we both knew it.

"Aaron, what's going on? It's just dinner, and I need to do this for Made in Heaven."

"Nothing's going on!" he snapped. "Whatever you want. Let's go get in line."

Sure enough, there was a line of tourists at the Needle, even on a Thursday night in November, but with restaurant reservations, we were ushered right into an elevator. Aaron kept his back to the glass during the stomach-swooping ride to the top, missing out on the gradually widening view of downtown and Elliott Bay. This was a new side of Aaron, this petulance at not getting his way. I hate men who sulk.

Inside SkyCity, things got worse. We lucked into a window table and ordered drinks, but Aaron barely glanced out at the spectacular nighttime scene of city lights strung along Puget Sound like jewels on black velvet. Instead, he looked fixedly over my shoulder, across the room. I tried to regain his attention.

"Aaron, how's Tommy doing?"

"What? Oh, no change. Paul's been calling the hospital a couple times a day and keeping us all posted." Then he went back to staring past me.

"Look, if you're that unhappy here, maybe we should just call it a night."

Aaron shook his head as if to clear it and forced a smile. "Sorry, I'm being a boor. I was just distracted. By *him*."

He nodded and I turned to look. Syd Soper, Death himself, was sitting at a table full of cocktail glasses with three other men in business suits, laughing loudly and kidding the waitress who had just brought us our steamed clams. She didn't look pleased.

Neither did Aaron. He stared at Soper and tapped his cigarette lighter against the tablecloth, flipping the little steel rectangle end over end after each furious tap. He didn't seem to notice he was doing it. "That's the son of a bitch who killed Mercedes, not your creep with the tattoos. And he'll probably get away with it."

"The police didn't listen to you?"

He waited till the waitress came and went, bearing our order for one seared ahi with wasabi mashed potatoes, and one prime rib, rare. *Thanks, Mom.*

"They listened, but they can't prove anything. Nobody saw her go down that corridor, and the party was so big that it's hard to piece together everyone's whereabouts or even who saw her last."

"But Aaron, the police aren't going about it the right way!"

"What do you mean?"

"They should be looking for the man who attacked Mercedes *and* Corinne. I know, you don't trust Corinne's story, but what if it's true? It gives us much more to go on."

He smiled again, a genuine smile this time. "Us?"

"Well, you're going to help me figure this out, aren't you? Remember, Corinne was smothered with a black cloak, and Soper was wearing one."

He nodded, intrigued in spite of himself. "So if we ask people whether they saw Soper go down the pier to where Corinne was—"

"Not just Soper, though. Anyone in a black cloak. I've got the guest list, and I can get the costume list from Characters, Inc. We can eliminate the people in black capes who couldn't have done it because they left the party before eleven o'clock—"

"Or because they're you and me."

"Oh, that's right, isn't it? We both had black capes. Well, we know we didn't do it, so that cuts the list down right there. Soper was Death, and someone was a magician—"

"That was Harry from Classifieds. He wouldn't hurt the rabbit in his top hat, let alone kill anybody."

"Let's think about motive later, OK? Who else wore a black cloak?"

"OK. There was a Batman, I remember, and Darth Vader..."

"...and the Three Musketeers!"

It was almost like a game, and I began to forgive his earlier bad manners, especially after dinner arrived. The food was better than I expected, even if I'd been paying for it. Joe might have curled his lip, but I was feeling well fed, right down to the slice of praline apple tart that we split between us. I paid the check, then sat back, replete, and closed my eyes to replay scenes at the Aquarium: the martini bar, the buffet tables, the dance floor...

"Rick," I said. "Rick the Rocket, the DJ, he was a medieval monk and his robes were black. There was someone else, too, in some kind of religious—oh, Angela Sims. She was a nun in black. She doesn't count."

"Why not?"

"You don't think *she'd* attack other women?"

"You said to leave motive out of it, Stretch. Angela's big and strong."

"Corinne was pretty sure it was a man," I said doubtfully. "But OK, we'll consider Angela. Who else?"

"That Dracula, the one who kept quiet all night so no one could identify him. Who was he?"

"I don't know, but Characters, Inc. can tell me. I'll call the shop in the morning. Oof, I'm half-asleep with all this food. Let's go out on the deck and look at the lights."

But Aaron dug in his heels again. "It'll be freezing out there. Drink your coffee and let's go home."

"Look, I'm the host here tonight, and I want to go out on the deck." I tried to keep it good-humored, but it came out peevish.

"Well, I'm your guest here tonight, and I don't." He didn't even try for humor. "I'll be at the bar."

"Well, OK."

"OK."

We parted ways, each in our own separate huff. It *was* freezing out there, with a big wet wind, but I was determined to stay long enough to make Aaron uncomfortable. Like a mule with red hair, my father used to say.

My father, I thought suddenly. *Of course.*

I marched back inside and found Aaron sitting with his elbows on the bar, a drink and an ashtray between them. I felt so contrite I didn't even care about the cigarette. He deserved one.

"It's acrophobia, isn't it?" I said quietly.

"How did you know?"

I sat on the barstool beside him. We were enclosed in a buzz of voices, over which floated the pianist's haunting rendition of "Send in the Clowns." I love that song. "I should have known right away. My dad had a fear of heights, a bad one. He hid it as best he could. I tried to take him and Mom up here once for their anniversary and she had to explain why it wouldn't work. Aaron, why didn't you just tell me?"

"Why do you think?" He angled his head and ran one thumb along his eyebrow, hiding his face from me. "I was embarrassed. I know how you feel about big, strong men—"

"What are you talking about?"

He turned to me. He had the nicest eyes, a dark, polished brown. "I'm talking about how you can hardly stand to go out with a short guy, let alone a short guy with phobias."

"Aaron, that's not true! Look, I was tall and gawky as a girl, and I'm still a little self-conscious about my height. That's all. Doesn't mean I'm looking for some macho monster."

"So who are you looking for, Stretch?" He put out his cigarette and finished his drink. "Are you looking for me?"

"Wel-l-l, that's what I wanted to talk to you about tonight."

"So talk."

The bartender showed up just then, which bought me a few minutes. I ordered brandy, inhaled the golden fumes, and took a sip. And then I took the plunge.

"Aaron, I need some time. I'm still shaken up by what happened this summer with Holt, and I feel like you're trying to rush me into bed."

"Rush you?" He looked genuinely puzzled, and laid his hand on mine. "I'm not trying to rush you, Slim."

"But you talk about sex all the time—"

"That's just talk!" He smiled, that wonderful, winning smile. "You know, repartee, wordplay, romantic banter? I'm just letting you know how attractive you are to me. I'm not laying down an ultimatum."

"So you don't mind waiting?"

"Of course I mind! You drive me crazy. But if you need some time, you've got it. I'm not going anywhere."

I felt a warm glow of relief, and brandy.

"Of course, there is one problem," he went on. "You're going to have to help me out tonight. 'Cause if I don't get what I want from you tonight, then it's all over."

The glow faded. "What do you mean?"

"Well..." He was trying not to smile, but it broke through. Zorro was back. "Well, I am shit-scared of that elevator ride, and if you don't hold my hand on the way down, I'm going to have to jump down to the monorail."

I began to laugh. "I think that can be arranged."

Chapter Sixteen

REHEARSAL DINNERS CAN BE MORE FUN THAN WEDDINGS—more intimate and relaxed, imbued with hospitality instead of stage fright. They're flexible, too, having evolved far beyond the simple function of nourishing the wedding party after the rigors of the rehearsal. Sometimes the dinner is a formal first meeting of the bridal pair's parents; sometimes it's a casual thank-you evening for all the friends who have pitched in with the wedding preparations. I'd organized everything from pizza feasts to private sushi bars for my clients, and my batting average was close to perfect. But this was the first time I got to plan my dinner and eat it, too.

Paul and Elizabeth's Friday-night rehearsal dinner was taking place a week before the rehearsal itself, to accommodate Paul's parents. They had an overnight layover in their flight from Minneapolis to Maui, where Howard had a sales conference and Chloe was going to see a real palm tree for the first time.

I'd ordered Hawaiian flowers for our table for twelve: the engaged couple, their parents and attendants, and Valerie Duncan, the *Sentinel*'s managing editor, who had graciously agreed to fill in for Roger Talbot tonight. It was an amiable group, and the evening took on the air of a bon-voyage party for Paul's homey, unassuming parents. I was especially taken with Chloe, who took me aside to thank me for filling in as bridesmaid. I just hoped she never found out I'd been paid.

"It's so important to Enid," Chloe said to me over cocktails and appetizers, blinking her pale brown eyes behind their thick glasses.

"Is she your aunt, or Howard's?"

"Mine, though I hate to admit it."

"I'm sorry?"

"Oh, Enid can be such a . . . a *bitch*," said Chloe daringly, savoring the word. "She's very demanding, and she just hates Elizabeth! Don't tell anyone I said so, though."

"Trust me."

Family drama was a pleasant distraction from thoughts of murder, and from the dense November fog pressing in at the windows. Elizabeth's father—in town for the week to get some business done before the wedding—groused a bit because he couldn't see "this famous so-called waterfall" from our private terrace. He was a self-made real-estate tycoon of the old school, proud and loud, and he wanted his money's worth.

But the rest of us enjoyed our beautifully presented dinners, sipping the fine wines appropriate to each course, and making conversation about every imaginable topic except murder. Afterwards, we settled cozily in the glow of the leaping, aromatic fire. When the combo in the foyer began to play, I opened the French doors to let the music drift in, then took my coffee from the sideboard and sat a little apart to try and clear my head.

Elizabeth's father soon joined me, cradling a snifter of brandy against his beltline. "Well, Miss Kincaid—"

"Call me Carnegie, please."

"And I'm Burt. Carnegie, this is a nice little party you put on. We've got some fine-looking women here tonight, start-ing with my daughter."

He nodded across the room at Elizabeth. She wore a chic little black number, outshining her sister's long-sleeved floral print, as she must have outshone her in general for most of their lives. Patty, trying out her new French twist, began the evening animated and almost pretty, but her father gave her only cursory attention; his compliments and smiles were all for the bride. Now his older daughter had grown silent, al-most sullen, frowning into her coffee cup as if the bitterness she felt was concentrated there.

Over by the fireplace, Angela Sims lounged on a hassock, negligently lovely in a dove-gray tunic and long skirt. She was deep in animated conversation with Valerie Duncan. Valerie, a handsome dark-haired woman in her forties, had been a bit reserved at first. But she was growing more voluble as the night went on, and had gratified Paul's parents no end by praising their son during dinner. Valerie and Angela were both sharp-witted professional women, and they looked to be well on the road to friendship.

Still seated at the dinner table was Corinne, overripe but succulent in a short peach-colored frock, working on her sec-ond slice of vanilla bean cheesecake with raspberry coulis. No wonder her bridesmaid gown was tight. She was talking shop with Aaron, who looked quite urbane in a herringbone jacket and charcoal slacks. He laughed heartily at some anec-dote of hers about a recent benefit ball, and then moved off to chat with Patty.

With no best man on hand, and Scott, the third grooms-man, detained back in Baltimore by a crisis at work, Aaron was doing his duty and being attentive to all the ladies. I was grateful to him, because Zack was no help at all. Woefully

underdressed in cords and a misshapen green sweater, Zack
spent most of the evening moping around and gazing at me.

"This Roger Talbot, the publisher who couldn't make it
tonight," Burt was saying. "He's the one whose wife died?"

"Yes."

"Poor bastard." He stared into his brandy. "Still, there are
worse things."

I kept tactfully silent. Elizabeth's mother, Monica, had
also recently departed from her marriage. But instead of
heading for heaven, she had gone straight into the arms
of Burt's private Norwegian tennis coach. The specter of
Monica and Lars attending the wedding had raised some
very sticky seating questions.

Now, however, it appeared that a killer backhand might
come to the rescue. Lars was slashing his way through the
semifinals of a tournament in Connecticut, and if he made it
to the finals, Monica would fly in solo for the wedding. That
would be uncomfortable enough, but nothing compared to
putting Lars and Burt in the same building. *This interactive
rock-and-roll museum ain't big enough for the both of us, you
ornery sidewinder.*

Joe Solveto, a major tennis buff, was keeping me posted
on the tournament results. Elizabeth seemed to find the
whole thing mildly amusing.

"And who's the kid again?" asked Burt. "I didn't catch all
the names."

"That's Zack Hartmann. He's been working at the
Sentinel."

"Something funny about that kid. Won't look me in the
eye."

I was saved from replying by Aaron's approach. Corinne
had disappeared, presumably to the ladies' room, but since

she didn't seem to be drinking tonight, I wasn't worried about a repeat of last Saturday. Aaron held out his hand.

"Mr. Lamott, may I steal the lady from you? They're playing her song." The combo had begun "Lady in Red," and I was wearing my best dress—a deep clear red with a full, fluid skirt.

"Be my guest," the tycoon replied, knocking back his brandy. "I'll just chat with Karen when she gets back. Seems like a nice young lady."

"It's Corinne," I told him. "Yes, she's very nice."

As he escorted me out to the foyer, Aaron murmured, "Gorgeous as you are, Ms. Kincaid, I have decided not to make passionate love to you on top of the piano. But it was a near-run thing."

That's how he was handling my need for breathing space in our relationship: with patience and a laugh. Some men I knew would have dropped me at the nearest corner and never looked back.

"You're being so *nice* about this," I said.

"A man will do anything," he replied in a confidential whisper, "if he thinks it's foreplay."

We circled among the other couples, many of them from a family reunion being held in one of the larger dining rooms. As our own room came back into view, I saw Burt talking intently to Corinne, and Paul's parents coming out to the foyer to dance. Howard had tucked an orchid behind Chloe's ear, and she was smiling like a bride. How nice to know little, and care less, about Mercedes Montoya.

"So what's the word from the costume shop?" asked Aaron.

"Nothing yet. Apparently Characters, Inc. always closes down for a week after Halloween, to give the owners and the staff a break. I keep leaving messages, but I don't know when I'll hear back, and the owner's home number is unlisted. I bet we could put together the list of black cloaks from memory, though."

Aaron nodded. "You know, I'm beginning to come around to your view of Corinne's story. She's trying to cover it up, but she's really frightened."

"So can we get together tomorrow and go over the guest list?"

"I'll come by early and take you out to breakfast."

"Sounds good. Oh, no—" As the song ended I saw Zack approaching, his jaw set in grim resolution. "Aaron, be a prince and fend off Zack, would you? I'm just not up to conversations about the Internet tonight."

He turned. "Zack, my man! Come have some brandy with me on the terrace. I need a smoke."

I cut through the dancers to the concierge desk, just to let them know how well our evening was going. An unnecessary errand, but it would save me a phone call tomorrow, and I really was pleased with the Salish Lodge. If the Buckmeisters started to dither again about their rehearsal dinner, maybe I'd bring them here.

"Message just came for you, Ms. Kincaid," said the bright young man at the desk. "I haven't even had time to write it down yet."

"From Joe Solveto?" I'd accidentally left my cell phone at home, and felt naked without it.

"Yes. He said Lars Kvern won in straight sets, and you'd know what that meant."

"Oh, thank God! You just made my night." I paid my compliments to the chef and the lodge, and returned to my party.

Howard and Chloe were still dancing, and Zack and Aaron were out on the terrace with the French doors shut, but most of the other guests were nowhere to be seen. Valerie Duncan, still ensconced by the fire, told me why.

"It seems that Burt Lamott simply had to see the Falls, so they've all gone trooping across the parking lot to that viewpoint pavilion farther along the canyon. He must think the fog is going to lift and the Falls are going to light up, just for the VIP. I decided to stay here and stay warm."

"Very wise," I said. "But I'd better get out there and make sure no one goes astray."

"Carnegie, before you go—"

She looked so grave that I sat down beside her.

"What is it, Valerie?"

"Why didn't Roger come tonight? It's because of Mercedes, isn't it?"

Oh, hell. "I, um, couldn't say."

"You don't have to. Your face is too honest." She sat back and sighed, fingering the fringe on her challis shawl. "I always wondered if they were lovers. Roger's terribly discreet with all his women, paranoid, really, so there was never a sign. But she was so beautiful. And young. I'm not young anymore."

"Valerie, I shouldn't be discussing this."

She seemed not to hear me. There were two snifters on the table beside her, one of them already empty. She reached for the other, with a hand that was blunt and mottled, not slim and brown like Mercedes'. She drained the brandy. "He's been completely cold to me since we . . . since *he* . . . He can make you feel so cherished, and then be so cruel."

"I'm afraid I can't really follow what you're saying," I said neutrally. "There's so much noise from the dancing. I'm going to go check on the others."

It was the best I could think of, to save her dignity later. I grabbed my coat and left. Outside in the dank, chilly night, guests from the lodge were coming and going in the parking lot, and pale bands of headlights crisscrossed against the blanketing fog. As I strode along the walkway towards the pavilion, the sound of voices dropped away abruptly, muffled by the fog and then lost in the roar of Snoqualmie Falls, which thundered and raged like an invisible beast in the gorge below.

After a few minutes, cocooned in a strange isolation of sight and sound, I began to make out dim figures coming toward me, barely discernible in the swirling darkness. Burt was coming back, his arm around Corinne's shoulders, and the rest of the party seemed to be following.

Small talk suddenly seemed like too much effort. On impulse, I stepped off the walkway among the parked cars, far enough to lose the others from sight. I needed time to think. If Roger Talbot was juggling multiple affairs, maybe Mercedes had become inconvenient. But inconvenient enough to murder? Why not just set her aside, as he'd done with Valerie? Anyway, Corinne insisted that the killer had a cloak, not a topcoat.

Their voices faded quickly, leaving only the white noise of the Falls. I went ahead to the pavilion, a small concrete platform circled by railings that hung out over the gorge. It was empty, save for a brandy snifter on one of the benches. Cold white beams from the ceiling lights fanned out through the pillars and rails, laying crosshatched shadows onto the pale walls of mist. I crossed to the far side and peered out, but of course the Falls were invisible. As I stood there, I quit brooding over Valerie's remarks and lost myself in the crashing roar of the waterfall. It reminded me of the otter's little waterfall at the Aquarium, back before this dreadful thing had happened—

"Carnegie."

"Oh! Zack, you scared me."

"I'm sorry. You keep avoiding me, but I, like, really have to talk to you. I'm going crazy about this."

"About what, Zack?" It was utterly private here; we could have been miles from the lodge. *Might as well get it over with.*

He moved toward me and I retreated. I was willing to be kind about a declaration of affection, however misjudged, but I preferred to fend off another kiss before it happened.

"I can't . . ." he stammered. "I didn't mean . . ."

I was getting chilly. "Zack, please, just say what you want to say."

He turned his face away for a moment and then looked full at me, a wild spark in his shadowed eyes. Suddenly he wasn't a nerdy kid anymore, attractive but immature, easy to flirt with but easy to dismiss. Suddenly he was a man, blazing with a strange intensity.

"Carnegie, I killed Mercedes."

Chapter Seventeen

I FROZE. THE WHOLE SAFE, SANE WORLD WAS SUDDENLY very far away. Zack and I were marooned on an island of stark white light, surrounded by a sea of fog and thundering darkness. My little theory about Skull evaporated on the spot. Not a party crasher, but a party guest, had lured Mercedes down that corridor. Not a black cape but a dark green one had dropped over Corinne's head to blind her before she drowned. Robin Hood, not Death or Darth Vader, had gone home with blood on his hands.

Zack stepped closer. The mist made silver beads on the dark wool of his sweater, and clung to his fair hair.

"You have to listen," he said hoarsely.

"I am listening, really I am." But I was also edging slowly backwards, determined to run for it when I had the chance. I kept seeing the bloody wound beneath Mercedes' perfumed hair, and the way her slender arms had floated, limp in the water.

My retreat was blocked by something hard and cold at my back: the steel bars of the railing. With a quick glance I saw that they stretched for three or four yards to my right along the pavilion's edge before the opening to the pathway. The path to safety. I could slip under the lower bar, but that would take precious seconds, and very likely send me tumbling down the steep slope into the gorge. If I screamed, would anyone hear me over the roar of the Falls, or would it just panic Zack into action? He looked barely in control of himself.

"She was...She said..." His dark blue eyes were wide and fixed, his mouth working soundlessly. I sidled along the rail, one step and then another, my eyes locked on his.

"Go ahead, Zack. Tell me about Mercedes."

Two more steps. A third, a fourth. Zack mirrored my movements, but unconsciously. All his conscious thought seemed bent on getting the words out before they choked him.

"She laughed at me, so I shoved her over. I didn't mean—"

I flung myself toward the pathway. Zack grabbed me, locking my arms against my sides.

"You have to listen!"

I struggled, frantic to get away, but he was shockingly strong. I tried to stamp on his instep, as I'd learned to do, but stumbled instead. It pulled him off balance, so I hooked one foot behind his knee and turned the stumble into a fall, hoping to bring us both down and then pull free.

Only the first part worked. We crashed to the concrete floor, hard enough to knock the wind out of me. I went limp for a moment, gasping, but Zack held on.

"Carnegie, what are you *doing*?" he said plaintively, his voice breaking like a teenager's, his breath hot on my face. The words tumbled out, faster and faster. "I'm not going to hurt you, I just want you to *listen*. I didn't mean to kill her. I've been going totally crazy ever since you told me she was dead. I just shoved her, I thought she'd fall in the water and have to go back to the party all wet and that would serve her right. The water was so shallow, I never thought she'd drown! You've got to believe me...."

His face was wet, but not from the fog. Zack was crying. He disentangled himself from me and sat up, his entire body heaving with anguished sobs that tore themselves from his chest. I could have run away then, but instead I sat up and put a hand on his shoulder.

"You *shoved* her? That was all?" That was bad enough in itself, of course. But Mercedes' head wound came from a deliberate attack, not a simple fall. And a shove was not a murder....

"Yes!" he cried bitterly. "I pushed her over the railing and left her there and she drowned. Oh God, Carnegie, I'm so *sorry*."

"Help me up." We got shakily to our feet, and I led him over to the bench and handed him a handkerchief. I carry three, from habit, but they're usually for brides.

"Zack, sit down. Tell me exactly what happened at the party, OK?"

He nodded, scrubbing at his face, and drew a long uneven breath. "It was just before you and I danced together. Remember?"

"Yes, I remember." I spoke softly, careful of his precarious composure. "Go on."

"Tommy asked Mercedes to dance with me—I wish he'd quit doing that—so she did, and for a while she was, like, really friendly, and kind of sexy even. I mean, she danced real close. I thought...I thought..."

"Just tell me what actually happened, Zack. It's important."

"OK, so we danced, and then she said, let's walk, and we

went past the barrier into that shorebird corridor. You know the one?"

"I know."

He gave a little laugh, with a wavering edge of hysteria to it. The smooth young man I'd found so attractive was gone, reduced to a very vulnerable youngster. "Of course you do! You found her. You found the ... the ..." He couldn't say the word.

"The two of you went past the barrier and into the corridor," I prompted. "Then what?"

"She sat up on the railing. She looked so pretty! And she was laughing and kind of flirting with me, hiking her skirt up and saying wild stuff. It was like she was high."

I could see what was coming, because I'd seen Mercedes high and happy myself, in the ladies' room, and seen her mood alter in the blink of an eye.

"So at first you thought she was enjoying herself with you."

"I thought she *liked* me! I was always watching her at the *Sentinel,* but she totally ignored me, and then here she was, smiling and saying I was handsome and stuff." He flushed darkly at the memory. "And then I tried to kiss her and she laughed right in my face! She said I was boring, and she didn't have to waste her time with a boring boy. She got, like, really nasty."

"And so you shoved her over the rail?"

"Yeah." He hung his head, his eyes squeezed shut and his fists clenched with the effort to undo what he believed was a murderous act. "I can't believe I did that, but I was half-drunk and she got me so excited. . . . She went over backwards and I heard a splash but I didn't stay to watch, I just got out of there and back to the party and got another drink. Then Tommy saw me, and then you know what happened after that."

I knew. I remembered Zack's rigid tension on the dance floor, and how he began to relax as he talked about his website design work. "Some people think it's boring," he had said. Now I knew that "some people" meant Mercedes. When he kissed me, Zack was trying to recover his masculine pride. He didn't know that the woman who had humiliated him was soon to die.

"Zack, listen to me, and tell me if this is right. You pushed Mercedes over the rail, into the water, but you didn't touch her after that?"

"You mean help her out of the water? No." He groaned. "Oh, God, I wish I had. You've got to believe me, if I'd known she was drowning—"

"Zack, she didn't drown."

He stared. "But everyone's been saying that somebody drowned her. The police are looking for whoever did it. They're looking for *me*!"

"Listen to me. The police are looking for whoever took a rock and smashed Mercedes' skull with it. Did you do that?"

"No!" He looked at me in horror. "No! I didn't...I couldn't..."

"Of course you couldn't." I sat beside him, the two of us isolated in our cave of fog and thunder. "The worst you may have done was to leave her there stunned so that someone else could come along and kill her, but we don't even know that for sure. Mercedes could have picked herself up and had a conversation with the killer. We just don't know. But we *do* know that you didn't murder anyone, on purpose or by accident."

The tears began again, this time in a cathartic flood of joy and relief. I found myself smiling inanely, and crying a little as well. It was like bringing someone back from the dead. I couldn't condone Zack's aggressive behavior, but between the alcohol and Mercedes' taunting, I could understand it. The main thing, to him and to me, was that he wasn't a murderer.

"You don't know what it's been like," said Zack, sniffing. I handed him another hankie. "Ever since you told me in your office, I've been trying to act normal on the outside, but inside I was losing my mind. I felt like some kind of monster, and I kept imagining her lying there in the water."

"Shhh. Try not to think about it anymore. All you have to do now is explain to the police—"

"No!" He sprang up from the bench. "No, I can't! And you can't tell them either."

"But Zack, we have to! The more they know about what happened that night, the better. You can tell them what time you saw her alive, and if you saw anyone else in the area."

He shook his head violently. "I didn't see anybody, and I don't know what time it was. I can't tell them anything they don't already know. Don't ask me to!"

He strode to the railing and gripped it with both hands. I followed, trying to sound calm and persuasive, and get this settled while we were still alone. No one else had come out from the lodge, and now I prayed they wouldn't.

"Zack, the police will understand what you did. They won't blame you. You can tell them you didn't even know how she was killed—"

"But now I *do* know, don't you see?"

"That's only because I told you! You can skip that part, just tell them you've decided to come forward with your story about seeing Mercedes alive."

"If I did that, they'd question me over and over, and I wouldn't be able to pretend I don't know about her getting hit with a rock."

I looked at his profile, young and tear-stained, and realized with dismay that in my rush to reassure Zack, I'd stolen his innocence. If he had gone straight to the police with his story, not knowing how Mercedes really died, his ignorance would have been obvious and unshakable. But now . . .

"I'll go with you," I told him. "I'll convince them that you didn't know until I told you. The police are reasonable people. Lieutenant Graham will listen."

"Oh, right," he said hotly. "Like you would know. Have you ever been interrogated?"

"No, but—"

"Well, I have. They just pound away at you till you say what they want to hear. The cops believe what they want to believe, and the prosecutors believe the cops. They'd take one look at my record and lock me up."

"Your record?" I asked uneasily. "What's on your record, Zack?"

His voice dropped to a sullen mutter, and I had to strain to hear him. "I was driving some friends, back in St. Louis. I was just driving! I thought they bought this booze, but they stole it, and beat up the liquor store guy. I was in for five months and it felt like a hundred years. Somebody like you, you can't even imagine what it's like in there. Especially for guys like me."

I didn't have to ask what kind of guys he meant: young and good-looking, and nowhere near tough enough to make a true criminal back off. I pictured a man like Skull alone all night in a cell with this youngster, and shuddered.

"Carnegie, please." Zack turned to face me. "I came out to

Seattle to get my act together. Nobody here knows about me being in jail. I got my web business going, and now that I know that I didn't kill Mercedes, I really do get to start over. I'll never touch anybody again, I swear, and I'll never drink like that again. Please. You saved my life. Don't take it away again, *please*. I'm, like, begging you."

"All right, Zack. All right."

He clutched my hand. There was hope in his eyes, hope after long days and nights of despair. "You promise you won't tell the cops? Or anyone, ever?"

"I promise."

"Oh, *Carnegie*."

Zack embraced me, and this time I welcomed it. I had some qualms about keeping his secret, but they were swept away in the exhilaration of delivering him from his tormented guilt. And when he began to kiss me, well, it was a highly emotional moment. Anyone would have kissed him back. And besides, I was chilled to the bone by that time, and it felt good to get wrapped up in his arms. It was only reasonable.

Well, all right. So it wasn't reasonable. I really had no business standing out in the middle of a brightly lit pavilion smooching with a handsome guy some years my junior—a fact which occurred to me instantly and with compelling force when Aaron Gold tapped me on the shoulder.

I was too flabbergasted to speak. Unhappily, Zack wasn't.

"Hey, Aaron, my man!" Zack greeted his friend with a nervous grin. To me, Zack was still the picture of restored innocence, but to Aaron he must have merely looked smug. "We didn't see you coming!"

"Obviously." Aaron's voice was calm enough, but he had to step close to be heard over the Falls, and in the harsh light of the pavilion I could see a vein jumping at his temple. I knew him well enough to know he was furious, and trying not to show it. "Carnegie, the party's breaking up. I came out to tell you."

"Thanks." The word caught in my throat. How could I possibly explain the scene he had just witnessed, without betraying Zack? I settled for a feeble smile. "We were just going to—"

"Save it," he snapped. "I can guess what you were just going to do. Good night."

"Will . . . will I see you in the morning?"

"Oh, right, our breakfast date." Aaron glared at Zack, then at me. "I think I'll pass."

"But—"

But Aaron was already striding off into the fog. Instead of returning to the lodge, he headed out to the far end of the parking lot where he'd left his yellow Bug. I'd seen it there when I parked my tin can of a rental car.

"Damn," I groaned. "Damn, damn, *dammit.*"

"Carnegie?" Zack looked blank at first, then the light dawned. "Oh, I get it. Aaron's, like, mad about us being here together."

"Aaron is, like, royally pissed off," I said. "And now he's not going to help me figure this out."

"Figure what out?"

"The murder," I told him. "Because if you didn't kill Mercedes, then who did?"

Chapter Eighteen

I SLEEP NAKED. EVEN AS A KID I FELT STRANGLED BY PAJAMAS, and as an adult I go without, keeping a big fuzzy robe on a chair by the bed in winter. So when Aaron knocked on my door early Saturday morning, I threw off my flannel sheets, threw on the robe, and rushed through the kitchen to let him in, grateful that he'd relented and eager to explain away, somehow, the awkwardness of the night before.

Except it wasn't Aaron. It was Zack, standing on my doorstep with a huge grocery bag and a carrier tray of take-out espresso cups. He was still in his cords and green sweater from the party, and clearly still riding high on the news I'd given him. Even in the half-dark of a November morning, Zack was radiant with happiness.

"I brought you breakfast," he announced, "since Aaron cancelled on you. I didn't know what kind of coffee you drink, so I got, like, four different ones."

I should have sent him away. I knew that. But the aroma of coffee, life-giving coffee, rose up through the chilly air and addled my brain. I opened my mouth to tell him "Thanks anyway, but—" and heard myself saying, "Is one of those a double latte?"

Zack radiated even brighter. "Yeah! Right here—oops!"

As he proffered the tray, the grocery bag slipped from his

grasp and spilled its contents at my bare feet. I rescued the coffee and backed into the kitchen, while he gathered up his treasures and piled them on the table: a half-gallon of orange juice, a cardboard supermarket box holding a dozen syrupy cinnamon rolls the size of my head, a baton of somewhat dented French bread, a big tub of cream cheese with chives, an even bigger jar of orange marmalade, and, retrieved from where it had rolled up against the stove, an entire pineapple.

Zack frowned uncertainly at the pineapple, then set it on the table, where it rolled again and knocked over the marmalade. "Do you, like, eat fruit for breakfast?"

"All the time," I said, hiding a smile in my latte. How many men, far more mature than Zack, turned into clueless adolescents in the supermarket? "But there's enough here to feed me and everyone I know!"

"I guess I got carried away." He gazed at me earnestly. "But I just wanted to *do* something for you. I mean, I want to help you figure out about Mercedes, too. I couldn't really think straight last night."

That was an understatement. Zack had floated back to the party with me, said his good-byes in a kind of oblivious daze, and only looked a little crestfallen when I packed him off to Seattle with Valerie Duncan instead of taking him myself. He'd ridden to the Salish with Aaron—a favor that would probably not be offered in the future.

"I heard Valerie offering you your job back," I said, setting my coffee safely out of his orbit. "Did you take it?"

"Yeah." Zack's all-too-easy blush surged up from his throat to wash across his fair-skinned cheeks. "She said I was doing to-tally great stuff for them. I want to keep going with the Made in Heaven web site, too. I couldn't really, like, concentrate, before."

"I understand. Here, have one of these rolls. They look . . .

large. And delicious, I'm sure. What are the rest of these drinks?"

"There's an Americano, and a cappuccino, and I think this one is just plain."

"Which one's yours?"

"Oh, I don't drink coffee."

"Really? I can't even imagine—"

There was another knock on the door. Zack, eager to please, jumped up and pulled it open, giving Aaron a full view of me, still not dressed, having breakfast with Robin Hood, still wearing his same clothes from the night before. Wonderful.

Zack stood there tongue-tied while Aaron and I had a stilted conversation, with a silent but thoroughly understood subtext conveyed by our eyes and, in his case, one eyebrow.

"Aaron," I said. *This isn't what it looks like.*

"Carnegie?" The eyebrow went up. *Looks pretty clear to me.*

"Aaron, would you like some coffee?" *Be reasonable, please.*

"Well . . ." *That's asking a lot.*

"Come on, sit down." *Please?*

"I just got here!" Zack blurted. "Honest!"

Aaron couldn't help it. He laughed, though it was an edgy laugh, one that ended abruptly. He shook his head and pulled a small paper sack from the canvas carry-on bag over his shoulder. I hadn't noticed the bag at first, or the jacket and tie Aaron was wearing—not his usual working clothes.

"Whatever," he said. "I was going to drop off some bagels, but you seem to be well supplied."

"I'd love a bagel," I told him. "Have a seat."

"Can't. Got a plane to catch, to Portland."

"Portland! For how long?"

"Couple days, maybe. It's hard to say. See you." Without another look at me, Aaron turned away to leave. At least he tried to. The door behind him, still ajar, swung open yet again, propelled by the volume of a familiar voice.

"Carnegie! We brought you breakfast! You see, Mother? I said it wasn't too early. She's got company!"

I sank my head in my hands, rearranged my face in a courteous smile, and looked up. The kitchen was teeming with Buckmeisters. This time the sweatshirts said "I Love Washington."

"Good morning, Buck. Hi, Betty. Where's Bonnie?" The three of them usually came as a set.

"She's doing an all-day beauty spa kinda thing," Buck told me. "Isn't that something? We just dropped her off and picked up some Egg McMuffins, and I said, Mother, let's bring a couple over to Carnegie. She's so darn skinny, I bet she just drinks black coffee for breakfast! That's not enough for a working girl like her, I said, and Mother agreed with me, didn't you, Mother?"

"I surely did, Father, but now look at all this nice food that's here already. My goodness, a pineapple! Is that what they eat in Seattle, pineapple for breakfast? Good morning, dear," said Betty, addressing herself to a baffled Zack. "Are you getting married?"

Zack's reply, if any, was lost as her husband seized Aaron's hand and shook it. "No, I bet this is the groom over here, Mother! Am I right? Bruce Buckmeister—call me Buck—and that's my wife Betty. Our little girl Bonnie is the bride in the family! Pleased to meet you!"

"Likewise, Buck," said Aaron, amused in spite of himself. I could tell he was taking notes in his head. Aaron loved a colorful character, and Buck was Technicolor, even without his red-checked bandanna. "I'm Aaron Gold, and that's Zack Hartmann. But neither of us is walking down the aisle just yet. Unless there's something you and Zack haven't told us, Stretch?"

"Don't start," I warned him. "Just wait while I get some clothes on and I'll walk you to your car, OK? Folks, Aaron has to leave, but take a seat there with Zack. He's a web-site designer, isn't that interesting? Have him tell you all about it."

I dressed fast, afraid that Aaron would miss his flight. Not that I wanted him on it, if he was heading for an interview at *The Oregonian*. I wanted Aaron Gold right here in Seattle, where I could feel ambivalent about him. It wasn't raining, for a wonder, so I skipped my jacket and hurried back to the kitchen. Buck and Betty had settled cozily at the table while Zack, Egg McMuffin in hand, was solemnly explaining JPEG files and animated GIFs and why frames, like, totally suck. I still didn't understand it, but the Buckmeisters were charmed.

"Imagine," Betty kept saying. "Just imagine, someone as young as you knowing all that."

Aaron was at the door checking his watch, so I just waved at the Killer B's and followed him outside, wrapping my arms around myself against the chilly salt air.

"You're going to freeze out here," he said, striding down the dock to the parking lot. His footsteps rapped hollowly on the fog-dampened planks. The low gray sky was getting lighter, paling the porch lights of the other houseboats. One of my neighbors, stepping out to pick up her newspaper, called out a cheery good morning. I smiled mechanically and kept going, trying to keep up with Aaron.

"I can't let you leave without explaining."

"So explain." He shot me a sidelong glance, but he didn't slow down. "Start with the pineapple. The pineapple fascinates me."

"Aaron, be serious! I mean, not too serious." I was beginning to sound like Zack. "It's not a serious situation, is it?"

"You tell me." He unlocked his yellow Bug and threw his carry-on into the miniscule trunk.

"Back in the kitchen you were joking about it."

"What was I supposed to do, play the jealous lover in front of the Buckmasters?"

"Buckmeisters. Look, Aaron, last night I was helping Zack sort out a . . . a personal problem. He was happy about solving it, and grateful, and so he hugged me. And this morning he just showed up. That's all."

"That's all? I'm supposed to feel better because you're not sleeping with him just like you're not sleeping with me?" He slammed the trunk lid with a violence that made me jump. "You tell me you need some space, then you fill the space up with Zack Hartmann. Who's next, your Russian guy? What kind of high-school bullshit is this?"

"Don't talk to me that way!"

"Well, don't treat me this way." Aaron's deep brown eyes looked suddenly vulnerable, and I might have apologized if he hadn't pulled out a pack of cigarettes and lit one. The morning air was dead still, and as he exhaled, the smoke made a little cloud between us. "Carnegie, I can't talk about this now. I've got a plane to catch."

"Why Portland, anyway? Is it a job offer?"

He frowned. "Maybe. Mostly I'm going down to do some research for a series on mass transit. I better go."

"Well, could you call me later?" *I'll miss you. I want you here.* I didn't say it, though. Too high-schoolish. "We were going to sort out that list of people in black costumes—"

"Sure, I'll call you," he said from behind the smoke, "but let's forget all this amateur detective crap. Stay out of it. Leave it to the cops."

"You said yourself you were starting to believe Corinne."

He shrugged. "How do I know she's not playing games, too?"

"What do you mean, too? I'm not playing games, not with you and not about Mercedes! I need you to identify some of the *Sentinel* people, and—"

"So ask Zack," he said flatly. "It'll give you something to do while you're not having sex."

That tore it. I turned around and marched back inside. I was trembling, more from anger than cold, and I wanted hot coffee. Or a drink. Inside, Betty was bustling around my kitchen putting away the jam and cream cheese, her pert black curls bouncing as she went.

"Carnegie, there you are!" said Buck. "Mother and I have to run, but we had some ideas about place cards—"

"Monday," I snapped, and then softened my tone. "We'll talk about place cards at the cake tasting on Monday, all right? Thanks for breakfast. Betty, I'll finish that, really."

"All done, dear. Except for the pineapple. I wasn't sure where to put it."

"Just leave it there. It, ah, makes a nice centerpiece."

"So it does!" She beamed at me. "Isn't she just clever, Father? I wouldn't have thought of that."

And they beamed their way out the door. Zack, still sitting at the kitchen table, waved good-bye and reached for another cinnamon roll.

"Zack, have you got some free time today?"

"Sure! All day, if you want."

"That's great. Let's go up to the office and look over the guest list from the party."

I'd finished my latte, so I reheated the cappuccino in the microwave. But only because it was too early for wine.

Chapter Nineteen

"CARNEGIE?"

"Hmm?"

"Are you going to finish your pizza?"

"Help yourself." I slid the Pagliacci's box across my desk without taking my eyes from the list I was scribbling. After making a final notation, I looked up. "How can you *eat* that?"

"It's good!" Zack protested, his mouth full.

"No, I mean how can you eat pepperoni on top of all those cinnamon rolls?"

He shrugged. "That was, like, hours ago."

Not all that many hours, really, but we'd made a lot of progress. After explaining my original and now discarded theory about Skull—Zack had heard about the purse-snatching incident—I laid out my current plan. Mercedes was killed after eleven o'clock, and Corinne was smothered with a black cloak; if the police wouldn't put those two facts together, then I would. No more harebrained notions about tattooed party crashers, and no speculation about motives. Just solid reasoning that Lieutenant Graham couldn't dismiss out of hand.

Zack wasn't my first choice of a partner to tackle this puzzle—for all his good resolutions of the night before, I wondered if I'd been too accepting of his unpredictable tem-per. But I needed help, and he'd been at the party and knew a lot of the guests. And besides, I was still angry at Aaron. I'd be damned if I'd let him dictate who I spent time with.

So Zack and I combined our memories of the party to come up with the names of guests who wore black-caped costumes. Then I made a couple of dozen phone calls to those people and others, claiming to be checking on the re-turn of their costumes and the level of satisfaction with my work as a party planner. Most people were happy to gossip about the behavior and attire of their fellow guests, and as they reported on who left early and who stayed late, our list began to shrink. I also called Elizabeth, and heard just what I hoped for: everyone was delighted with the rehearsal dinner, and her mother, Monica, would definitely be at the EMP sans Lars.

While I worked the phone, Zack kept busy over at Eddie's desk, scoping out the wonderful world of weddings on the Internet and making notes about his Made in Heaven pro-ject. He took his work seriously, I was glad to see. At one point he discovered Dorothy Fenner's elaborate web site, and raved about it until I asked him to stop. Dorothy, gracious and wealthy, was the premier bridal consultant in the Northwest, and I'd lost more than one potential client to her. We were on reasonably friendly terms, but I didn't need to hear about yet another thing she did better than me.

"OK," I announced. "Here's our tally so far. Twelve people wore black capes or cloaks. If you subtract me and Aaron, that leaves ten. The magician was Harry from Classifieds, and he went home with his wife around nine-forty-five. So Harry is out. Ditto Batman, the product manager from Microsoft, who had another party to go to that night. That leaves eight people.

The Three Musketeers were delivery drivers for the *Sentinel*, and they left early to go drinking together in Pioneer Square. That leaves five. The DJ was a monk, but he was sitting out in public all night. Four."

"What about breaks?" asked Zack. He shut down Eddie's computer. "DJs take breaks."

"True. Do you think he could have killed Mercedes and then gone back to playing music?" I shivered. It was too easy to make this into an intellectual puzzle and shy away from the thought of what one of these people actually did, there in the darkened corridor. "All right, Rick the Rocket stays on the list, at least until I get him on the phone and ask him some questions. Where was I?"

Zack pulled his chair closer to mine. He smelled like soap. Nice soap. "Five."

"Right. The other four are Darth Vader, Dracula, the pregnant nun, and the Grim Reaper. What a crew."

"Darth Vader was Doug Rawls," Zack pointed out. "No way did he do it."

"No, I don't suppose he did." Rawls, the paper's copy editor, had cerebral palsy. He'd spent most of the night sitting quietly aside, his black helmet on his knee, enjoying the spectacle of his coworkers cavorting.

"OK, I'll cross him off. We still don't know who Dracula was, but one of the bartenders saw him just before midnight, so he stays on the list. The nun was Angela, and she was definitely at the party right till the end, because I saw her leaving. But I just can't see her as a murderer. Can you?"

"She seems really nice," said Zack doubtfully. "But—"

"Yeah, but." But *someone* had killed Mercedes, and tumbled Corinne into the harbor. "All right, we'll keep Angela. That just leaves—"

"Death," said Zack.

"Death." I drew a black box around the last name on my list. "We don't know for sure that Soper was at the party after eleven, but we don't know that he wasn't, and he hasn't returned my calls. Aaron thinks he did it because Mercedes knew about...knew something incriminating about him." I remembered just in time that Aaron wanted the bribery issue kept secret. Not that I gave a damn about Aaron Gold anymore. "But why would Soper attack Corinne?"

Zack frowned. "Maybe Corinne knows the incriminating stuff, too? Except I didn't think she and Mercedes ever worked on the same kind of stories."

"No. And besides, Corinne would have said something if she had an enemy at the party. Wait, we're getting into motives again. Let's just concentrate on who and when, like we've been doing, and let the police worry about why."

"OK," said Zack. He started decorating my list with doodles as he talked: crescent moons and rocket ships. No hearts with arrows through them, fortunately for my composure. "So, like, we need to find someone who knows if Syd Soper stayed late. And also keep asking if anybody saw someone follow Corinne down the pier."

"And who on earth Dracula was." I wiped the tomato sauce off my fingers and picked up the phone. But I got the same old answer.

"Thank you for calling Characters, Inc., Seattle's finest costume shop. We're taking a vacation after Halloween, but if you leave your name and number—"

I'd already left them a couple of messages, so I hung up, but it rang right away.

"Hi, Carnegie? It's Angela. I think I've got the wrong dress. Does yours come with this weird bra?"

I laughed, glad to think about something frivolous. "That sounds like mine. Let me call you back."

I ran downstairs and checked the garment bag from Stephanie's Styles hanging on the back of my bedroom door. Sure enough, the pink gown inside had a strip of tape on the shoulder marked SIMS. When I went back up to the office, Zack had finished the pizza and was poking through the candy dish out in the good room.

"The ones in red wrappers are the best," I told him. "Want to go see Angela with me? Maybe she can tell us something."

We took my rented tin can down to the Harbor Steps complex on First Avenue, where condos rise high above trendy restaurants and antique shops. Zack spotted a parking space not too far from Angela's building, and carried the garment bag for me. We cut across the polished granite steps, which lead up from the waterfront to the Seattle Art Museum on Second, and serve as a long slanting public plaza for outdoor concerts and lunchtime picnics.

No picnics today, with the gray skies and the chill, but a valiant street-corner fiddler had drawn a little audience. We paused to listen, and Zack shyly dropped a dollar in the open instrument case. Zack's fuse might be short and his conversation might be limited, especially compared to Aaron's, but he was pleasant to have around.

"Must be cool living right downtown," he said as we rode the elevator to the thirteenth floor. "She could have walked home from the Aquarium."

I remembered Angela laughing as she left the party. In innocent merriment, or in guilty relief at getting away with murder? When she opened her door to us, smiling like a cheerleader, wearing electric-purple leotards and a messy ponytail, the idea seemed absurd. Although Aaron was right: she did look strong.

"Hey, thanks," she said, turning off the exercise video she had running on a big flat-screen TV in the corner. "But I could have come to your office. Hi, Zack."

"No problem," I told her. "We needed to get out for a breather."

"Oh, really?" Angela pulled on a purple sweatshirt. "I didn't know you two were—"

"A breather from working on the web site for my business," I said firmly. "That's all."

She tilted her head archly. "Whatever. I'll get your dress."

While she was gone, I crossed the cheery, cluttered living room to a pair of sliding glass doors, drawn by the view. From the tiny balcony with its tiny potted junipers you looked south over downtown, past the faded old brick buildings of Pioneer Square and the stark new baseball and football stadiums, to green hills and the soft gray horizon.

"You can see Mount Rainier from here when it's clear," said Angela, returning with the other Stephanie's Styles bag. "Sunrise and sunset both. Incredible! It's why I bought the place. And now that Microsoft has a building downtown, I don't have that awful commute."

It was quite a panorama, but even through the glass I could hear the traffic noise a dozen stories down. Give me the lapping of lake water anytime. Angela swapped garment bags with Zack, dropped hers over the back of a chair, and looked pointedly back at her VCR.

"Well, thanks again."

Zack turned to go but I lingered. "Angela, at the Aquarium that night—"

"Yes?" Angela's eyes were a light, clear hazel, with glints of gold. Innocent-looking eyes.

"Did you happen to see Syd Soper, the man dressed as Death, during the last part of the party? Bald guy in a black robe, with a long sickle?"

"The one who was dancing with Mercedes?" The eyes were troubled now. "Carnegie, do you think he killed her?"

"I don't think anything, honestly. We're just trying to sort some things out. Did you see him, say, after eleven?"

She nodded, slowly and dramatically. "He was in the Dome room right near the end. Almost everybody was dancing, you know, for the last dance, but he just stood and watched. He had a really spooky look on his face, too."

Zack and I exchanged glances. Death was still on the list.

"What about Corinne?" I said. "Did you see Soper anywhere near her, or following her?"

"You mean when she went off by herself? No. But you don't really believe she got pushed in the water, do you? Elizabeth thinks she jumped."

"And what do you think?"

"I don't know." She shook her head, sending her ponytail swinging. "She's kind of strange, isn't she? Well, I've got to finish working out, OK? Thanks for bringing the dress."

And with that, Angela hurried us out the door.

"Funny how urgent that workout was, all of a sudden," I commented to Zack in the car. I meant to try Characters, Inc. again, but I'd left my cell phone in my other bag. That was getting to be a bad habit. Sighing, I promised myself to get extra-organized as soon as I got Vanna back. Not having my own wheels was throwing everything off.

"Yeah," said Zack, his brow furrowing. I found myself wishing I had eyelashes like his, long and curly. "She was, like, so quick to jump to conclusions. I mean, you didn't even *say* we suspected Soper."

"No, I didn't, did I? She just assumed he was capable of murder. Or she wanted us to assume it. And she acted funny about Corinne, too, as if—Who's that?"

A bulky figure, made even bulkier by a huge navy pea coat, was stomping up and down the dock near my front door. Shaggy black hair, bull-like shoulders, and an almost visible aura of hysterical indignation. Who else?

"Hi there, Boris."

"Those Buckmeister people!" he thundered. "They make me betty!"

"What about Betty?"

"They are driving me betty with their poinsettias, their meeny poinsettias! Kharnegie, there is no such thing as a meeny poinsettia! You said ruby amaryllis, I have supplier for glorious ruby amaryllis, hypericum berries like jewels, perfect for Christmas wedding! Poinsettia is trite, is vulgar! I am not a vulgar man!"

That was debatable, but it was raining again and this was not the place to debate.

"Boris, come upstairs and calm down. Zack, this is Boris Nevsky. Zack Hartmann." They shook hands, Boris still smoldering and Zack looking startled, as well he might. I led the way upstairs. "So I take it the Buckmeisters came to see you?"

"They would not *leave*," Boris said tragically. He collapsed onto the wicker loveseat, which cried out for mercy. "I came to you, to get away from them! So *cheerful,* and all the time *talking.* You must keep them away from me, Kharnegie!"

"I will, I promise. Absolutely. Was there anything else?"

"No. Except you should come out for a drink with me."

"Boris, I can't. Zack and I—"

Boris rolled his eyes and grinned, a huge grizzly bear grin. "Aha! So this is the one?"

"What one? Oh, you mean...Listen, Zack and I have been working on the Made in Heaven web site. That's all." *Have I got a sign on my back saying The Older Woman, or what?*

"Of course!" Boris lumbered to his feet and clapped Zack on the shoulder. "Web sites, of course! Zeck, listen to me."

Zack could hardly help it. Even when Boris whispered, he was loud.

"Zeck," he whispered now. "Be careful with my Kharnegie. She...is...very...*ticklish!*"

"Out! Now!" I yanked the door open and then slammed it behind him, though I could hear him laughing on his way down the stairs. Zack stood staring at me owlishly.

"OK," I said, sighing. "Let's just get this clear. You and I are friends, right? You're working for me, and we're friends, and that's all. Right?"

"Sure. Whatever you say. Are you really ticklish?"

That did it. "Zack, thanks for your help today, but I'll take it from here. I'll see you Friday at the rehearsal, OK?"

After he left, I checked the answering machine. Nothing from Aaron, but there was one message, loud and lively:

"Yo, Carnegie, Rick the Rocket here. Got your message, but I'm real busy today. I'm doing a wedding gig at SAM tonight. I'm leaving right after on a red-eye for Vegas, so if it's important, come on down and I'll talk to you when I'm on a break. Dorothy Fenner's in charge, she says it's OK, and maybe you'll pick up some pointers. See ya."

Chapter Twenty

SAM WAS THE SEATTLE ART MUSEUM, NOT A STARTLINGLY original venue for a wedding reception, but very nice, very upscale. My mental Rolodex said it had room for five hundred guests stand-up, or two hundred at a seated meal, and a good marble floor for dancing at the foot of the grand staircase. Catering by the Seattle Sheraton, on exclusive contract. Joe Solveto would love to get a foot in the door at SAM; when he heard where I'd been, he'd want a close critique of the food and the service.

As I steered the rental car into a cavernous parking garage near the museum, I wondered which of Dorothy Fenner's clients had chosen this venue for a Saturday-night reception. Then, as I was fussing around trying to lock up—why do the cheapest cars have the fanciest electronic gizmos?—I remembered: Mayor Wyble's daughter Sarah. The bride's mother had interviewed me for the job, after a nice recommendation from Joe's partner, but then she went with the silver-haired Dorothy. "Someone just a bit more experienced" was the way Mrs. Wyble put it. Those were the breaks, but still, it rankled. Pointers, my ass.

The museum's grand staircase is flanked by a wall of windows facing a terraced plaza along University Street. Waiting for the light at the corner, I could see animated people in gowns and tuxedos moving up and down in a silent, brightly-lit pantomime of festivity that glowed against the evening's gloom.

A familiar face met me at the upper level entrance: Marvin, doing another off-duty stint as a security guard. Dorothy had told him I was coming, so he just nodded and pulled open the door. Inside, in the roaring clamor of voices, laughter and music, I was intercepted by a glassy-eyed young usher who was starting to fluff his lines.

"Hi! I mean, uh, thank you for joining us. The coatroom is around the corner there, and the buffet is open, and, and everything. Thank you for joining us."

"You're welcome."

I stepped around him and looked down the staircase, past the people dining at the midway landing, to the jam-packed dance floor at the bottom. This was a more sedate crowd than we'd had at the Aquarium, but Rick the Rocket, in a tux and a party hat, had coaxed them out of their seats with some Rolling Stones. His mike was on, and he was making crowd-pleasing comments about the bride and groom, who were getting down and dirty in the middle of a ring of dancing friends. There was a spark in the air that was both familiar and exciting to me: the contagious, spine-tingling sizzle of a successful event.

"Carnegie, how lovely to see you!" Dorothy, in floor-length lavender chiffon and ever-present pearls, swept over to greet me with her usual aristocratic charm. We exchanged air kisses, and I smelled liquor. *Interesting*. I had never, but never, seen Dorothy tipsy. There was a wistful, faraway look in her eye that suddenly sharpened to something less re-fined. "I suppose you'll be fishing around for my prospective client file."

"Pardon me?"

She shook her head as if to clear it. "Sorry. You don't know yet, do you? I'm retiring. This is almost my last Seattle wedding."

"*Oh.*" I'd been competing with Dorothy Fenner—often in vain—since I started Made in Heaven. She was a pain in the neck, but sort of a fixture in my professional life.

"I'll miss you," I said, and I almost meant it.

"I'll miss the business!" she exclaimed, a little shrill, and definitely inebriated.

"Then why—"

"My *husband*," she said, as if the word tasted bad, "wants to play *golf.* In *Scottsdale.* Says he's tired of the rain. I'll fly back for the Tyler girl's wedding, but after that I'm finished."

Sally Tyler's mother was the CEO of MFC, Meet for Coffee, and even richer than her own espresso. Yet another account I had lost to Dorothy—but maybe the last one I would lose. *Hooray for Scottsdale.*

"You came to see the disk jockey?" Dorothy was asking.

"Yes. It looks like he's going on break, so I'll go down and catch him right now."

It took me a while to push my way down the staircase through the crowd, making mental notes as I went. The waiters weren't clearing the dirty dishes fast enough, and there weren't quite enough places to sit. Yet even the guests who were stranded standing up, balancing champagne flutes and plates of poached salmon, were laughing and talking in great good humor. *Well done, Dorothy.* Everywhere I looked I saw familiar faces from the upper echelons of the city: the mayor and his wife, a brace of CEOs, board members of the opera, the ballet, the symphony. If only I'd landed this account, it would have paid my rent for months. *Bon voyage, Dorothy.*

In the midst of all this happy commotion, I had the sudden, isolating sense that I was being watched. I paused on the stairway to scan the crowd. Standing all alone by the windows was Syd Soper, observing me balefully. Death in a tuxedo. It's hard to look bad in a tux, but Soper had no neck at all, so he was getting there. I nodded politely and kept going. Soper could wait; I had to catch Rick before he left town. I thought I'd be able to track him down between sets, but there he was, heading back to his sound board already.

"Rick, aren't you on break?"

"No way!" he said from the side of his mouth, all his attention on the dance floor. The party hat was gone. He'd gotten a haircut since I saw him last, leaving a neat straw-colored fringe around his pink dome, but he was sweating and jittery, and his clip-on tie was crooked. "Just takin' a leak before the big finish."

"I need to ask you—"

"Kincaid, it'll have to wait. Gig's over soon."

"Of course, I'm sorry." Abashed, I retreated—right into wallflower city. I was accustomed to being busy at weddings, but now all I could do was stand around admiring Dorothy's success, drinking too much champagne, and wishing someone would ask me to dance, which of course no one did. Aaron was right, all this wedding stuff can make you feel extra-single.

Rick did a letter-perfect last set, bringing the crowd to a paroxysm of high spirits, and even some high kicks, with "New York, New York." He finished off with the latest Hollywood love song and then "The Way You Look Tonight," a wedding reception classic that had everyone—except me—embracing. Some of the dancers went over to tip Rick and get his business card, and I saw several people hugging Dorothy as they left. She was winding up her Seattle career on a high note.

I talked to Rick during his teardown. He was brisk and efficient, stowing speakers and cables, making notes on his play list for the event, and still buzzed on adrenaline.

"Nice job," I began. "Those were great songs."

"You think so?"

"Don't you?"

Rick pulled out a handkerchief and ran it across his glistening dome. "Tell you the truth, I hate that shit. You know how many times I've heard 'Satisfaction' in my life? Or 'The Macarena'? But the customers like it, and I am all about pleasing the customers. So, whaddya want to ask me about? You got a gig for me?"

"No, though I probably will in the future. It's about the other night at the Aquarium. Do you remember the woman dressed as Venus?"

"The blonde with the big—I mean, with the nice figure? Oh yeah, I remember her." He snapped shut the latches on his equipment cases, and hefted a stack of them onto a small dolly. All the while he kept smiling agreeably at departing guests, and talking faster and faster to me. "You want to walk me out? I don't have much time before my flight. Got some serious gambling to do for the next seven days and nights. Lucky seven! I been looking forward to this for months."

The night outside was loud and windy, with gusts ripping up from the waterfront. We crossed the lower level plaza past the base of Hammering Man, the fifty-foot sculpture that Seattleites love to hate. Or used to. By this time the lanky steel silhouette, forever raising and dropping its hammer with a monotonous clank, was so familiar as to be invisible.

Summer tourists still posed for pictures on the big guy's feet, but the guests from today's reception didn't even glance up.

"I was just wondering," I said, above the wild flapping of the museum banners, "if you noticed anyone in particular hanging around Venus. Or if you saw the man dressed as Death follow her out of the Dome room?"

I'm also wondering if you killed Mercedes Montoya. But how do I ask you that?

"I remember the Death guy, he was around right at the end, but I didn't see him follow anybody." We got to a bright green van that read Rick the Rocket, Hot Music for Good Times! across the sides in orange. Rick swung open the back doors and we stepped between them, out of the wind. It didn't occur to me that the doors also shielded us from the view of passersby until he grabbed my arm and gave it a painful twist. The jolly smile was gone. "OK, where's my money?"

"Your *what*?"

"Montoya owed me a bundle, and she said she gave it to you. I want it back, and I want that ring."

My heart was stampeding, but I tried to rein it in. Even if Rick was the killer, he obviously wasn't going to do anything drastic here in public, and if I could keep him talking I might learn something.

"So you know about the diamond ring."

"Of course I do, the bitch promised it to me!"

"What for?"

"Never mind. Business." He dropped my arm, as if the adrenaline had ebbed abruptly. Or maybe there was another substance at work. Rick was acting a lot like Mercedes had the last time I saw her. "Look, Kincaid, I'm not a bad guy. We can cooperate on this. I got a line in to the cops, I know they're looking for that diamond, so I figure either the murderer took it, or you did. Unless maybe it was you—?"

"You're accusing *me* of killing Mercedes?"

"Nah, not really." He shoved his hands in his pockets, and I relaxed a little. "But everybody knows you found Montoya's body. You got my money, and I figure maybe you've got the ring, too. Not that you stole it, you know, maybe it was just lying there and you picked it up. I'm not asking any questions, but that ring is worth plenty, and I got debts to pay. How 'bout we go half and half? I know a guy can sell it for us."

That clinches it, I thought. *I don't have to ask. If you had killed Mercedes, you'd have taken the diamond yourself.*

"Listen to me," I said. "If you want that money you'll have to ask the police for it, because I turned it over to them." I probably shouldn't drink champagne, but sometimes overconfidence is just what's needed. "I have no idea where that ring is, and if you bother me about it again, I'll turn you over, too, for assault. Now you'd better go catch your plane."

And with that I strode away. My mind was racing. No doubt about it, Mercedes had something shady going on that night at the Aquarium. But when it came to murder, Rick the Rocket was off the list. I was down to three names: Angela, Soper, and the mysterious Transylvanian. They made a pretty short list; maybe it was time to turn this over to Lieutenant Graham. But no, I was hooked. I wanted the satisfaction of giving him a single name. And, I admit, the satisfaction of throwing my success in Aaron Gold's face.

I was concentrating so hard as I walked that I almost overshot the parking garage, and once inside I didn't immediately notice the footsteps behind me. But when I glanced around, I stopped pondering and realized two things.

The footsteps belonged to Syd Soper.

And there was no one else in sight.

Overconfidence is not the same as stupidity. Soper was advancing rapidly towards me. I gauged the distance to my car and saw that I couldn't beat him there, not with the time it would take to fool with the electronic remote and unlock it. So instead I ran toward the nearest stairwell, my own footsteps clapping loud against the dirty cement. Just as I got there the door opened and a party of wedding guests emerged, looking at me curiously. I stopped short, gasping.

"Carnegie, wait a minute!" Soper's voice sounded calm, even friendly.

One of the party, a middle-aged woman in a leather coat, looked past me and waved a hand at him. "It was nice to see you tonight, Syd!"

"You, too, Margaret," Soper replied, walking up to me. "I'll call you tomorrow about that committee. Good night."

They proceeded on to their cars, and as they did, more people emerged from the elevator nearby. This was a public garage, after all—hardly the spot for a solitary ambush. And now that I could see him clearly, Soper looked puzzled, not dangerous.

"You called me today. What about?"

"I . . . I'm just checking back with people after the party at the Aquarium. Making sure they got their costumes back, that kind of thing."

He wasn't buying it. "Then why'd you run away? What's Gold been telling you? I saw you with him at the Space Needle."

"Aaron hasn't told me anything, Syd. I just heard footsteps behind me, and I didn't realize it was you. I'm a little jumpy these days. . . ." That was when I had my brainstorm about how to test him. *Why didn't I think of this before?* I watched his expression carefully and said, "I found Mercedes' body, you know. It was pretty gruesome, the way she was stabbed. And molested."

Soper flinched and grimaced as if someone had struck him in the face. "The bastard *raped* her? Oh, Jesus. Oh, Jesus, a beautiful woman like that. And these goddamn liberals protest against the death penalty! I'm telling you, if it was *their* wife, or *their* daughter—"

He went on at length, but I tuned out the words and focused on his face. Syd was passing the test: his shock and disgust looked absolutely genuine. I said something vague in agreement, and he walked me solicitously back to my car. Death was worried about me, for crying out loud. I drove home with a headache, and fell asleep thinking about Angela Sims.

Chapter Twenty-One

I SLEPT LATE ON SUNDAY MORNING, AND MY PHONE RANG just as I was waking up. It was Lily.

"Carnegie, can I come over for a few minutes? I need to talk to you."

"Of course. Something wrong?"

"No, not exactly. I'll be there soon."

"OK. I'm leaving for Mercedes' funeral at two, but I'll be around till then."

At least today I had time to get dressed. When Lily arrived I was stumbling around the kitchen in jeans and a sweat-shirt, reluctant to put on my black slacks and sweater too soon. If Tommy Barry died, I was going to have to buy a proper black dress. Berating myself for such pessimism—and superficial pessimism at that—I pulled open the door to greet her.

"Hey, there! You hungry?"

"Not right now, thanks." Lily settled comfortably at the kitchen table while I went back to the stove. She was wearing a royal-purple sweater with black leggings and the silver ear-rings I'd given her for her last birthday. "I had a phone call this morning. From Aaron."

I dropped the egg I was holding, and watched the shell crumple and the contents ooze across the counter. Then I swiped a paper towel over the mess and turned to look at her, all thoughts of murder suspects flown from my mind.

"Aaron called you from Portland? Why?"

"Why do you think?" she said peevishly. "I don't like being in the middle of things like this, but he's a nice guy, so I said I'd talk to you."

I abandoned the eggs and sat down. "OK, let's talk."

She sighed. "He's thinking about leaving Seattle for a job in Portland. He cares a lot about you, but he can't figure out how you feel."

"That's the trouble, neither can I."

"Well, maybe you should try harder!" There was an edge to Lily's voice that I seldom heard. "Good men aren't exactly easy to find, you know. If you're waiting for somebody perfect, you're going to have a long wait."

"Maybe I'm waiting for someone who doesn't smoke like a chimney." I was a little edgy myself. This was embarrassing.

"For God's sake, Carnegie, you've never smoked. You don't know anything about it."

"But you don't smoke either—"

"I used to! Two packs a day, at one point. I quit when I got pregnant with Ethan, and then I started again during the divorce, and then I quit again."

"I had no idea." I recalled with a wince all the comments I'd made to Lily about Aaron's filthy habit. "Why didn't you tell me?"

"I just didn't feel like talking about it. But honestly, you can't *imagine* how hard it is to kick cigarettes."

"Aaron's not even trying."

"Why should he? Why should he rearrange his life to suit you, when you won't even make a commitment to him?" Lily stood up and paced around the kitchen. "You've got to accept people the way they are, whether it's their habits or their careers or . . . Are you going to offer me a cup of coffee, or not?"

I laughed in spite of myself. "Of course. You know, I appreciate your trying to help—"

"Well, I just hate to see you mess up a good chance like this." She accepted the mug I gave her and took a healthy swallow. "I'd give a lot to find a man just like Aaron for myself and my boys."

"But he's—"

"White?" She took another sip and said softly, "Why do you assume I'd only want a black man?"

"I'm not assuming anything, Lily. But a while ago you said that a mixed-race marriage would be hard on Ethan and Marcus."

"Well, that was a while ago. Mr. Right African-American hasn't shown up yet. And I'm lonely. Don't I deserve somebody to love?"

I looked at her, and for the hundredth time or more, I marveled at this strong, beautiful woman who was my friend. "Of course you do, Lily. And the boys deserve a dad. Maybe—"

"Never mind." She set the mug down. "I don't want to talk about it right now, and I don't want to talk about Aaron anymore either. I said my piece. What I want is some lunch."

"Eggs?"

"I had eggs hours ago. Let's go out."

"OK, but someplace cheap." I kept talking as I went into the bathroom to brush my hair. "I've got a lot to tell you while we eat."

It was my morning for breaking things. As I tossed the brush onto a shelf, it caught the corner of the black-and-gold powder compact, sending it cartwheeling to the floor. I grabbed but missed, and it splintered open with a sharp little crackle, releasing an avalanche of tiny identical pills that rolled and slid across the tiles. "What on *earth*?"

Lily came to the doorway. "Did you break someth— Carnegie, what are you doing with those?"

"They're not mine! I don't even know what they are." I bent down to look. Weirdly, each pill had a minuscule smiley face impressed into one surface. I reached to pick one up, but Lily put out a restraining hand.

"This is serious, Carnegie. If they're not yours, whose are they?"

"The compact belonged to Mercedes Montoya. I picked it up at the party, and then after she died I just kept it. I'm not sure why. What do you mean, serious? What is this stuff?"

"I think it's Ecstasy. I'm going to go call Lieutenant Graham. Don't touch anything."

Lieutenant Graham, when he arrived, was not a happy man. He didn't seem to mind being called on a Sunday, but he was indignant that I'd "concealed" an item belonging to a murder victim. He was also skeptical of my ignorance about Ecstasy, and annoyed that I'd been talking to Rick the Rocket, even though my conversation seemed to clear the DJ in Mercedes' death.

"Ecstasy is MDMA," said Graham, sitting in my living room after bagging up the compact and pills. In a handsome blue fisherman's sweater, snug jeans, and shiny loafers, he was nobody's stereotype of a cop. "It's a neurotoxin, a middle-class party drug that makes you feel wonderful while it's destroying some of your brain cells. And half the time it's mixed with something else—MDA, GHB, rohypnol— that's even worse. You see it at raves, clubs, house parties, everywhere. People who should know better go on the Internet and explain how to use it. Manufacturing costs are about two dollars a pill, and then the pills retail for forty or fifty dollars apiece. Quite a valuable stash you've got here."

"It's not mine, I *told* you that. It belonged to Mercedes, and she must have gotten it from Rick."

"Who has now disappeared, by the way. He had a plane reservation for Las Vegas, and never used it."

"Well, that's not my fault!" My headache was back, and now my stomach was rumbling.

Graham leaned back on the couch and closed his eyes for a moment. He looked infinitely tired. "Some people are going to think it is. Some people are already wondering about you. You take money from Mercedes Montoya, and she turns up as a homicide victim. You talk to Richard Royko, and he vanishes. And now you're in possession of a Schedule One drug, in a quantity that strongly suggests not just using but dealing."

"Lieutenant, what exactly are you accusing Carnegie of?" Lily, hands on hips, was standing her ground in the middle of the room. The sun had come out, a rare phenomenon this time of year, and she was surrounded by a corona of silver light reflecting off the lake through the sliding glass doors. Talk about your warrior princess. Lily might be annoyed with me, but she was still in my corner.

Graham smiled at her, a gentle, tired smile. "Nothing. Strangely enough, I believe that Ms. Carnegie Kincaid is an innocent bystander in this situation, and I'm going to record these pills as evidence that was discovered by accident and immediately turned over to the proper authorities."

Lily smiled back, and I was about to offer scrambled eggs all around when Graham said, "*But* there is a multi-agency

task force addressing the party-drug trade in this area, and
the DEA is not going to be pleased that they didn't get this
evidence sooner. So, Carnegie, is there anything further you
want to share with me about Mercedes Montoya or Rick the
Rocket or anyone else connected with the case, before you
promise to stay out of police business altogether?"

"Wel-l-l," I said, and he rolled his eyes. "There is just one
thing I'd like to pass on about Syd Soper."

"And that is?"

"He didn't kill Mercedes." And I explained how I knew.

Graham actually laughed. "Sydney Soper was one of your
suspects?"

"He was wearing a black cloak, and he was at the party after eleven!" I said defensively. This was not exactly how I had
planned to present my findings to the police. "He could have
been the one who attacked Corinne—"

"If anyone did."

"I believe that someone did! And I believe that we should
find out who it was. Corinne is scared to death, and
Mercedes may have been dealing drugs but she still deserves
justice."

"Of course she does," said Graham. He stood up. "And
she will get it. But from the criminal justice system, not from
wild guesses and woman's intuition. All right?"

I opened my mouth to argue, but then I caught Lily's
glare and the shake of her head. "All right. Thank you,
Lieutenant."

The phone rang as I closed the door behind him. Hungry
as I was, I stopped to answer, half-hoping it would be Aaron.
Instead, I heard a fussy, familiar woman's voice, one that
never seemed to stop for breath.

"Miss Kincaid, this is Georgette Viorst, at Characters, Inc., and we're opening the shop on Monday, so I came in this weekend to get things organized, and saw that you left several messages, so I thought I'd better get back to you, in case it's important and you didn't want to wait until business hours. So, you were wondering who rented a Dracula costume for the Lamott party? I'd like to help you out, really I would, but I checked our inventory twice, and I could check it again but I don't think so, really I don't."

"You don't what? I'm sorry, I'm a little confused here. What are you telling me?"

"Miss Kincaid, we don't have a Dracula costume."

"What?"

"No, we had one, but you see the last person to rent it left it lying on his sofa and his cat just shredded the cape into ribbons! It was very careless of him, really, and he brought it in and offered to have it fixed, but you can't fix something like that, can you? You have to replace it entirely, and we've been meaning to do that because it's a popular costume, well, not that popular but it's a standard, and we like to have all the standards in stock for when—"

"Wait! Please, let me get this straight. You didn't rent anyone a Dracula costume for the party at the Aquarium last Saturday night?"

"No."

"Or for any other party, any other night?"

"No. You see—"

"Thank you, Georgette. I'll call you tomorrow to check up on the rest of the costumes, OK? Good-bye." I hung up, and said to Lily, "That does it. I'm scrambling some eggs. If I don't eat in the next ten minutes, my head's going to explode."

Over eggs and toast and a lot more coffee, we talked about Dracula.

"Dracula was Skull!" I insisted. "He had to be. That's how he got into the party unrecognized. He wore a full rubber head mask that covered his tattoos."

Lily wasn't convinced at first. "What about height and build? I don't quite remember—"

"Medium-sized guys, both of them," I said. "It all fits! None of the other guests could figure out who Dracula was, and now we know why. Because he wasn't an invited guest."

"It does make sense," she said with growing enthusiasm. "And he didn't talk so he wouldn't give himself away."

"*And* he wore a black cloak, *and* he was on the premises after eleven. And even if his motive is kind of bizarre, at least he's got one, which Angela never did. With Rick and Soper in the clear, the list is down to one name. Dracula, aka Lester Foy."

"I'm not quite as sure as you are," said Lily, "but say you're right. What are you going to do next? I don't think Mike Graham wants to hear any more theories from you."

"No, I don't suppose he does."

As we looked at each other, perplexed, the phone rang yet again. And yet again it wasn't Aaron.

"Kincaid? Juice. I saw your guy."

"What guy?"

"With the tattoos!" She sounded quite pleased with herself. "I was getting off the bus on Olive and there he was, getting on, so I just sat down again, right next to him, and started talking. Man, he is a walking work of art, you know?"

"Juice," I said, feeling a little sick, "did you tell him I was looking for him?"

"Well, no. See, you got it wrong, it's not Les that's in the band, it's his girlfriend Mandy. They're called Slippery When Wet, and he's sort of their manager. I've heard them at clubs, and Rita even knows Mandy. Isn't that a coincidence?"

"Yeah, a coincidence. Did you mention me at all?"

"No, I thought I'd better talk to you first. Are you sure you want this particular band for your client? I don't wanna tell you your business, but if you think I'm scary, you should see these girls. Mandy's really hot on guitar, but still—"

"I'm sure you're right," I said hastily. "Sounds like the wrong band. Absolutely. But thanks for letting me know."

"You're welcome," she said. "Tomorrow at seven for the tasting, right? I'm bummed that it has to be so early, but they're rewaxing all the floors at nine. BBA's closed on Mondays, remember, so I'll let you in the side door. . . . Are you still there?"

"Yes. The side door. See you then." I hung up the phone and stared at it for a moment without seeing it. Thank goodness Mandy's band was so scary. The last thing I needed was for Skull to hear that I was asking around about him.

"Now I know what I'm going to do next," I said, turning back to Lily. "First I'm going to call Graham and tell him just the facts, ma'am, about the Dracula costume. Then I'm going to install a floodlight over my front door. And then I've got a funeral to go to."

Chapter Twenty-Two

FUNERALS SHOULD HAPPEN IN THE RAIN. THERE SHOULD be dark clouds, at least, and a doleful wind, and a decent dimming of the light.

But when I arrived, late and flustered, for Mercedes Montoya's graveside service, the low-hanging November sun shone, bright and almost warm, from a sky of extraordinarily clear, deep blue. The priest, a small man built like a wrestler, cast a blocky shadow across the casket, already lowered into the gaping grave. The sun's glare made the mourners squint and shield their eyes with their hands, and illuminated the faces of the grieving family with cruel precision. Clouds would have been kinder.

I'd hit a traffic jam on I–5, then gotten lost trying to find the church in the southern suburbs, so I missed the funeral mass entirely. But I'd spotted the hearse and followed the short procession of cars to Greenwood Memorial Park, a modest cemetery with an adjacent funeral home. Another burial service was just getting started, a larger one than Mercedes', and other visitors, solitary or in pairs, were walking the paths across the flat green plane of grass and headstones and bouquets, all of it far too gay and colorful in the sunshine.

From the edge of our little assembly I stood scanning all

the faces, while Mercedes' brother Esteban, a gangling, good-looking youth, made some remarks in Spanish. His voice broke several times, and his mother, standing tall in her black suit and long veil, wept silently but without pause. Among the mourners who were strangers to me, some were surely Spanish-speaking family friends, while others—the young and stylish ones—were probably colleagues from the TV station where Mercedes had begun her rise to fame.

I saw Paul with Elizabeth, and several more people from the *Sentinel,* including Corinne Campbell and Valerie Duncan, both wearing sunglasses. I wondered if Aaron would have attended had he been in town. *He should have called me, not Lily, the bum....* I noticed that Angela Sims was there as well. I'd almost forgotten that she and Mercedes were not just bridesmaids together but sorority sisters. The one figure missing, besides Aaron, was Roger Talbot. Was he too grief-stricken to attend, or just wary of letting his grief be seen in public and interpreted for what it was, mourning for a lost lover?

"Um, hi," murmured a voice behind me.

It was Zack, solemn and wide-eyed. I touched his arm briefly, then returned my attention to the priest, who was pronouncing a final prayer. Several people made the sign of the Cross; Corinne was one of them, and I recalled that she was Catholic. Valerie Duncan was not, apparently, but she was murmuring a private benediction to herself. Or was it something else? She had little reason to bless Mercedes. At the grave's edge, Esteban and his mother each dropped a blood-red rose onto the casket. I don't cry easily, but I felt tears on my face. *Good-bye, Mercedes. We'll find out who did this. You would have been a lovely bride.* Beside me, Zack gave a sharp little sigh.

The crowd stirred and began to drift apart, some people stepping forward to offer their condolences to Mrs. Montoya. I moved to follow, but Valerie Duncan came across the grass and drew me discreetly aside.

"Valerie—" I began.

"Please forget I said anything," she whispered, not meeting my eyes, and keeping her back turned toward her coworkers. "At the rehearsal dinner. You know what I mean."

"It's completely forgotten, believe me."

The rest of the *Sentinel* crew came over to join us, looking at a loss about what to do next.

"Of course Roger cares," Paul was saying, in answer to someone's question. "It's just that he's not up to another funeral so soon after his wife's death."

"I'm sure that's why Roger isn't here," said Valerie smoothly.

Given that she knew about Roger and Mercedes, it was a nice job of acting. But I guess if you're going to have affairs with married men, you learn how to act a part.

"This has been difficult for everyone," Valerie continued. "Why don't we go back to the Two Bells for a drink? I know I need one. Carnegie, you're welcome to join us."

There were murmurs of agreement, and they set out toward the parking lot. Zack lingered behind with me.

"What happened with the DJ?" he asked.

I told him about Rick the Rocket's demand for money, and my deduction that he was innocent. I didn't mention the diamond ring; Mercedes' affair with Roger Talbot was none of his business.

"Syd Soper is off the hook, too," I concluded. "When I told him that Mercedes had been stabbed to death, he believed it."

"Hey, that was smart!" said Zack.

"I thought so."

"So that just leaves Angela and the Dracula guy." As he spoke, I could see Angela over his shoulder, her smooth hair gleaming and her willowy form casting a long shadow on the erratically-trimmed grass. She stared after the *Sentinel* people, then suddenly hurried after them and spoke intently to Corinne. I wondered why.

Zack turned and followed my gaze. "You think it was Angela after all?"

"What? No, I was just being nosy. My *big* news is about Dracula. Characters, Inc. never rented a Count Dracula costume! I've been thinking it over, and I'm sure that my first idea was right. This guy Lester Foy is on some kind of bizarre revenge trip, and he crashed the party."

"But that means you're in danger, too!" Robin Hood was back on the scene, ready to defend Maid Marian. "You should tell the police."

"I already did. At least, I left a message for Lieutenant Graham about the costume. And I'll keep calling to make sure he follows up. Meanwhile, I'm being extra-careful."

"I'll totally hang with you as much as you want," said the hero of Sherwood Forest. "I got a ride here with Valerie, but I'll go back with you and we can meet up with them at the tavern."

"Oh, Zack, I'm in no mood for a bar right now." *And in no need of more gossip about me and the younger man.* "You go ahead, please. It's broad daylight. I'll be fine."

"Are you sure?"

"Yes. Go."

He grinned and loped across the grass after his friends. And why not? Zack was still basking in his deliverance from guilt, back in the land of the living after his nightmare. As they climbed into their cars, I noted with interest that Angela was still talking to Corinne, two blondes in black dresses in the bright sunshine. They both seemed tense.

I considered strolling over to eavesdrop, but Corinne made a sudden sharp gesture with her hands and turned away. She nearly bumped into Valerie, who had just come after them, apparently to say that her carload was leaving. As Corinne entered Valerie's sedan, Angela looked after her with a puzzled expression. Then she got into her own sporty model and drove off.

I was left alone, wondering idly about that encounter, and pondering, much more seriously, about Aaron. Lily was right, good men were hard to find, and perfect men were impossible. I stood there in the peaceful hush, wishing for a bench where I could sit in the sun and think. Maybe Aaron's phone call to Lily just proved how serious he was about our relationship. Maybe the only unknown in this equation was me. How could I calculate how serious *I* was? Should I ask Aaron to stay in Seattle? And if I did, what then? And why on earth had I ever kissed Zack Hartmann? It was all very—

"Excuse me, lady."

I was so lost in thought, it took me a moment to peg the man with the shovel as a gravedigger. He wore a gigantic handlebar moustache and a look of long-suffering patience.

"Do you mind if we finish up here? I don't mean to rush you if you need some one-on-one time with the deceased and all, only my crew is going off shift—"

"I'm sorry! Please, go ahead." Embarrassed, I strode off toward the far end of the cemetery, looking for some privacy and maybe a bench.

What I found was Skull.

He was standing alone, his thick arms folded and his

booted feet planted wide, glaring at me as I walked toward him. *Oh, God.* He must have come to gloat over the woman he killed, and stayed to watch the rest of us with murder on his mind. I could feel the heat rush to my face as I veered aside, trying to act as if I knew where I was going.

Fortunately, the other, larger burial service was still underway a few hundred yards across the cemetery from my nemesis. Ignoring the curious glances from the family members seated in folding chairs, I took a place on the other side of the grave, among the standing mourners, as far as I could get from Lester Foy. What could he do, jump over the casket and attack me? I kept a close watch on his inked-up bald skull beyond the heads of the peevish silver-haired widow and her brood of antsy teenagers. Whoever the dear departed was, nobody seemed all that sorry to see him go.

Skull hadn't followed me. In fact, he didn't move a muscle as the presiding minister droned through the eulogy. No wonder the widow looked peeved; this guy was a lousy preacher, and he didn't seem too inspired by the life and death of Harold Baird. That was the departed's name, evidently, though at one point the clergyman called him Howard.

"*Har*old," snapped the widow, and one of the teenagers snickered. The minister frowned, corrected himself, and droned on. I was determined to stay safely inside this group until we all drove away, but after a few minutes I was longing for hymns or hysteria or something to break the monotony.

". . . that he may rest in peace. Amen."

And about time, too. I exchanged polite half-smiles with a few of the mourners, and turned to accompany them along the path to the parking lot. Suddenly my way was blocked by the widow.

"It was you, wasn't it?" she hissed. No kidding, she actually hissed. "You *bitch*!"

I glanced around, hoping to see the guilty party standing behind me, but no, I was the only one in her crosshairs. Everybody else was steering clear, leaving us alone on the path.

"I'm sorry, I don't understand—"

"I knew it was a redhead. Did you think I didn't know? How *dare* you come here!"

"Mrs. Baird," I said firmly, scanning over her shoulder for Skull. He was walking toward the parking lot, and, to my surprise, there was a woman with him. *Mandy?* "Mrs. Baird, I think you've confused me with someone else—"

"Don't give me that, you—"

I pressed on boldly, my blood prickling with relief at Skull's departure.

"You see, I just had to pay my respects after Harold was so kind to me. So kind to a *stranger*," I added hastily. Skull and Mandy were climbing into a battered red pickup with a skull-and-crossbones flag on the antenna. "You see, I...I had an accident once, in my truck, and he drove me to the police station. I've always been so grateful." The pickup pulled out of the lot and disappeared. "Harold was such a modest man, that's probably why he never told you about it. Nice meeting you. Lovely ceremony. Fabulous sermon. Bye!"

I left her sputtering behind me. Inside ten minutes I was cruising back up the freeway, with no red pickups anywhere in sight, and inside the hour I was home with my doors and windows locked against the gathering darkness, on the phone to Lieutenant Graham.

"I got your message, Ms. Kincaid. I really don't see that the absence of a Dracula costume at that particular shop means much, but in any case—"

"But there's more!" I told him. "Skull is following us again. He was at Mercedes' funeral!"

"You *saw* Lester Foy? When and where?"

I gave him the details, including the flag on the truck. "So you're looking for him now? You believe me?"

"Ms. Kincaid, I was about to say that in any case, Lester Foy has moved out of his apartment without notifying us, which means he has jumped bail. So yes, there's a warrant out for his arrest, but only on the robbery charge. As I said, I don't think this business about the costume means much."

"But—"

"Ms. Kincaid, it's Sunday afternoon. I'm still at the office, and I'm going to be here all Sunday night, too, if I don't get back to work. Call me immediately if you see Lester Foy again. And please, leave the homicide cases to me."

Chapter Twenty-Three

UP NORTH IN SEATTLE, YOU PAY FOR THE LONG JUNE AFTER-noons with the dark winter mornings. It always seems like a good deal in June, but never in November.

I had expected some nightmares about Skull, but instead I slept dreamlessly until Monday morning. A good thing, too, since I had to be up early for Juice's audition with the Buckmeisters. It seemed extra-early when my alarm went off; the weather had shifted yet again, to the kind of dank, cold fog we'd seen up at the Salish Lodge, and between the fog and the time of year, it was still half-dark.

I scanned the dock carefully from my front door, but the only people I saw were various neighbors setting out for work. Grateful for their presence, I scurried out to the park-ing lot, locked my car doors and drove off, keeping a wary eye out for Skull's red pickup. I didn't see it, and by the time I stopped for my usual latte and bagel, and then parked downtown, the streets and sidewalks were so full of cars and people that the day quickly took on a more prosaic atmo-sphere. Cold and gray, but prosaic.

"Hey, Kincaid, you're late!" said Juice, letting me in by the side door to By Bread Alone. She wore a white apron over a T-shirt, along with her usual short shorts and cowboy boots—brown ones this time—and her hair was its usual violent green. "Sucky time to get up, isn't it? 'Course bakers have been awake for hours by now. Your clients are late, too."

I wondered again how the Buckmeisters, especially Betty, would take to Juice. "They'll be here. They only show up early when you're not expecting them at all. Aren't you ever cold in those shorts?"

"I'm hot-blooded. Just ask Rita."

Laughing, she led me through the kitchen, with its giant mixers and long counters for kneading, to the café section out front. Most of the tables were bare, but one was set with dessert plates, cake forks, coffee cups, and a vase of carnations. The table beside it was spread with a white cloth, an empty stage waiting for the star's big entrance. Presentation is half the battle in the food business, and Juice knew it.

"So what have you got to show us?" I asked.

"Surprise," she said smugly. "You're gonna have to wait."

I noticed she had blisters along one forearm. "Let me guess. Something wonderful in pulled sugar?"

Pulled sugar creates lovely, brittle fantasy shapes—not unlike Dale Chihuly's blown glass—but it has to be kept hot while it's worked, and even careful bakers end up with a burn or two. The smart ones keep a bowl of ice water close at hand.

"You got it," said Juice. "But I'm not saying anything else."

She went back to the kitchen, and I went to look out the window through the thin hazy fog, in case the Buckmeisters came to the wrong door. Across the street, up on the utility roof of a south-facing apartment building, I saw something odd: a uniformed policeman, visible only from the waist up, behind some ventilation equipment. There was no one else around, but he wasn't slouching, or smoking, or fidgeting. He was standing very still, and something about the somber look on his round young face made me curious to know what he was doing up there.

"Carnegie! You ready for some cake for breakfast?" The familiar voice boomed across the empty room and resounded from the plate-glass windows. Buck, Betty, and Bonnie trooped in, bundled against the chill, all six cheeks rosier than ever. Juice followed them in, and when they reached the center of the room and turned to get a better look at her, I held my breath for the reaction.

"Goodness!" said Betty, her black curls bouncing. "I can't believe it!"

For all her bravado, Juice looked a bit discomfited. "Believe what?"

"Ray Jones peanut-brittle lizard! Look at that toebug!"

I thought Betty had lost her mind, but Juice smiled broadly and stuck out one foot. "Like 'em?"

"Dear Lord," said Buck, in the quietest tone I'd ever heard from him. Then he reverted to his usual bellow. "Young lady, where in the name of I don't know what did you get a pair of handmade Ray Jones boots? He's been gone for decades!"

"My girlfriend found them for me at a pawnshop in Oklahoma. And they fit *perfect*. It's like they were destined for me, y'know?"

"I'm giving my fiancé a pair of Henry Camargos for a wedding gift," said Bonnie, blushing like, well, blushing like a bride. "Cognac alligator."

Juice sighed. "Cooool."

The Buckmeisters went on exclaiming and admiring and agreeing about the destiny of footwear for about ten minutes, and by the time they took their seats at the tasting table, the color of Juice's hair was clearly immaterial. So far, so good. But could she get Christmassy enough for these Yuletide fanatics?

I shouldn't have doubted. Juice swaggered into the kitchen—now that I was looking, they *were* pretty nice boots—and reappeared with a tray bearing three small, exquisite cakes decorated as Christmas gifts, wrapped in three different and elaborate ways, swathed in gossamer ribbons and bows, and surrounded by Christmas tree ornaments in glittering, stained-glass colors. The Buckmeisters were struck dumb—for once—so I spoke up.

"Juice, those are fabulous! But we have three hundred guests—"

"I'll do a different cake for every table, like centerpieces," she said, trying to be nonchalant but brimming with pride in her creations. She set the tray on the second table so we could marvel at it from all sides. "This one is white chocolate hazelnut torte with raspberry liqueur filling, then there's mocha mousse torte, and this one is 'lemon impossible,' that's golden sponge cake with lemon curd filling. It's awesome."

Buck found his voice. "I have never seen anything so pretty that you could eat!"

After four other tastings, Betty was learning the lingo. "Is that what they call gum paste?"

Juice bridled. "I freakin' *hate* gum paste. You can model it like clay, but it tastes gross."

"Sorry, dear. No offense. What is it, then?"

"The wrapping is poured fondant, the ribbons are pulled sugar, and the ornaments are blown sugar."

"It's a very tricky technique," I told them. "Juice is a real artist when it comes to sugar work."

"She surely is!" said Buck. "I could look at these all day."

"You look all you want while I get you some coffee," Juice offered, then winked at me. "You wanna help me back here?"

I followed her into the kitchen. As we assembled a thermos pot and the cream and sugar tray, I whispered, "Juice, are you crazy? You can't possibly charge enough to cover that many individual cakes. Not ones that elaborate, anyway. It would cost a fortune!"

"I'm only gonna charge them three-quarters of a fortune. I'll still end up working for chump change by the time I do all the custom work on these puppies, but I figure it'll make such a splash that snotty guys like Joe Solveto will start taking me seriously."

"Still, that's an immense amount of work."

She shrugged. "Rita's out of town the first half of December. When I'm not getting any, I got energy to burn."

We poured coffee for the Killer B's, now looking sweet as honeybees, and Juice began slicing cake. I declined—I can't handle sugar that early in the day—and took my coffee cup over to the window again. It was lighter now, the flat shadowless light of winter in Seattle, and I could see the rooftop scene across the way with eerie, two-dimensional clarity.

The policeman was still there, joined now by three men in suits. One of them carried what looked like a doctor's bag. The others deferred to him, and when he knelt down with his bag, out of my line of sight, the young policeman grimaced and turned away. Off to one side, a janitor in coveralls stood holding a bucket and wearing long rubber gloves. The hair on the back of my neck began to stir.

"Come taste this lemony one!" Betty called to me. "It's just divine."

"No, thanks," I said faintly. I was trying to remember the cross streets in this part of town, and figure out which building that utility roof belonged to. I had a guess, but maybe I was wrong. "I'm really not hungry."

"These are dee-lish, every one of them," Buck announced. "Now, young lady, what's all this pretty cake going to set me back?"

I turned to watch, expecting some price resistance, or at least shrewd negotiation. Juice looked Buck right in the eye and named an astounding sum of money. The ladies fluttered a bit, but Buck just half-closed his eyes and worked his jaw for a minute.

Then he slapped a hand on the plate-filled table and said, "Done! You get what you pay for, isn't that right, Mother? Juice, honey, you got yourself a deal."

It's the boots, I thought, trying not to think about the man with the doctor's bag. And then, absurdly, *Maybe they'll start showing up at Juice's place for breakfast instead of mine.*

The Buckmeisters began the long happy process of deciding on flavors, and as the delectable terms filled the air— cappuccino truffle, strawberry buttercream, Grand Marnier praline—I signaled to Juice that I'd be right back. I jaywalked across the street, glancing down the block as I approached the sign at the intersection.

My guess was right. The utility roof was on the south side of a building whose main entrance was around the corner, facing west. A building I had been inside just two days before. I hurried around the corner, into the lobby, and onto an elevator, passing clusters of people with eager, horrified faces. As the doors slid closed I heard one of them say to a new arrival, "Some woman fell—"

The moon-faced young policeman stopped me partway down the hall of the thirteenth floor.

"Excuse me, miss, may I ask where you're going?"

I pointed silently to the door beyond him.

"Did you know the occupant?"

Did. Not do. Past tense. Oh, God.

Angela Sims was dead.

Chapter Twenty-Four

BY THE TIME I GOT BACK TO BY BREAD ALONE, THE Buckmeisters were gone and Juice was clearing away the cake plates.

"Hey, where'd you go, Kincaid? Buck and the gang said they'll see you later. Man, they are *great* people! And you were afraid—What's the matter? You look like death."

I heard someone laughing, as if from a distance. It was me. She left the plates and came over to take my arm.

"No kidding, you look like you're gonna keel over. Here, sit down." I sat, taking long shuddering breaths, while Juice brought me a mug of milky coffee. "Lots of sugar. Good for shock. Now, what's up?"

"I...had some bad news about a friend," I said at last. I didn't feel up to explanations. Not that there were any; the cop had just taken my name and address and sent me on my way. I knew what had happened, though, as surely as if I'd been there myself. But why hadn't Angela secured her door? And why, I asked myself painfully, why hadn't I warned all the attendants about Skull the day of the dress fitting? *I could have saved her life.*

Juice was staring at me, waiting for more, but I shook my head.

"It's a long story, and I have to get back to the office. Um, congratulations about the Buckmeisters. You really impressed them. I'll get back to you later about the cake contract, OK?"

"No prob. Sorry about your friend." Then she frowned angrily. "What the hell does *she* want?"

Someone was banging on BBA's locked front door. Juice stomped to the window and gestured at the Closed sign, but the pounding continued, and I heard a woman's voice.

"Carnegie, open up!" It was Corinne, wild-eyed and frantic. I pointed toward the side entrance, and went through the kitchen to let her in.

"I saw him!"

Corinne stumbled through the door and into my arms. Her raincoat was unbuttoned, the belt dangling, and her upswept hairdo was coming down. For a moment I felt her panic infecting me as well. But only for a moment. It's funny; nothing helps you pull yourself together like somebody else falling apart. So I reacted as I usually do in a wedding crisis, and started ordering people around.

"Juice, lock that door, would you? It's OK, Corinne, you're safe, he's not coming in here." It didn't sound as though she knew about Angela, and I didn't intend to tell her until she calmed down. "Now sit here and tell me what's going on."

"I saw the tattooed man! I was going to have breakfast at the Athenian Café, but when I saw him I just kept going through the Market and I think he followed me! I was looking for a policeman but then I saw you through that window and, and..."

"Here, take a swig of this."

Juice, instead of interrupting with questions, had very sensibly kept silent and brought over the rest of my coffee. As Corinne sipped at it, there was another knock at the front window, businesslike this time, and Juice went to unlock the front door for three burly men in coveralls—the cleaning crew, here to do the floors.

"Kincaid, I kinda need you to leave, I gotta help these guys. If your friend's OK now?"

"She's fine," I said firmly. "Come on, Corinne, let's go back to my office for a little while, and then you can go home, or to the *Sentinel*, or wherever."

"I should go to work," said Corinne. She put down the coffee and rooted in her pocket for a tissue. "I have a deadline—"

"OK, but we'll stop at my office first, and we'll call Lieutenant Graham. Juice, thanks a million."

On the way to the houseboat, I tried and failed to reach the detective on my cell phone. Just as well; I didn't want to break the bad news to Corinne until I had her safely in my office. Climbing my stairs, the two of us kept glancing anxiously around, as if Skull had the powers of Dracula himself and could come swooping at us like a bat. It would have been laughable if I wasn't still imagining Angela's plunge from her balcony. *Thirteen stories. Did she know what was happening? Did she scream?*

Eddie looked up from a snowstorm of printouts and welcomed us with his customary savoir faire.

"So how'd it go with the cake? And who's your friend?"

My partner rarely meets the attendants for our weddings. I introduced Corinne, then settled her on the wicker love seat in the good room while I spoke to him privately, with the connecting door shut.

"Eddie, another one of the Lamott bridesmaids has been killed. I have an idea who's doing it, but—No, don't interrupt, I need your help. Call Lieutenant Graham—here's his card—and tell him Lester Foy was in the Pike Place Market this morning. Then call Elizabeth and her sister, tell them Angela is dead and the purse-snatcher is on the loose, they'll know what that means. Tell them to be very, very careful, and I'll talk to them soon. Got that?"

"Got it." And he picked up the phone. Eddie was a master of fuss and sputter when it came to the small stuff, but he knew a crisis when he saw one.

Back in the good room, I sat next to Corinne and took her hand. It was cold, and she was trembling.

"Corinne, you understand that you're safe now, don't you?" I said gently. "OK, I have to tell you something, about Angela. The police found her this morning, down below her balcony. She's dead."

I was right about the hysterics. Corinne wrenched her hand away and leapt to her feet with a wail of horror. Then she threw herself against me, clutching me like a life preserver, and sobbed aloud. Always over the top, that was our Corinne.

Suddenly I was overcome with distaste for her dramatics. I had felt obligated to break the news to her, but now I wanted her out of my office so I could have my own reaction to Angela's death, and get on with my own work. I wondered, with a horrible sense of déjà vu, if Paul and Elizabeth would still want to carry on with the wedding. Beyond the expense issue and the heartbreak for dear old Enid, lay a grim question: What good would it do to cancel? Skull would still be lurking around, whether Elizabeth and her attendants spent the evening at a wedding or home watching TV.

This nightmare would continue until he was caught. Or until Elizabeth, Patty, Corinne, and I were all dead.

Gradually the sobs died away, and Corinne slumped back into the love seat, hiccupping.

"What are we going to do?" she whispered. "He's going to get us all."

"The first thing to do is get you over to the *Sentinel*. You'll be safe there, and they're bound to arrest this guy soon. Do you have someone who could stay with you tonight?"

She nodded, just as Eddie came to the connecting door to say that Lieutenant Graham was on the phone.

"Tell him I'll be right there. And, Eddie, would you mind driving Corinne to her office?"

I locked the door behind them, then picked up the phone. The detective was all business. "You were at Angela Sims' building this morning. Why?"

"I saw the police and went in, that's all. Lieutenant, you've got to find Lester Foy. He murdered Angela."

"You're sure of that, are you?"

"Don't tell me you think she *fell*, for God's sake! People don't fall off their own balconies. He broke in there last night and—"

"What makes you think someone broke in?"

"Don't tell me Angela *let* him in! A guy with a bat tattooed on his head?"

"We don't know who she let in, if anyone. What we do know is that two weeks ago a woman was raped in a building two blocks away. Her assailant threatened to push her out a window if she resisted him."

"And you think the same 'assailant' killed Angela?"

"All I think is that it's a far more likely hypothesis than your obsession with Lester Foy. He has no record of violence."

"It's not an obsession! He was stalking me at the cemetery, and this morning he chased Corinne through the Pike Place Market."

"Chased her?"

"Well, followed her."

"Did he threaten her in some way? Were there witnesses?"

I kept forgetting: in Graham's eyes, Skull was still just a petty thief and Corinne was still the girl who cried wolf. "I don't think so. But you should talk to her. She'll be at her desk at the *Sentinel* in a few minutes."

"Excellent idea," he said dryly. "Any more suggestions about how to do my job?"

"No, I guess not. Wait, what about Tommy Barry?" I'd been calling the hospital every day to check on Tommy's condition. Some slight improvement, they kept telling me, but still no visitors. "Are you still guarding him?"

"Round the clock."

"Good." I could imagine the scene the sportswriter must have witnessed. The dim corridor, the shallow water lapping on stones, and Dracula looming over the fallen gypsy queen. Did Foy know there was a watcher in the shadows? Maybe he hadn't seen Tommy clearly enough to identify him again. Or maybe he was casing the hospital as well as stalking the women who turned him in. "Tell your people to look out for those tattoos. Or maybe a rubber Dracula mask."

"Ms. Kincaid, I really don't believe that Lester Foy was at that party."

"Why not?"

"In any case, he'll be picked up on the bail violation."

"And how long will that take? Foy must know that Corinne saw him at the Market today. He'll go into hiding for a while, and then come after us again!"

"I assure you, we're doing all we can. Good-bye."

I hung up, frowning in concentration. Skull had to be

drawn out into the open before he killed again. And I thought I knew how to do it.

I paced along the picture windows lining the front of the office, and stared out unseeing at the pewter surface of the lake. *It won't really be dangerous, if I handle it right. And what else can I do? I just have to get a message to him...*

By the time Eddie returned, I had my plan. But first I had to make some explanations.

"What in the Sam Hill is going on around here?" Eddie demanded. "Who's Lester Foy?"

"He's the purse-snatcher from the bridesmaids' luncheon last month. Have a seat and I'll tell you the whole story."

Of course, I edited the story, telling him about Angela's death and Corinne's panicked flight, but nothing of my newly hatched scheme. Eddie seemed to take it all very calmly, until I told him I was going downstairs to rest for a while. He insisted on coming with me, peering ferociously up the dock toward the parking lot with every step. Then he checked through all the rooms, including the inside of my miniscule bedroom closet. If Graham was right, this was sheer paranoia and a waste of time. But I didn't object.

On his way out my front door, Eddie inspected the dead bolt. "You keep this locked, sister."

"I promise."

"And you should have one of those peephole things. For Christ's sake, anybody could be standing out there and you wouldn't—"

"I'll have one put in tomorrow! Besides, it's daytime. Foy's not going to show his face until—I mean, he's probably lying low."

"Yeah, but you don't know that. You want me to sleep down here tonight?"

"Thanks, Eddie, but I think I'll have company."

"Zack, you mean?" His clear gray eyes were uneasy. "Carnegie, it's none of my business, but . . ."

"But what? That's never stopped you before."

"Dammit," said Eddie, who actually seemed to be blushing under his leathery tan. "Dammit, maybe he's a nice enough kid, but he's too young for you! And besides, I thought you and Aaron were all set."

"Aaron and I are anything but 'set.' As far as I know he's in Portland and not speaking to me, so let's drop that subject, OK? And *of course* Zack's too young for me. We're just friends. I'm seeing someone else tonight. It's . . . it's a first date. Honestly, Eddie, let me run my own life, would you?"

"Suit yourself," he grumbled. "I'll let you know when I'm ready to go home."

"I'll be back up before then. I just want to nap for a bit, and maybe make some calls."

But once my partner was safely upstairs, I skipped the nap and went straight to the phone.

"Juice, I need a favor."

"You got me another client!"

"Sorry, no. That guitarist you told me about, Mandy. Do you know how to reach her?"

"Sure. Rita's got her number."

"OK, I need you to call Mandy and tell her I want to see her boyfriend Lester. I think he's probably staying with her, or at least she'll know where he is."

"OK, but—"

"Have her tell him that I've got a business proposition for him, and he should come to my houseboat. Tonight, at nine o'clock. Give her my address, directions, anything she wants. Tell Mandy . . . Tell her to say to Lester that I know all about Angela."

"Kincaid, is this gonna make sense to her? 'Cause it sounds pretty weird to me. Like blackmail or something."

"Trust me, Juice. Just do it, and call me back after you reach her, OK?"

"OK."

Juice called back an hour later. It was a long hour. I clean house when I'm anxious, so I set about dusting my bookshelves, book by book, whether they needed it or not. I worked my way across the living room and then to the coffee table, and when the phone finally rang I dropped the biography of John Adams on my foot.

"Ouch! Hello, Juice?"

"Yeah. Mandy says he got the message, and he'll be there. Are you going to tell me what's going on?"

"No."

"That's what I figured. Watch your ass, Kincaid."

I assured her that I would. Then I called Lieutenant Graham and requested the pleasure of his company that evening.

Chapter Twenty-Five

GRAHAM WAS FURIOUS, OF COURSE, AND TREATED ME TO A short, sharp summary of his views on civilians who meddle in police affairs. He scrupulously avoided profanity this time—a waste of effort on my account, really—but the words "harebrained" and "dangerous" cropped up repeatedly. I made myself comfortable on the living room couch and waited for him to run out of steam before I replied.

"Look, Lieutenant, you keep saying that you don't think Lester Foy is the murderer."

I could almost hear his teeth grinding. "That's beside the point."

"No, it's not! If you're right, then all I'm doing is inviting over a small-time thief who jumped bail. You've had trouble finding him so far, but now you know exactly where he's going to be at nine o'clock tonight."

"Unless he comes early."

"So, you can come earlier. I'll feed you dinner." Graham might even be good company, once he forgave me.

But forgiveness was in short supply. "Never mind dinner. You just stay in your office with your partner until I get there. And don't ever, *ever,* even *consider* pulling this kind of stunt again, or I will do my best to have you incarcerated myself. Understood?"

"Understood." I said it meekly enough, but I climbed the stairs to the office nursing a flicker of quiet triumph. *This will work, I know it will. Then we can all stop being afraid.*

Meanwhile, though, the fear was still there. I spent the afternoon in a state of numb determination, going through the motions of a normal day just to pass the time until Skull's arrest. Not that it's ever normal to call a bride and ask her if she's still alive.

"I'm OK," said Elizabeth, when I reached her at home. "Paul's here, and he's not letting me out of his sight. Patty's at work, and she's going to spend the night with friends." I heard Paul's voice in the background. "He says Zack is staying with Corinne at the newsroom."

"I know. She's pretty upset."

"I bet she is, with this guy stalking her again."

"So you believe Corinne's story now, about being attacked at the Aquarium?"

Elizabeth laughed, a brief and bitter sound. "Angela didn't, and look where it got her. Jesus, how long is it going to take for them to catch this maniac? I could have found him myself by now."

It struck me, suddenly, that for this particular warrior princess, losing control of a situation was almost worse than being in danger. Maybe making some bridal decisions would help.

"Elizabeth," I said briskly, "let's assume, hypothetically, that the police arrested Lester Foy, like, maybe tonight. Would you and Paul want to go ahead with the wedding, do you think? I'm sorry to press you about it, but we'll have to make some decisions soon. The cake, for one thing. It's a three-day job, and I see I've got a message here on my desk to call the baker."

"Wel-l-l," she said. And then, in the take-charge voice that made her so valuable at Microsoft, "Yes. If the cops can get Foy out of the way, then we'll get married Saturday as planned."

Again I heard Paul's voice, raising a question, and Elizabeth saying to him, "Postpone for how long? It won't help Angela any, and I'm damned if some tattooed son of a bitch is going to spoil my wedding."

"That's the spirit," I told her. "You and Paul hang in there. I'm betting we'll have good news before too long."

Eddie pounced the minute I hung up. "What makes you think they're going to arrest this fellow so soon?"

"Nothing in particular, Eddie. I'm just trying to put a good face on the situation. You know, keep up the clients' spirits."

"Hmph."

I picked up the phone to head off any more questions; I wanted Eddie well clear of the houseboat before nightfall. There really was a message from Elizabeth's baker, so I started with him. I knew the overall design—the swooping curves of the Experience Music Project would be carved from a block of cake layered with buttercream—but the last time we had talked, the details were still in question.

"Hi, Todd. How's the masterpiece coming?"

"Super." Todd was a laconic Scotsman, re-transplanted from British Columbia. He had a lucrative business in special-occasion desserts, and even more freckles than me. Juice's bias notwithstanding, Todd did amazing things with gum paste. "Got just the right effect for the colored aluminum skin of the building."

"How?"

"Edible pearlescent dust. Liquefy it with vodka, brush it over rolled white fondant. Super."

"What about the glass panels on the roof?" It was bizarre

but comforting to turn away from the dark undercurrents of this day and stay safe in the shallows.

"Simple. Cast sugar."

"And the monorail tracks?"

"Modeling chocolate."

"Yum. Will you assemble the cake on site, or—"

He made a disparaging and Scottish-sounding noise. "I'll be assembling all week, d'you see? So when it's done, it's to be transported all of a piece."

"Right. Of course."

We settled the delivery details, and I moved on down my checklist. Eddie had lectured me on the ease of inputting and amending data with his new software, but I was still clinging to my outdated ways, scribbling notes in colored ink with stars and arrows to keep track of changes. It all made sense, at least to me. And scribbling helped to distract me from more pressing questions, like how Skull had gotten Angela out onto that balcony. No signs of a struggle, Graham had said. It didn't make sense.

The hours crept by, and finally it was time for my "date." A rap sounded on our outside door, and Lieutenant Graham stepped into the good room. He wore the same jacket and sneakers I remembered from the Aquarium, and a handsome ski sweater that made him look almost cheerful. And certainly plausible as a man I might go out with. More plausible than Boris, come to think of it.

"Hello . . . there," I said lamely. I could *not* remember my date's first name. "Eddie, I think you've met—"

"Of course I've met the lieutenant," he growled, barely civil. "Nice to see you. Have fun." And he plucked his coat from the rack and marched out.

Even Graham's poker face couldn't withstand Eddie

Breen. Both eyebrows went up, and once the door slammed he said, "Fun?"

"I didn't tell him."

"So he thinks it's a social call?"

"Yes. Sorry."

I *was* sorry, too. As we descended the stairs, I decided that the lieutenant was quite attractive, in a somber sort of way. And it would serve Aaron right if I started seeing someone else while he was gone. Or would it? He might reciprocate—if not with Corinne, then with someone else—and I wouldn't be at all happy with *that* scenario.

A moot point, in any case. My personal charms were clearly far less interesting than my home-security precautions. Graham stalked around my humble abode with a deepening scowl of disapproval, and pointed out the fact that my front door had no peephole, and my sliding glass door had no dead bolt.

"There's a wooden dowel in the groove at the bottom," I countered. "That holds it closed."

Graham took hold of the handle and jerked it, hard, with a single rapid pump of his arm. The dowel arched up from its channel and cracked like a pretzel stick.

"Jeez, you're strong!"

He slid the door open and gestured out to my narrow little deck. Night was falling fast, and the wind that invaded the room had an icy edge. "Might as well put down a welcome mat."

Then he returned to the kitchen and unscrewed the head from my dust mop. He laid the mop handle down where the dowel had been, brushed off his hands, and sat down on the couch. His poker face was back in place, his hazel eyes expressionless.

"Well!" I said brightly. "Well, thanks. That takes care of that. Now what?"

"Now we wait." He pulled out a sheaf of official-looking paperwork, and a pair of wire-framed reading glasses.

"But don't you have to station your men? Or are they already out there?"

"What men?"

"Your officers. For the stakeout."

Graham smiled mirthlessly. "There is no stakeout. I can't just whistle up surveillance units because someone has a hunch."

"But did you talk to Corinne?"

"I did." He sighed, a deep, disappointed sigh. "Ms. Campbell is a remarkably vague witness. She saw a man in the Market. She is 'pretty sure' he was Foy, and she 'could swear' he was following her. He didn't speak to her, or even get close enough to do so. And so far we have no other witnesses to the incident. Such as it was."

"So you're here on your own?"

"That's right."

"Oh."

"I had theater tickets, too," he said.

"Oh."

Another sigh. Graham began reading in disciplined stillness, while I wandered the room, fidgeting and checking my watch. *I should have said eight o'clock, not nine. I shouldn't have done this at all. What was I thinking?* It began to rain. By seven-fifteen, my stomach was growling worse than Eddie, and I recalled that I hadn't eaten lunch. No wonder my head hurt.

"Do you mind if we wait in the kitchen?"

I nuked a box of frozen lasagna and made a spinach salad.

Graham unbent enough to eat with me, though he declined a glass of Pinot Noir. I made stilted attempts at conversation, speaking in low tones that wouldn't carry through the front door. Over the thin hissing of the rain, the scrape of our forks on the plates seemed unpleasantly loud. Neither of us actually ate much.

Finally I got up to make coffee, eking out a half-pot from the last handful of beans in my cupboard. Murder really screws up your grocery shopping. Behind me, Graham cleared the table with quick, economical movements.

"What if Skull doesn't show up at all?" I asked, pouring coffee for him and more wine for myself. *Might as well drink for both of us.*

"If he doesn't show up, we have a problem," said Graham. "I can request ongoing protection for you, but we're short of people and it's not automatic. You haven't actually been threatened."

"No, I've just been stupid, haven't I?"

He looked at me with those intriguing, disillusioned eyes. "Yes. Very."

We took our beverages back to the living room and waited some more. Eight-fifteen came, and eight-thirty. Eventually Graham loosened up a little, and even asked me about life in my floating home.

"I love it. It's a nuisance in a lot of ways, but I swear, regular houses seem landlocked to me now. I always want to get back on the lake."

"Is this where you met Lily James? On her houseboat?"

"No, Lily's got a house near Woodland Park. It's a great location for her kids."

We chatted on aimlessly, about kids in general and Lily's in particular, then fell silent. Nine o'clock. No sound. Nine-ten. Nine-thirty. I had picked up a book at random, and as I turned the pages, that same sense of unreality settled over me again, of idling in the shallows while a deadly, invisible undertow slides silently past. The wine didn't help.

I noticed Graham glancing at the photographs on a side table. "That's Lily with Ethan and Marcus, on a camping trip we did to Deception Pass."

"And who's this?"

"My mother, back in Idaho."

"I can see the resemblance," he said. "Your eyes—"

A double knock, so sudden that I bit my lip and let the book fall in my lap. Another knock, faint and somehow furtive. It was past ten o'clock. Graham motioned me to keep still and stepped silently to the front door, pulling out a gun as he went. It looked huge in his hand. I waited a moment, then tagged along behind him. I couldn't help it. I had put this thing in motion. What if something went wrong and he needed me? I couldn't catch my breath, and a pulse was thudding in my ears.

Graham leveled the gun at the door, then stretched his hand slowly for the knob. He wrenched the door open, side-stepping quickly as he did, and aimed the gun straight at the chest of the man standing in my doorway.

"What the *hell*?" said Aaron Gold.

Chapter Twenty-Six

"AARON, WHY DIDN'T YOU *CALL*?"

After an exchange of explanations and apologies, Lieutenant Graham left us to keep watch in the parking lot for another hour before heading home. Not that he thought Lester Foy would show up this long past the appointed time, and after all the commotion at the front door.

So now Aaron was standing in my living room with his arms crossed and his shoulders hunched, looking haggard and disgruntled. He wore rain-spattered khaki slacks and jacket, and there was a Rorschach blot of airplane coffee on his yellow oxford cloth shirt. Zorro was having a bad night.

I should have been grateful for his arrival—he had caught the first flight north when Paul called his Portland hotel room with the news about Angela—but my nerves were flayed by hours of tension, and the near-disaster in the doorway was the last straw. All I felt now was unreasoning resentment, and Aaron was the only target within range.

"Why didn't you call me from the airport, or from your place?"

He threw up his hands. "I didn't *stop* at my place. Why are women so fixated on the telephone, anyway? 'When are you going to call me?' 'Why didn't you call me?' It's like a hobby, nagging men to call."

"But Graham could have shot you!"

"You think I don't know that?" He closed his eyes and kneaded the back of his neck with one hand. "I felt like an idiot, charging in here to protect you and getting scared out of my wits. Can't you at least offer me a drink?"

"Of course." I looked doubtfully back toward the kitchen. "I think the Pinot Noir is gone, but there's some white wine I could open? . . ."

Aaron rolled his eyes. "I mean a *drink*. As in Scotch?"

"Sorry." I almost laughed at his woebegone expression, but caught myself in time. *I really should be grateful, having Zorro gallop into the hacienda to rescue me.* "Please, sit down. You look exhausted. Was it a hard trip?"

"No, I just stayed up late with some friends, and did an interview early this morning. It's no big deal." Still, he slumped onto the couch and let his head fall heavily back against the cushions.

"Have you eaten? I could make you an omelet."

"Scotch would be better," he said to the ceiling, more in sorrow than in anger. "But an omelet would be nice."

I bustled into the kitchen, wondering belatedly if I had any eggs. There were just two left, small ones at that, but I searched further and exhumed a weary half of an onion and a stub of cheddar. It took only minutes to sauté the one and grate the other, and slice the last of the French bread. I even arranged the omelet and toast on a tray, and added a glass of Chardonnay in case Aaron changed his mind. I finger-combed my hair, put on a gracious smile, and carried my handiwork into the living room.

Zorro was deep asleep.

I stood irresolute, listening to the whisper of rain on the lake, wondering whether to wake him. Aaron was always so animated, hectoring me with questions and wisecracks, that I rarely just looked—really looked—at his face.

His lips were parted slightly now, showing neat white teeth, and his hair, shiny-straight and almost blue in its blackness, tumbled across the high forehead and nearly touched the smooth, arched eyelids. His exposed throat made him seem young and vulnerable.

But only briefly. With a gasp and a snort, my handsome houseguest began to snore, which pretty much killed the mood. I shook my head, smiling, and bore the tray back to the kitchen. The omelet smelled wonderful, so I ate it, and tossed off the wine as well. Then I covered Zorro with a blanket and went to bed.

I was a long time drifting off. Questions kept marching through my mind, relentless ranks of soldiers on parade. Was Skull ever going to show up, or would I have to look over my shoulder for days on end? Or more than days? What if my call stampeded him into attacking one of the other women? Would Tommy Barry pull through, and would he be safe if he did? What if the guard at the hospital slept at his post...slept...

I slept at last, fitfully, plagued by dreams. In the midst of one nonsensical nightmare—something about a thunderstorm, and being clawed by a cat—somebody slid a hand up my leg, from ankle to knee. I gave a little screech and sat up, clutching the comforter around my bare shoulders.

"Leave me alone!"

"I've been trying to, Sleeping Beauty."

It was Tuesday morning, and Aaron was sitting on the edge of my bed with a Cheshire-cat grin. His jaw showed a heavy stubble and his clothes were a crumpled mess, but aside from that, he was repellently brisk and bright-eyed. "I gave it my best shot, but I can't stand it any longer."

"Stand what?"

"Starvation. There's nothing in your kitchen but Zack's pineapple and a bottle of cheap white wine, and they both smell rotten. I'm perishing out here! Get your clothes on and we'll go out for breakfast."

I sank deeper under the covers, whining. "It's too early for breakfast. I'm not hungry."

But the issue wasn't hunger, it was hangover. Unconsciousness, I was sure, would be infinitely preferable to this all-too-familiar combination of flannel mouth, sledgehammer head, and remorse. *Did I really drink a whole bottle of Pinot Noir?*

"I'm going back to sleep. Go away."

"No deal, Stretch. Come on, up and at 'em. Or would you rather I joined you under there?" The hand slid under the comforter, higher this time.

"Cut it *out*, Aaron! Can't you wait a while?"

"You're awfully crabby for a damsel in distress, you know that? Here I came all this way for a false alarm, and you—"

"What false alarm? Skull is after us! He killed Angela."

"That's not what Graham seems to think." Aaron began to pat his pockets, hunting for cigarettes.

"Well, Graham is wrong, and so are you. And don't you dare smoke in here. Go outside."

"Not unless you get up." His dark eyes held a spark of irritation now. "I mean it. If you want a bodyguard, you've got to feed him."

"I don't want a bodyguard!"

"Well, what do you want?" He stood up, rifling his pockets in earnest.

"I want you out of my bedroom. And then—"

The phone rang, which was just as well since I didn't

really know how to finish my sentence. *And then what? Hide out from Lester Foy forever?* Aaron left the room and I grabbed the receiver.

"Ms. Kincaid? Graham. There was another sexual assault last night, right near the Sims woman's building."

"Not a murder?"

"Not this time. We've got a chance to make an arrest today, so I can't spare the time for your . . ."

"My hunch?"

"Exactly. Just take sensible precautions, and stay in touch with my office, all right?"

"Of course. Lieutenant, about last night, I really appreciate—"

"Got to go." And he hung up.

When I emerged from the bedroom, dressed but still cranky, Aaron was out on the deck in his shirtsleeves, grinding one cigarette underfoot while he lit another. Last night's rain had emptied the lower clouds, and the sky showed a high, faded blue streaked with fast-moving mares' tails. His khaki windbreaker was lying on the couch, so I carried it out to him, holding it distastefully with two fingers.

"This smells of smoke."

"Excuse me for living. Who was that on the phone?"

"None of your business."

"Come on, Stretch, I can read you like a book. Something's happened."

I related Graham's call about the rapist downtown, and as I did, I felt a sneaking qualm of doubt to go with the queasiness in my stomach. Was I wrong about Skull after all? Maybe Angela's death *was* unrelated to Mercedes'.

"You see?" said Aaron triumphantly. "That's who killed Angela Sims, not your phantom Dracula. And I bet I was right all along about Corinne. She was telling tall tales again, looking for sympathy."

"But she saw Skull in the Market!"

"No law against being in the Market. Maybe he's a big fan of vegetables. Come on, let's get going."

"I'm not going anywhere," I said stubbornly. "I . . . I'm not feeling well."

I went back inside and he followed, his thin East Coast voice raised in protest. "Look, Stretch, don't be embarrassed. You just got carried away with your serial-killer theory, that's all. This kind of violence would make any woman paranoid. You'll feel better with some food in you."

"I'm not paranoid!" I snapped. "And I don't want any food."

"Well, I can't just leave you here."

"Why not? According to you, I'm not in any danger, I'm just a hysterical, paranoid woman."

"Calm down!"

"I am calm!" I shouted. "Stop patronizing me, and go get your damn breakfast."

"Fine." He shoved his arms into the tangled sleeves of his jacket, got one arm stuck, struggled a bit, and yanked the jacket off again, glaring all the while. Then he stalked through the kitchen and out the front door, banging it behind him and leaving me with the world's worst headache.

"Fine!" I said to the door. Then I flipped the dead bolt and glared around the kitchen. *That pineapple smells perfectly nice,* I thought defiantly. I returned to the living room, sniffing the air. The reek of cigarettes was even stronger than I thought. *Where does he get off complaining about smells—*

"Who the fuck is Angela?"

The reek was coming from Lester Foy, who was standing

just inside the glass door to my deck. He wore motorcycle leathers and massive boots looped with silver chains, and his face held an expression of such brute malevolence that meeting his gaze felt like warding off a blow.

I opened my mouth, but nothing emerged except a feeble gasp. Then last night's omelet tried to follow the gasp out, and I felt the cold sweat of nausea on my face. The room seemed to tilt.

"Answer me!" His voice was harsh and raw. "You got Mandy so pissed off—"

I may scare easy, but I don't scare for long. The room straightened out, the omelet stayed put, and I inflated my lungs like bellows and shrieked for all I was worth.

"Get AWAY-Y-Y!!"

"Jesus!" said Foy.

I fled into the kitchen, meaning to grab my chef's knife, but when I heard Foy's boots clumping behind me, I snatched up the next best thing and whirled to face him.

"Don't touch me!" I warned, brandishing the pineapple. Granted, it wasn't much of a threat, but it made him hesitate. Then came a shout and a rattle at the front-door knob, and Foy retreated back to the living room.

"Aaron!" I hollered. "He's in here! Help!"

Still clutching my tropical weapon, I unlocked the front door, but no one was there. Aaron must have gone around to the back. I rushed into the living room with the vague notion of catching the intruder between us.

Foy was standing outside on the narrow wooden deck. The weak winter sun, reflecting off the water, illuminated the dark designs on his skull and the backs of his hands. I could see the bat wings above his left ear as he faced the south end of the deck, the way he had come. But he wasn't moving, and his jaw was agape in astonishment.

I ran to the glass and saw, not Aaron but the beautiful, the glorious Buckmeisters, surging around the corner like the flying squad of some good-natured, unstoppable football team. Foy spun on his heel to flee the other way, then stopped again, stymied. My deck doesn't run all the way around; it dead-ends at the north corner. He turned back to glare at me, with murder in his eyes. I knew I'd never get the sliding door closed in time, let alone fumble the mop handle into place.

So I launched the pineapple.

It sailed heavily through the open doorway, losing altitude fast and coming in at knee level. Foy deflected it with one grimy hand, and with the other flicked open a wicked-looking knife. But those precious seconds brought Buck Buckmeister bearing down on him like vengeance itself in a red bandanna. Snarling obscenities, Foy backed away from this new opponent and raised the knife.

Unfortunately for Lester Foy, he backed up one step too many. He seemed to hang suspended for a moment, and then fell, spread-eagled and howling, into Lake Union. The enormous splash he sent up spattered the Buckmeisters and sent an arc of drops rat-a-tatting across my windows. I fell into Betty and Bonnie's solicitous arms while their patriarch stared down into the water, breathing hard.

"Who is this bastard?" Buck demanded. "Did he touch you? By God, I'll kill him."

"I don't think you have to, Daddy," said Bonnie. "I think he's drowning."

"Serves him right," rumbled Buck. "Probably faking it."

But Foy was flailing around in a genuine panic, propelling

himself farther away from the safety of the deck with every thrashing movement. His tattooed head slipped beneath the surface, reappeared, then went down again with a gargling shout.

"Boots!" I said. "He's wearing big leather boots."

"He'll die," said Bonnie.

"Let him!" said Buck.

"Oh, for heaven's sake," said Betty in a small, vexed voice, and shucked off her jacket and shoes.

She executed a neat, shallow dive off the deck, coming up plumb in the center of the foamy ripples created by Foy's struggles. Treading water and gasping from the cold, Betty stared at us bug-eyed for a moment, with her black curls plastered straight and streaming around her face. Then her apple cheeks puffed out as she took a big breath, upended herself and dove straight down, her diminutive feet in their gay plaid socks twinkling and then vanishing in the dark water.

Bonnie grabbed my arm and moaned, but Buck was smiling.

"Relax, honey," he said. "Don't forget, your momma was a lifeguard in Galveston when I met her. Just the prettiest little lifeguard you ever saw."

Chapter Twenty-Seven

WHAT A DIFFERENCE A DAY MAKES—OR AN HOUR. ESPECIALLY if, in a single hour, your nemesis is arrested; your beloved van is pronounced ready to come home; and your not-quite-boyfriend apologizes abjectly after leaving you in the hands of a murderer for the sake of two eggs over easy and a side of home fries.

"I just hope it was a good, filling breakfast," I said earnestly, "to tide you over while you identified my body."

"Enough with the guilt!" Aaron replied. "I've said I was sorry about ten times now. Any more of this and I'll throw *you* off the deck. I should anyway, just to teach you not to lure psychos to your house when I'm not around."

But he held me tight while he said it. We were nestled together on my couch, exchanging small, comforting kisses while I calmed down. It was quite a relief to have the place to ourselves. Lieutenant Graham was still out hunting the downtown rapist, but the SPD dispatched some uniformed cops to haul Lester Foy off to jail, mute and soggy in his leathers. The combined clamor of that many loud-voiced men, plus the Buckmeisters, had been a bit much for a woman with a resounding hangover.

With Skull safely gone, Betty had brushed off my concern about hypothermia, asking only for a towel and some hairspray, and the loan of some dry clothes. Once she was dry and curly again, I sent the Buckmeisters away with my heartfelt gratitude and a promise to discuss Christmassy place cards in exhaustive detail—some other time. Meanwhile, Pete the mechanic had called with the good news about the newly-repaired Vanna, and Aaron had returned from his breakfast to find me shaken but safe after the springing of my trap. Good news all around.

"Tell you what," I said, lifting my head from Aaron's shoulder. "I'll accept all ten of your apologies if you drive me to Pete's to pick up my van."

"Deal. You want to tell people about Foy first?"

I nodded. "I think I've got my breath back now."

Elizabeth was my first call, though it was Paul who answered her phone.

"Thank God," he said, "and thank God he didn't hurt you." Then, with his reporter's curiosity kicking in, "I wonder why he went after you instead of Corinne this time?"

"Who knows?" I lied. No point telling anyone else how foolhardy I'd been. "Right now I just want Elizabeth and Patty to know that they're safe."

"They got him?" Elizabeth had picked up an extension. "They got the bastard?"

"They got him."

"All *right*. I'll call Patty. Carnegie, when can we meet? I need to talk to you before the rehearsal."

"So the wedding is still on?"

"Absolutely. I'm going out right now to buy some shoes. These pumps just aren't breaking in right."

She didn't mention hiring another substitute bridesmaid, and I didn't raise the issue. So what if we had an extra groomsman? Aaron could still escort Corinne, and maybe after the ceremony I'd walk back up the aisle with Zack on one arm and Paul's brother Scott on the other.

Elizabeth and I set a time to meet the next morning, and then I called Corinne. She was nearly incoherent with relief, and handed the phone to someone else, who turned out to be Zack.

"So everything's OK now?" he said. "Awesome!"

"My sentiments exactly. You did bodyguard duty with Corinne, I take it. How is she holding up?"

He lowered his voice. "She was, like, awake all night being bummed out about Angela and everything."

"Well, tell her to call in sick and go back to bed."

"Sure." Zack sounded a bit deflated, now that his heroic mission was over. "Can I, like, help with anything else?"

"Just be at the rehearsal on time," I told him. "Front entrance to EMP, seven o'clock Friday evening."

"No, I mean before that." The petulant tone was back in his voice. "I want to *see* you."

"Zack, I'm going to be really busy for the next few days."

"Not every minute."

"Yes, just about every minute."

"But—"

"But nothing." It's hard not to scold when someone's acting like a child. "I appreciate all your help, I really do, but I can't see you till Friday night. Just get Corinne calmed down, OK? She's been through a lot."

After the calls I went to rejoin Aaron on the couch, but he was getting to his feet.

"Sorry, Stretch. If you want that ride, it has to be soon. I want to go home and shower before I check in at work."

"And explain why you came back early? I hope it's not a big problem."

"Nah, I was pretty much done."

I took a deep breath. "Aaron, Lily told me about the job offer in Portland."

"I knew it!" He surprised me by laughing. "I told her about it in confidence, but I had a bet with myself that it would get back to you. I'll have to give her hell about being such a blabbermouth."

"Never mind that." I was still holding my breath. "Are you going?"

For reply, he kissed me, not a small comforting kiss but a long, provocative one. Then he slapped me on the fanny. I would have sworn that only my father could slap me like that and live, but I was so off-balance from the kiss that I let it go.

"I told them I needed time to think about it," said Aaron. "A long time. Come on, let's go rescue Vanna."

As we drove, I spared a thought for Zack. I shouldn't have spoken to him that way, but preserving his manly dignity was becoming a bore.

And Aaron was becoming a mind reader. "Sounds like Robin Hood's getting to be a pain in the ass."

"What do you mean?"

"I couldn't help overhearing. You know, Stretch, you might want to keep your distance with Zack. He's been acting kind of strange since Mercedes died."

So would you if you thought you were the one who killed her. But of course I couldn't say that. "Surely it's not all that strange to enjoy my company?"

"That's not what I mean, and you know it. He just strikes me as being kind of a weird kid. And I think he might have lied about his background to get on at the *Sentinel*. I was talking to a friend of mine in Boston—"

"Boston? I thought he was from St. Louis."

"No, he told Paul he was with an on-line start-up in Cambridge, and he came out here after the company went belly-up. But my Boston buddy says he never heard of them."

Poor Zack, trying so hard for his fresh start. He must not even want to mention St. Louis.

"These little companies come and go all the time," I said. "Your friend can't know all of them. Why were you investigating Zack, anyway?"

"I wasn't investigating," he said sheepishly. "I just thought it was odd. Besides, Zack is starting to look familiar to me, like I've seen his picture somewhere."

A likely story, I thought. *You're jealous!* Zorro was jealous of Robin Hood. I was tempted to tease Aaron about it, but really, it was kind of sweet. So I changed the subject instead.

"There's a left turn coming up," I said. "Pete's is two blocks after that. I can't *wait* to get my van back."

Pete had Vanna parked right out front. The repaired fender was smooth and seamless, the copper-colored Made in Heaven logo gleaming in the mild winter sun. I could feel my cramped muscles relaxing just to look at her. No more soup cans! I gave Pete a hug and a hefty check, and climbed happily behind the wheel, sliding the driver's seat all the way back with a satisfied sigh.

"You look like a kid with a new toy," said Aaron, smiling at me through the open window.

"Now if I could just sleep for about sixteen hours, I'd feel like a kid. Thanks for the lift. And . . ."

"And what?" He paused in the act of pulling out a cigarette, and quirked one eyebrow.

"And thanks for galloping in to my defense. Really."

"You're welcome. Really."

Aaron leaned into the window for a kiss, and this time I gave as good as I got. Then he walked over to his VW—he looked good from the back, too—and drove off. His apartment building was on the shore of Lake Union, not far from my houseboat, and somehow I liked that sense of him being nearby.

As I put Vanna in gear, marveling at the absence of clanking noises, I decided that Bonnie Buckmeister's wedding wasn't the only thing I'd have to focus on after the EMP ceremony. My relationship with Aaron Gold was right up there at the top of the list. Maybe I wasn't quite so wounded after all.

Back at the office, Eddie had arrived—he kept his own hours—and was playing with his pet software, his white hair ruffled and an unlit cigar clamped in his teeth. When I came in he stood up and stretched, then squared his shoulders. Eddie has the best posture in the world.

"I saw the note you left me," he said over the hum and grunt of our bottom-of-the-line printer. "How's Vanna?"

"Good as new, if not better."

"And this fellow that killed the bridesmaids, he got arrested downstairs this morning?"

"Yep."

"Right after you start dating a cop. Funny coincidence."

"It is, isn't it?" I said airily.

But he wouldn't be put off. Folding his arms, he said, "Carnegie, you been up to something?"

"Not a thing! All that matters is that Foy is locked up, and Lamott/Wheeler is on schedule for Saturday. In fact, I have Elizabeth coming by tomorrow morning, so could you update her budget report?" Cunningly, I went for the sure-fire distraction. "I don't suppose you've got it in your new program yet..."

Eddie snorted, happily indignant. "'Course I have! And it's *our* program, sister. We're in the twenty-first century now. You better start learning this stuff yourself."

He went on grousing gently, while I settled in at my desk with a smile of contentment. You couldn't say all was right with the world, but it was a damn sight righter than it had been yesterday. I called Lily at the library to tell her so but got her voice mail, so I left her a cheery message, made myself a cup of stomach-settling instant soup at our little one-burner kitchen in the corner, and got down to work.

Ten minutes later, I gave up.

"Eddie, I'm half-asleep. I'm going to take Vanna to the supermarket, and then I'm going to shut off my phone and crash."

"Let me take a look at her before you go."

"Sure."

We stepped to the office door, but when I opened it there was a woman standing outside, evidently about to knock. An attractive woman: a youthful fifty, maybe fifty-five, small and slender with a tip-tilted nose, warm wide eyes the color of maple syrup, and chestnut hair that fell in loose waves against the shoulders of her stylish wool coat.

"Oh!" she said, in a soft, burbling voice. "You must be Carnegie Kincaid. And this is your partner, Mr. Breen. I looked you up on the Internet, you know! Now, is it Ed or Eddie? No, never mind, it doesn't matter, because I'm going to call you Edward. You have that kind of dignified air about you."

"Well..." said Eddie, who never bantered with women. Ever.

She was inside by this time, looking around delightedly. "What adorable wicker furniture! You know, Edward, I'm the kind of person who loves things or hates them, and I just love wicker. Wicker and chintz." She perched herself on the love seat and sparkled up at Eddie, who was still finding his voice. "I guess I'm just a country girl at heart."

"I'm so glad you like the office," I said, assuming an air of suave professionalism while I futilely racked my brain for a name, or at least a function. Vendor? Potential client? It wasn't like Eddie to forget an appointment, but the way things had been going lately, it was a lot like me.

"I'm afraid I don't recall—"

"How silly of me!" She laughed, one of those silvery-ripple laughs that some women have. "I thought you knew I was coming. I'm Monica Lamott."

O-ho, I thought. *So this is Monica, lover of Lars, betrayer of Burt. So much trouble in such a sweet little package.*

"Nice to meet you," I said, sitting down myself, though even then I topped her by a foot or so. "I wasn't expecting you until the rehearsal."

"Well..." Eddie muttered. "Well, I'll just take a look at that fender on the van."

Monica watched regretfully as he sidled out the door. She had a sweet tooth, I could see, not so much for men as for men's attention.

"You've been on the East Coast?..." I said delicately.

"With Lars. We hardly got out of bed for *days*." The mother of the bride shook back her hair and closed her eyes with a reminiscent sigh. So much for delicacy. Then she frowned a pretty little frown. "But all that changed when he made it to the semifinals. When Lars is this close to winning, he gets ridiculously single-minded, if you know what I mean. An absolute monk! He's afraid I'll break his serve."

I murmured my sympathy and offered her coffee, which she declined. Feeling my eyelids droop, I poured myself a hefty mugful. *Just a grocery run and an early bedtime, is that so much to ask?*

"—and there is only so much tennis a girl can watch," Monica burbled on, like a mountain stream that's going to make it to the ocean, no matter how long it takes. "So I just hopped on a plane! That's the kind of person I am. Impetuous. You never know what I'll do next. Besides, now that the wedding date is upon us, I knew that Liz would want my advice. I used to give fabulous parties, you know, when we lived in Santa Barbara. I was interviewed in the newspaper about my parties! But then Burt insisted on moving to Seattle, where we didn't know a soul."

Except Lars, I thought dryly. "That's so interesting, Monica. It's actually a little late to make changes now, but Elizabeth and I are meeting on Thursday, so maybe you could join us—"

A sharp, no-nonsense knock, and the door swung open to reveal the bride herself, with a furious glint in her own wide brown eyes.

"Mother! Paul said you called from your hotel. What are you bothering Carnegie for?"

Monica stiffened but maintained her smile. "Since you were out shopping, I just thought I'd stop by to introduce myself and share a few of my tips for successful parties. I told Paul that on the phone."

Elizabeth smiled back quickly and coldly, a fencer deflecting her opponent's blade. "And I told *you* last week that we have everything under control."

They held each other's gaze, the family resemblance quite

striking now, as their lips tightened and nostrils flared. When dogs get to this point in a conversation, the growls are low-pitched but the teeth start to show.

"Control is hardly the right approach to a festive affair." Monica sounded like one of my least-favorite bridal magazines. "Proper planning allows you to 'go with the flow' and—"

"Is that what you and Mr. Swedish Open have been having, a festive affair?"

Monica gasped, then shifted her stance like a pro.

"Lizzie, you know perfectly well that Lars is Norwegian," she said sadly, a faint tremble in her voice, then turned her syrupy eyes to me. "You'd think my own daughter would want to see me happy after all I've been through...."

"Your own daughter is not named *Lizzie*," said Elizabeth, with a flash of fangs.

Normally I'm willing to give my all for the pre-wedding peace process. But I'd had enough drama for one day, and decided to bail out before I got bit. "We can talk about the reception details Thursday—"

"Hi, Monica." Paul was in the doorway, looking like the soul of reason. "Hi, Carnegie. Took me a while to park. Did I miss anything?"

"Nothing to miss," I said decisively. "We were just confirming our meeting for Thursday. Elizabeth, I'll have all your paperwork ready then, and I'll look forward to hearing Monica's ideas...."

I was herding them all to the door when a cell phone chirred. The women dipped into their purses, but it was Paul's. He spoke a few words, listened intently, and broke into a huge, elated grin.

"It's Tommy!" he told us. "That was Roger, calling from

the hospital. Tommy's awake, and he must be doing OK because they're allowing visitors. Honey, let's go over there right now."

This last to Elizabeth, but she balked. "I've got a million things to do this afternoon. I'm still looking for shoes, and—"

"Lizzie hates hospitals," Monica confided to me in a perfectly audible whisper, getting in one last thrust. "She thinks sick people are weaklings. She doesn't mean to be unkind, but I always notice, because I'm the kind of person who notices things like that."

Elizabeth's face darkened dangerously, and I hastened to intervene.

"Paul, why don't I take you to Harborview? That way Elizabeth and Monica can go on...chatting." Relief was fizzing through me like champagne. "I'll be *so* glad to see Tommy."

Family feuds could wait, and so could groceries and sleep. This day was getting better and better.

Chapter Twenty-Eight

TOMMY LOOKED GHASTLY. THEY HAD SHAVED HIS BUSHY gray hair to stitch up various head wounds, and the face below the naked, knobby skull was slack and weary. But his leprechaun's eyes lit up at the sight of us, and when Paul embraced him gingerly, bending over the hospital bed, Tommy smacked him on the back with vigor.

"What a sight you are, Paulie!" he said. "And you brought my favorite redhead! Carnegie, dear, you look like a bride yourself."

He meant my armful of flowers. I had stopped at Nevsky Brothers on the way, where Boris commanded Irina to turn over what seemed like half her stock. What a summer's treasure to enjoy in November: sheaves of royal-blue irises, glossy tulips like huge crimson goblets, and an entire thicket of sweetheart roses in white and blush pink.

I held my armload aside while I kissed Tommy's forehead, then set them down on the vacant second bed and went out to beg some vases from the nurses' station. As I went, I could hear Paul explaining that Aaron and some other friends from the *Sentinel* would be coming by the next morning so as not to overwhelm him with too many people at once. Likewise, I planned to refrain from asking Tommy what he had or hadn't seen at the Aquarium. At least for a few minutes.

Of course, maybe the police had already questioned him. There was still a patrolman stationed outside Tommy's door, a gray-haired man who looked bored and cross. I nodded at him in passing, figuring that he'd be relieved of this dull duty soon enough. Down the hall, Roger Talbot emerged from the men's room.

"Carnegie!" In the cold fluorescent hospital light, I could see the strain and sorrow in Roger's dark eyes, but his clothes were pressed and his silver hair recently trimmed. He no longer had the haunted look of a man on the edge. "Is it true? They found the one who killed her?"

"Her," not "them." Of course, he barely knew Angela, the other victim. Just a quick introduction at the Aquarium to a nice-looking blonde who then disappeared, leaving hardly a memory.

"It's true, Roger. I don't know if he's been charged with murder yet, but he jumped bail for the purse-snatching, so he's not going anywhere."

His face twisted in a spasm of pain. "Purse-snatching! A petty criminal does something as stupid as purse-snatching, and Mercedes ends up . . . ends up . . ." His eyes filled, and he looked away, blinking hard.

"Hey," I said gently, "let's get some coffee and sit down for just a minute, OK? And then you can help me with Tommy's flowers."

We sat in the little lounge with our Styrofoam cups, and as usual, I thought about my father. But only for a moment. Over the years, the pain was fading to something softer and easier to bear. How long would that process take for Roger Talbot, who had to do his grieving in secret?

He sipped mechanically at his coffee, then set it down and sighed. "Tommy doesn't remember what he saw."

"How do you know he saw anything?"

"It's obvious. With the guard there, he's either a witness or a suspect. So I simply asked him. He remembers being at the party, but that's all. Then I had a word with his doctor."

"And?"

"His memory may return all at once, or in fragments over time, or not at all."

It's interesting what people will tell an influential man. I bet the doctor in question would have stonewalled someone like me. Well, now I wouldn't have to distress Tommy further by asking him myself.

"Maybe that's for the best," I said. "Now that the police have Foy in custody, they'll be able to check for DNA traces and all that. They won't need an eyewitness."

"*I* need one," said Roger fiercely. "I need to know how it happened."

"No, you don't," I insisted. "Whatever Tommy did or didn't witness, you need to remember Mercedes as *you* last saw her. She made such a beautiful gypsy!"

"She was always beautiful." He smiled bleakly, and I could see that the healing had begun, however long and slow it might be. I tried to nudge it along.

"Roger, are you coming to the wedding?"

"Of course!" His public persona roused itself. "People expect me there."

"I'm glad to hear it. Come on, let's get back to those flowers."

When we reentered the room, laden with vases, Paul was recounting a football game to his bedridden best man. They both seemed quietly satisfied by the humiliation of some team I didn't recognize, and by the victory of some other.

To say that I don't follow football is to vastly understate how mind-numbingly tedious I find it, so I busied myself with the flowers at the tiny sink in the corner of the room. Roger loaned me a slim gold penknife to trim the stems, and dutifully set the bouquets around the room at my direction.

"There you are, Tommy," I said when we were done. "You could practically hold a wedding in here. I'm sorry you can't be with us on Saturday."

"Who says I can't?" he demanded, looking up from his pillows with a rebellious gleam. "They tell me I might go home in a couple a' days, and if I can get dressed and go home, then I can surely put on a monkey suit and see that this character doesn't leave his girl at the altar."

Paul shook his head fondly. "You take it easy, Tommy. I'd love to have you there, but you do what the doctors tell you, all right?"

"Ah, you're just afraid I'll frighten the ladies with my new hairdo." Tommy gave a pat to the grizzled stubble atop his head. "I think I'll keep it this way. Aerodynamic."

We all laughed, and didn't notice at first that the door had opened on two more visitors: Corinne, her heavy makeup not quite masking the effects of a sleepless night, and Valerie Duncan, brisk and tailored with her dark hair tucked back behind large copper earrings. Beside me, I felt Roger shift uncomfortably. Valerie's eyes went flat and cold.

"I'd better be going," said Roger curtly. "Tommy, you take care."

"Oh, don't leave—" Corinne began, but the publisher pushed past them both and left the room. Tommy let him depart with a wave, happily distracted by the influx of "ladies." As they fussed over the patient, Paul drew me out into the hallway, out of earshot of the policeman. Roger, just ahead of us, strode down the hall to the elevator without looking back.

"We can't let Tommy come to the wedding," Paul said

urgently. His kindly young face was shocked and troubled. "He looks *horrible*."

"Well, he could hardly look good at this stage," I pointed out. "And who knows, maybe it would help his recovery to have something to look forward to. Let's leave it up to him and his doctors."

"But—"

"Look, if Tommy does come, I'll keep an eye on him, and make sure someone takes him home early. How's that?"

Paul nodded, not quite mollified. "He just looks so *old*, you know? Of course he's older than me, I know that, but I've never really thought about it. I guess I didn't want to."

"I understand. My partner Eddie is my mother's age, and I keep thinking they'll both be just the way they are forever. All you can do is be Tommy's friend, here and now."

He nodded again, and set his face in a cheerful expression that looked almost natural. "We should go back in with the others." Then, switching gears, "Corinne must be relieved to have that guy off the street."

"She's not the only one."

Corinne was sitting on the edge of Tommy's bed, flirting outrageously, while Valerie watched with an indulgent smile. Tommy was lapping it up, but I could see that his strength was flagging, and I was relieved when an amiable Filipina nurse looked in to tell us we really should leave soon. Aaron's opinion notwithstanding, I don't always want to take charge of things. I'd be ordering most of these people around soon enough.

I thought Corinne and Valerie had come to the hospital together, but it turned out they'd only met on the way in. Down at the lobby, Valerie said good night—which made me realize that it was indeed evening already, and that I had a post-hangover hunger for a nice bland meal. Corinne, riding the elevator down to the parking garage with me and Paul, took the words right out of my mouth.

"Y'all want to get something to eat?" Seeing Paul hesitate, she added, "But I suppose Elizabeth's waiting for you."

He gave a small, rueful laugh. "Her mother got in today. I think I'll let them entertain each other."

"Don't you like your mother-in-law?" Corinne teased him.

"Oh, she's fine. But she and Elizabeth really set each other off." He frowned, resisting an unwelcome thought. "I guess they're both pretty strong-willed. So's her father. I don't think he approves of us getting married."

Corinne seized his arm in that melodramatic way she had. "Don't worry about other people, Paul! If you truly love someone, that's *forever*. No one can stand in your way."

Paul, taken aback by these greeting-card sentiments, said, "Um, thanks. Carnegie, you up for dinner?"

I hesitated. I was so damn tired, but I knew there was nothing edible back at the houseboat. Starve a fever, feed a hangover, right?

"Sure, why not?"

"Great. There's a sushi place up the block."

"Well, maybe not sushi . . ."

We ended up having Chinese, which in my case meant lots of rice, a few pea pods, and careful sips of tea. I was off Pinot Noir for life. Corinne ate her own dinner and most of mine, chattering away about how nice it was to see Tommy. She had certainly rebounded quickly from her fear of Lester Foy.

"Now what was that policeman for?" she asked, popping one last sweet-and-sour shrimp between her lips. "I didn't say anything, in case Tommy was under arrest for drunk driving or something embarrassing like that. Are y'all going to eat your fortune cookies?"

"I've been wondering that myself," said Paul, and he didn't mean the cookies. "My guess is that Tommy saw something at the Aquarium, so he's a murder witness and they're protecting him. What do you think, Carnegie? You were there yourself that night. Afterwards, anyway."

Corinne gazed at me, her blue eyes round and spooked, a glistening dab of shrimp sauce on her chin. "That's right, you were. Did Tommy see that tattooed man, do you think? Or did you?"

"Well, I wasn't supposed to talk about it, but now that he's been arrested, I guess it doesn't matter." I was suddenly exhausted, and sick of the whole dreary business. "But this is off the record, Paul, OK?"

"Swear to God. So tell us, did Tommy see the killer?"

"I think so. Once his memory comes back—if it ever does—his testimony could nail down the case against Lester Foy. But I'm sure they'll charge Foy anyway. Someone must have spotted him at Angela's building."

"Even if they didn't," Paul said, "he showed up at your house-boat! Why would he do that if he wasn't stalking all of you?"

Why, indeed? It occurred to me, disconcertingly, that Foy could always claim that he only came to my house because of Juice's phone call. But no, Graham would find more evidence, now that he had his man. I'd done part of his job for him—with a little help from the Buckmeisters—and now he could do the rest.

"The important thing," I said to Corinne, as we parted ways in front of the restaurant, "is that Lester Foy is in jail, and we can all concentrate on the wedding. We're safe now."

"That's right," she replied, buttoning up her raincoat for the solitary walk back to her car. "We're safe now."

Chapter Twenty-Nine

THE FINAL DAYS BEFORE A MAJOR WEDDING HAVE A HEAD-long momentum that can be nerve-racking, but also a hell of a lot of fun, an adrenaline high. I started this particular final lap by going straight home from the Chinese restaurant, calling Lily for a cathartic conversation about my escape from Lester Foy, and then sleeping like a baby with a clear conscience until nine o'clock Wednesday morning. It felt wonderful.

On Wednesday, with the help of Eddie and his magic software, I threw myself into the final preparations for Lamott/Wheeler. As usual, we had a slew of little snags and surprises, but after the recent horrors, they seemed pleasantly mundane. The wedding announcements, for example. To be strictly proper, announcements should be postmarked on the wedding date itself. Elizabeth might be wearing an unorthodox gown, but she wanted propriety elsewhere, so I had lined up a calligrapher for the envelopes well ahead of time. Fran was a single mom who worked at home, using a spare bedroom as an office.

Unfortunately, Fran's oldest daughter chose this particular week to learn how to operate a doorknob. Result: A through L tipped over on the floor (mussed but salvageable), and M through Z smeared with peanut butter (a total loss). There was nothing else for it; I swallowed my pride and called Dorothy Fenner.

"The other calligraphers on my list are busy doing holiday invitations, but I was hoping you could—"

"Why, Carnegie, I'm always here to help you with your little problems," said Dorothy, graciously complacent. "I'll just make a few calls. I'm sure I can find someone who'll make a special effort for *me*."

I thanked her effusively, all the while thinking *Scottsdale, any day now she's moving to Scottsdale.* Then I pressed on with my telethon, calling to confirm with the photography studio, the videographer, the judge, the jazz trio for the ceremony and the sound man for the dancing, and the stylist who would do the bride's hair and touch up the bridesmaids' faces—including mine.

The knowledge that I'd soon be slinking around in a bridesmaid's gown added a certain personal frisson to my professional frenzy. So after Eddie left for the day, I squeezed in a call to Lily at the library, just to calm my own jitters.

"That pink satin's so clingy, it's not going to cover even one sin, let alone a multitude," I fretted to her. "What if my invisible bra comes unstuck?"

"Just reach down your cleavage and pull it out," she suggested. "You can throw it to the crowd when the bride tosses her bouquet. Start a whole new tradition!"

"*Lily.*"

"You'll be fine. Want me to come over Saturday and help you get dressed?"

"Would you really? You're my hero."

"That's what they all say. Listen, before I forget, you're still coming for Thanksgiving, aren't you?"

"I wouldn't miss it." I always spent Christmas in Boise

with my mother, and she always traveled to either my home or my brother's for Thanksgiving. This year she'd be at Tim's house in Illinois, so I could eat turkey with Lily and her boys.

"How are you and Aaron doing? I was wondering if he'd like to come, too."

That gave me pause. "It's nice of you to offer, but . . ."

"But what?"

"Well, it might seem kind of like bringing him home to meet the folks, or something." I leaned back in my chair and stared out the window. The silver expanse of Lake Union offered no guidance on the matter.

"The reason I ask," said Lily in a too-neutral voice, "is that I'll have a friend there myself."

"You mean a friend of the male persuasion? Lily, I didn't even know you were dating anyone! Who is he?"

"I don't want to talk about it yet," she said. "It might jinx things. Besides, he might not even make it that night. But think it over about Aaron, OK?"

I promised I would, then got back to work myself—nailing down minor assignments like tending Elizabeth's guest book, which Valerie Duncan had offered to do. I could have asked her to distribute the corsages and boutonnieres, too, once Boris delivered them, but I couldn't resist just a tiny bit of matchmaking: I assigned flower duty to Corinne. Maybe if Boris saw her all dolled up in pink, he'd have second thoughts? I only remembered the wife in St. Petersburg after I'd made the calls. *Oh, well.*

Some event services were already provided for; we'd use EMP employees to check coats, stash gifts, and bus tables in the restaurant and lounge. But because it was my first wedding at this venue, I tried to double- and even triple-check every little detail. Except for one detail—inviting Aaron for

Thanksgiving. I mulled that one over all Wednesday evening, coming to the firm, decisive conclusion that I'd wait until I saw him in person at the rehearsal, and then wing it from there.

On Thursday I started making the really dicey phone calls, not to any of the vendors but to the guests who had written in their children's names on their RSVP cards. This was an adults-only affair—a fact that certain doting parents had trouble understanding.

"But little Mason won't be any trouble," one mother told me.

"It's not a question of his behavior," I said easily, having rehearsed my script. "It's just part of our contract with the Experience Music Project. They're giving us special access to all the exhibits, and we've agreed to have no guests under eighteen."

Which was true enough, though the EMP would have been flexible on the issue if we'd pressed it. The strict decree had come from the bride, whose thoughtful rationale had included the phrase "no screaming brats underfoot." But Mason's mother didn't need to know that. She also didn't need to know that she and Mason's dad had barely missed the cut for the A-list. Two hundred guests would actually attend the ceremony in the EMP's small but sophisticated theater, and four hundred more would come an hour later for the reception.

And what a reception it would be. How often do you have 80,000 popular music artifacts to look at while you sip your champagne? Not to mention the Sound Lab, where you could seclude yourself in a soundproof booth and play guitar, bass, keyboard, or drums, all interactively wired to help you along. Or the Sky Church, the great hall of the EMP.

The Sky Church, I had read in the visitor's guide, was built in homage to Jimi Hendrix' vision of communion through music. It was dominated by the world's largest video set-up, forty feet high and seventy feet across, which could be fragmented into different projections or treated as one huge screen for concert footage and video art.

For the wedding, the sound man had orders to keep things hot, fast, and loud. He had awesome equipment to work with: a 24-channel sound system that created layers of amazing sound throughout the vast space, dozens of speakers hanging from the Sky Church ceiling like futuristic chandeliers, and four towers of spotlights, two rising up on either side of the screen and two more flanking his control balcony on the opposite wall. I had been on that balcony during one of my planning visits, and marveled at the dizzying drop to the dance floor and the complexity of the space-age consoles. This was going to be some dance party.

Although the planning for this extravaganza rivaled a space shuttle launch, one of my tasks was actually simpler than usual. Joe Solveto's delectable food would be served buffet-style, and the seating would be casual, with suit-yourself clusters of tables in the restaurant and lounge areas, and scattered throughout the exhibits as well. So I had no place cards to design and no seating charts to develop, except for the head table. Which, inevitably, turned out to be the stickiest wicket of all.

The fuss started late Thursday afternoon, barely forty-eight hours before the big moment, when my meeting with the bride turned into tea with Great-Aunt Enid. Elizabeth was putting up all the out-of-town guests at the Alexis, a bijou luxury hotel near Pioneer Square that was swankier than anywhere I'd ever stayed in my life. The formidable Enid was presiding over a tea table in her suite, with Paul, Elizabeth, and a nurse in dutiful attendance.

Monica, in fawn-colored cashmere that set off her chestnut hair, sat stiffly on a needlepoint chair looking like she wanted a cup of something stronger. Burt wasn't there; he and his errant wife were doing a Clark Kent and Superman act, never to be seen together.

"So you're the big-deal wedding expert." Enid was as short and tough as a tree stump, with a wide flat face rayed with wrinkles and square bony hands that trembled badly. Nothing trembling about her gaze, though. She surveyed me like a horse trader assessing a decidedly sub par nag. "In my day, a girl had her mother to help her get married, not some expert. I bet you charge a fortune."

"But Monica *is* helping me, Aunt Enid," said Elizabeth. She and her mother had apparently called a truce in the face of this larger threat. "It's just such a big wedding that we need Carnegie to handle some of the details."

Enid made a rude noise. "What kind of a name is Carnegie, anyway? And who has hair that color?"

"Well, I do," I said, sitting down and smiling. After all the diplomacy entailed by my job, there was something appealing about Enid's rough candor. "My dad was a redhead, and I can promise you that *he* didn't dye his hair."

The old lady nodded, satisfied. Or maybe she was just tired. After a few minutes' chat, she turned to the nurse, a sturdy Jamaican woman with a good-humored manner.

"Time for a little lie-down, don't you think, Irene?"

"Just a little one," Irene agreed, and helped her shuffle slowly into the bedroom.

We rose to leave, but Monica beckoned us across the hallway to her own suite, whose luxurious furnishings she had nearly obliterated with scattered clothing and fashion magazines. There were no chairs clear, but Monica had a stand-up conversation in mind.

"Lizzie," she said, "I went through those notes you gave me, and I've changed my mind."

"But you already agreed!"

"I just can't do it. I cannot sit next to that man."

Was it my imagination, or was that smoke rising from Elizabeth's ears? "'That man' is still your husband. And if you call me Lizzie one more time I'll—"

"Elizabeth, honey," said Paul, while he telegraphed me a look that said *Mayday*. "I'm sure we can figure this out—"

"There's nothing to figure," said Monica crisply. "Put him at one end of the table and me at the other."

"That would look ridiculous!" Smoke, and possibly flame. "If you think you're going to make a big dramatic statement at my wedding—"

"Isn't this wedding dramatic enough?" flared Monica. "You could feed a third-world nation with what you're spending."

"At least I'm spending my own money," said her daughter, "which is more than you've ever—"

"You know," I said loudly, "I think it's time for Plan B."

The three of them looked at me blankly.

"What Plan B?" demanded Elizabeth.

"The table for two, of course." I smiled my very best back-me-up-here smile at the groom. "You remember, Paul, we talked about this?"

"Y-yeah," he said. "I guess I do."

"Of course you do. It's a European tradition, Monica, that's becoming quite popular at sophisticated weddings back East. The bride and groom have a flower-decked table for two, very romantic, and the guests stop by their table to wish them well. Much less stuffy than a reception line."

"But then where would I sit?" asked Monica, intrigued but not won over.

"Well," I said, "maybe you could do me a favor. Let's talk about it over a drink in the lobby, shall we? Paul, it was lovely to meet Enid. I'll call you two tomorrow, all right?"

Once Monica and I were alone with a couple of gin-and-tonics, I gave her my pitch.

"Paul's publisher is a man named Roger Talbot—"

"Oh, I met him!" she said. "When Paul showed me around at the *Sentinel*. He's very attractive."

"Isn't he? And very prominent here in Seattle. The next mayor, everyone says. Well, he recently lost his wife, and I know he's going to feel all at sea at the wedding. Could I possibly prevail on you to have dinner with him, keep him company a little?"

Monica glowed at the prospect, as I hoped she would. "I'd be glad to. Poor man..."

Now I just had to ask Roger to do me a favor and tend to Monica, and we'd be all set. I drove home feeling highly self-satisfied, and pleasantly hungry for a real dinner, a meal beyond pea pods. But when I entered the office and picked up the ringing telephone, my appetite vanished.

"Carnegie, it's Corinne," she said in a quavering voice. "I'm in terrible trouble!"

Chapter Thirty

As I stood there, alone on my darkened houseboat, fear rippled over my skin like wind on water. *Foy got away, he tracked her down...*

"Corinne, where are you? Is Lester Foy there?"

"Oh my God!" she gasped. "He escaped! Oh my God—"

"Calm down and tell me where you are so I can call the police." I fumbled for my wallet, where I'd tucked Lieutenant Graham's card. Calling his direct line might bring help faster than 911.

Corinne said, "I'm at home—"

"Are you alone? Are the doors locked?"

"Yes, everything's locked, but—"

"Where did you see him?"

"See him?" she parroted.

"Lester Foy! Where was he when you saw him?"

"But I didn't see him."

I sat in my desk chair and took a deep breath. "Then how do you know he escaped?"

"You just said so! You said he was coming here—"

"No," I said wearily. "No, no, no. Do over. As far as I know, Foy's still in jail."

"Thank goodness! I thought you meant—"

"Yes, I understand what you thought. Now, what's your terrible trouble?"

"It's my dress," she said defensively, as if this critical topic had been outshone by the mere threat of murder. "It's too tight. I tried to let out the side seams but one of them tore and now it looks *awful*. What am I going to do?"

I could think of several things for Corinne to do, none of them polite, so I moved on to practicalities. "I'll call Stephanie Stevens at home, and arrange for a quick repair. But I don't think there's much fabric in those seams to let out. Can you get the zipper closed even partway?"

"Oh, the zipper closes all right, but my tummy pooches out and the dress hangs funny."

Quelle surprise. You've only been eating like a horse for weeks.

"Well, Stephanie can stitch up the tear," I said, as if speaking to a child. A dim child. "Beyond that, you'll just have to suck in your stomach and hope for the best."

"But, Carnegie!" Corinne wailed. "I have to look my very, very best on Saturday. It's important!"

Of course, I realized ruefully, *she wants to dazzle Boris. A matchmaker should be more sympathetic.*

"You'll look fine," I soothed. "Honestly, that shade of pink is just gorgeous with your hair and complexion."

"You really think so?"

"Absolutely. And the neckline is perfect for your . . . for you. You'll be irresistible. Try not to worry about it, OK? Just drop off the gown at Stephanie's tomorrow morning, and I'll see you tomorrow night at the rehearsal. Everything will be fine."

As it turned out, the rehearsal could not have been farther from fine.

I assembled my motley crew at EMP's main entrance and

led them down to the private theater, with its state-of-the-art seating and display screens. A rather severe background for a wedding, but Elizabeth had vetoed having the ceremony out in the Sky Church, on the grounds that it would be a nuisance to clear the chairs afterwards for dancing. I suspected her real reason, though: in a huge space like the Sky Church, with its 85-foot ceiling, a mere bride would be barely noticeable. In the small, plain theater, her appearance would be electrifying.

The rehearsal could have used some electricity, or at least a smile or two. I had rarely seen a more disgruntled wedding party. For starters, the bride and groom weren't speaking to each other. Elizabeth wore that smoke-and-flame expression I had seen at the Alexis, and Paul was maintaining a dogged silence quite unlike his usual affability. Evidently the path of true love had developed a pothole that afternoon, but no one was saying why.

I considered playing therapist, then let it go in favor of my role as stage manager. Which was tough enough, given my cast of characters.

"It's not very *pretty*, is it?" mused Monica, gazing critically around. "Not like a church."

"When's the last time you were in a church?" Burt inquired sardonically. "You some kind of Swedish Lutheran now?"

"He's Norwegian," she pronounced, as if Burt were hard of hearing. "And I'm just saying that it's not a very decorative place. I'm the kind of person who—"

"I think we know what kind of person you are," snapped Burt, and everyone in the room stiffened, like dogs hearing distant thunder.

"We'll have some fabulous flower arrangements, Monica,"

I said, cheerfully deaf. "And softer lighting, and the music. Now, if you could all just take a seat, we'll get started in a moment...."

Monica subsided—at a pointed distance from her husband—and her daughter Patty, red-eyed and pale, sat next to her. Not that Monica seemed to care. *Patty must be working night shifts,* I thought. *Nurses lead a dog's life sometimes. And so do least-favorite daughters.* The maid of honor wore white slacks and clunky white walking shoes, along with a shapeless rain parka that she kept clutched around her, as if to emphasize the fact that she'd rather be elsewhere.

That was the bride's family; the groom's kin was hardly in better shape. Paul's brother Scott, the third groomsman, was a slight, balding fellow who seemed to be surgically attached to his cell phone. He had barely arrived from Baltimore, jet-lagged and cranky, and his mind was still back in his office three thousand miles away. Howard and Chloe, the groom's parents, had returned early from Hawaii with the most spectacular sunburns I'd ever seen. Their faces were puffed and scarlet, the skin stretched tight and shiny over the affronted flesh. It hurt just to look at them.

Chloe merely sat and winced, but Howard had bought himself a digital camera for the trip, and was conquering his pain by annoying his wife and everyone else in a relentless pursuit of close-up candids.

"Big smile," he kept saying, as he zoomed in on one victim after another. "Come on now, big smile!"

I wondered if the lobsteresque in-laws were the source of Elizabeth's pique. In the heady rush of getting everything they desire for their special day, some brides lose touch altogether with the real world, and expect their wedding photos to look like movie stills. But you can't get friends and relations from Central Casting. At Elizabeth's orders, the two mothers had bought dresses in harmonious shades of coral—which would now clash with Chloe's peeling countenance.

Well, the bride would have to get over it. At least Howard and Chloe had showed up, unlike Aaron, who was inexplicably late. Zack told me that "something, like, happened to him at the newsroom," which would have sounded ominous except that he smirked when he said it. Zack was the only person present who seemed to be in a good mood, smiling at nothing and almost bouncing in his seat with youthful energy.

Corinne, meanwhile, sat eating celery sticks from a plastic bag, looking ravenous and despairing. I'd seen brides try to lose weight at the eleventh hour, but never a bridesmaid. I felt for her, but the crunching was getting on my nerves. The three musicians, a hotshot local sax player and two cronies on bass and clarinet, stood in one corner exchanging sardonic remarks and looking bored. Or maybe that's how jazz players are supposed to look. Their music certainly bores me.

The ceremony was to be simple enough: jazz stylings for the prelude, processional and recessional, readings by both bride and groom, and brief remarks before the vows from an eminent judge too busy to join us tonight. Much as I disliked the music for this wedding, I loved the readings, which were just as quirky and personal as such things should be.

Paul was going to recite a Yeats poem, *Had I the Heavens' Embroidered Cloths,* and Elizabeth would reply with the lyrics to a charming song from the 1940s, "Come Rain or Come Shine." Monica thought it was all very odd, which pleased Elizabeth no end.

"How nice to see all of you," I said brightly, deciding to

press on without Aaron. "This will be an informal run-through, and then you can all go out and enjoy the museum." *Or jump off the Space Needle, for all I care.*

As the music started, I had Zack and Scott practice escorting Chloe and Monica to their seats, and then lining up at the front of the room with Paul. Corinne came down the aisle, stiff and self-conscious, with me following, and with everyone in the room trying not to think about Mercedes and Angela. Tommy Barry made a happier thought; he was home from the hospital, in his daughter's care, and might actually make it for the ceremony.

"All right, Patty," I called to the sisters, now waiting at the theater's doorway. "You'll be next. Listen for your cue from the trio.... OK, nice and slow... now Burt, you take Elizabeth's arm..."

We made it through the processional, and Paul delivered his poem in a rushed, impersonal voice; the last line—"Tread softly, for you tread on my dreams"—was certainly ironic, given Elizabeth's demeanor tonight. After he finished, there was a long pause, as she stood facing him but not meeting his eye, her lips tight, too irritated to speak words of love.

"Elizabeth?" I prompted.

"I've rehearsed it already," she snapped. "I'll be fine."

I couldn't stand it anymore. "Elizabeth, if there's something you're not happy about concerning the ceremony, please say so now—"

"Hi, guys! Sorry I'm late."

We all looked back, startled, toward the doorway. Aaron's sudden entrance set off a barrage of reactions: Paul and Zack erupted in laughter, the fathers grinned, the mothers gasped, and the bride boiled over.

"How am I supposed to be happy with *that*?" she wailed.

She was referring to Aaron's face, and she had a point. Aaron was sporting a black eye of spectacular magnitude, swollen almost shut and positively pulsating in shades of deep purple and olive green.

"What happened?" Chloe and I asked simultaneously, but by now Aaron was chortling as well and couldn't answer. Howard and Burt joined in the hilarity, and even the musicians looked entertained.

"They were playing football in the *office*," said the bride venomously, over the men's howls of laughter. "Like a bunch of children."

"Honey," Paul managed to get out, "be a sport, would you? It's no big deal—"

"It is to *me*! You've ruined everything!"

And with this histrionic pronouncement, Elizabeth stalked up the aisle, past Aaron, and out of the building, leaving an uncomfortable silence in her wake. Everyone looked at me uncertainly.

"Well..." I said. *Why is it again that I love weddings?* "Well, I think we're done for this evening. Good night, everyone." Then, as the room emptied, "Aaron, can I talk to you for a minute?"

He came down the aisle, looking a bit guilty, and then a bit irked as he tried to kiss me and I turned my face away. "Hey, is it my fault if I fumbled a pass?"

"Shut up and listen," I told him. "There's going to be a stylist here tomorrow, an hour before the ceremony. I'll tell her to bring stage makeup for you, so for God's sake, be on time."

"Oh, no," he said. "I'm not wearing makeup just so some self-centered bride can—"

"Self-centered! You think *she's* self-centered? Tomorrow is one of the most important, most public moments of

Elizabeth's life and everyone will be looking at *you*. She'll have photographs she'll want to show her grandchildren, and all they'll want to know is the story behind your goddamn eye. Grow up, Aaron."

"Grow up? You of all people—"

"What about me of all people?" I'd been restraining myself all evening. If he wanted to fight, I was more than ready. "What's that supposed to mean?"

Aaron looked away, and I could see the muscles in his jaw go taut. Then he turned a cold gaze back to me. "Forget it. It's not worth the trouble."

And he walked out, leaving me to stew in my own complicated juices. *Forget his objection to makeup? Or forget about him and me?* I jammed my clipboard into my tote bag and pulled on my coat, muttering savagely under my breath all the while.

"How did it go?" Rhonda Coates, the EMP's chic and ultra-efficient coordinator for private events, poked her head in from a side door. "Anything I can do to help?"

Only if you've got a magic wand to wave, I thought. "We're all set, Rhonda, thanks."

"Are you going to stay tonight and cruise the galleries? There's a new exhibit on honky-tonk artists—"

"Wish I could," I fibbed, "but I've got more paperwork to do tonight. You know how it is."

"All too well," she said. "Break a leg tomorrow."

"That or somebody's neck."

She grinned and said good night. I walked up the aisle to the theater exit, and gave a silent groan when I opened the door: Zack was waiting for me right outside, slouching against the wall with his arms folded and his brow furrowed. He perked up visibly when he saw me—a warning sign right there if I hadn't been too preoccupied to notice. "Are you all done now? We could have dinner in the café here."

"Oh, I've already eaten. But thanks, Zack."

"Where should we go, then?" He fell in step beside me as I cut through the EMP gift shop, crowded with visitors, on my way to the Fifth Avenue exit and Vanna.

"Go?" I said absently. "I'm going back to my office."

Our way forward was blocked by a couple of teenagers, oblivious in their headphones at a demo kiosk for CDs. We were surrounded by shelves of souvenirs, coffee-table books, T-shirts and leather jackets, all celebrating rock and roll in one way or another.

As I edged my way around the teenagers, Zack stopped me with a hand on my arm. "You said on the phone that you'd, like, see me tonight. We have a date."

He looked so hopeful, and vulnerable, that I bit back an irritated reply and said patiently, "When I said that, I meant I'd see you at the rehearsal, that's all. I thought we agreed that we're just friends."

He frowned stubbornly. "I wanted to talk to you about that."

Oh, lord. "Zack, I've got a screaming headache, and a million things to do before tomorrow evening. Let's talk some other time, OK?"

He began to protest, but I turned my back and fled. I'd filled my quota of ill-tempered individuals for the day, and something told me that the Lamott/Wheeler wedding was going to set a new record.

Chapter Thirty-One

WHAT'S A WEDDING MORNING WITHOUT ONE LAST DISASTER?
Friday night, after a grueling round-robin of tactful phone calls, I persuaded Paul to apologize to Elizabeth on Aaron's behalf—Aaron himself being incommunicado—and then got Elizabeth to accept the apology and simmer down. By Saturday morning I was checking off details and hitting on all cylinders—food, flowers, liquor, limos, table linens, glassware, music, parking, coat check, gift table, *everything*, even Corinne's dress—when I got a call from Todd, the cake baker, at his studio on Queen Anne Hill. The ordinarily terse Scotsman was overflowing with apologies, anxiety, and bad news.

"I never screw up, Carnegie, you know that. I keep my truck tuned like a bloody piano. I've got Triple A here, but they can't start it either, and once they tow it to a garage there's no telling when I'll get it back. I've been calling round to borrow a vehicle but—"

"No need," I told him. "I'll come over there myself. Vanna should be just big enough."

"Who's Vanna?"

"Sorry, I mean my van. If you can help me secure the cake in the back?"

"Aye, I've got all sorts of padding and tie-downs, we'll make it work. You're a bloody angel, Carnegie." As he said it,

I could picture the relieved smile on Todd's long, freckly face. "This is the grandest piece I've ever done, and I want those on-site photos."

"You'll get them," I promised. "Will you ride down to the EMP with me?"

"I'd rather follow you in my car so I can go tend to my truck afterwards."

"Fine. I'll be there in half an hour." I put down the phone and turned to Eddie, who was knee-deep in printouts and happily gnawing an unlit cigar. "Looks like I'm on cake patrol. I might as well stay at the EMP once I'm there, and just run back home later to suit up."

"I meant to mention," said my partner, his voice oddly casual. "I'd, ah, kinda like to see you in that gown."

"Why, you sentimental son of a gun! Sure, I'll model for you. We'll get a picture of the two of us and send it to Mom." Eddie was still one of my mother's oldest and dearest friends. "Lily's coming by at five to help me dress, you can come down then."

Eddie turned suddenly brusque and bashful. " 'Course I might not be in the office that late. Probably will, though. Say, you better keep that cake dry, sister. It's raining again."

It was indeed, a slanting ice-water rain that popped off the wooden surface of the outside steps as I descended them. I wished, for the millionth time, that my houseboat had interior stairs between my home and office, although I knew full well that a stairwell would eat up half the floor space of both. I darted into my kitchen, grabbed my old goose-down parka with the more-or-less waterproof shell, and then rushed out again. Straight into Zack Hartmann.

"Hey, what are you doing here?" I said. "Oops, sorry—"

Zack bore a cellophane-wrapped bundle that slipped to

the ground in our collision. He retrieved it while I unfurled my umbrella, and handed it to me: a sorry-looking supermarket bouquet of desiccated carnations and skeletal mums. The poor things would have done better out in the rain.

"It's to, like, apologize for last night," said a blushing Robin Hood. "I think I made you mad."

"Oh, Zack, I wasn't mad! I was just frustrated by all that fussing around at the rehearsal. These are very nice, thank you. I'll put them in water, and then I've got to run."

"I thought we could talk...?" he began.

"We will talk, but not right now. I've got to get up to Queen Anne and fetch Elizabeth's cake."

He brightened. "I'll come and help you."

"No, that's not—Actually, yes, I could use an extra pair of hands, to sit in back and keep the cake steady. Better yet, you can drive while I ride shotgun. I've still got phone calls to make."

"Cool! Good thing I came over, huh?"

You'd have thought it was me doing Zack the favor. I felt a brief pang at taking advantage of his infatuation, but on a wedding day I'll dragoon anybody to do anything, just to get the job done.

I stayed busy on my cell phone the whole way up to Todd's, raising my voice above the thrumming of the rain on Vanna's roof. Zack drove in silent concentration, apparently determined to be the world's best assistant cake picker-upper. But both of us broke into awed exclamations when Todd wheeled out the low cart bearing his tour de force.

And it was awesome. The confectionary Space Needle was a good two feet tall, and the cake itself covered an area almost three by four. I'd know the Needle if it was carved in Spam, but I was amazed at how instantly recognizable the

EMP was, with undulations of rolled fondant re-creating the glistening swerves and curves of the building in silver, gold, red, and bright blue. The final flourish, a marzipan monorail on chocolate tracks, was so cute you could eat it up. So to speak.

"Todd, this is extraordinary," I told him. "I've never seen anything like it."

"Well," he said, taking a stab at modesty, "it's a fairly interesting building to start with. Now, young man, if you'll get that side of the board..."

The cake rested on a thick sheet of plywood covered with silver plastifoil, and boxed around the sides with heavy cardboard. No top on the box, though, not with the Space Needle rising high. But Todd's little loading bay was covered from the rain, and we all stayed dry, including our irreplaceable cargo, while he fussed over the loading like a hen with one chick.

It took all three of us to lift the thing—I wondered how many thousands of calories we were hefting—and quite a while to secure it in the back of the van. Then I belted myself into the backward-facing seat, where I could hold the plywood steady if we hit any bumps.

"It'll do," said Todd. "I'll meet you down there, Carnegie. Young man, you drive slower than you've ever driven in your life."

Zack pulled smoothly away from the studio, while I braced myself in my seat and watched the cake. The Space Needle vibrated ever so slightly, but otherwise all went well, until I realized that Zack was heading down the fearsome slope of Queen Anne Avenue. It's a twenty-degree grade that was once called The Counterbalance, because trolley cars had to be counter-weighted by a subterranean railcar full of concrete just to descend it safely, or to climb it in the first place.

As we angled downward, the plywood platform began to shift forward towards me. And were the upper curves of the EMP bulging out as well?

"Zack, I should have told you to take a different route." I craned around to look at him, hunched over the dashboard with his knuckles white on the wheel. "You can still turn off, just take any side street. And for heaven's sakes, buckle your seat belt. You could get a ticket."

"I don't think I better turn when it's this steep," he said. "Not too much farther..."

At least he was heeding Todd's warning and creeping along slowly, much to the displeasure of the drivers behind us. So far, so good. My cell phone chirped, and I fumbled it out of my bag without taking my eyes from the precious payload.

"Hey, Stretch, it's me. Eddie gave me your number."

"Nice of you to call," I said acidly. "I was trying to reach you all evening. Are you going to let the stylist paint over that eye, or not? We've got one groomsman too many right now, and I promised Elizabeth—"

"OK, OK!" he said. "I'll get painted. You're going to need me in the line-up."

"What do you mean?"

"You're about to lose your not-very-secret admirer, Babyface Hartmann," he said gleefully. "Guess how old he is?"

"Aaron, this isn't a good—"

"He's twenty-nine! And he's got a prison record in Massachusetts, for date rape no less. I *knew* I'd seen his picture somewhere. Paul brought his folks through the newsroom this morning, and old Howard let me download his digital snapshots from the rehearsal. I e-mailed the close-up of Zack to the Boston police, and I just heard back. His name's not Zack, by the way. It's Tyrone."

I felt dazed. "Tyrone?"

The instant I said the name aloud, I knew I'd made a horrible mistake. Zack straightened convulsively and whipped his head around to stare at me. I stared back, seeing a strange light in his shadowy blue eyes that brought back the roar of Snoqualmie Falls and the look in those same eyes when he said, "I killed Mercedes."

In the distance, a siren sounded. I began to hyperventilate.

"Yeah," Aaron's voice chattered on, distantly. "And Tyrone Peters broke his parole when he came out here. The SPD's going to pick him up today, so you'll have to do without him at your shindig tonight—"

"Aaron," I shouted, as Zack turned his back to me and hit the gas. "Aaron, Zack is with me!"

That was all I got out, because Vanna went barreling down the grade and pancaked at a levelled intersection. The force of the impact flung the phone from my hand and set Todd's beautiful Space Needle rocking on its foundation. Instinctively, I lunged forward to try and steady it, but the lunge turned into a lurch and my outstretched fingers administered the coup de grace. The Needle toppled backward, still in one exquisite piece. Then it made contact with the edge of the box and smashed itself into a sweet, sad wreckage.

"Goddammit, Zack!" For just that moment, I was more worried about the cake than my own well-being. "Look what you—"

But Zack gunned Vanna's engine and we raced downhill

once more. Now I had time to get good and scared. All around me, horns blared and brakes squealed, and the shops and restaurants of lower Queen Anne went whipping past the side windows behind dense silver curtains of rain. That first siren hadn't been pursuing us, of course, but soon a second one began to wail, and then a third, as Zack tore through one red light after another in his panicky flight.

"You're going to kill us!"

Bouncing and jolting, my head snapping back and forth like a doll's, I pulled my shoulder belt even tighter and watched in horrified fascination as the inevitable catastrophe unfolded. Todd's magnificent cake trembled, shifted, and heaved itself out of its box like some clumsy, primitive beast.

As the leading wall of the cake smacked against the rear door of the van, deep crevasses opened into its layered innards, panels of fondant shattered into whirling fragments of red and silver, and the little monorail flipped into the air like the victim of some Candyland earthquake.

Suddenly a whirling blue light strobed across the devastation, and I twisted around to look through the windshield. There was a police car dead ahead, lying in wait for us with its siren snarling. Zack hauled at the steering wheel to throw us into a skidding turn, left and then right.

The EMP cake—unrecognizable now—disintegrated further as it smashed from one side to the other, bombarding the interior of the van, and me, with flying gobs of mousse and buttercream and tumbling chunks of bitter chocolate cake.

I scraped sweet goo from my eyes and looked again. We were racing down First Avenue. The sirens had cleared the traffic lanes, so Zack had a clear shot, and he was pushing Vanna to her limits and beyond.

"Zack, please, this is crazy—"

"Shut UP!" he yelled, his voice breaking. "Shut up, shut up, shut up!"

Then his voice was lost in the scream of our tires. A glaring barrier of headlights and police lights lay straight across our path, setting the rain on fire. The lights tilted and swung away as Zack stood on the brakes and hauled at the wheel, sending us spinning and lurching across the road with our side door flapping open like a bird's broken wing.

Vanna went careening across the plaza of the Seattle Art Museum—for that's where we were—spilling her luscious contents as she went, and smacked abruptly against tall, unyielding steel. I screamed, but only in alarm; strapped in tight, I was badly shaken but intact. Zack, however, was thrown from the driver's seat and ended up on the ground several yards away, unconscious and bleeding. And Hammering Man ended up with pulverized fondant and rain-streaked French buttercream all over his shoes.

Chapter Thirty-Two

LUCKILY FOR MY DEBUT AS A BRIDESMAID, I WASN'T TOO badly bruised, having been cushioned by goose down and buttercream, and securely belted down.

In one of the three ambulances that came wailing up to SAM, I was poked, prodded, and pronounced to be remarkably undamaged, though a visit to my doctor was strongly advised. The police on the scene were inclined to detain me, until Lieutenant Graham appeared to assess the situation.

"You sure you're all right?" he asked, smiling ever so slightly at the frosting in my hair. The rain had stopped, at least for the moment, and we were sitting in his car while a maelstrom of emergency vehicles and news cameras swirled around us.

"I'm fine. What's going to happen to him?" Zack—I couldn't think of him as Tyrone—was departing the scene in serious but not critical condition, with a police escort for his ambulance.

Graham shrugged. "As soon as he's fit to travel, we'll ship him back to the Commonwealth of Massachusetts."

"What about the murders here?"

"Oh, he'll be charged, once we put a case together. But Boston wants him first. Got to follow procedure." He hesitated. "If we'd known about his background, we might have kept him away from Angela Sims. And from you."

"But that's not your fault." *It's mine. If only I'd gone straight to you after he confessed at Snoqualmie Falls . . .*

"I know it's not," said Graham, and sighed wearily. "With so many people at the Aquarium, and then Montoya's drug connection, we had too many backgrounds to check and not enough time. Peters is a pathological liar, and a damn good one. Excuse my French. He could be Ted Bundy all over again."

"Oh, surely not!"

"That's what everyone said about Bundy."

I shuddered, and once I started I couldn't stop.

"Let's get you home," said Graham. "I'll call you tomorrow about taking a full statement."

The first thing I did when he dropped me off was to totter into my bedroom, unstick myself from my high-calorie clothes, and remove the slinky pink gown from its garment bag. Yes, it would cover the nastiest bruises, and for the rest, I'd just unfold the pink chiffon stole to its full width and wrap myself in it, as mummylike as possible. I was damned if I'd let this wedding party lose one more member. Not so much for Elizabeth's sake—I had to admit, I'd be glad to be rid of her—but for Paul's, and for my own professional pride. The show, after all, must go on.

Which was why I was trying so hard not to think about Zack right now. I had to pull off this wedding first. But the questions kept surfacing. Was the black cloak I'd been hunting for merely a dark green one? Was my brave-hearted Robin Hood truly a cold-blooded killer? Date rape, Aaron had said. Could Mercedes' death have been a simple flirtation that turned deadly? Hard to imagine . . . horrible to imagine . . .

"Stop right there," I said aloud to my reflection in the bathroom mirror. "It's Scarlett O'Hara time. I'll think about that tomorrow."

Tomorrow was also the time to think about poor Vanna White, with her new fender all accordioned and her new engine traumatized. Graham had arranged to have her towed to Pete's, and beyond that, I'd have to worry about insurance and temporary transport and maybe even a car loan. *But not now, not now.*

For now, I washed that mocha mousse right out of my hair and pulled on some nice soft sweats. Then I pulled myself up to the office, clutching the stairway railing and groaning as I went. Scarlett was going to be slow off the mark for a while.

"What the hell happened to you?" Eddie had the phone in his hand, but clapped it down at the sight of me. "I told Aaron you were getting the cake, and then he called back and asked me where Todd's place was, and that's the last I heard. Except from Todd, and he's practically hysterical, says you went speeding off in the van. I've been calling your cell phone every two minutes!"

Then he looked more closely as I levered myself into my desk chair. "Jesus H. Christ, Carnegie, you look like something the cat dragged in."

"You should have seen the other guy. Listen, Eddie, it's a long story, but the punch line is that we need a new wedding cake for the EMP tonight."

I filled him in, as economically as I could, and headed off his exclamations of anger at Zack and dismay over Vanna by asking him to call Aaron.

"Just tell him I'm OK, and I'll talk to him later. I have to get on this cake thing right away."

I began by breaking the bad news to Todd. That went better than expected: after a single gargling groan, the Scotsman had the grace to pretend that my personal survival was some consolation for his ruined masterpiece, and rang off to do his grieving in private.

Then I started calling bakers. We needed something that would look good and taste decent and be ready in one afternoon. How hard could it be?

Hard. I made call after call, but many of my usual cake purveyors were closed, and the others reminded me huffily that they booked months in advance and could hardly fit in another project at such short notice. It was understandable, but disheartening. Joe Solveto was out on another job, and he didn't do baked goods anyway, though he could probably come up with some truffles and chocolate-dipped fruit for the buffet.

But a wedding cake isn't just dessert, it's an icon of the celebration, with centuries of tradition behind it, and plenty of modern hype as well. It just had to be there. I was mulling the possibility of a frosted cardboard box when Juice Nugent called. I hadn't tried her because she didn't work Saturdays, and I figured she couldn't commandeer the ovens at By Bread Alone except by prior arrangement.

"Hey, Kincaid, I've got some questions about the Buckmeister deal."

"They'll have to wait, Juice. I've got an emergency here. Do you know any other bakers who could take a quick job, as in right this minute?"

"I'm not sure. What's up?"

Quickly, I explained the sad demise of Todd's masterwork. "I need a substitute, just something big and pretty. It's too late to play out the rock-and-roll theme—"

"Maybe not," she said thoughtfully. "Thin layers would bake and cool pretty fast. . . . I'll call you back in ten."

The door swung open as I set down the phone. It was
Aaron, his hair wet with rain and his black eye only slightly
less ghastly for a night's rest. Before I could stop him, he
rushed across the good room to the office and embraced me
fervently.

"Oh, God, Carnegie, I was afraid—"

But I was not feeling embraceable.

"Don't *do* that!" I yelped. "It hurts."

Aaron backed off, startled, and perhaps a bit embarrassed
about exposing his feelings like that. "Sorry, Stretch.
Shouldn't you go to a hospital or something?"

"The medics said I don't have to. Didn't Eddie tell you?"

"Yeah, he did. Hello, Eddie."

"Hello, yourself." My partner stood up, with a conspirato-
rial gleam in his eye. "I'm going to get myself some lunch.
You two want anything?"

We declined, and he left us alone. I wouldn't have said no
to a hug then, a gentle one, but Aaron perched on one corner
of my desk and resumed his normal impertinent air. "So. You
really hammered Hammering Man."

"How did you know—?"

"You're on the local news, Slim. The Made in Heaven logo
showed up nice and clear."

"Oh, *no*."

"They say all publicity is good publicity, but don't you
think you went too far this time?"

"Never mind that," I told him sternly. "Are you going to
let the stylist fix up that eye for tonight?"

"I already said I would. You never listen to me, that's
something I've noticed about you. But we'll work on it.
Meanwhile, aren't you going to thank me for exposing the
real killer?"

I frowned. "I still can't quite believe that Zack *is* the real killer."

"You mean Tyrone. Maybe you just can't believe you were so blinded by flattery."

"Flattery!"

"Come on," he said, folding his arms and cocking his head smugly. "Tell me it wasn't flattering to have a younger man following you around like a pet puppy. The whole thing was getting ludicrous."

"What's ludicrous is your being jealous of Zack!"

"Jealous? Is that what you think? This isn't some soap opera, Stretch. The guy murdered two people."

"We don't know that for sure. What about Lester Foy? I still think he was Dracula. Corinne saw him in the Market the morning of Angela's death, and then he came to the houseboat to get me—"

"Foy came here because you asked him to, remember? And Corinne only *thinks* she saw him in the Market. And even if she did, so what? He's just a petty thief. But Zack—I mean, Tyrone—he could easily have found out where Angela lived—"

"Actually, he knew," I admitted. "He was there with me."

"What did I tell you?" Aaron stood up and began pacing along the picture windows, thinking hard, talking as much to himself as to me. Beyond him, I could see another rain squall moving across the lake, drawing a gray veil over the opposite shore. "Zack knew you were trying to figure out Mercedes' murder, so he hung around here acting innocent and helpful. But it was just to keep an eye on you, in case you were starting to suspect him. And you fell for the whole thing."

"There was nothing to fall for!" I rose, stung into anger by his condescending tone. "If he was trying to act so innocent, why would he tell me about shoving Mercedes?"

He whipped around to stare at me. "Shoving her? What are you talking about?"

Too late I realized what I'd said. Well, it was going to come out anyway in my statement to Graham. I looked down, twisting my hands together. Might as well face the music.

"That night at the Salish Lodge, Zack told me he had pushed Mercedes into the water at the shorebird exhibit. He got angry, because she was flirting with him, leading him on, and then she laughed in his face." I looked up defiantly. "Why would he tell me that if he actually murdered her? He was afraid she had drowned after he left her there, and he was so relieved when I told him—"

"Are you *crazy*?" Aaron grabbed me by the arms, his eyes wide and furious. "Zack confessed and you didn't go to the police? Do you know what you've done?"

"He didn't confess! You don't understand—"

"No, I don't!" he shouted. "You play around with a homicide case like it's one of your little weddings—"

"Stop it!" I was shouting now as well. My head was throbbing, and I was sickeningly aware that Aaron might be right. But that didn't justify his sneering at my livelihood. "Just leave me alone, would you? Stop pestering me when I'm trying to work."

"*Pestering* you? You think I'm just here to—"

The phone rang and I grabbed it.

"Hey, it's Juice. So how's this? We do a mess of half-depth sheet cakes, cut 'em in circles, and use a poured chocolate glaze to cover them so it won't take a lot of hand work. Then we pipe song titles around the centers."

"Song titles?" I repeated stupidly.

Aaron watched me for a moment, his face perfectly impassive, and then left, closing the outside door behind him with exaggerated care. I closed my eyes.

"Yeah, so they're like forty-fives, get it?" said Juice's voice in my ear. "Records, EMP, rock and roll? You can put 'em on all the tables. And we'll do an oversized one for the cutting, with the bride's and groom's names on it, like some kind of love song duet."

"That's . . . that's a good idea." I wondered, irrelevantly, how a cutting-edge type like Juice even knew about artifacts like vinyl records. "But can you get the oven space?"

"The BBA honchos said I can take over the kitchen this afternoon and call in some friends to help, on account of this being so important to my career."

"Important?"

"Well, if I pull this off, you're gonna want to feature me on your web site and urge all your clients to hire me and shit like that, right?"

"Right." I even smiled. "OK, get started."

"Already did. There's a batch of batter in the mixer now. Lemon cake OK?"

"Anything, as long as they arrive on time."

"I'm all over it."

I sighed and slumped down in my chair. "Just so it doesn't end up all over me."

Chapter Thirty-Three

THERE'S A SAYING AMONG THEATER PEOPLE, AFTER A DISAS-
trous dress rehearsal: "It'll be all right on the night." After all
the tragedy and farce, Paul and Elizabeth's wedding ceremony was all right on the night. More than all right, in fact.
And it brought out the best in everyone.

Everyone including the bride, surprisingly enough. When
I called Elizabeth to relate the fate of her cake, bracing myself
for the explosion, she astonished me by asking first if I had
had been hurt, and only second whether her special-event
policy would cover the cost.

"It should," I told her, "and if it doesn't, I bet my car insurance will. We'll work it out. Meanwhile, listen to this
great back-up plan . . ."

"That sounds fine," she said, when I explained Juice's
idea. "Cake is cake, at this point. The important thing is that
they've got the killer. Zack Hartmann, of all people! It's unbelievable. Thank God the police are keeping a lid on it until after the wedding. Paul and I will be in Venice by the time this
all hits the headlines."

"It's unbelievable, all right. In fact, I'm not sure I do believe it. I'm still wondering about Lester Foy."

"But he's in jail, too, the bastard. So either way, Tommy's
safe to be best man."

"Tommy's going to make it tonight?" My spirits lifted at the thought.

"Yeah, his daughter told us that he's still pretty shaky, so she'll have to take him home soon after the ceremony. But he's determined to be there for Paul."

"Has his memory come back yet?"

"It's starting to. Once it does, we'll know for sure who murdered Mercedes."

She went on, but I lost the thread of the conversation momentarily. *Have I got a best man's boutonniere? Better call Boris and make sure.*

"That's wonderful, Elizabeth. I've got to get back to my phone calls. You and Paul get going on that list of your favorite songs. Juice is waiting to take dictation."

So the bride and groom had a hilarious afternoon, calling each other with musical ideas while they made ready for their big night. And Boris assured me that he had Tommy covered.

"Of course! Boutonniere for best man is more special than for groomsmen, and for groom, more special than that. Everything perfect. You will dance with me tonight, Kharnegie? I have good news, and all bridesmaids must dance."

"Not this bridesmaid, not this time. You can dance with Corinne."

I could almost hear him shrug, and see the full lower lip jutting from his thornbush of a beard. "Perhaps."

Eddie and I plowed through the rest of the Lamott/Wheeler checklists, and then he went off to mail the announcements while I hobbled downstairs to meet Lily. I was running too late to use Elizabeth's stylist, who would be leaving the EMP while I was still checking in with my vendors, so Lily and I poured some wine and got to work. We spent half an hour giggling in my tiny bathroom, employing the entire contents of my cosmetics case to prepare me for my supporting role.

Lily was as good as any stylist—you can learn a lot playing Cleopatra. My hair is curly to start with, but she fluffed it out even more and gelled it into a dramatic coppery mane. Then she used three different eyeshadows and a lot of liner to make my so-so hazel eyes look huge and luminous, and finished off with shimmery lipstick and a spritz of perfume.

I blinked at the face in the mirror. "Wow."

"Wow is right," said Lily. "Come on, let's get you into that bra."

I held and she taped, and once the underpinnings were in place, I gingerly inserted my stiff and aching self into the slithery pink satin. Thank heaven the gowns weren't scratchy brocade. Still, I tucked some extra-strength pain pills into my purse.

"I can't believe you're going through with this," said Lily, as she camouflaged the minor bruises on my back and shoulders with face powder. "What if you've got a concussion or whiplash or something? Jeez, if the back of this dress was any lower you'd get arrested."

"I keep telling you, the medics said I'm OK. Are you sure the bra is going to stay on?"

"Girl, that adhesive's so strong, the problem is going to be getting it *off*. You may have cleavage for the rest of your life. There, now, that's my best shot. Let's show you to Eddie, and I'll drive you over there. Maybe you'll even have fun."

"Fat chance." I sashayed, sort of, over to my long mirror. The result of Lily's labors, except for my worried expression, was pretty damn glamorous. "I'd settle for no more catastrophes."

Eddie bestowed his highest praise—"What a tomato!"—

and then Lily and I set off through the early-evening darkness for the EMP. In the kitchen of the Turntable Restaurant, I found Joe Solveto choreographing his cooks and waiters with theatrical fervor, and wearing his designer tuxedo as though he'd been born in it.

"Joe, you and the food both look scrumptious."

"As do you! Pink may not be your color, my dear, but that bias cut does wonders for your...mmm...lines." He kissed me on the cheek, mindful of my lipstick, and directed my attention to the glossy chocolate 45s, which his people were just now unboxing. The piped-on titles ranged from old ballads to the latest hits, all of them celebrating love. Or at least lust. "Did that clownish Juice person really create all these this afternoon? I'm impressed."

"You should be. Are the flowers here? I'm running a little late."

"That's understandable, given what I saw on the news. Yes, the Mad Russian has been and gone. He says he'll be back for the party. Oh, and he said he heard from St. Petersburg, and he's a free man. Was he having green card trouble?"

"Something like that." So Boris was going to be single again! Maybe Corinne's heart could be mended after all. "Thanks for letting me know. If you need me, I'll be in the bride's dressing room."

"Break a leg." Joe's attention was already straying back to the buffet platters. "No, no, *no*! The aioli goes on the crab cakes, you cretin, and not until the last minute!"

Elizabeth, Patty, and Corinne were gathered in the women's rest room outside the theater door. I gave the theater a quick inspection—the judge's lectern was in place, the flowers were glorious—and then joined them. I stayed out of sight while the guests arrived, and stayed in touch with Rhonda, the EMP coordinator, on the cutting-edge little walkie-talkie she had loaned me for the night. It featured a handy clip on the back, but of course I had nowhere to clip it on my barely-covered person, so I'd brought along a little beaded purse on a narrow strap. Somehow my canvas tote bag just wouldn't cut it with the pink chiffon stole.

Rhonda reported that all was well out there, so as the guests chatted and the jazz trio noodled away on some tune or other, I concentrated on the bride and her attendants. Elizabeth, sensational in her hot-hued ensemble, held her postmodern bouquet to one side and gave me a quick hug and an air kiss.

"Carnegie, I'm so nervous! Is that normal?"

"Absolutely," I told her, secretly pleased that even hard-bitten software types could get butterflies. "That's where the bridal glow comes from. Enjoy it. So, Corinne, you and Boris got the flowers distributed? . . ."

I was fishing for a hint about their possibly renewed romance, but Corinne was too busy to notice. She was striking poses, frowning intently into the full-length mirror as she tried out different ways to drape her chiffon stole across her bulging midsection. Stephanie's alterations had added maybe an inch of breathing room, but she could have used more. Corinne's gown had gotten tighter across the bust, too. *If only I could gain weight in the chest,* I thought, comparing my own reflection to hers, *I'd eat hot fudge sundaes for breakfast.* As it was, I had to be content with the modest curves created by my invisible bra—which was beginning to itch.

But I soon forgot the itch—and Corinne and Boris, too—in the flurry of final niceties before the ceremony. I will never, *never* double up as consultant and bridesmaid again. Between fielding queries from Rhonda, temporarily losing one of my pink pearl earrings, and retwisting Patty's French twist, my nerves were in shreds before I set one high-heeled foot out in public.

But still I kept a cool and professional façade, barely registering Aaron's chilly glance at me—and his double take at my dress—as he entered the theater. I was more concerned with his carefully disguised black eye, and the effect of the tiny calla lily boutonniere on the lapel of his tux. *Nice work, Boris.* Scott went next, looking far more alert and involved than he had at the rehearsal, and when he joined the men up front, the two brothers winked at each other over Aaron's head.

Then the music changed, and everyone craned around from the raked rows of seats to watch Corinne come down the aisle. At the first glimpse of her gown and flowers, an appreciative murmur arose from the guests over the jazz trio's silky sounds. *Wait till they get a load of the bride,* I thought. This was going to be fascinating, taking in every detail of a Made in Heaven wedding as seen from onstage instead of the wings.

I counted a slow ten, stepped into the aisle, saw all those eyes staring at me . . . and lost consciousness of the entire ceremony in a blur of stage fright and fatigue. I heard later that everything went beautifully, but the only detail that stayed with me was Tommy Barry's face. He looked like a man who should still be in bed, yet his expression held such fondness, such pride and triumph as he watched his protégé Paul say "I do," that the happy tears in my eyes were more for him than for my client.

The next thing I knew, Scott was escorting me back up the

aisle, behind Aaron and Corinne. I glimpsed Chloe and
Howard, all sunburn and smiles, and Monica Lamott, in a
coral-colored number about a quarter-inch inside the line of
decency for the mother of the bride.

But for haute couture chutzpah, you couldn't beat Great-
Aunt Enid, who had deliberately worn the one thing that etiquette forbids to the wedding guest: a white lace dress. It
was a hollow victory, though, since at her age the effect was
less bridal than funereal. She could have been buried in that
dress, and maybe she would be. But to judge by the tender
looks she was sending Paul, she'd die happy.

Meanwhile, though, Enid was safely whisked away to her
hotel by her nurse, and the rest of us were plunged into the
biggest, loudest, most over-the-top party of the year.

"This is *awesome!*" I heard one guest saying half an hour
later, and I had to agree. Hundreds of people, all dressed to
the nines, had spread out across the pulsating dance floor of
the Sky Church, up the stairs to the exhibits, and along the
snowy-linened, colorfully laden buffet tables.

One group was clustered in wonder at the base of Roots
and Branches, a fabulous, towering sculpture of 600 guitars,
all wired together, with a few accordions and banjos thrown in
for good measure. The tornado-shaped assemblage rose from
the main floor up through an atrium to the Sound Lab mezzanine, where a gleeful melee of guests were having a go at the
drum kits and electric guitars. Rising up with it, the rock music from the Sky Church permeated the air and carried everyone along on a current of rhythmic energy. I've never seen so
many people having such a good time all at once.

But I wasn't one of them. All I could think about, now
that we'd gotten through the ceremony, was Zack. My young,
earnest Robin Hood, so eager to help Eddie with his soft-

ware, so guilt-stricken that he might have accidentally caused Mercedes' death—could he have been faking all that, every single expression and emotion? Surely not. *Surely not.* A criminal past was shocking enough, but the idea of Zack as a brutal murderer made me dizzy. Or was it just stubborn denial about my own foolishness, as Aaron claimed?

Of course, I was dizzy anyway. I hadn't eaten since breakfast. I stashed my bouquet and purse at a table in a semiquiet corner of the gift shop, and hit the buffet for a plate of Joe's crab cakes. A quick protein fix, and then I'd radio the limo drivers and guide the videographer and do everything else I needed to do, including to stop obsessing about the guilt or innocence of Zack Hartmann.

Exhilarated wedding guests flowed through the aisles of the shop, but no one paid attention to me. I had almost cleaned my plate when I saw Aaron making a beeline through the crowd. He was pocketing his cell phone, and by the look on his face he had news. "There you are, Wedding Lady! Hiding out from the adulation of the masses?"

"Just regrouping." Neither of us was going to apologize, that was clear, but I was up for a truce. "Your eye doesn't look bad."

He touched his eyebrow gingerly with a fingertip as he sat down. "Yeah, your makeup artist used putty or something. You're not half-bad yourself in that dress. Very sexy."

Some idiot impulse drove me to demur. "Oh, well, it's not really a good color for me. And, of course, I don't fill it out the way Corinne does. I mean, my figure, if you can call it that, isn't exactly—"

"Look at me, Stretch."

I hadn't realized that I wasn't, until he said so. I met his gaze. "What?"

He leaned toward me and whispered, "When you get a compliment, try saying 'Thank you,' and nothing else. For instance, when I tell you that your naked shoulders could start a major world religion—"

"Aaron!"

"No, not 'Aaron,' just 'Thank you.' You'll get the hang of it." He leaned back and rapped the table with his knuckles. "Now, listen, I just heard something interesting about Lester Foy from my source at the SPD. They've been backtracking his movements lately."

My mental gears were grinding. "Foy? He's the killer after all, isn't he?"

"*Not.* Sorry, Stretch, your little friend Zack is still the prime suspect. On the night of the Aquarium party, Lester Foy was up in Blaine, making an unsuccessful attempt to cross the Canadian border."

"Are you sure?"

Aaron nodded, and a lock of black hair flopped across his forehead. "Positive ID from the customs guys. When they asked him to pull over for a spot search, he took off and they lost him. Blaine's a two-hour drive from here. Whoever Dracula was, he wasn't Lester Foy."

"Oh." I took a minute to digest this news. "But that still doesn't prove that it was Zack who killed Mercedes. Dracula could have been..." *Who?* I couldn't think straight. "OK, I'm not sure about Dracula. But I know Zack wasn't the murderer. I just know it."

"Come on, Mrs. Robinson, give it up. Zack fooled all of us, not just you. Admit it, and try to forget the whole thing."

"I can't forget it. I'm sure I'm right, and once I get some sleep I'm going to figure it all out, you wait and see."

"More power to you, Sherlock." Aaron stood up and straightened his bow tie. "Want to come up to the Sound Lab and jam with me? I'll play 'Wipe Out' for you."

I smiled. "Maybe later. I have to get back to work."

"Kharrnegie!" A vast and crumpled tuxedo front was hovering over me like a Slavic storm cloud. "I have found you!"

"So you have. Aaron, this is Boris Nevsky. Boris, Aaron Gold, a good friend of mine."

"And so, a good friend of mine also!" Boris enveloped Aaron in one of his patented Russian bear hugs, then set him down and extended one huge paw to me. "You prromised to dance! Come!"

"I did not promise! Boris, I'm in no condition—"

"Yes, I know, you were in car smash. I will hold you gently, like flower. Come!"

"Oh, all right." If I didn't keep moving, I'd probably stiffen to a complete halt. So I picked up my purse and followed Boris up to the main floor, leaving Aaron to arrange his tie all over again.

Chapter Thirty-Four

"BORIS, YOUR FLOWERS ARE WONDERFUL!" I HAD TO SHOUT to be heard. High over our heads in the Sky Church, Travis Cook, an elfish fellow with long lank hair and the best sound technician on the West Coast, made magic at his control panels on the balcony. Like a latter-day wizard, he was conjuring up waves of music and dazzling, shifting video projections, filling the vast space with a pulsing phantasmagoria that throbbed through our bones as we stood at the edge of the crowded dance floor. "Corinne loved her bouquet! Did she tell you?"

The Mad Russian didn't answer, but instead scooped me delicately into his arms for an impromptu tango. We angled across the floor, with smiling guests parting before us, then reversed course and thrust back into the throng.

Most of the faces that swam past were unfamiliar, but I saw Chloe and Howard dancing together, equally oblivious of their sunburns and the beat. Also Valerie Duncan, partnered with Paul's brother Scott but gazing wistfully over his shoulder at someone else. *Who?* Ah, Roger Talbot, resplendent in white tie. He looked like a head of state at the very least.

Roger was squiring Monica Lamott, as requested, but smirking over *her* shoulder at a gorgeous young thing I recognized from the *Sentinel*'s art department. *Another conquest so soon?* He was incorrigible. I returned my attention to the path ahead and jerked my partner to a halt just before we clipped the metal struts of one of the light towers.

"Boris, slow down, please! Now tell me, did you talk with Corinne? I thought maybe after your divorce—"

"Corinne! Why always do you talk of Corinne?" He blew out a gusty breath, like an exasperated horse. "Corinne is no more fun since she stopped to drink."

"Corinne stopped drinking?" Corinne had passed on the tequila shooters back at the bridesmaids' luncheon, but I remembered all too vividly how sick she was in the Aquarium ladies' room. "I don't think so, Boris."

"*Da!* She stops to drinking, she cries, she gets fat, she vants to get married. Please, no more Corinne."

"Sorry . . ."

He kept on talking, but I had ceased to listen. *No alcohol . . . weeping . . . nausea . . .* As soon as I could, I extricated myself from Boris and made my way to the edge of the dance floor. *Corinne?* I grabbed a glass of sparkling water from a passing waiter. I had to think, though the pounding music and strobing lights made it nearly impossible. *Perrier, Aaron said she was drinking Perrier. . . .*

"Great party, Carnegie!" Burt Lamott patted my bruised shoulder heartily and jostled my water glass so that it spilled on my dress. *Filling out her dress . . . eating like a horse . . . What was it Valerie said? "Roger's terribly discreet with all his women."* The memories were connecting so fast I could hardly follow them. *All his women . . . and she was in the ladies' room when Mercedes told me . . .*

I left the Sky Church in a daze, feeling feverish, as if an electrical charge was flickering through my brain. *Venus had long red fingernails . . .* I pushed rudely through the milling guests... *but when she came out of the water her fingers were cold and blunt, no long nails. What did that mean?*

Valerie Duncan walked past, and I stopped her, fumbling to formulate my question, stumbling over the words. "At the, the cemetery, the funeral, Angela talked to Corinne about something, it seemed to make her angry. Just before they got in your car. Do you know what they were talking about?"

"Not really." Valerie was in party mode, and did not look pleased at the reminder of recent events. "Something about a necklace. I didn't pay much attention."

"No, of course not... Sorry."

A necklace. A necklace, or a ring on a gold chain? And the man in a black cloak... I stopped dead. *What if the man in the black cloak never existed?*

"Isn't this *great*?" Paul Wheeler, buoyant and beaming, stepped back from the guitar sculpture and stood before me, blocking my way.

I clutched his arm. "Have you seen Tommy?"

"It's like a, a super wedding. Elizabeth's a super girl. And you're a super—"

"Paul, *where is Tommy?*"

He frowned, blinking his glazed-over eyes. "I think they went upstairs. Why?"

" 'They?' He's with his daughter?"

"No, with Corinne." The bridegroom smiled at me reassuringly. "Don't worry. She'll take care of Tommy."

The next few minutes were the stuff of nightmare: surrealistic lights and ominous sounds, seemingly infinite obstacles, an overwhelming sense of urgency and dread. I rushed past Paul and up the stairs to the mezzanine, fighting the crowd all the way, then stopped to catch my breath at the railing that ran around the atrium and the wide, glittering head of the tornado of guitars.

Across the atrium were the Milestones galleries, behind me the Sound Lab, and off to my right a glass wall that overlooked the Sky Church and formed the rear of the technical balcony where Travis was working. And everywhere were wedding guests by the dozen, blocking my view and confusing me further. *Where would she take him? Was he beginning to remember?* And, most critical of all, *did Corinne have her gun with her tonight?*

My first thought had been to contact the EMP security guards on my walkie-talkie, and have them apprehend Corinne even if they had to clear the building to find her. If I was wrong, well, better safe than sorry. But then I held off. If I was right, Corinne would be armed, and a challenge from a guard could easily spook her into harming the already fragile old sportswriter.

Because, whether Tommy remembered it or not, I was certain that I knew who smashed that jagged stone into Mercedes Montoya's skull, as she lay helpless in the water where Zack had pushed her. Corinne Campbell, one of Roger Talbot's many mistresses, who seemed "so ordinary and tedious" by comparison with the haughty Mexican beauty. Corinne, who by some evil chance had overheard her rival gloating about the engagement ring, the ring she coveted for herself.

Corinne, who was carrying Roger Talbot's child.

I stepped back from the railing, collided jarringly with someone who moved away with a laugh, and reeled against a small window that looked into one of the soundproof practice rooms. Aaron was inside, alone, with his eyes closed and his bow tie pulled loose, flailing away on a drum kit for all he was worth. I banged on the window, but he couldn't hear me, just as I couldn't hear his drums.

I had begun to turn away when I saw his hands blurring with the speed of a silent crescendo. He whacked the high-hat cymbal one last time and opened his eyes, grinning like a boy. I gestured wildly, and ten seconds later he was out the door, through the Sound Lab, and at my side.

"What's happening? You look—"

"Aaron, it was Corinne!" I glanced around to see if anyone was listening, but the party noise was roaring over us like surf. "She killed Mercedes and invented the attack on herself to cover it up. There was never any man in a black cloak."

"*What?*"

"Please, there's no time to explain, we have to find her before she hurts Tommy. She owns a gun!"

"Hang on, Stretch." He put his hands on either side of my waist. His palms felt warm through the thin satin. "You really think Corinne is the murderer?"

"I'm sure of it. She's pregnant by Roger Talbot, that's why she suddenly wanted Boris to marry her, to be a father for her baby and—"

He was shaking his head. "Even if Corinne did kill Mercedes, how would she know that Tommy was a witness?"

"Because I *told* her. God help me, I told her and Paul after we visited Tommy in the hospital. And now she's off with him somewhere and if I tell the guards to stop her she'll panic!"

Aaron's eyes were fixed and intent; I could almost see him thinking, faster and more clearly than I could after the day I'd been through. Was that crash in Vanna only this afternoon? My sense of time was distorted, and the roar of sound around us felt like a suffocating physical pressure, mounting by the minute and battering at my senses.

"All right," said Aaron. "Tell the guards to find Tommy, not Corinne. Tell them to say his daughter's looking for him, he needs to take some medicine or something. That shouldn't tip her off. Meanwhile we'll tell other people the same thing. I'll search the main floor galleries and you do the ones up here. We're bound to find them soon."

But it wasn't soon. I called the guards, and we all worked the crowd, but it was a harrowing, endless half hour later before I got a response. It came when I related our little fiction to one of the *Sentinel*'s receptionists in the Milestones gallery.

"Oh, poor Tommy!" she said absently, absorbed in a display on hip-hop artists. "He looked kinda sick, so I wondered why Corinne was taking him into that Lab place—"

I was gone before she finished, racing around the atrium and into the Sound Lab. It was full of guests, mostly younger ones in a state of inebriated hilarity, pounding on the huge electronic drum in the center of the space and moving in and out of the various practice rooms. The lights were low, and I had to peer into faces and haul open the heavy door of each room to make sure I wasn't overlooking my quarry.

But it seemed that they must have gone elsewhere. In the booth where Aaron had been, two hulking fellows were savaging the drums and singing along to an indecipherable tune. A larger chamber, with drums, guitar and keyboard, held five young women who were squealing with laughter while making passable music. And in the microphone room, Boris Nevsky was belting out the Russian national anthem to a stunned-looking audience of three who were probably afraid to walk out on him.

"Boris, come help me!"

He looked affronted. "I am not finished!"

"You are now." I towed him out by the elbow and cupped my hand to his ear to make myself heard in the din. "I have to find Tommy Barry. Have you seen him?"

"Who is that?"

"The best man, the old guy with the shaved head? Help me look for him, Boris, please."

He shrugged affably. "I forget second verse anyway."

We searched the rest of the rooms, to no avail, and then Boris gestured at some steps in a far, dim corner. They led up to two more practice booths, but a chain was draped between the railings to keep tonight's crowd off the Lab's upper level. I remembered the barrier across the shorebird exhibit at the Aquarium, and groaned aloud.

"*Tommy*—"

Boris, sensing my urgency at last, forged ahead of me through the crowd like an icebreaker and flung the chain aside. We mounted the steps and checked the first room: empty. But the second room was dark, and when we pulled open the door, the shifting light from the party below faintly illuminated an overturned chair, a guitar dangling by its cord over the edge of an electronic keyboard—and the body of Tommy Barry.

He was sprawled facedown, halfway under the keyboard stand. His outflung hands were still, and between his shoulder blades, just barely discernible as a dim gleam against the matte black of his tuxedo jacket, was a patch of blood spreading darkly outwards from a large, ragged wound. The exit wound from a bullet.

Boris lifted the guitar away so I could crouch down and

feel Tommy's throat for a pulse. "I think...yes! He's still alive. I'll call—"

But I couldn't call Rhonda, or the guards, because the walkie-talkie was in my purse and my stupid goddamn bloody purse was lost in the shuffle somewhere. "Boris, stay here. Try and stop the bleeding, and don't let Corinne anywhere near him. I expect she's left the building by now but—"

"*Corinne* did this?" His eyes were round. "Did she vant to merry him, too?"

But I was already halfway down the steps, and shouting out the request that no event planner ever, ever wants to utter: "Is there a doctor here? Anybody know if there's a doctor here?"

The only response was alarm and perplexed confusion, so I pushed through the crowd and out to the atrium, heading for the little glass-walled balcony that hung over the Sky Church. Surely Travis would be able to communicate with Rhonda, and she could find a doctor and mobilize the guards and the police. I could see him in the gaps between the milling people, apparently giving a couple of guests a private tour of his electronic marvels.

As I toiled through the crowd and got closer, the two guests were revealed as Roger Talbot and the girl from the art department. Irrelevantly, some part of my mind groped for her name: Ruby? Jewel? Crystal, that was it. Crystal was a pocket Venus, five-one or so with short, feathery white-blonde hair, and she was gazing up at Roger with a different kind of high voltage in mind. The publisher, forgetting for the moment that the wall behind them was made of glass, had let one hand slip from Crystal's waist down to her velvet-clad derriere. They jumped apart when I pushed open the door, calling out as I went.

"Travis, we need the police!" He looked at me—or was it past me?—with blank dismay. "Call Rhonda and—"

A scream, an anguished shriek of pain and outrage, froze me in my tracks. Roger and Crystal were staring past me at the person who had screamed. Slowly, with a dreamlike dread and yet certainty about who I would see, I turned around.

Corinne Campbell, with her lush figure straining against her rose satin gown, and a demented light shining in her aquamarine eyes, was pointing a wavering pistol at Roger Talbot's head.

Chapter Thirty-Five

MY FEET HURT. I'D BEEN RUNNING AROUND ALL EVENING IN rose-pink dyed-silk stilettos instead of my usual comfy flats, and now I couldn't sit down because I was stuck on a tiny balcony overhanging a fifty-foot drop with three other terrified people and a crazy lady with a gun, smack in the middle of somebody else's love triangle, except one side of the triangle was already dead. Or would it be one angle?

This must be what hysteria feels like, I mused, as my thoughts rear-ended each other like cars in a freeway pileup. *Interesting.*

"You said you loved me!" Corinne whimpered—the old, trite, unbearably painful plea of the spurned woman. And in this case, in these circumstances, tantamount to a confession of murder. After the secret killings, and all the clever deceptions to maintain her innocence, she had cracked and revealed herself at the sight of her lover with another woman. A woman he had only just met.

Corinne stood just inside the balcony door, her back to the atrium. Although a few heads had lifted when she screamed, most of the crowd outside had shrugged it off as mere high spirits, and went on with their party. But then Roger tried to speak, and an upsurge in the music erased his words.

"Stop the noise!" said Corinne, desperate, but still—barely—in command of herself. The ugly blind eye of the gun swung toward Travis. "Make it stop!"

The sound man gulped and nodded, his long locks brushing at the shoulders of his EMP T-shirt. He moved his hands slowly, slowly to one of his consoles, and as if he had lifted the needle from some gigantic record, the music instantaneously ceased.

The abrupt and utter silence in that great space was shocking, and somehow beautiful. But it was quickly sullied by a rising drone of voices, like the buzz of baffled and then angry bees, as hundreds of dancers and diners and general merrymakers questioned and then protested this break in the action.

"Hey, whassup?" An amiably drunk young man with a girl in each arm marched across the atrium to our glass wall.

His sloppy smile froze as Corinne's gaze, and her gun, swerved in his direction. One of the girls screamed, long and piercingly. This time everybody heard it. Revelers poured out of the Sound Lab and the galleries, at first to gape, but then to flee, as news of the situation rushed through the crowd like toxic fumes. Within minutes, the mezzanine was empty—except for the two people that only I knew about: Boris, faithful at his post up in that soundproof booth, and Tommy Barry, bleeding his life away.

"Corinne," I said gently. She stared at me with blank, panicky eyes. "It's me, Carnegie, remember? I've been so worried about you lately."

Behind me, Talbot stirred slightly, and I tried to will him into silence. If Corinne stayed focused on her sorrow, instead of her wrath, maybe we could survive this. She continued to stare at me without answering, but at any rate, I didn't seem to be making things worse. Her chest rose and fell in short, shuddering breaths, as if she couldn't quite take in enough air, and her round, fair face was misted with perspiration. She backed away from me with uncertain steps, until she felt the balcony railing at her back.

"You've been very unhappy, haven't you?" I said.

The murmuring from the dance floor down below had subsided to a mass shuffling of footsteps and the occasional clipped sound of someone giving directions; Rhonda must be clearing the building. We were marooned up here, hanging over open space, flanked by the light towers and dazzled by the monster images that were still moving on the enormous video screen, the huge mouths of singers working silently, giant hands playing soundless guitars.

That was the view before us, across the Sky Church. Behind us lay the empty atrium, the guitar sculpture spreading above deserted corridors and stairs. No rescuers could approach us from the atrium or reach the Sound Lab without Corinne seeing them through the glass wall. And there was no telling what she would do when that happened.

"You've been unhappy, and worried about the future," I continued in a low, lulling tone. "You're scared about what's been going on lately. It must seem like a nightmare."

Corinne nodded at that, and her grip on the pistol seemed to relax ever so slightly.

"You must be tired," I said. "Has it been difficult to sleep?"

"Yes," she whispered, in a voice like a weary child's. The blue eyes blinked back tears. "I have dreadful dreams."

"That's hard," I said sympathetically, staying perfectly

still, trying to reach her with my voice and my eyes. "It's hard when you can't get any rest. It makes everything so confusing. But you need to rest."

Corinne was listening, wavering a little, and for a moment I could feel her exhaustion and despair. But my own exhaustion was so intense, and my sympathy for her so vivid, that I made a ghastly mistake.

"You need to rest," I repeated. "You need to take care of your baby."

"Roger's baby," she said reverently.

"Mine?" Roger Talbot, the philanderer, the moron, the monster of ego, actually stepped past me and confronted her, his bold dark eyes blazing under the patrician silver hair, for all the world as if he were just as invincible to bullets as he was to any sense of decency or conscience. "I don't believe for a minute—"

"It's true!" Corinne howled, and the gun swung wildly from him to me and back again. "You wouldn't listen, you didn't want to hear, but once I found out about the baby I never let another man touch me again. I was faithful to you, and all the time you were fucking that snotty Mexican bitch. She wasn't even an *American*!"

This last bit of lunacy seemed to startle her as much as it did the rest of us. Talbot retreated a step, and young Crystal began to cry, in little hiccupping gasps that were sure to catch Corinne's attention at any moment. From the corner of my eye I saw Travis take Crystal's hand, and she managed to silence herself. All four of us knew what might happen to any rival for Talbot's interest, however recent or casual that interest might be.

"How could you, Roger?" Corinne herself was sobbing now, but they were angry sobs, and her knuckles were white once more on the handle of the gun. Beyond her, on the screen, a woman's giant face was contorting in pain or ecstasy as she sang words we couldn't hear. "How could you give her the ring? It was *my* ring, you said so when you showed it to me, you said we just had to wait, but you lied, you gave it to *her*!"

She was working herself up to a climax, I could see it coming, and all I could think to do was interrupt. "Is that why you killed Angela, Corinne? Because she saw you throwing a necklace into the harbor? It wasn't a necklace, it was the diamond ring on a long gold chain, wasn't it?"

That broke her momentum, and she looked at me like a scolded puppy. The mood swings reminded me, horribly, of the last time I saw Mercedes alive.

"It wasn't my fault," she whined. "None of this was my fault."

"Of course it wasn't, honey. You couldn't help it. But don't make it any worse, all right? Corinne, *Tommy is still alive.*" The others stared at me as they absorbed this new horror, the idea that she had already attacked someone, here, tonight. "He's alive, but he needs a doctor. Let Travis go and find him a doctor, OK? You don't want to hurt Travis, do you? Just like you didn't really want to hurt Tommy. You want to help Tommy, don't you, Corinne?"

She looked baffled by all the questions, but at least I was distracting her from Roger, who was surely the short fuse to her final explosion.

"Won't you let Travis go help Tommy? Please?" I made a small, appealing gesture with one hand. Another mistake.

"No!" she shrieked, and we all recoiled, waiting for the shot. But Corinne Campbell had more to say.

"Don't move, don't anyone move, y'hear me? And stop

talkin' at me. Just listen." Her Southern drawl was coming back, and with it a subtle shift in her mood, a sense of power, even pleasure, at finally having the upper hand over the man who had tormented her. "Are you listening, Roger?"

He licked dry lips and nodded, finally understanding just how close we were to the final disaster.

"This is *your* fault," she said, using the little gun like a pointer to gesture at Talbot's impeccably tailored trousers. He flinched, and she gave a foolish little giggle. "You're the one who should have gone overboard, not me."

I tried to calculate the best way to move, once Corinne fired at him, as she inevitably would. Drop to the floor? *But what if she keeps shooting? Rush at her? And send us both over the railing?* I was closer to her than Crystal or Travis, so anything I did would protect them for a few critical seconds, but the thought of plummeting through all that empty air, of the floor below rushing upwards to meet us, sent a paralyzing chill through me that seemed to freeze both breath and blood, thought and action. *But I'll have to do it. When the gun goes off, I'll throw myself at her—*

"Hey, Corinne, look at me! Is this wild or what?"

Comically, insanely, Aaron's head and shoulders had appeared in midair, six feet or so beyond the railing. He was forcing a grin, but his face was blanched white as his shirt, and the sweat pouring from his forehead had dissolved the makeup and exposed his black eye. This man, this wonderful foolish man who was afraid of heights, had climbed the struts of a light tower, fifty feet into the air, leaving his tuxedo jacket and shoes behind and moving silently in his socks until he could give us the distraction that we needed to save ourselves.

Corinne whirled to face him, bringing the gun around

with a wild cry of alarm. Aaron, exposed on his perch, clung to the metal bars and closed his eyes. In the same infinite moment, Roger Talbot bolted for the balcony door, Crystal slumped over in a faint, and Travis and I launched ourselves at Corinne. He went high and I dove low—the side slit in my gown ripped almost to the waist—as we knocked the gun from Corinne's hand and brought all three of us crashing to the floor in a chaotic and very painful heap.

Travis seemed to have stunned himself, and Corinne went completely limp and began to weep and moan. As I struggled out from under their combined dead weight, I heard the pistol strike the Sky Church floor far below with a tiny, harsh clang and a drawn-out metallic clatter that seemed to go on echoing forever in my mind.

Chapter Thirty-Six

THANKSGIVING IS THE PERFECT HOLIDAY. YOU COOK, YOU eat, you count your blessings. Except for the dirty dishes and the indigestion, what could be better?

One of my blessings in recent years—having Lily as a friend—brought with it the fine fringe benefit of a turkey feast at her house. Who knew that I'd also be thankful for not getting splattered all over the floor of the Sky Church? But on this particular Thanksgiving morning, less than a week after the crisis, it was much on my mind. Especially with my mother on the phone talking about it.

Mom had called the day after the wedding, of course, because she buys *The Seattle Times* in Boise, and could hardly miss "Shooting at Experience Music Project Leaves One Critical, Suspect Arrested" on the front page. Now she was calling again, from my brother Tim's home in Illinois, to wish me happy Thanksgiving and to fret some more.

"I'm fine, Mom," I said again as I sat in my chilly kitchen, muffled up in my robe, and contemplated the culinary adventure before me. In a fit of holiday spirit I'd promised Lily a pie, and although she assured me that store-bought would be fine, I was determined to concoct the thing myself.

"But this crazy woman could have *shot* you," said my

mother. Now that she knew her darling daughter was safe, she seemed to almost relish the idea. What a story for her poker club. "You could have been *killed*."

"Well, I wasn't, and you're beginning to sound ghoulish about it."

"Don't be silly, Carrie!" Only my mother called me Carrie. "I was worried sick. You should have called me before I read about it in the paper."

"I was busy, Mom. It was a long night, and Tommy was in surgery for hours. I'm sorry, I just didn't think about it."

"But he's all right now? The poor man."

Lucky man was more like it. Boris had stopped Tommy's bleeding with his wadded-up dress shirt, and clever Rhonda had summoned an ambulance crew the minute she heard there was a gun in the building. Tommy was back in a room at Harborview, but in satisfactory condition, and managing a faint wisecrack or two for his constant stream of affectionate visitors. The whole affair, dreadful as it was, could have been far, far worse.

Mom went on, "I read that the publisher, is his name Talbot? I read that he's running for mayor over there. It's wonderful, how brave he was."

I sank my head in one hand, listening to her rattle on and deciding not to disabuse her of the heroic impression that Roger Talbot had managed to convey to the press. The man was a master. While the rest of us were at the hospital worrying about Tommy, he gave a long, nonexclusive interview to anyone with a mike or a pen.

Somehow the ugly little scuffle that brought Corinne to the floor of the balcony had evolved into a denouement featuring Roger and Travis as coolheaded heroes, with Crystal and myself as adoring onlookers, and Aaron as an anonymous EMP employee who had merely shouted at Corinne to distract her.

Talbot even called me "plucky," the son of a bitch. By the time I was aware of his manipulations, the next morning, a call to the paper with my own version of events would have seemed like self-serving mudslinging. Besides, the last thing I wanted was more column inches associating Made in Heaven weddings with gunfire.

What I wanted was to have Aaron write up an accurate account of the incident, for his own paper or someone else's. But Aaron refused to talk about his role—his truly heroic role—because he had frozen up on the tower afterwards and had to be helped down, step-by-step, by a police officer. He saved our lives, and he was embarrassed about it. Men are so odd.

I would have argued with Aaron about his reticence, but between both our jobs and all our statements to the police, we'd hardly seen each other. I was eager to talk with him tonight. And not just talk, either. I'd made a decision.

"I've got to go, Mom. I'm working on a pumpkin pie."

"Oh, good! Are you using my recipe for butter pastry?"

"Not exactly." Of course, maybe the packaged pie shell in my freezer had some butter in it. I hadn't read that label, only the label on the back of the pumpkin can, where it said "Quick 'N' Easy!"

"Well, I'm sure it will be delicious. And you say your friend Alan is going also?"

"His name's Aaron, Mom." *And I'm going to have sex with Aaron tonight, how about that?* But what I said was, "He's very nice. You'd like him. Lily likes him."

"Then he must be nice. You tell Lily Happy Thanksgiving for me."

Mom rang off, and I got dressed and got busy. The kitchen had warmed up nicely with the oven preheating, and my enthusiasm grew as I measured out brown sugar, hunted out the cinnamon, and whisked some eggs and evaporated milk. *This is so simple, I should do it more often.* I was cranking the can opener when Aaron called.

"So, Stretch, is this thing tonight formal or anything? Both my good shirts are at the cleaner's."

He sounded disappointingly matter-of-fact, but then he didn't know about my secret plan for our night of passion.

"No, not at all," I said casually. "In fact, wear some walking shoes. We usually go around Green Lake after Thanksgiving dinner."

"Oh. Do we have to?"

"Aaron, it's less than three miles on a paved path! Come on, it's the Seattle thing to do."

"OK. So long as it's not a no-smoking lake." I had told him Lily's house rule about cigarettes. "You need anything for this pie deal?"

"Nope. I'm just getting it into the oven now."

I suppose I shouldn't cook and talk on the telephone simultaneously, but I'm on the phone so much that it's second nature. Cooking isn't, however. I carefully closed the oven door, wiped my hands in triumph, and went about my business, enjoying the spicy smell that spread through the house. But when I passed through the kitchen a little while later, I spotted something odd on the counter: the measuring cup of brown sugar.

"Oh, hell!" I grabbed some pot holders and hastily yanked out the pie. A dollop of pumpkin slopped onto the hot oven floor and began to blacken and smoke. "Hell and *damnation*."

I was afraid of more spillage if I emptied the pie into a bowl, so instead I sprinkled the sugar over the surface and tried to stir it in with a fork. But the filling had partly solidified by now, and the fork snagged on the bottom and tore up a flap of crust. I smooshed it down as best I could, returned the whole mess to the oven, and waited patiently for the timer to sound. Once done, the pie looked...funny, with lumpy brown spots and little bubbly craters all over the surface. Maybe I could tell Lily's boys it was a moon pie. Sighing, I set it cautiously aside to cool, and ran up to the office to check my e-mail and do some paperwork.

E-mail first, in case there was a message from the prominent young heiress who had actually responded to the Made in Heaven web site. *Thank you, Zack, wherever you are.* I had sent her a proposal for her wedding, along with an invitation to come in for a first consultation, and was eagerly awaiting her reply. And I got one, too, but not the reply I wanted. In my one Unread Message, she thanked me for my time, and said that she'd decided to use Dorothy Fenner instead.

"I thought Dorothy was leaving town!" I called Joe Solveto to whine, after gritting my teeth and sending the heiress a gracious reply. That's the nice thing about E-mail, you don't have to fake your tone of voice. "Why isn't she in Arizona where she belongs?"

Joe chuckled. "The word is that Dominatrix Dorothy packed her husband off to Scottsdale alone, and took an apartment near her office. She says he can come back to visit her, but only by invitation."

"Just what I needed," I grumbled. "Bad publicity, and Dorothy still on the scene."

"There is no such thing as bad publicity," he told me sternly. "You wait, brides will call you just to get the juicy details about Corinne Campbell. Now go enjoy your turkey. Give my love to the luscious Lily."

Aaron arrived almost half an hour late, and seemed preoccupied, so I decided to save the unveiling of my secret plan for the end of the evening. He apologized, then frowned as I climbed into his car and settled the pie on my lap. "Is pie supposed to look like that?"

"Of course it is. Listen, Aaron, Lily might have a friend there tonight, a man."

"Besides me?" he asked as he drove. "You know how I hate to co-star."

"Be serious. I mean, she's dating someone, and I haven't met him yet, so behave yourself, OK?"

"When do I not?" He glanced over at me. His shiner had faded to a repulsive yellowy-green. "Of course I will, Slim. I'm very fond of Lily."

It only occurred to me to wonder, as we entered her modest, happily messy house, if Aaron would be fond of Lily's sons, and vice versa. But he immediately began to wrestle with them, causing shrieks of delighted terror to bounce off the walls. Lily ignored them, and beckoned me into the kitchen.

"Let them wear themselves out before dinner," she said, pouring me a glass of wine. "How are you?"

"Never mind how I am, what about this new guy of yours? Are you going to tell me more about him before he gets here?"

She smiled mischievously. "You'll have to wait . . . no, you won't, he's here."

Marcus and Ethan had begun to shriek, "Mike! Mike!" so I stepped to the doorway—and saw Detective Lieutenant Michael Graham, a bottle of wine in one hand and a bouquet of white roses in the other, with both boys wrapped around his legs like curly-haired little octopuses.

"Hello," he said, as Aaron and I gaped silently. "Carnegie, was it Pinot Noir you liked so much? That's what I brought."

Lily pecked him on the cheek and relieved him of the wine and the flowers. I shot her a look that said, *You only met him two weeks ago!* and she shot one right back saying, *So what?* Then she laughed, and Aaron pumped Mike's hand, and we settled down to dinner.

The feast was wonderful—Lily did her famous Madeira gravy—and the walk around Green Lake was bracing, with the boys putting in double the mileage of the grown-ups with all their running around. On our return, my unfortunate pie was consumed with only a few witty comments about its interesting texture. The high-spirited atmosphere and the obvious chemistry between Lily and her new man—and maybe the Pinot Noir, too—got me counting the minutes before Aaron and I could decently leave and head back to my place.

Aaron seemed to be sharing my thoughts, sitting ever closer to me on the couch, and slipping a warm, massaging hand between my shoulder blades. I began to speculate about the location of his tattoo, and to lose the thread of the conversation.

But then the boys were carried off to bed, and the conversation turned, inevitably, to Corinne Campbell.

"It's the saddest kind of case," Graham said, leaning back in his chair with his hands wrapped around a coffee mug. "She might never have resorted to murder if Peters hadn't pushed Mercedes Montoya into the water. The way I figure it, Campbell killed her rival in a fury, got blood all over her white Venus costume, and then jumped into the harbor to

cover it up. She couldn't very well go back to the party looking like that."

"Her nails," I murmured.

"What?" asked Lily.

I told her, as I had already told the police, about Corinne's
long fake nails, the ones that were gone when she was "rescued" from the harbor. "She must have had blood under her
nails, too, and pulled them off in the water. But first she
threw in the diamond ring that Roger had promised her, still
on the chain that she took from Mercedes' neck."

The diamond that Roger Talbot wanted back as a memento, I
thought, *and Rick Royko wanted as payment on a drug deal, is
permanently sunk in the black ooze at the bottom of Elliott Bay.
Diamonds are forever.*

Graham—I'd have to start calling him Mike—nodded and
went on. "Campbell didn't find out until the funeral that
Angela Sims saw her getting rid of the ring. She might have
won a jury's sympathy about the first murder. The wronged
woman, a moment of madness, that kind of thing. But killing
Sims was almost certainly premeditated, and of course she
shot Thomas Barry in cold blood. No one's going to execute
a pregnant woman, though. She'll have the baby in prison."

The thought was so depressing that I couldn't speak. Lily
bit her lip and made a soft, distressed sound.

"Corinne must have thought about abortion, earlier on,"
she said sadly. "But being Catholic, and being in love with
Roger Talbot, that would have been a horrible prospect. And
then after committing murder, the deadliest sin, she just lost
her grip altogether."

Aaron seemed not to hear her. He was still putting the fac-
tual pieces together. "She killed Mercedes, and then claimed

that someone tried to kill her. She killed Angela, and made up that story about being chased by Lester Foy. Corinne was always the victim, always crying wolf. We just couldn't see that she *was* the wolf."

A silence fell. I tried to use Aaron's perspective, to think about the puzzle and not the heartbreak.

"OK, Mike, two questions." I held up my cup as Lily poured more coffee. "If Lester Foy wasn't Dracula, then who was? And what was Foy doing at the cemetery in Redmond, if he wasn't stalking us?"

"The first one's easy," said the detective, flushing a little, "though if you tell anyone I'll deny it."

We all leaned forward a little, and he rolled his eyes. "Dracula was a guy named—well, never mind his name. He's a hotshot DEA agent from the party-drug task force. He'd been tracking Rick the Rocket, and he wanted to try some close-up surveillance. Without telling us, of course. The goddamn Feds are always pulling stunts like that. Excuse my French."

Amid our exclamations, he continued, "But Lester Foy showing up at the cemetery is a mystery to me. He must have been following one of you for some reason, but I don't see why."

"I do!" Lily laughed her big, full-throated laugh. "I mean, I can guess why he was there, but he wasn't following anybody. Carnegie, didn't you say Foy was with his girlfriend, and that she's a guitarist?"

I nodded. "What's that got to do with it?"

"You were at Greenwood Cemetery in Redmond, right?" The phone started ringing, and as she stood up to answer it she said, "Girl, Greenwood Cemetery is where Jimi Hendrix is buried! Music people go there all the time. Excuse me a minute."

"Librarians are such show-offs," said Aaron, in mock indignation. "How did she know—"

"Aaron, it's for you," said Lily from the kitchen door. "Long distance, I think."

He grimaced and shut his eyes, as if something expected and yet dreaded had happened. "Sorry. My cell phone's on the blink, so I left your number with someone just in case."

Two minutes later, he returned from the kitchen with an odd, tight look on his face. "Well, it's getting late. Stretch, do you mind if we take off now?"

"No problem," I said. *Enough with the postmortem, let's go home and start the carpe diem.* But when I followed him into Lily's bedroom to fetch our coats, and tried to steal a quick kiss, he kept his distance. I touched his shoulder. "Aaron, what is it? Something wrong with your family in Boston?"

"Yeah," he said, shrugging into his coat. "Well, no, not exactly. But I do have to fly back there right away. There's someone I have to help out."

"Who?"

Aaron jammed his hands into his pockets and sighed. I was just thinking about how handsome he was, even with a black eye, when he said, "My wife."

About the Author

DEBORAH DONNELLY's inspiration for the Carnegie Kincaid series came when she was planning her best friend's wedding and her own at the same time. (Both turned out beautifully.) A long-time resident of Seattle, Donnelly now lives in Boise, Idaho, with her writer husband and their two Welsh corgis. Readers can visit her at www.deborahdonnelly.org.

If you couldn't wait to turn each page of

Died to Match

you'll be on the edge of your seat with

May the Best Man Die,

the next wedding planner mystery by
Deborah Donnelly,
on sale Fall 2003
Read on for a preview...

I don't do bachelor parties.

Wait, that sounds like I jump naked out of cakes. And who makes cakes that tall and skinny? What I mean is, I don't *plan* bachelor parties. Weddings, yes. Rehearsal dinners, of course. Bridesmaids' luncheons, engagement parties, even the occasional charity gala, when business is slow.

The business in question is "Made in Heaven, Elegant Weddings With An Original Flair, Carnegie Kincaid, Proprietor." I've got a pretty decent clientele in Seattle by now, and sometimes I get non-nuptial referrals. But I don't do bachelor parties.

First off, I resent the symbolism of the doomed groom enjoying one last spasm of freedom before turning himself in to the matrimonial slammer. I'm in favor of matrimony, after all. I might even try it myself—but that's another story.

The second and more compelling reason is that no event planner in her right mind wants to plan an event where the guests are hell-bent on drinking themselves to oblivion and behaving as poorly as possible en route.

So why, at ten o'clock on a frigid December evening, was I en route to the Hot Spot Café, inside of which were at least two dozen inebriated bachelors? Because of Sally "The Bride From Hell" Tyler.

Now, most brides are content to let the best man coordinate the bachelor bash. Not Sally Tyler, oohh no. Sally was a mere slip of a girl, with milky skin and smooth white-blonde hair, but she had cold agate eyes beneath dark, level brows. When she was displeased—a seemingly daily occurrence—her eyebrows drew together and her furious glare pierced your vital organs like a stiletto carved from ice.

I desperately needed the revenue from the Tyler/Sanjek account, but it was turning out to be hard-earned. My innards were practically perforated.

Sally's latest excuse for a temper tantrum was this bachelor party. Supposedly, she asked me to plan the affair so that my valuable services, along with the food and drink, could be her wedding gift to Frank Sanjek, her devoted (not to say besotted) fiancé. But I saw through that little fiction.

What Sally really craved was more scope to contradict, criticize, and in general control Frank's every waking moment. Though why she thought my involvement would prevent the best man from pouring too much booze, or screening porno movies, or doing anything else he pleased, was beyond me. I'm a wedding planner, not a chaperone.

Anyway, I declined, Sally fumed, and then Frank's best man, Jason Croy, came up with a perfect site for the party. A friend of his owned a café on the Seattle Ship Canal, complete with bar and pool table, and the place was closing for a major remodel. The guys could take it over for the night for free. They could do their worst, with Jason as master of ceremonies—but only if the event was held immediately, well in advance of the wedding date.

So, like a good best man, Jason set up the bachelor party venue, the guest list, and the entertainment. Meanwhile I made peace with Sally by arranging for a buffet of serve-yourself Greek appetizers catered by my friend and colleague Joe Solveto, while stipulating that I personally would *not* be visiting the party permises. Frank thanked his bride for her generous gift, and everybody was happy.

Until ten minutes ago. I'd been working late, digging through some files over at Joe's office in the Fremont neighborhood, when my cell phone rang.

"Carnegie, it's Sally. You have to go to the Hot Spot right away. Jason needs you."

"Why can't he just call me? What's wrong?" My stomach constricted at the sudden vision of all the things that might be wrong: property damage, an angry neighbor, an injured guest . . .

"Just *go*, OK? You're, like, two minutes away from there, aren't you?"

"Not exactly, but—" But if someone was hurt, or the police had been summoned, every minute would count. "I'll be there as quick as I can."

So I climbed into Vanna White Too, the new replacement for my dear departed white van, and drove through the Christmas lights and sights to the south side of the canal.

December in Seattle is usually gray and drippy, but this evening had a winter wonderland feel, with Christmas trees and decorations all a-glitter in the clear, crisp air. The "Artists' Republic of Fremont" has gone almost mainstream these days, now that a big software firm calls it home and the fancy condos have sprung up, but there are still plenty of funky shops and charming restaurants.

Everywhere I looked tonight, white puffs of frozen breath rose above the Yuletide shoppers and diners as they hurried cheerfully along the sidewalks. Too bad I wasn't one of them. I crossed the Fremont drawbridge to the darker, quieter blocks along Nickerson, then dropped down a side street.

The new Vanna rode like a Rolls after the clanking and stalling of the old one, and we pulled up smoothly to the undistinguished brick facade of the Hot Spot Café. At least there were no police cars in sight, and no ambulance.

The front entrance was locked, so I hammered on it, and tried to peer through the gaps in the curtained front windows; no telling if anyone could hear me over the guitar music throbbing inside. After one last pound, I gave up and went around back, hugging myself against the cold.

I'm not used to real winter weather. I still had on my most businesslike suit from a morning meeting, but the temperature had been plummeting all day, and the silk tweed blazer, though stylish, was no match for it. So now I was shivering as well as irritated and anxious.

Out back, a wooden dining deck extended over a wedge of patchy grass and shadowy bushes that sloped down to an empty bike path and the wide, cement-walled lane of dark, still water. The Seattle Ship Canal is a major waterway; on sunny afternoons, the Hot Spot's patrons could sit out on there with their beers and watch big sailboats and bigger barges move between Puget Sound to the west and Lake Union to the east.

Right now, though, the splintered planks of the deck held nothing but stacked plastic chairs and a silver coating of frost that sparkled in the light from the bare windows and sliding glass doors. The glass doors were unlocked, so I stepped gratefully inside.

A quick look around yielded a confused impression of milling young men, clouds of cigar smoke, puddles of spilled liquor, and a massive serve-yourself Greek mess. Empty plates and glasses littered all the tables, but the mess went far beyond that.

From the demolished dolmathes scattered across the pool table, to the bits of fried calamari stuck to the ceiling, to the smear of spanakopita on the big-screen TV, Joe's feast had clearly been enjoyed in ways he never intended. There was a bit of broken glass—apparently juggling retsina bottles is now a recognized indoor sport—but no broken heads that I could see, no blood, and no cops.

And no Jason Croy. Peering through the fumes, I spotted Frank Sanjek sitting stupefied near the television, on which two women with improbable physiques were cavorting in a hot tub. Though I couldn't fathom his devotion to Sally, Frank was a sensible fellow, with a cleft in his square chin and an amiable look in his light blue eyes. So far he'd been quite pleasant to work with.

Averting my gaze from the hot tub hotties, I headed toward Frank to ask for an explanation. But my path was blocked by three men, all of them in their early twenties and none of them sober.

"Hey, she's here!" shouted one, a beefy lad whose sweatshirt was adorned with something damp and garlicky. At least it smelled less disgusting than it looked. He was swaying a bit on his feet, and gazing at me with the oddest mixture of shyness and enthusiasm. He dropped a moist, heavy hand on my shoulder and repeated, "She's finally here."

"Yes, I'm here," I snapped, trying for patience and failing.

Someone turned off the music, and in the heavy-breathing silence I removed his hand. "Brilliant observation. Now where's Jason?"

"How come you're wearing, like, a suit?" inquired one of his companions, a sharp-faced sort leaning on a cue stick.

"How come she's so *flat*?" muttered the third, and there were nervous snickers all around.

This drunken discourtesy left me speechless for a moment, and while I gathered my wits to tell him off, some of the other men, the ones who were still ambulatory, began to congregate around us. Not quite a wolf pack—the eyes were too dull, the movements too clumsy. More like a herd of cows. But still . . .

"It ain't whatcha got, it's whatcha do with it!" yelled someone from the back. "Do it!"

Catcalls and more lewd comments followed. Make that a herd of bulls. A sort of testosterone bellowing arose, and emergency or not, I decided to bail out. I didn't have to put up with this. Then a new voice, familiar this time, cut across the others.

"Shut up, you jerks! Carnegie, what are you doing here?"

The speaker was a young black man, even taller than me and nearly as lanky, but with rock-solid biceps gleaming darkly against his sleeveless white T-shirt. He had large, ardent eyes, and a humorous curl to his wide mouth that I knew very well—from all the time I spent hanging out with his sister.

Darwin James was the younger brother of my best friend, Lily, and a coworker of Frank Sanjek's at the headquarters of Meet for Coffee. The MFC chain of espresso shops had been giving Starbucks a run for their money. Frank was a brand manager, and Darwin, formerly an underground comics artist, was now a hip, much-in-demand graphic designer. He was also one of Frank's groomsmen.

"What's going on here?" I asked him. "I had an urgent call to come talk to Jason. Is someone hurt?"

"Not that I know of." Darwin shrugged and gestured around the room with the bottle of orange juice he held in one long, muscular hand. "I think Jason's playing pool. You want me to get him?"

"Please." The herd was dispersing, though Mr. Garlic stood his ground. I stepped away from him and added, "Why's everyone staring?"

"Mistaken identity," said a light, mocking voice.

From the pool room beyond the bar, the best man sauntered towards us through the debris-laden tables. Jason Croy's face was long and lantern-jawed, with full, crisply carved lips and small gray eyes, just a touch too close together. His eyes held disdainful amusement, as they often did, and a spark of malice.

Or is that my imagination? I wondered. I didn't like Jason Croy.

"So Carnegie," he continued, "we need some more booze around here. Some of these gentlemen brought their friends. Make it a mixed case, OK? And another rack of beer."

"What?!" Curiosity about his first remark vanished in indignation about his second. "You called me over here to make a liquor run?"

The full lips stretched into a slow, arrogant smile. He, too, was weaving a little on his feet. "Well, you're in charge of the food and drink, aren't you? That's what Sally said."

"If Sally had told me this on the phone—" But of course, that's why she hadn't told me what Jason needed so urgently. Because I wouldn't have come.

"Come on," Jason wheedled, "you've got your car out anyway, why not do us a favor? All my plastic is maxed out."

"Listen up, Jason," I said, and I could feel my face getting hot. "If you want more liquor, you can get your ass to a Seven-Eleven. I'm off duty."

My exit would have been more dignified if I hadn't stumbled on a shish kabob, but I kicked it aside and strode over to the glass door. It slid open as I got there, and in walked, no kidding, Santa Claus.

I was still puzzled—*Salvation Army on overtime? A late guest with a sense of humor?*—when a howl went up from the men.

"That's her!"

"She's here!"

"Merry freakin' Christmas!"

St. Nick glared at me and said, in a low but distinctly female tone, "Hey, I work alone."

I took a closer look, past the rippling white beard and padded red suit, and realized that this particular Santa Claus was wearing glossy scarlet lipstick, extravagant false eyelashes, and high-heeled black boots.

Enter stripper, exit Carnegie. I spotted three other, legitimate Santas on my drive back to Joe's office, and I snarled at every one of them.

I don't usually work in Fremont. Under normal circumstances, I live in a houseboat on the east shore of Lake Union, with the Made in Heaven offices located conveniently upstairs. At the moment, and hugely inconveniently, I was working at Joe's catering office and sleeping on Lily's fold-out couch.

The culprit was that ancient enemy of damp wood, *Serpula lacrymans*. Dry rot. My houseboat was infested with the fungal friend, and my horrified landlady had launched a barrage of chemical and mechanical assaults to annihilate it.

Mrs. Castle barely gave me time to load up my PC and some file boxes, and stuff my suitcase, before she had the place cordoned off and swarming with guys in hazmat suits. At least I was saving some rent, which had gone to the down payment on Vanna Too.

So tonight, the award for My Least Favorite Entity on Earth was a split decision between *Serpula lacrymans* and Jason Croy. His outrageous demand for delivery service had interrupted a frantic search: I was trying to unearth a particularly nice photograph of one of my brides to show at a television appearance in the morning. I'd never been on TV before, so naturally I was nervous.

Not that I expected an interrogation or anything; this was just a segment about weddings on a local morning show, with a perky interviewer and some softball questions about my job. But my fellow guest would be Beau Paliere, a very hot wedding designer from Paris by way of Hollywood, who'd arrived in Seattle to keynote a bridal expo.

Beautiful Beau—as the celebrity magazines called him—was very big time, and I didn't want to look like a yokel in contrast. Besides, this could be terrific publicity for Made in Heaven—*if* I carried it off well.

All that anxiety has to channel itself somewhere, so earlier this evening I had become suddenly and unreasonably convinced that my on-screen success hinged on having the camera pan across this one damn photo. I'd riffled through each of my files at least twice, and now the minutes were counting down to zero hour. I had to be awake, dressed and mascara'd by five a.m.

How do TV people do it? I thought as I drove through Fremont. *They must sleep in their makeup.*

Back at Joe's building, I took the lobby elevator up four floors to his storeroom. Most of Made in Heaven's stuff was downstairs in my tiny borrowed office, but I knew that my partner Eddie Breen had dropped off a file box of his own before leaving town for a few days. Joe's staff had put it in the storeroom, out of the way, until Eddie could come sort it out on Monday. It was a long shot, but maybe that box held the photo I needed.

The fourth floor was dark and empty, except for the one light I'd left on, and my footsteps sounded loud in the corridor. I turned on the staff's radio in the corner—it was set to a talk station—and jingled my keys loudly, reminding myself to lock everything up before I went home for the night. Joe was pretty casual about security, but I wanted to be a good temporary tenant.

The storeroom was piled with treasure.

Like most caterers, Joe relied heavily on indestructible or inexpensive dishes and glassware; tonight's bachelors had gotten plastic only. But when Solveto's put on a festive meal for more responsible folk, the buffet table and the serving stations always included a few eye-catching pieces of hand-painted Italian ceramic, vintage English silver, or rare Depression glass.

Rumor had it that Joe began the practice so he could write off his exotic vacations as buying trips, but in any case the clients loved it. Sort of a signature Solveto's flourish.

The storeroom was lined on three sides with shelves bearing a splendid assortment of platters, pitchers, trays and tureens. When I flipped on the lights, reflections winked from massive gilt candelabras and sparked across to a cobalt-blue cut glass cake stand.

Along the fourth wall, under the windows, a long work table was stacked neatly with cartons and bubble wrap for transporting these treasures. A huge silver punch bowl sat ready, with a pad of inventory forms beside it for recording which items were in use, and where. Joe was brilliantly creative, but strictly organized.

Underneath the table I found Eddie's box. I hauled it onto the table top and began to lift out the top layer of contents: a squat steel pen and pencil jar, a favorite oversized coffee mug, none too clean, and a framed photograph of the freighter Eddie had sailed on, back when he and my late father were cadets together in the merchant marine.

Eddie's seagoing past explained the next item in the box: a pair of small, powerful binoculars that he used to observe the pleasure boats and sea planes on Lake Union. I set each item carefully aside, pulled out the stack of file folders at the bottom of the box, and sat down at the table to search.

No luck. There were checklists for the Tyler/Sanjek events, a detailed timetable for Bonnie Buckmeister's Christmas-themed wedding next week, and notes on all our current marketing efforts, including my TV appearance tomorrow and the Made in Heaven booth at the bridal expo. But no photos.

I propped my chin on one fist and stared absently out the windows. I'd just have to do without. There were other pictures I could use, a wedding cake, one of our bridal couples dancing, and of course the Made in Heaven logo in curly copper lettering, which I would try my hardest to get on camera. But first I had to get some sleep.

As I stood up to re-pack Eddie's box, something across the Canal caught my eye: a brilliantly lit window, with a tiny figure in scarlet clothing moving back and forth across it, like an erratic actor on a garish stage. Santa Claus. The Hot Spot was directly across the Canal from Joe's office building, and from my upper-story vantage point I could see right into the café. Not that I wanted to, of course. I swept up all the files I'd opened, tucked them back into the box, and set the mug and the pencil jar on top of them.

Then I picked up the binoculars.

I was innocently nestling them into Eddie's box when it occurred to me that maybe I had knocked them out of focus, or out of alignment, or whatever. And how else could I check except by aiming them at something? That brightly lit window, for example, would be a perfect way to test them out...

Whoa. Nothing wrong with the focus. With the lenses at my eyes, the Hot Spot's rear window leapt into brilliant clarity, as did the Saint Nick chick. She had shed the padded red trousers and the beard, and while I watched, fascinated, she strutted back and forth, moving to music I couldn't hear, in just her fur-trimmed jacket, tasseled red hat, and high black boots.

If I were a young man—or an old one, or one in between—I would have said she had thighs to die for.

Santa's audience, mostly cut off from my downward view by the edge of the café's roof, seemed not to realize that they were sharing the show with any passing sailboat—or hidden observer. But in fact, you'd have to be up in a crow's nest, or up where I was, to get just the right angle.

If the bachelors had thought of that, they sure didn't care. As I watched, Frank Sanjek sat heavily on the floor at his comrade's feet, and someone invisible to me poured a beer on his head. He didn't appear to notice.

I could see why. Dipping and swaying, always in motion, Santa dropped the jacket off one smooth bare shoulder, then the other, each time letting the white fur border of the garment slip lower and lower down the curves of her breasts.

Then, perhaps responding to some climax in the music, she suddenly turned her back to the boys and her front to me, bent forward, and flipped the jacket up behind. If she was wearing much of anything under the jacket, it was too small for the binoculars to pick up. Frank fell over sideways.

I was hastily putting the binoculars down—honest, I was— when my phone rang again. Something told me it wasn't Jason this time.

It was my erstwhile hostess, wondering when I'd be home for the night.

"Oh jeez, Lily, have you been waiting up for me?"

"No, but I'm going to bed now, and I wanted to be sure you have your key."

"Yep, I've got it. I'll probably be there soon."

"Did you find your photo?"

"No, I should have given up hours ago. Then I wouldn't have gotten dragged over to the Hot Spot." I told her about Jason's summons, and the arrival of Santa.

"So did you stay to watch?" she inquired archly.

"Of course not!" I glanced over at the binoculars. The back of my neck was damp. "Why would I do that?"

"Just kidding. Seriously, though, you didn't happen to see Darwin, did you? I shouldn't worry but I can't help it, I still feel like he's my baby brother. And he was so out of control before he got this job—"

"Actually, I talked to him," I told her. "He seemed OK. Come to think of it, he seemed sober. Doesn't he drink?"

"Not any more. He's been in AA for a year now."

Lily had never disclosed this about Darwin before, and I wasn't sure how to reply. "Oh . . . well, I wasn't at the party for long, but honestly, he was fine."

"Forget I asked, OK?" She hastened to change the subject. "Did you see Aaron?"

"Aaron *Gold*?" I almost dropped the phone.

"Are you in love with some other Aaron?" I could hear the wicked smile in her voice. "Dar said he was invited tonight."

"You know perfectly well I'm not in love with Aaron. I'm not sure I ever was."

Just to prove it, I should have changed the subject myself. But I couldn't. "I thought he was still in Boston, anyway. How does he know Frank?"

"I don't think he does, really," said Lily. "Darwin told me Aaron's working on some book about the CEO of Meet for Coffee. He's gotten friendly with the guys in Creative Services, so they asked him to the party. I guess he didn't go, though."

"I guess not." *Unless he was in that side room shooting pool with Jason. I wonder . . .*

"Um, Lily, I'd better get back to work here. I want to make one more pass through the files, and then get some paperwork done. This TV thing tomorrow has really thrown me off."

"Good luck. I've set the VCR for you."

"Thanks, Lily. Good night."

I did spend some time downstairs in my borrowed office— but not much. Aaron was on my mind, and so were those binoculars. Rolling my eyes at my own foolishness, I took the elevator back up and focused on the window again. Not that I cared whether Aaron was there. Not that I cared about Aaron. Not that I could see him, either. Santa had left the area near the lighted window, and the revelers seemed to be milling aimlessly inside, as if the party was winding down. I spotted Mr. Garlic, but no one else familiar—until a sudden tangle of movement drew my attention to the grassy slope below the deck.

There in the frost and the shadows, two tall, lanky figures were struggling together, dodging and flailing in clumsy counterpoint. I had no trouble recognizing them: Jason Croy, and Lily's baby brother. The best man was obviously drunk; maybe Darwin was taking his car keys away?

It was hard to tell if this was a ritual male scuffle—elk clashing their antlers—or a serious fight. Either way, I can't say it bothered me to see the supercilious Jason getting knocked around a little.

The third figure was less ambiguous: Frank Sanjek, the bridegroom, was kneeling on the grass and being hideously sick. Another male ritual. I sighed and shook my head. Time for me to go.

But once I went downstairs and finished some genuine work, a nagging question kept me from actually walking out the door. I had assured Lily that her brother was fine, and now he was apparently in the middle of a fistfight. Shouldn't I check on the outcome?

For that matter, shouldn't I make sure that the amiable, sensible bridegroom wasn't unconscious and abandoned by his drunken friends, out in the freezing night? Eddie tells me I fuss too much about our clients, and maybe it's true, but I couldn't wait to see Sally Tyler walk down the aisle and out of my life. And to that end, I needed Frank Sanjek safe and sound.

So I rode the elevator up to the storeroom one last time, and pulled out my illicit spyglasses. I had forgotten to turn the radio off, so as I scanned the scene across the canal the talk station provided an incongruous sound track: several snooty-sounding people debating the situation in Northern Ireland.

There was even less to see this time. The café's windows had gone dark, which made it hard to get a clear view into the shrubbery. But Frank was definitely gone. In fact, I couldn't see anyone at all except for Santa Claus. She was striding briskly down the street away from the café in her padded red suit, head up and shoulders back after a job well done.

All's well that ends well, I thought idly. *I'm just glad we didn't have a damage deposit—*

"Bird watching?"

I gasped and whirled around. Eddie's binoculars slipped from my nerveless fingers and landed in the silver punch bowl with a enormous and resounding *gonnng*.

I was shocked, and not just because a man was now lounging in the storeroom doorway. I was shocked by who it was.

Aaron Gold. The man I'd been dating, the man I'd been falling for. The man who had a wife back in Boston.

I hadn't spoken to him since I found out.

The air in the storeroom was clean and neutral; now that I was paying attention, I could smell a blend of cigars and retsina from where I stood.

So he was shooting pool in the other room. And then watching Santa...

Unlike the younger party guys, Aaron wore a tie, but it hung loose from his collar, and his crow-black hair was mussed. The deep-set brown eyes gleamed even more than usual, and when he smiled, his swift white grin came out lopsided.

"S' Christmas," he said, nodding his head sagely. A lock of hair flopped down into his eyes. "You're gonna find out who's naughty or nice."

I stood with my back to the reverberating punch bowl, and took a deep breath. I didn't know how long he had watched me watching, or whether he could guess that I'd been spying on the striptease. I also didn't know how I felt about him, after the last few weeks of angry silence and unwilling tears.

And what neither of us knew, and wouldn't learn until the next day, was this: of the three young men I had observed on the grass behind the Hot Spot Café, only two were still alive.